Advance Praise for
UNBOUND

"Dina's debut novel, *Unbound*, is a gripping and heartwarming family saga of love and betrayal, and of rebellion and restraint, in a time of war and peace. The journey of two strong women to break their visible and invisible bonds, and to search for freedom, resonates today."

—GELING YAN, author of *The Flowers of War*

"From the very first page—an ominous knock at the door—to the very last, *Unbound* binds us to an incredible story of heartbreak and passion, of dreams and desperation, of despair and unconditional hope. Through the eyes of Mini Pao and her granddaughter, Ting Lee, Dina Gu Brumfield weaves a masterful tale that not only starkly captures both the promise and oppression of twentieth-century China, but more importantly, brings to life the people who struggled to survive behind the facade. A master of her craft, Brumfield never hesitates to lure the reader in close, so that we breathe the sweat and feel the pain; because only then will true understanding emerge about the human need for freedom and the power of will. This book is not so much a novel as it is an event—one that singularly proves the adage that history told through story will never be forgotten. This is one debut not to be missed!"

—JAMES MATHEWS, author of *Last Known Position*

"In the tradition of *Wild Swans* and *The Woman Warrior*, *Unbound* follows the perilous journeys of three generations of Shanghai women navigating politics, Chinese tradition, and love. You will find much to learn from this amazing novel as well as much to identify with."

—BARBARA ESSTMAN, author of
The Other Anna and *Night Ride Home*

"Brumfield's novel is, at its essence, a well-paced historical novel that kept me turning pages. I know very little of Asian history—even the more recent chapters of the twentieth century when this book is set—but I learned a lot from the dramatic scenes that featured characters who are often thrown into the midst of political turmoil. Particularly interesting to me were the moments that dramatized the changes generated in Chinese society by the death of Chairman Mao. Vivid drama also surrounds the era from the Japanese invasion of the country to their routing by the American and British forces. Seeing history through the eyes of people on the 'other' side of the world, from the Western side that I am most familiar with, provided rich realism for this reader. And, of course, much of the suspense lay in wondering how, and if, Ting and her grandmother could survive the violence and heartbreak in their lives, to find safety and happiness at last.

I would recommend this novel to readers interested in learning more about Eastern cultures and history. The author not only instructs, she entertains. And we leave the book in sympathy with her appealing characters."

—KATHRYN JOHNSON, author and teacher

"Engrossing and filled with a host of richly drawn characters, Dina Brumfield pulls back the curtain in this informative and gripping tale on what it was to live in China. The book covers a span from 1935 to 1980, physically, politically, and socially."

—CHARLOTTE IRION, author of
Case Not Closed: Diary of a Court Reporter

UNBOUND

A Tale of Love

and Betrayal

in Shanghai

Dina Gu Brumfield

GREENLEAF
BOOK GROUP PRESS

This is a work of fiction. Although most of the characters, organizations, and events portrayed in the novel are based on actual historical counterparts, the dialogue and thoughts of these characters are products of the author's imagination.

Published by Greenleaf Book Group Press
Austin, Texas
www.gbgpress.com

Distributed by Greenleaf Book Group

For ordering information or special discounts for bulk purchases, please contact Greenleaf Book Group at PO Box 91869, Austin, TX 78709, 512.891.6100.

Design and composition by Greenleaf Book Group
Cover design by Greenleaf Book Group
Cover Images: ©iStockphoto.com/ake1150sb; ©iStockphoto.com/LeeYiuTung; ©iStockphoto.com/Bill Oxford

Publisher's Cataloging-in-Publication data is available.

Print ISBN: 978-1-62634-714-4

eBook ISBN: 978-1-62634-715-1

Part of the Tree Neutral® program, which offsets the number of trees consumed in the production and printing of this book by taking proactive steps, such as planting trees in direct proportion to the number of trees used: www.treeneutral.com.

TreeNeutral®

Printed in the United States of America on acid-free paper

20 21 22 23 24 25   10 9 8 7 6 5 4 3 2 1

First Edition

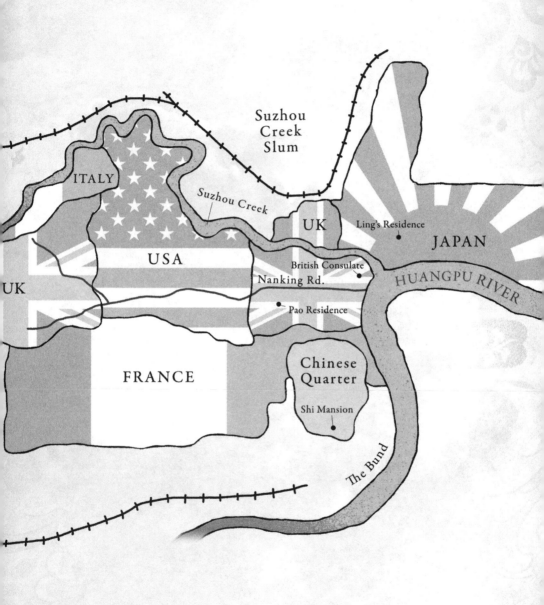

To Noah,
For convincing me that I can accomplish things I thought impossible.

1

IT'S NEW YEAR'S ALL OVER AGAIN

TING, SHANGHAI, 1975

We learned of my grandma's return late one December night.

Earlier that evening, the three of us had sat down and begun to eat dinner when we heard a knock on the door. Father opened it, and his pause made us turn from our dishes toward the door to see three officials in Public Security uniforms standing at our doorstep with the neighbors looking on. Father's face turned white as paper. I felt his fear from across the room as he stood and silently searched for his voice. I am sure his pause was but seconds, though it felt much longer.

"Officers, are you sure we're the ones you're looking for?" he asked.

"Yes. We are looking for Jing Ling Shi. Is she here?"

Mother froze in her chair at the sound of her name.

"Yes. Jing Ling Shi is my wife," Father said, turning to face us. "We were just . . . would you please sit down and have a cup of tea?" He bowed his head and motioned to the dining table and half-eaten food.

"No need," one of the officials replied. "You and Jing Ling Shi should go with us."

"Why? Did we do anything wrong?" Mother asked, reluctantly standing up.

"It's top secret," the official replied. "We cannot tell you now. You and your husband have to go to our local office with us right away. The leader in the office will tell you why."

"Can I take my daughter with me?" Mother asked. She was very pale.

The head of the three Public Security officials looked at me for a few seconds. "How old is she?"

"Eight," Mother answered.

"Well, she should be able to look after herself for a short while," the official said hurriedly. "Let's go now. We don't have time to waste."

Mother came to me, her hands shaking as she caressed my hair. "If we are not back by eight tonight, you should go to Aunt Fong's house."

I nodded my head. Aunt Fong lived a few blocks away. She was Mother's friend and had taken care of me when my parents went to the labor camp a few years before. Now, watching them leave with the officials, my heart was pounding so hard I could hear it. I wanted to run after them but I didn't dare. I just stood there watching, tears rolling silently down my cheeks.

I don't know how long I cried. I only know that I didn't touch my food. I dragged my chair to sit in front of the window and peered into the darkness, hoping to catch a glimpse of my parents' return. Three half-eaten bowls of rice sat on the table, slowly getting cold. I forgot to check the clock, refusing to believe my parents could be gone from my life. I told myself that they would return in an hour.

I waited for what seemed like an eternity. When my parents finally reappeared, I was still in the chair, half-dozing. I heard their footsteps and the jingling of keys before I saw them—and then they were in front of me, faces flushed from the cold. Mother was so relieved when she saw me; she ran over to me and scooped me into her arms.

"We went to Aunt Fong's house, but she said you weren't there,"

Mother said. "We were so worried." I noticed her eyes were puffy, like she had been crying.

"Mama, I'm hungry," was my only reply.

Without a word, Father put the bowls onto a tray and carried our now-cold dinner into the communal kitchen. There, Mother warmed the food on the stove and we had a very late, very quiet dinner. Whether in spite of my worry or because of it, I slept very well that night.

It wasn't until the next morning that my parents told me my grandma was coming to visit us in March.

"How?" I asked.

"She will take a big plane to Hong Kong," explained Mother. "Then she will take a train to Guangzhou, and switch trains to Shanghai."

I knew very little of my grandma at that point. I didn't even know I *had* a grandma until two years earlier. It was just thirteen months after Nixon visited China that we received the Red Cross letter telling us that my grandma was looking for us. The letter encouraged us to contact her. Included with the note was an address—she lived in the United States.

After obtaining permission from their work unit leaders, my parents sent a letter in reply, enclosing a black-and-white portrait of our family. Soon after, we received letters from her directly. She sent along a few pictures, too. Hers were in color, and it wasn't so much that the pictures were in color, but that they were bathed in *so many* vibrant colors that I had never experienced before. My grandma looked so glamorous in the pictures, a tiny dog sitting in her lap. She had the elegance of Jackie Kennedy—coiffed and polished in a slim, fitted dress—except with an Asian face. Her home was clean and spacious. Each picture was taken in a different part of her house: by the pool, at the garden, and of course—as I was to appreciate later—in a living room with a huge TV and a cream-colored sofa for a backdrop.

Having always lived in our small two-room apartment, I had never seen rooms like these belonging to my grandma, let alone all the objects decorating her home. Behind my parents' backs, I'd look at those pictures over and over, each time noticing some new detail: a tiny flower, a beach chair in the background, and so on. I would tell my parents about what I found, but they weren't interested. They warned me not to share what I saw in these pictures with my friends.

I ignored their warnings, of course. Grandma's pictures were so interesting, and I would show them off to any close friends who came over. All my friends had grandparents waiting for them at home when they returned from school. I was excited to finally have one of my own. "I have a grandma, too," I would tell them.

Soon, everyone at school knew I had a grandma living in the United States. During recess one day not long after, some kids pointed at me, lowered their heads and whispered, and then approached me, asking to see the pictures. I said I didn't have the pictures with me because my parents kept them locked up. At that they started laughing and said I must have made up the whole story.

Each school day started with a chant, all of us shouting, "Down with American Imperialism!" But after I made the mistake of sharing the photos with my classmates, each day several kids started turning and grinning at me, raising their voices as they chanted. Soon enough they had given me the nickname of "American Spy."

I had suffered their mocking before. I had even tried to fight back when they made fun of my family's "bourgeois" or "black" political class. But now I was even worse than that: I was the "American Spy." I was torn. She was my grandma, but I knew better. I should have listened to my parents and kept the pictures and news about her to myself.

This fresh torment didn't end my curiosity, though it did dampen my enthusiasm for sharing the pictures with friends. Still, I pressed my parents relentlessly for information about my grandma. Eventually I learned one fact, one inconceivable to me: Grandma had left China in 1947, when my mother was nine years old, and she had not returned since.

Now she was returning. It was not just that I would finally see her. Her return, to me, carried the hope that I would be different no more. At last, my family would be just like everyone else's: I would have a grandma.

It was a busy three months before Grandma arrived.

Mrs. Yung, our neighborhood party leader, called a meeting the next day, inviting all the immediate neighbors who shared the kitchen with us. I went along with my parents.

Mrs. Yung began the meeting by announcing my grandma's visit. She instructed our neighbors to show the warmest hospitality to our overseas brothers and sisters. While my grandma was staying with us, our family would be given priority in using the kitchen sink and bathroom. Mrs. Yung also handed my parents extra rations for food and other essentials.

"Thank you, thank you very much," my parents replied, many times. They were so grateful and touched by the support from our neighbors. I was so proud to get this special treatment, too—all because of my grandma.

Surprisingly, getting the extra ration tickets was the easy part; the real battle turned out to be buying what we needed. To win, we needed two things: time and information. The former was in the hands of Mother and Father's work units—their work unit leaders would spare them from the many endless meetings so they could attend to preparing for their guest. More difficult to come by was the information we needed. It was no easy thing to know when rations would be available, or where. Store supplies were scarce and the choices were limited. Mother used up all her contacts finding what we needed.

Getting fabric to make new clothing was the only easy task. We lacked decent clothes for the big day. This hadn't been a problem before, because we had been wearing, like everyone else, the same gray or blue woolen or cotton outfit modeled after Chairman Mao's suit. Mother and Father knew better than to spend their precious rations on clothing. But with Grandma coming it was time, Mother said, to finally have some suitable clothing. Fortunately, Aunt Fong worked at one of the fabric stores. She had just been moved to a new position and so she knew firsthand when and what the store was going to get.

One day, the person who operated the neighborhood phone came with a message from Aunt Fong: The store was getting new supplies, and could we please be there quickly. Mother rushed home and grabbed the clothes-ration tickets, and then we went straight to the store. By the time we got there, a line had already formed, people stomping their feet to stay warm in the frigid January air. We waited patiently, and finally got what Mother was waiting for.

Aunt Fong was a good tailor and volunteered to work on the jackets for Mother and me—a red jacket for Mother, and a polka dot jacket with a pretty white lace collar for me. After the jackets were taken care of, Mother undid two of her old sweaters—one gray and one pink. She washed the wool carefully in warm water and soap, then hung it out in the sun to dry. When the yarn was clean and dry, she used it to knit new sweaters for Father and me.

As Grandma's arrival approached, we cleaned our house inside and out. Mother made new bedding with some of the fabric she was able to get with the extra ration cards. After much debate between my parents about the sleeping arrangements, they agreed that I would sleep with Grandma in the big room. It was my parents' usual room, and the nicer one, with a big window and plenty of light. My parents would sleep in my windowless room in the back while my grandma was visiting.

The last couple of weeks before Grandma's arrival were the busiest. Mother saved all the food shopping for last. One of her friends worked at the grocery market, and she gave Mother daily information about what was going to be available the next morning. Each morning, I was dragged from my warm bed at the crack of dawn. After quickly swallowing our bowls of porridge, Mother, Father, and I bundled up and rushed to the open-air grocery market while the streets were still empty and dark. I felt like a sleepwalker, holding onto my parents' hands. Yet once we reached the market, it seemed that the whole city was already there.

Like experienced soldiers on the front line, Father and Mother leapt into action. They separated wordlessly, Mother pulling me along purposefully in the ordered chaos around us. People were yelling and arguing, each one jostling to claim their position in line. Mother put down a small bench to mark her place in the fish line and told the lady behind her that she'd be back. She would then run to the mushroom line, or the scallion or another vegetable line, and put down a large stone that she had picked up on the walk to the market. Each time, she obtained the acknowledgement from the person who came behind her that her place was saved. At last, she would march me to yet another line and tell me to stay there.

"Don't move until I come back and don't let anyone cut in front of you." She flashed a weary smile to whoever joined up in line behind me before disappearing into the crowd. I knew the drill because we had just celebrated Chinese New Year. The market battle usually lasted a few hours. Each day we brought home what we could.

Typically, arguments would break out, but they never went anywhere. Maybe some shoving or a thrown elbow was necessary to stake a claim, but that was to be expected. During these trips, the market seemed full of raw excitement, as if the city were building anticipation along with us. A fistfight even broke out in one of the meat lines near me. Apparently, a young man tried to cut the line. Father and Mother were in their own lines and could do nothing to shield me from the scene, as they might have done.

Finally, the food ration tickets were all used up. Mother was happy that the weather was still cold enough to preserve the food for a long time. We hung the chickens, ham, and fish in the cold air outside our apartment windows.

"We keep the fish whole as a symbol of completion—a full cycle in life," Mother reminded me. "Its head represents the start and its tail represents the end. And we make round dumplings, too, because they mean the family will be together always."

Whether there are similar meanings behind the other foods, I don't know. These were Mother's most special dishes, those we looked forward to once a year. *It's New Year's all over again*, I thought.

2

JASMINE IN SPRINGTIME

Trucks and buses bustled among the unstoppable waves of bikers, and angry horns filled the air. The street was a sea of blue and gray Mao uniforms. Against this monochromatic backdrop, the pink bows in my hair and the red jacket Mother wore seemed like unexpected flowers blooming in the late winter. People stared at us curiously at the bus stop.

As usual, the bus was late. We waited patiently until finally a bus approached. By then, the waiting crowd had grown large enough to fill an empty bus. The mob ran toward the still moving bus, surrounding the doors, ready to push their way on board even before it stopped completely. Father positioned himself at a right angle as he pulled Mother and I onto the bus, shielding us from the violent pushing of the crowd.

It seemed like countless minutes until the conductor was able to close the door, pulling it shut on those passengers still halfway on board with nowhere to go, yelling at the passengers who hung on and tried to pry the door open. I felt relief when I finally heard the hiss of the air-pressured doors closing and the bus started rolling seconds later. The scene would replay itself over and over during the forty minutes it took to get to the train station. At each stop, Father and Mother would do their best to shelter me from the crowd crushing in around us. My parents held my hands tight, managing to create a small cushion of space around me. It seemed like it took forever to travel the several kilometers to the station.

It turned out we arrived way too early, and were stopped at the entrance to the train platform. An expressionless, uniformed man shouted loudly: "Document." Father handed him the letter from the local authorities. The man took his time studying it.

"Who is Jing Ling Shi?" he asked.

"I'm Jing Ling Shi," Mother said. "And this is my husband and this is my daughter Ting Lee." She managed a smile, her slightly shaking finger pointing to our names on the document.

The guard looked at us coldly, one by one. I lowered my head and studied my shoes to avoid his scrutiny.

"The train is delayed today. But you can go in and wait at the platform." He waved us in.

This was no ordinary platform: It was one of a few windows China had opened to the outside world, Father told me. It was the only passageway for foreigners who were not dignitaries to visit China.

The platform stood empty. A few benches in the middle served as a divider for the incoming and outgoing waiting areas. We seated ourselves and waited. Out on the open platform, the early March wind cut my face like a knife. Mother tried to shield me from the wind, but she was distracted, and could only do it for a few minutes at a time before she forgot, staring off down the tracks.

More people began to appear on the platform, but it was never as crowded as elsewhere in Shanghai. Once the loudspeaker announced the arrival of the train from Hong Kong, Mother couldn't keep still. She stood up, paced back and forth, and constantly looked in the direction the train would be coming from. I held her hand tightly.

Her nervousness passed to me, and I felt equally uneasy. I was shivering in the wind, my face pink from cold as my own anxious thoughts ran through my mind. *Who is my grandma?* I understood she was my mother's mother. *Will she like me? Why was it she was never mentioned to me before?*

I heard the loud whistle of an incoming train. The crowd had by now grown, and pressed toward the platform anxiously. The rail station police desperately tried to maintain order. Mother grabbed my hand tightly and pushed forward. After that, everything happened in slow motion.

The train approached. Mother looked up through its windows and doors, her eyes searching. At first, nothing happened. Then all the train compartment doors opened at once, like magic. Mother moved forward, her uncertain expression changing—she smiled, though her lips trembled so much that the smile seemed sad. She let go of my hand and rushed toward a woman who had just emerged from the train. They embraced and tears rolled down both their cheeks. The woman wiped Mother's face dry, and they walked back toward us together.

"This is my husband and daughter," Mother introduced us.

I looked up. The woman was tall and slim. She looked young for a grandmother, unlike the grandmothers I was used to. Her hair was combed into a bob with curls on the side. She wore a stylish light-yellow suede jacket that fit her like a second skin. She hugged me, her scent making me think of white jasmine in springtime. She smelled so good.

This was my grandma. Her name was Mini Weingardener and she was from America, a place far away and full of wealth.

3

GRANDMA BEGINS HER STORY

Turning from us to the conductor, Grandma smiled and reached into her purse. "May I take my son-in-law aboard to help collect my luggage?" she asked, offering him a pack of Winston cigarettes she had pulled out in a fluid, practiced motion.

"Of course, Madam," the conductor replied politely. Mother and I followed on behind her.

The corridor of the train car was lined with several small benches beneath the window overlooking the platform. Opposite the benches was a rather posh compartment with two soft-looking bunk beds on each side of a small tray table that attached to the wall under the window, with a view of empty train tracks. Two porcelain teacups stood with a pot of hot water, an ashtray, and a tiny vase with a single pink plastic carnation. Grandma led us into the compartment and pointed underneath the bunk bed that held her luggage. I skipped past and sat on the bottom bunk, bouncing up and down, feeling the cushiness of the bed.

The adults pulled out three large, bulging suitcases, each one seemingly as large as me, and a small travel bag. Mother handed me the travel bag and took another smaller suitcase. She ordered me off the train, while the conductor and Father managed one of the larger suitcases out of the compartment and down the train steps together. I followed Father back onto the train again for the second large suitcase. By the time the last piece of luggage was on the ground, Grandma had a luggage cart waiting for us. It took a little time for Father to load all of the luggage onto the cart. I could no longer stand still, hopping up and down with excitement beside Father.

"Can I push the cart?" I asked.

Mother pulled me aside. "Behave yourself," she warned.

"Let her push the cart," Grandma said indulgently. "She's a big girl." She winked at me, as if to signal a conspiracy between us. I grinned back. I liked her already.

A guard stopped us at the station exit to inform us that the luggage cart could not leave the station. My parents realized a bigger issue: How would we get all this luggage on the bus? It would be difficult enough for the four of us to get on together, let alone with a pile of luggage. My parents argued in a hushed voice, each proposing a different plan. I stood between them, glancing back and forth. Grandma strolled purposefully over to the guard, fishing out a silver cigarette case and matching silver lighter from her brown leather purse. She took a cigarette for herself and held the case open for the guard. Eyeing the cigarettes, the guard's serious face gave way to a smile.

"No, thank you," he said politely.

Even *I* knew he wanted one. No one could refuse foreign cigarettes.

Grandma held the case out long enough to overcome his polite hesitation. Stepping closer and flipping the silver lighter, she lit her cigarette and then his. She put the case and lighter back and tilted her face up, blew out a breath of smoke. There was something indescribable about *how* she did it, the way she never looked away from the guard.

"Can we get a cab, mister?" she asked, as simple as that.

"Oh, yes, Madam. Let me get one for you," he replied.

Within minutes, I was sitting anxiously between Grandma and Mother, the guard directing the cab driver how to pack and then rearrange the luggage so it would all fit into the trunk. Soon enough the cab driver and Father closed the trunk and got in the taxi. As the cab started up and glided past crowds of people hugging themselves tight to keep warm at the bus stop, I enjoyed the toasty back seat, as soft as a sofa. The driver navigated a sea of people on bicycles, competing with buses and trucks. Looking up, I watched laundry flapping in the wind outside the cement-gray buildings. Higher still, the blue sky looked sunny and warm.

This was my first ride in a taxi. I didn't want it to end, though it did, and much quicker than the morning bus ride.

Soon we were pulling up to our neighbors, who huddled together at the curb outside of our building. Mr. and Mrs. Yung were there, along with their two children, Tai Pao and Lily—my tormentors. I also spotted the Tang family, and the Yis, and the Wangs, all busily chatting and staring as we pulled up. Were they waiting for us? No one had *ever* waited for us before.

Mrs. Yung was the first to approach. Once we were out of the cab, she stepped forward and forcefully grabbed Grandma's hand with both of hers.

"Welcome, welcome!" she exclaimed. "We are the neighbors of your daughter. You had a long journey. You must be tired."

Grandma leaned back a little, as if in response to the forcefulness of Mrs. Yung's greeting.

"Thank you very much for your warm welcome," she replied, steadying herself. "It's nice to be home."

Grandma took a look at the group of our neighbors assembled before her. "You all are so nice. Why don't we have a cup of tea at my daughter's home?"

Mr. Yung—a rude person who deliberately occupied the kitchen sink for longer than necessary whenever he saw us—carried one of Grandma's suitcases over Father's polite protests. Other neighbors came forward, too, all reaching out to help with the luggage. We climbed upstairs, with the luggage and neighbors cramming into our little apartment. Father directed the suitcases into the back room, while Mother and I busied ourselves in the communal kitchen making hot tea for everyone. We didn't have enough cups so we borrowed some from Mrs. Wang and Mrs. Yi, along with some extra chairs. It took three trips just to serve tea to all the adults, each one nodding in thanks.

Quietly the adults sipped their tea, smiling at Grandma. Even the children were awkwardly silent. After a moment of this, Grandma stood up and disappeared into the back room, only to reappear holding two colorful packages. She whispered something in Mother's ear. Mother ran to the kitchen, brought back a few plates, and put them on the table. Grandma opened one of the packs, revealing a tin of butter cookies. She opened the other one—a pack of chocolates.

"Please try these cookies. They are good with green tea," she said to no one in particular, shaking the cookies and chocolates onto the plates. No one moved to take the food.

Grandma motioned to the kids. "Come on, have some chocolates. Don't be shy. They're yummy."

The children looked to their parents for approval and, upon seeing a collective nod, mobbed the plate of chocolate all at once, snatching the candies with both hands. They filled up their small pockets and then their fists. I looked at Mother. She nodded slightly and I went to the plate, but by then it was empty. I was so disappointed—almost in tears. Chocolates are my favorite, and I only had them on very rare occasions. Grandma pulled me aside and whispered into my ear: "No worries. There are plenty for you later." A smile broke across my face.

The adults, more restrained, reached out for the butter cookies once the candy was gone, each person commenting on how good the cookies tasted.

"Hong Kong products taste better than local food because they have more cream and milk in them," someone said knowingly.

The kids finished the chocolates and moved on to attacking the butter cookies. The room had come alive: Children were darting around, comparing who got more of the chocolates, while the adults talked over each other.

The whole time, Grandma sat on the only sofa we had, in the center of the group, smiling pleasantly and responding to Mrs. Yung's questions with one or two words—drowned out by the collective noise filling our small room.

My parents sat in a corner of the room, looking tired, waiting for these people to leave. After an hour of this, Mother announced in an unusually sharp voice: "It is time for me to prepare dinner." She stood up abruptly.

The neighbors took the cue. One by one, they stood and thanked Grandma for the tea and snacks before leaving. Father and I started to clear the room as they left, gathering the dirty glasses and plates and taking them into the kitchen. Mother changed out of her red jacket and made Father and me change, too. I did so reluctantly. Once the new outfits were back in the dresser, we were our normal selves again.

However, we had the kitchen sink all to ourselves, which was a rare treat, especially at this time of day, when the kitchen was usually full of neighbors preparing dinner. Today it was empty, reserved for our use, and the three of us worked as a team to clean. Mother washed, I dried, and Father put everything away in our tall wooden cabinet. Every family had their own cabinet, next to their stove top, and beside a small table for cooking oils and soy sauce that marked out our respective territories within the room. On our table sat baskets of washed greens, bowls of shelled shrimp, and plates of cut raw meat. Mother had Father and me take the thinly sliced five-spiced beef, the cold chicken marinated in wine sauce, and the bowls of jellyfish and pickles out of the cabinet and into the main room of our apartment.

Mother was heating oil in a wok and started on the hot dishes when I returned to the kitchen.

"Take the smoked fish, also," she said, pointing to a large serving plate with fish nicely placed in the center and garnished with green vegetables around the sides. "Then come back and help your father with the sesame dumplings."

Sesame dumplings were a delicacy only served during the New Year celebration, yet Mother was determined to serve them to Grandma. She had managed to buy sweet sticky rice that she soaked in water for a week, which she then had us grind into powder in the water. We prepared the filling by pounding sesame into a fine powder and mixing it with sugar and oil. The process had taken more than a month, as we could only do a little at a time every night. Father and I labored throughout the process, as Mother barked out orders. Now it was finally time to taste the fruits of our hard work.

The kitchen filled with a delicious aroma as Mother sautéed the shrimp, greens, and meats that she had laid out on the kitchen table. Father and I kept busy folding dumplings—a delicate process that required light fingers. I was very proud that I was twice as fast as Father, who wasn't good at housework as he usually didn't do much around the house.

A neighbor or two appeared in the kitchen once in a while to get hot water, or food that was already prepared, looking over their shoulders at the three of us preparing dinner. They were likely surprised to find that Father was also busy in the kitchen. Children passed by on their way to the communal bathroom and peeped in quietly to see what we were doing. Their eyes were full of longing when they saw the enticing food set on the table. We were so focused on the tasks at hand that we nearly forgot the purpose of the feast until we noticed Grandma standing quietly in the kitchen doorway, observing us. Her hands were full of things wrapped in pretty packages.

Mother wiped her hands on her apron, her face red, as if the dark, messy kitchen embarrassed her. She went to her mother.

"Mother, you needn't come out," she insisted. "Please go back. Sit down and rest. Dinner should be ready in a short while."

"I'm not tired," Grandma protested. "I started emptying my suitcase while you were busy in the kitchen. I brought some food for you. I thought you would want to keep it in the kitchen."

Mother glanced over Grandma's shoulder into the hall, and then looked back at our open cabinet. "No, I will keep them in the apartment," she replied. "See, we don't have a padlock to lock our cabinet." She pointed to the padlocks that others had placed on their cabinet doors. Grandma nodded her head knowingly and went back to our room with the packages.

Dinner was delicious. Father served rice wine for this special occasion, but conversation was scarce. It seemed they had little to say. Grandma asked how old I was, which grade I was in, and what I was learning. She asked Mother about her job. Along the way, she told us a little bit of her life in America. She had just been on a trip to Europe, which greatly aroused my curiosity.

"Which country did you visit?" I asked.

"France and Germany."

I was only vaguely aware of these countries, and I paused, taking that in.

"What did you do there?" I asked when I had recovered.

"I went with a group of tourists," she told me. "We took a train from city to city, and then a bus would take us around to see lots of beautiful, old places in each city."

"What did you do in France?"

"I went to the museums."

"Museums?" *How boring*, I thought to myself. "I went to the Shanghai museum once and all I saw was old pottery," I told her. "Did you eat lots of cream?"

"Shush, let your grandmother eat in peace," Mother interrupted.

I had wanted to try French food ever since the day I passed the Red House with Mother. It was one of only two Western-style restaurants in Shanghai. Mother told me this place specialized in French food, or at least it had at one time. French food was the best, she told me. I asked her whether she had tried any before.

"No. I don't like too much cream in food," she replied.

I like cream, the little bit on top of cakes. I'd like to have *lots* of it. From that point on, France had stuck out in my mind.

After I had eaten a big helping of sautéed shrimp with green peas, I forgot Mother's chiding. "What do you eat in America, at home, I mean?" I asked.

"I eat Chinese food," Grandma replied. "I am the only one who eats Chinese food at home. Bob, Lidia, and Bill eat Western food. I have to prepare two sets of meals each day."

"Who is Bob? Who are Lidia and Bill?" I asked, curious. I had never heard about them before.

"Bob is my husband. Lidia and Bill are our children."

I was puzzled by this. My grandpa died in Shanghai about ten years ago, before I was born.

"But Grandpa is dead," I said.

"Leave your Grandmother alone," Mother said. "Little people shouldn't speak too much. Mind your manners."

I didn't like being considered a little person, but I knew better than to talk back.

After a few minutes' silence, Grandma said to me, "It's a long story. I promise I will tell you eventually. Now, I want you to study hard in school and to be the first girl to go to college in our family."

"College?" I laughed out loud, my mouth full of food. "There is no college. College is closed."

"Then you can come to America and live with me. You can go to college there." Grandma smiled at me.

"Don't plant unrealistic ideas in her head like you did when I was little," Mother snapped.

Grandma looked at Mother as if she was about to cry, and then looked away. When she turned to face me, she was smiling again. She helped herself to two spoonfuls of tofu and bok choy.

"I miss these foods so much," she said cheerfully. "I can't get them back at home."

Mother smiled too. "Come on. Have more."

A meal like this was a rare treat, and I took the opportunity to have another helping as well.

With the mood lightened, I continued on, jabbering away. I couldn't quit talking, even though Mother told me many times to mind my manners and to stop talking with my mouth full, only to have Grandma give me nods here and there, encouraging me. I felt like I was an adult, almost, suddenly grown up.

By the time we finished dinner, darkness had long settled outside. With every light in the apartment on, the bright room reflected the cheerfulness of our mood.

"Why don't you help Grandma unpack in the back room while your Mother and I clear up the dinner table?" Father asked.

"Of course. Can I?" I asked Grandma, eager to be her assistant. Already, I would do *anything* for her.

She nodded and the two of us went to the back room together. One of the suitcases was open, empty except for a few cartons of cigarettes. She took out her small suitcase and opened it, producing a small makeup case.

"Please put it on the vanity in the big room," she instructed me.

The big room, an all-purpose dining, sitting, and bedroom, wasn't all that big except in comparison to the back room, a dark, windowless room where the suitcases were. That windowless room was usually my bedroom, but on this night I would sleep with Grandma in the big room. I did as she said, and eager to do more, I took her makeup out of the case as well. I opened the first thing I pulled out: a short, gold-colored tube, only to find a red, waxy stick inside—lipstick, I guessed. There were a few smooth-shaped bottles of perfume, a brush, a case of powder, and a few jars of something else I didn't recognize. I unscrewed the tops of all the jars and bottles and smelled every one of them carefully. I dabbed a little lipstick to my lips, and then I touched the powder. Just then, Mother came in and noticed what I was doing. She snatched the powder case out of my hand, scolding me.

"Stop messing around. Clean up your face." Mortified, I cleaned my face as best I could with the back of my hand, and ran back to the back room, where Grandma was waiting.

"I have something for you," Grandma told me as I walked in. She had opened one of the other big suitcases. "Close your eyes," she said playfully.

I closed my eyes, anxious, and extended my arms and hands. An object touched my palm, a little hairy thing. I opened my eyes. I was holding a doll: a yellow-haired, long-legged girl doll with breasts and a figure like a woman. The doll was in a tight, white, short-sleeved knit top and a slim miniskirt. She had on a pair of red high heels. Her eyes were blue and deep; her lips were pink and smooth, parted slightly as if she was smiling—but not exactly smiling. Also in my palm was a small brown toy suitcase. "Her changing clothes," Grandma explained. What a glamorous doll, I thought.

I played with the doll until I went to bed. Her name was Barbie and I made her change into all the outfits that came along in her suitcase. After trying every possible combination, I undressed her and studied her. Without her clothes, Barbie was too skinny; her body looked like a piece of light pink plastic, not as attractive as when she was fully dressed.

After Mother and Father went to sleep in my bedroom, Grandma sat next to me on the bed. She took out a photo from her purse. She showed me Bob, Lidia, and Bill. Bob was a tall man with curly, salt-and-pepper hair, a big nose, and steel-gray eyes. He wore a busy Hawaiian shirt and shorts; he stood next to Grandma, holding her shoulder and smiling, his big grin glittering in the light. In front of them stood Lidia, a sullen, black-haired girl in a green dress and white shoes, and Bill, a pimple-faced boy who stared straight into the camera. Behind them was a Christmas tree decorated in gold, silver, red, and green balls that hung from its branches. At the foot of the Christmas tree were piles of boxes that reflected the shine of the light, with red bows on top. A happy family, I thought. I stared at the picture for a long time.

Finally, I found my courage to ask: "Is Bob, your husband, a foreigner?"

"Yes. He's an American," Grandma confirmed.

I was shocked and awed by the news. I knew of *no one* who had married a foreigner. There were so few big-nosed and blue-eyed foreigners in Shanghai that everyone would stop and stare if we ever saw one. One time I saw a mob of people try to touch a blond boy about my age. The boy had been so scared that he burst out crying.

"Where did you meet him?" I asked. "Mother told me you left Shanghai a long time ago."

"I met him in Shanghai, a long time ago. Little Treasure, I am very tired now."

"Tell me how you met him," I demanded.

"I will tell you." She pulled the picture out of my hand gently, as if she was afraid of hurting either me or the picture. "Now, let's go to bed." She turned off the bedside light.

"When?" I didn't give up.

"Tomorrow."

"You promise?"

"Yes, I promise." She walked around to the other side and got into the bed next to me.

I lay awake next to her, reimagining the Christmas tree, Lidia's green dress, Barbie's many different outfits, and all the presents under the tree. I sensed Grandma was still awake, too, but she didn't say anything.

I don't know when my imagination ended and my dreams began. But in my dream, I was playing with Barbie—a real Barbie who laughed, talked, and moved—on a big lawn of green velvet under a bright blue sky. I was in a green dress, like Lidia's. The dress clung to my legs as the wind pulled it behind me. I was laughing and Barbie was singing. No one called me "American Spy," just Ting, my name.

The next day, Grandma began her story.

4

LING'S BIG LIFE EVENT

The afternoon sun was strong for late September. Mini stood in the doorway of the living room looking out into the front atrium. In the distance, she could hear the crisp clicking of ivory Mahjong tiles being pushed around in the drawing room, where her mother was playing her daily game. Ai May had just served afternoon dim sum to the Mahjong party, and so it was about time for Mini to see to dinner. Today's meal would be more complicated than usual: Ling and her new husband, Jie Xing, would be joining the family.

This was the first time Mini had seen her elder sister since Ling became the second wife of a prominent silk merchant and left home to live with her husband, his first wife, daughters, and parents in the Wang family mansion in Suzhou. Mini hadn't had much of an opportunity to speak to her sister these last nine months. The Wang family had a telephone in the house, but Ling preferred letters, even if those were written sparingly. The telephone was in the sitting room where everyone gathered when they were not in bed, Ling had explained. She felt uncomfortable using it too often, but her last call home was an exception: Ling was pregnant. Her usually hurried conversation was altogether different, and Mini could feel her excitement—her higher pitch and animated words conveying much about her new status. "I might even move back. I so miss Shanghai and the family. Jie Xing promised we can set up our own household. Then I can visit home more often. He's in Shanghai all the time anyway—for his business." The last part she said proudly, but Mini thought she also heard worry.

Ling's pregnancy put her in a very favorable position. Mini was very happy for her sister. She looked forward to being able to see her again and talk freely. Mini had never asked what life was like in the Wang household—having to share everything with the first wife, all under the watchful eyes of the in-laws and their servants.

The arrangement had held such promise, and it seemed Ling's wish was about to be realized. Aunt, of course, was to be credited, especially if Ling were fortunate enough to give birth to a son. It was Aunt who wrote to introduce the young Mr. Wang to Ling and Mini's mother, Mrs. Pao, about a year and a half ago.

Mini remembered her mother calling her into the drawing room and telling her to read the letter aloud.

"It's from Auntie," Mini said, and began reading:

> *Dear Elder Sister,*
> *I hope this letter finds you well. My family is doing well here in Suzhou. My husband, Dai Lian, was recently promoted to head accountant at the Wang silk factory. We are all happy about our good fortune.*
> *The reason I am writing is that Dai Lian learned his boss is looking for a wife. You see, Mr. Wang is married, but his wife has not been able to give him a son. Being the eldest son of the most prominent family in town,*

he needs a male heir. Now he is looking for a second change. He does not want to marry any girl, but one from a decent family. Of course, I thought about Ling. Ling is such a pretty girl, even though she is a bit old at twenty-two. Forgive us for not asking your permission, but we showed Ling's picture to Mr. Wang. He expressed great interest.

Please let me know what you think.
Sincerely,
Your Little Sister

Mrs. Pao took the letter from Mini's hands.

"You know better than to mention this until Father and I speak," Mrs. Pao chided.

Mini nodded and helped her mother walk to the adjacent study, where Mrs. Pao carefully placed the letter on her husband's desk.

At dinner that evening, Mrs. Pao broached the subject of her sister's letter.

"My sister mentioned Mr. Wang of Suzhou is looking to marry," Mrs. Pao said. "She kindly offered to introduce our family."

Ling was visibly interested at this, but their father did not say anything—Mrs. Pao's sentence left hanging over the dinner table. On retiring to his study that evening, Mini watched as her father read the letter for himself and promptly tossed it into the wastebasket without comment.

The next day, Mrs. Pao called Mini into her drawing room. "Mini, I want you to write to my sister." Mrs. Pao proceeded to dictate her reply.

Dear Sister,
Thank you very much for thinking about Ling's life event. As you know, Ling is a nice girl with exceptional taste.

I remember the Wang family. Our father used to work for old Mr. Wang. I would never dream that

Ling might have the opportunity to marry into the Wang family. Mr. Wang sounds almost perfect, except that he is already married. As I remember, his current wife was his second wife. She was promoted to the rightful position after his first wife died in childbirth, am I right?

I talked to Mr. Pao. I don't think he will agree to the proposal.

Please do visit me if you can. I miss my family.

Sincerely,

Your Elder Sister

Mini read the letter back and then sealed it, giving it to Ai May to post.

Two weeks passed without discussion of the proposition before Aunt appeared, unannounced, on their doorstep. Mrs. Pao let out a sharp shriek upon seeing her sister, excited as a little girl, dropping the clothes she was mending with her daughters onto the floor.

"Little, is that you?" Mrs. Pao struggled to get up from the chair, but her sister was faster. Aunt helped Mrs. Pao to stand up. Little was just a nickname, but an accurate one: She was *much* smaller than her sister. Otherwise, the likeness between them was striking—they each had high, arched eyebrows and bright eyes, surrounded by flawless skin. Other than their height, the only difference between the two was Aunt's unbound feet.

"Yes, elder sister. It's me. So nice to see you and the girls."

Aunt was to stay for a week, the maximum amount of time her husband allowed her to be away. As the two ladies were catching up, Ling went to fetch hot tea while Mini directed Ai May where to place the luggage. Ling and Mini returned to find their aunt already discussing the virtues of her proposed arrangement.

"Sister, Ling is not young anymore. You need to think about her big life event. You cannot keep her home forever."

"I know," Mrs. Pao conceded. "But finding the right suitor is so hard. And what about the rumor? About his frequent visits to the dance hall and pleasure houses?"

"Oh, big sister. You worry too much," Aunt replied. "He is a businessman. It is his business to entertain his clients. Mr. Wang is perfect for Ling. Ling could find no better family. The Suzhou Wangs go back for generations and he is an honorable man. You see, his first wife has been dead for five years now, and his current wife has only given him two daughters. He needs a son to take over his business and carry on the family name. Imagine if Ling gives him a son. Ling will be the rightful wife, even without a title. Sister, this is one opportunity in a thousand years."

"But why would he be interested in Ling?" Mrs. Pao asked. "Ling is from a working family."

"Ah, but your husband is not an average working man," Aunt explained. "He is an educated man who works for the British. I heard the Wang family wants to expand their business beyond Asia. They want to do business with the Americans and the British. You see, it works out just fine."

"But he is too old for Ling."

"He is only forty-four," Aunt rebutted. "He is still in his strong years. He keeps up his appearance, too. You see, he doesn't look old." She took out a photo of Jie Xing to show Mrs. Pao, but quickly drew it back to her chest upon noticing Ling and Mini as they leaned in, craning their necks to peek.

After that, Aunt would bring up the subject of marriage whenever she could, careful to avoid discussing it openly in front of Mr. Pao or the two girls. Ling and Mini couldn't help but tiptoe around them, trying to catch every word they exchanged. Their aunt's message varied little that week as she pled Mr. Wang's case.

Mrs. Pao agreed to keep the photo and had promised to seriously consider the opportunity when it was time for her sister to return to

Suzhou. She was more direct with Mini: "If Ling can give birth to a couple of boys, she can return home with the title of Mrs. Wang, the legitimate wife of the wealthiest man in Suzhou."

Ling's marriage was a constant subject for Mrs. Pao over the next few months. At first Mr. Pao would simply cut her off, but Mrs. Pao didn't give up. She continued bringing it up: at the breakfast table, at the dinner table, and—Mini guessed—in the bedroom as well.

Mrs. Pao told Ling and Mini about the Wang family in great detail: how big the house was—*"not a house but a compound of buildings in Suzhou, with rock gardens by a manmade lake"*—how almost the entire town of Suzhou worked for the family. Mini sensed that her mother's stories had aroused a strong desire in Ling's heart to be part of this wealthy family.

One Friday evening, Mr. Pao took both Ling and Mini for dinner at the Red House, a well-known French restaurant in the heart of the tree-lined French district. It was their standing weekly dinner outing when their Father was alone with his daughters. Mrs. Pao never joined them, as she had no stomach for the bloody meat or creamy chicken served there.

As dinner drew to a close, the waiter brought coffee, and Mr. Pao became serious: "Ling, what do you think of the prospect of marrying Mr. Wang and being a second wife?"

Ling's face flushed pink. Unlike Mini, she wasn't used to her father's directness. She lowered her head and shifted in her seat. Her cup of coffee sat on the table, untouched. She stared mutely at the silk handkerchief in her hand.

Mini answered instead: "I think Ling likes the idea. She wants to marry into the Wang family."

Mr. Pao sat up straight and looked at Ling. "Ling, I want to hear from you. It is your marriage. I want you to feel comfortable with the arrangement."

Ling lifted her eyes and made brief eye contact with her father, only to look down again. Mini turned to her sister, watching her.

"Ling, you don't have to say a word," Mini said. "Just nod your head if you agree with it."

Ling nodded her head slightly. Mr. Pao sighed a long sigh. They finished their cake and coffee in silence.

The next day, Mr. Pao wrote to his sister-in-law and her husband giving his consent. Ling was brought up a little differently from most girls her age, he explained: She had eight years of missionary education and was used to living a not-so-restrictive life. Ling, he wrote, would be happier if she could remain in Shanghai.

The reply this time came from Mrs. Pao's brother-in-law, who addressed Mr. Pao's concern as he would a business matter for the Wang family. He promised to bring up the idea with Mr. Wang, but the bargaining chip would likely be a baby. If Ling were to have a child—a male heir, specifically—then it would be much easier for Ling to persuade her husband to allow her to live in Shanghai.

Because Ling was going to be the second wife of Jie Xing Wang, there was little formality to the engagement. The elder Wang did not pay an official visit to the Paos, and Ling did not need to go to Suzhou to meet her future in-laws. Instead, she received a letter from the elder Wang with the family's blessing. With the engagement now official, the Wang family moved quickly, as if they were afraid Mr. Pao would change his mind: They sent Ling several trunks of assorted silk and wool fabrics, high-heeled shoes, satin-embroidered slippers, and both long and short fur coats.

A tailor was brought in and a workshop was set up in Mrs. Pao's drawing room. Mrs. Pao stopped her daily game of Mahjong to supervise the preparations over the next several weeks. Ling and Mini busily assisted the tailor, from giving him their views on what was fashionable to picking out the right buttons for various dresses. Ling was excited to try on the dresses, and she insisted Mini try them on as well—always pointing out when the dresses didn't complement Mini's dark complexion or her other imperfections.

Mrs. Pao made the arrangements for the prewedding banquet to formally introduce Jie Xing. She invited all the relatives and family friends she could think of. The event would be at the newly erected Park Hotel, the most prominent establishment in Shanghai.

"Why give a banquet at the Park Hotel?" Mr. Pao asked when Mrs. Pao described her planning. "Don't you think it's too extravagant? Mind you, Ling is going to be a second wife."

"Don't you worry—Ling will be the rightful one," Mrs. Pao told her husband. "It's just a matter of time. And the Wangs, they have showered Ling with their generosity. We need to do our part as well. Jie Xing should be introduced to our side of the family properly."

"All right, you arrange it," he said. He wrote a check and had nothing further to do with the matter.

On the day of the party, their families arranged for Ling to meet Jie Xing. The two would exchange pleasantries briefly in the banquet hall before receiving guests. Ling was dressed in a sleeveless turquoise silk qipao, with side slits reaching up to her thighs, giving a glimpse of her pale and shapely legs as she walked. A pair of ruby and diamond earrings peeked out from beneath her waves of jet-black hair, which was pulled back to rest elegantly on her shoulders. She smiled at Jie Xing shyly, red lips parted slightly to show her pearly white teeth.

Jie Xing was pleased; Mini could tell, because he held out his arm to Ling immediately. By the time the first guest arrived, Ling was hanging on Jie Xing's arm. She constantly looked up at him, smiling, and he squeezed her hand gently and smiled back. She waved at each person coming through the door of the banquet hall with her right hand raised high, the blinding sparkles from her diamond ring dancing in the light.

Mini looked on at this match made in heaven, busily receiving guests, only to realize that her father had separated himself and stood well off to the side. Indeed, even as the evening wore on with rice wine flowing and fireworks cracking amidst toasts and laughter, Mini noticed that Mr. Pao remained in the shadows, as if he didn't want to be seen. Mini did not ask her father, as proud as he was, why he had agreed to the match. She thought then of another who was missing from the festivities—Jie Xing's first wife. *How did she feel?* Mini wondered. Mini would never know, of course: The first wife wasn't invited.

A light tap on her shoulder brought Mini back to the present. Ai May was standing next to her, holding a large basket full of vegetables, fish, and beef. It was time to help Ai May prepare dinner. It had been only this morning that Mini had learned Ling was coming for dinner—just as Mini was about to go to the market for the day's shopping. Mrs. Pao had hobbled over on her three-inch feet, her bound "golden lilies" far too delicate for a lengthy walk.

"Mini," Mrs. Pao said. "Ling is coming home for dinner."

"Ling? Is she in Shanghai? How did you know?" Mini asked.

"She telephoned yesterday while you were out. I was busy with the game when you returned. I forgot to tell you," Mrs. Pao added in a way that told Mini to stop with the questions. "Get a big fish. Your sister is pregnant, and fish is good for a pregnant woman. It will make the baby smart. Get some beef. Jie Xing likes beef cold cuts. It's a family dinner—no need to buy a lot. Get an eastern melon. And let's have salted pork soup, plus two vegetable dishes and rice. That should do. Of course, make some porridge and get some pickles as well. Your father likes his cold porridge in summertime. Oh, I hope today isn't going to be too hot. We've passed the *bailu* already, but it's still so warm . . ."

It was another steamy morning, and the cooler autumn weather that was typically signaled by the day of bailu seemed far off still. Mrs. Pao wobbled towards her bedroom slowly on her tiny feet, fanning herself with a large silk fan.

In reality, Mrs. Pao's direction was no longer necessary. Mini had been running the household far better than her mother for some time now. Still, Mrs. Pao continued to instruct her on what to buy and how much to spend, even though Mini had come to manage the budget and their meals so well that her father gave the expense money to her directly.

On this and every other day, Mini would spend less than her daily allowance. She would return from the market and place the day's change in a small wooden box that she hid under her bed. Mini decided long ago the money was hers—a reward for her hard bargaining and good judgment.

Dinner that night would take longer and be more complicated than usual, so Mini volunteered her help to Ai May, for whom there would be no relief from the sweltering heat. The only shade in the courtyard was one small patch created by the tarp that hung over the outdoor sink. The air was still, but it was more bearable than the western-facing kitchen, soaked in the hot sunlight. These days, it was impossible to stay in the kitchen for more than a few minutes at a time, let alone prepare an entire meal there. Ai May, a tall and skinny girl about Mini's age, had moved the portable coal stove and a table outside to set up a makeshift kitchen. At least it was in the open, and although Ai May managed to conserve her movements and stay in the small patch of shade, beads of sweat formed on her forehead, threatening to roll into her eyes. Her thin cotton top stuck to her back. Ai May had been working for the Pao family for over nine years, since she was thirteen years old. She was very close to Mini. They played together when they were young, and Mini was the only one who took care of Ai May when she was sick.

"Ai May, dinner should be ready for everyone by seven," Mini told her. "Do we have enough time to cook the cold beef?"

"What time is it now, Miss Mini?" Ai May asked, throwing a piece of beef into a pot of water and putting the pot on the coal stove.

Mini looked at her small silver wristwatch. "It's half past three."

"Don't worry. We have enough time. Beef should be done in two hours and the rest doesn't take much time," Ai May said confidently.

She turned to gut the fish while Mini chopped green onions. The fish would be steamed and served with green onions sautéed in hot vegetable oil.

"Miss Ling must be happy now that she is living in Shanghai," Ai May began chatting. Mini had always treated her as an equal and, being close since childhood, Ai May was comfortable speaking to Mini without the formalities she used for the rest of the Pao family.

"I bet," Mini replied. "Ling said she hasn't gone out dancing once since she moved to Suzhou."

"Suzhou is a small place."

"Oh, I forgot to tell you," Mini said. "Ling promised to bring a few of her dresses for you. She's gained weight and cannot fit in them anymore."

Actually, Ling had offered her dresses to Mini, but Mini had politely declined.

"For *me*?" Ai May asked incredulously. "What am I going to do with them? They are too good for me to wear." She was pleased but practical, too.

"You can wear a new dress when you meet your beau." Mini winked at Ai May. Mini had recently overheard her mother telling a friend that Ai May was getting older, and the family wouldn't be able to retain her much longer. One day she was going to marry someone.

"Miss Mini, you know I will not leave this family. Who am I going to marry?" Ai May asked. "City people don't want me, and I don't want to go back to the country." She silently continued cleaning the fish for a while, then turned to face Mini: "Mr. Shi really is a dashing young man."

Mini's cheeks flushed light pink.

"Are we going to see him again tomorrow?" Ai May pressed.

"Perhaps."

They continued to wash the greens, sauté the onions, and so forth, until Mrs. Pao appeared in the courtyard.

"Don't you think you should change before your sister arrives? You smell like cooking oil."

Mrs. Pao had already changed into her shapeless formal wear: a brown satin tunic that reached above her knees and a long skirt that covered her feet. Her hair was tied into a bun and she wore a silk headband with a round jade cabochon in the middle of her forehead. Short and stout, she held fast to the edge of the wooden table to steady herself.

Mini was still in her cotton housedress and wasn't about to change, given the preparations she still needed to attend to. She looked in the direction of the drawing room, where her mother's Mahjong game should still have been in progress.

"Where are Wu Ma, Chang Ma, and Tang Ma?" Mini asked.

"They're gone," Mrs. Pao said. "We finished our game early today. I told them Ling and Ling's old master are coming. They left through the kitchen door."

Though Mrs. Pao routinely called her husband "old master" after the old custom, it was odd to Mini's ears to hear her mother refer to Ling's husband the same way.

When Mini didn't respond, her mother asked more directly: "Are you going to change?"

"I still have work here," Mini replied. "And it's much too hot. Ling won't mind seeing me like this."

"Leave it to Ai May," her mother suggested. "Jie Xing is with your sister. You must change and look decent. Jie Xing may find you a good husband." This, of course, was Mrs. Pao's ultimate hope for her unwed daughter.

Mini shrugged. She had never really cared for Jie Xing. She thought his voice sounded greasy and she had no desire to impress him, but it wouldn't help for Mini to say anything further. She walked her mother back into the house and went to her bedroom upstairs, where she changed into a short and simple white muslin qipao.

When the grandfather clock in the living room struck six times, as if on cue, there was a commotion outside the front gate. A car door slammed, and then came a knock on the front door.

"Ai May, go get the door," Mrs. Pao said as she checked to make sure her headband was in place.

Ai May was in the middle of setting up the dining table. Her hands were full of plates and chopsticks.

"I'll go," Mini said, walking out and opening the front door to find a filled-out Ling, with Jie Xing behind her. Her dress was tightly wrapped around her bust, and her waist and her rear seemed to have expanded. Her oval face was fuller too, and a pair of lustrous gray pearl earrings complemented her jet-black hair. She threw her arms around Mini.

"So nice to be home," Ling said. "I missed you. Of course, Mother and Father, too." She held Mini tight and the two sisters looked each other over.

Mini carefully put her hand on Ling's belly, as if she were afraid to hurt the unborn baby.

"I missed you, too," Mini said. "Now you're back for good! We can see you and the baby more often. Oh, congratulations!" Mini spoke as if the baby were already there. Nine months of living apart seemed to have dissolved the constant, subtle competition between them.

Jie Xing, wearing a gray silk robe, came up and casually placed his right hand on Mini's back. Mini stepped forward quickly to avoid his touch, and Jie Xing's hand fell away.

He smiled at her. "You look wonderful!"

"Thank you," Mini replied politely. "Please come in. Ma is waiting for you both."

Ling turned to the chauffeur. "Bring in the presents, and you don't need to wait for us. Please come back at nine to pick us up," she instructed.

"Yes, Mistress." The chauffeur followed them to the living room and laid a stack of boxes and a big bag on the coffee table, bowing to Ling and Jie Xing on his way out.

"Ling, my baby—how are you doing?" Mrs. Pao held Ling's hand.

"Ma, I'm doing fine. My morning sickness is not too bad. I can hold down food all right," she smiled up proudly at Jie Xing.

"Good, good. You need to eat more for the baby," Mrs. Pao responded. "Eat more fish so you will have a smart child. How are you, Jie Xing?" Still holding Ling's hand, Mrs. Pao half-turned to face Jie Xing.

"Very well, Ma." He bowed his head slightly.

"Come in," she implored. "Please sit down. Ai May, bring tea."

"Ma, I brought some Suzhou dried tofu and some other delicacies for you and Pa," Ling pointed at the boxes on the table.

"Thank you for thinking of me." Mrs. Pao turned and bowed to Jie Xing.

As they were chatting, a rickshaw stopped outside the house. Ai May ran and opened the door. Mr. Pao walked in wearing a cream-colored linen suit and panama hat, wiping his forehead with a linen handkerchief.

Mini stood up. "Pa, Ling is here."

"Jolly good," their father replied. "I need to change out of this suit. It's much too hot." As he passed the living room and entered his bedroom, he nodded to both Ling and Jie Xing.

Mini adjusted the electric fans and turned all three standup fans to face the group. Ai May brought in tea for everyone. Mrs. Pao opened a few boxes of the dried tofu to snack on.

Mr. Pao emerged from his bedroom in a light cotton robe. He had salt-and-pepper hair and wore a pair of rimless round glasses. His lean body held erect, he walked with energetic steps. He sat down in his usual chair. Mrs. Pao came up with a small plate of dried tofu and set it on the rosewood side table next to his teacup.

"Jie Xing, how was the journey back to Shanghai? How is the house hunting?" he asked, sipping his tea.

"Uneventful," the younger man replied. "I found a three-story western-style house in the Hongkew district. It's close to a park and also not too far from my new factory in the Japanese concession."

"International settlement," Mr. Pao corrected him.

"I am going to close the purchase tomorrow afternoon."

"Where are you staying now?" Mr. Pao inquired more politely.

"I booked a suite on the fifth floor in the Cathay Hotel on the Bund," Jie Xing answered. "Ling likes Western luxury hotels. The Cathay Hotel is a treat for her. They serve Chinese food too, so Ling and I can each have our own food when we feel like it. You spoiled Ling—she has such a taste for foreign foods, especially now, as she is in such a delicate situation. She was miserable in Suzhou."

Ling cut in: "Suzhou's gardens are beautiful, but I like Shanghai better. I'd like to have some Western food once in a while, and Suzhou is not good for that. Pa, when are you going to take us to the Red House again?"

"If you like, we can go this Friday," Mr. Pao offered indulgently. "What do you say, Jie Xing? You don't mind me taking Ling, do you?"

"No, no," Ling's husband replied. "I have some business to attend to this Friday. See, Ling, how nice it is for you to be back in Shanghai?" He winked at Ling and she smiled behind her silk handkerchief.

"How is your new factory doing?"

"Doing well," Jie Xing said confidently. "The machines are all up and running and I have received some orders from Japan already."

Mr. Pao's cup stopped in mid-air, though he didn't say a word.

"Congratulations!" Mrs. Pao said enthusiastically to fill the silence left by her husband.

"I hope to land some orders from the British," Jie Xing pressed on, ignoring Mrs. Pao. "I will truly rely on you, Mr. Pao, for that. You are the expert. What do you think will be the next step for these Japanese? There is so much tension in the North. How will the British deal with their aggression?"

Mini frowned. She disliked the fact that Jie Xing did not address Mr. Pao as "father," the way most Chinese sons-in-law would do. She gave Jie Xing a hard look, though no one paid her any attention.

"I suspect the British will do something. But I cannot say what," Mr. Pao said. He had been working at the British consulate in Shanghai for twenty-five years.

Mr. Pao had been born to a poor family. His father had worked as a cook for a German family, and Mr. Pao managed to get into St. John's University on scholarship. Even though he was one of the top students in his class, he could not travel abroad to continue his studies as he wished, lacking the connections and funds required to leave. He watched as many of his wealthy classmates went on to London or New York to study and returned to home to run their family businesses.

Instead, Mr. Pao settled into a position at the British consulate, working as a clerk. His services proved to be quite invaluable, bridging many commercial deals between his wealthy, Western-educated college friends and his new Western employer. He became as respected by his British employer as any Chinese employee could hope to be, and along the way he acquired a few rental properties.

Mr. Pao was not wealthy, but with rental income and a handsome salary from the consulate, he provided a very comfortable life for his wife and daughters. Though loyal to the British, he was fully aware he was only their *employee*, not one of them, and they had no duty to protect China. Still, Mr. Pao had been very frustrated by British inaction in the wake of the Japanese invasion of northern China during the Mukden Incident in 1931.

Ai May announced dinner. Everyone stood up and moved into the dining room. Mr. Pao changed to a lighter subject.

"How did you spend your day today?" he asked Mini.

"I went window-shopping with Miss Yee," she replied. Miss Yee was the daughter of their next-door neighbor.

"Mini, please visit me at the hotel tomorrow," Ling said. "You have to see the shopping arcade on the ground floor. The most recent fashions from London and Paris are there!"

"Did you review your English?" Mr. Pao asked before Mini could respond.

"No," Mini replied honestly. "I was too busy today. You see, I had to help Ai May get ready for Ling's visit."

"Excuses, excuses. What I am going to do with you?" Mr. Pao smiled at Mini. "Ling, do you keep up your English?"

"No, Pa. I have no need," Ling replied.

Mr. Pao made his two girls continue their English study long after they left the missionary school, though both of them kept at it halfheartedly, owing to the encouragement of Mrs. Pao, who never understood why her husband wanted their daughters to learn a foreign tongue. Ling had never been a diligent student, and it wasn't long before she forgot all she had learned in school. Mini, on the other hand, could still keep a simple conversation going in English.

"Ling, don't be shortsighted. You never know when your English might come in handy," her father chided. "Mini, you and I will practice each day. We will start today."

"Why, Pa?" she asked.

"I am going to take you to a picnic at the British consulate."

Jie Xing shook his head slightly, giving Ling a look as he picked up a piece of beef with his chopsticks. Mrs. Pao was embarrassed.

"Old Master, do you think this is a good idea? Bringing a maiden to a party full of foreigners?" Mrs. Pao said, more statement than question.

"Foreigners are people, too," her husband replied. "Mini knows how to behave and I am not worried."

The matter was settled. Ling and Mrs. Pao looked down at their plates, avoiding Jie Xing's disapproving eyes.

5

ENCOUNTER IN THE MARKET

Mini waited off to the side of the market entrance. Ai May stood two steps behind, holding a large bamboo basket, her hair woven into a thick, single braid. The entrance was less an entrance than an opening into a long back alleyway that stretched four blocks deep, selling everything from fresh vegetables, meat, and fish, to dry goods, fabric, and footwear. Vendors shouted their prices loudly, each one trying to outdo the others and lure in customers. It was a cacophonous, smelly place where the well-to-dos wouldn't set foot. It was also where Mini did her daily shopping. She had honed her form over years of practice and had filled up the wooden box under her bed with the savings.

She wore a red cardigan that, unbuttoned, modestly revealed a light-blue cotton qipao that complemented her tall, slim figure. Her shining, wavy black hair was combed back to reveal her long neck. As she turned her head impatiently, teardrop jade earrings trembled at her earlobes. Suddenly, she smiled. A young man in an off-white linen suit dashed toward her from across the street.

"You're late." Mini tried to act annoyed, but her eyes smiled brightly.

"I'm so sorry," Mr. Shi said apologetically. "Mother wanted me to run an errand because she didn't trust the servant."

He put his hand on her shoulder, turning her slightly toward the market. They entered together, with Ai May two steps behind.

The singsong-like chants from merchants swallowed them as they crossed the market threshold. It was crowded, as usual. Knowing that no one would notice them, they locked hands and closed the distance between their two bodies. The young man whispered something into Mini's ear, and she giggled.

From behind, Ai May pretended not to watch, looking down at her feet as if counting her steps. They stopped at a stall bloody with fish entrails, the merchant gutting fish for a customer.

"Good morning, Miss," he shouted to Mini. "I have good prices today. Pick anything you like, and I'll give you a ten percent discount."

A tank was set up, fish swimming happily within, oblivious to their fate.

Mr. Shi pointed: "This one."

"Right away!" The merchant signaled to a teenage boy next to him. The boy picked up a stick with a round net at the top and scooped up the fish. Ai May held out her basket.

"Gut it," the young man said to the merchant.

"That's extra," the fishmonger replied.

"No matter." Turning to Ai May, Mr. Shi said, "Save you some work."

Ai May nodded her head appreciatively. "Thank you very much, Mr. Shi."

As Mini fiddled in her purse to get exact change, the young man extended a large note to the merchant.

"No need to worry, Mini," Mr. Shi said generously.

"It is very kind of you, but I cannot let you do this often," Mini said. "It is for my family."

"Ok, I won't do it again today," he promised. "You take care of the rest."

At their leisurely pace, it was already nearly noon by the time they finished shopping and Ai May's basket was full. Ai May was impatient, eager to head back home. She still had to prepare lunch for Mrs. Pao and her Mahjong party. Mini felt it was her duty to leave the market as well.

"Wait, Mini, can you stay with me a little longer?" Mr. Shi pleaded in a low voice. "I would like to talk, maybe somewhere quieter."

Mini hesitated, looking from Ai May to Mr. Shi and back again.

"I will tell Mrs. Pao you bumped into a friend and decided to go to the Bund," Ai May offered.

"What a wonderful idea!" Mr. Shi exclaimed, eager for the excuse.

"I don't like to lie," Mini protested. "What if Ma asks who I bumped into?"

"I would say Miss Yee," Ai May replied at once.

"That's not going to work," Mini reasoned. "Ma will mention it to Miss Yee, since she lives next door."

"What about Miss Chang?" Ai May offered. "She was your classmate and you don't see her often."

"No, I don't like to lie. I should go home," Mini said, though she didn't move an inch as she said it.

"It's okay, Young Mistress," Ai May assured her. "Your mother is busy with her game, so she won't notice. I'm not lying to harm anyone."

"Ai May, you're a smart girl." Mr. Shi turned to Mini. "Ai May's right. Your mother won't miss you. I promise to send you home before your mother's game is over."

Mini hesitated, but finally nodded her consent. A broad smile swept across Mr. Shi's face.

"I'll see you in a few hours, then," Mini said.

"Yes, Mistress." Ai May turned and left.

Mini felt a faint sense of guilt. She didn't want to lie, but her desire to be with this young man was overwhelming. They had been meeting daily, always at the market, their walks through the shops taking longer and longer as Mini extended the trip as much as possible. Of course, they were never alone—Ai May always trailed behind them. But now she was gone. Holding hands and facing each other, they suddenly felt lost, unsure of what to do next.

"Where do you want to go?" he asked.

"Let's go to the Bund," Mini suggested.

Mr. Shi put his fingers to his mouth and whistled to a passing rickshaw. The coolie made a sharp turn and stopped his rickshaw in front of them. Mini climbed into the seat as Mr. Shi gently supported her elbow in his hand. He climbed in after her and, pausing to make certain Mini had settled in comfortably, instructed the coolie: "To the Bund."

The ride passed quickly. On this day, as every day, the road was busy with people navigating the sea of coolies, cars, and trams that carried traffic to the Bund, a part of the city that ran parallel to the Huangpu River and defined Shanghai's international settlement. Mini pointed to a café and suggested they go there. It was a small place and one she had been to before.

A quiet overtook the two once they were seated inside. Until now, they had really only exchanged a few words. The din of the marketplace had always made conversation unnecessary. The chaos of the street had provided a similar distraction on the ride over. But now that they were alone, an awkward silence fell between them, neither knowing how to start a conversation. Mini thought it was always so much easier with Ai May around. She was relieved when a waiter came by to take their order.

"A cup of coffee with milk and sugar for me," she said.

"Anything to eat?" the waiter asked.

"A ham sandwich, then."

He turned to Mr. Shi. "What about you?"

"I'll have the same," he told the waiter. Mini knew he wasn't as familiar with Western food and would have preferred to take her to a Chinese place where he would've been more comfortable. She had intentionally chosen this little café frequented by foreigners, avoiding the ones where she and her father normally went. Mini was convinced that if any family friends or relatives saw her with Mr. Shi, they would not be able to meet again. Besides, Mini longed for a cup of coffee after the long walk in the market.

It had been almost a year since they met, when Mini accidently stepped on Mr. Shi's foot in the market. He had been in pain and very annoyed by the slight, until he turned to take notice of who had stepped on him. Mini had been so apologetic.

"I'm so sorry. I hope I didn't hurt you too much," she had fretted, repeating the apology over and over.

Though his face was contorted with pain, Mr. Shi had calmly replied, "No, not at all. Don't worry."

He had limped away then, and Mini followed—just to make sure he was okay. They made their introductions, and from then on, Mini would bump into him every few days. After a few weeks, their meetings became intentional. As their daily walks through the market continued, familiarity grew between them and fondness began to creep in. It wasn't long before she found herself looking dreamily into the sky, as if in a daze, on those occasions when she arrived early and stood waiting for him.

Breaking the silence, Mr. Shi reached across the table for her hand.

"Mini, I'm so lucky I met you. I'm glad you stepped on me." Mini laughed at this, and he continued on: "You know I don't go to that market very often. It was just chance I went that day. But I'm sure glad I did."

Mini knew this in her heart and was flattered. She had guessed he only went there for her, because he never bought anything.

The coffee arrived. They retracted their hands to their own sides of the table, making room for their cups and saucers. Mini fidgeted with her napkin, folding and unfolding it on the table, until he reached for one of her hands and began kissing each of her fingers. Mini tried to pull back.

"People will see," she warned.

"It's dark here. It's hard to see," he said, holding her hand tight.

"Oh, Mr. Shi, please don't."

"Call me Kung Yi," he replied. "You are so beautiful, Mini." His eyes held her. Mini smiled and her face flushed. She was glad then that it was dark.

He paused, then continued on: "My mother wants me to get married. She called a matchmaker today to discuss the possibilities."

"Oh?" Mini feigned cool interest, though her heart sank. Even though she hadn't really thought about marriage, she did have the vaguest fairytale of an idea that floated across her mind when she was daydreaming at home.

"I don't want to marry someone I don't know," he replied. "I can imagine what kind of girl my mother will choose for me."

"What kind of girl?" Mini asked, her voice barely audible.

"A country girl, of course. Someone from the land," he said directly.

"That is good then, for your family."

"Precisely."

She paused.

"What do you want to do?" Mini asked abruptly, breaking their silence.

"I want to marry someone like *you*," he blurted, only to fall silent once more, embarrassed by his outburst.

Mini stared at him, barely aware of the server setting out the sandwiches for them. She didn't know what to say.

"I don't think I'd suit your family," Mini finally said.

Kung Yi looked defeated. She looked down. *If only, but how could I hope for anything like that? Was I stupid to put him on the spot like that? To lead both of us on all this time?* Mini noticed her plate and halfheartedly picked at it, though her appetite was gone. It was several minutes before he spoke again.

"Mini, what about you?" he asked. "Are your parents arranging your marriage, too?"

"My father doesn't believe in arranged marriages, but my mother does," Mini replied. "She's working on it. She had my father send word out to his friends that he's looking for someone for me."

"Do you want to marry a stranger?" he asked.

"No, I don't. But I trust in my father's choice." She spoke confidently, but Ling's marriage was on her mind as she said this. Mini didn't want to become someone's second wife.

"I will talk to my mother and see if she can send the matchmaker to your house," he said.

"You're kidding, right?" Mini looked up, her heart pounding.

"I'll try," he offered.

Music had started up for the afternoon crowd. It was a melancholy violin. Mini noticed that the café was filling up with foreigners.

"Oh, I'm attending the annual picnic party at the British consulate in two weeks," she said cheerfully, changing the subject. "My father will bring me with him. He doesn't go every year, only goes when he's invited—and always alone. This year he decided to take me along. I'll have an opportunity to practice my English with real English-speaking people."

"I thought you went to a missionary school before. Wasn't that run by the English?" Mr. Shi asked.

"Yes, but most of our lessons were in Chinese," Mini replied. "An English lady taught us English, but we didn't have much opportunity to speak to her one-on-one."

"What will you do there?" Mr. Shi asked. "I read about them in the gossip column, but those only say who was seen and nothing about what foreigners do at those parties."

"I don't know," Mini admitted. "This is a first for me. Father said many of the British officials bring their family. I will meet many girls my age."

"Except they're foreigners," Mr. Shi responded. "And foreigners are very different from us Chinese." He had tried to sound lighthearted, but it came out harshly.

"You think so? I'm nervous," Mini confessed.

They finished their lunch quietly. He asked to accompany her on a rickshaw home, at least partway, but Mini refused. She wanted to be alone to think.

As she arrived home, Mrs. Pao's voice carried above the crisp sound of Mahjong, breaking into Mini's reverie.

"Mini," she called out. "Where have you been?"

"The Bund, Mother. I had a light lunch," Mini answered, walking in on her mother's game.

"The tailor has been waiting for you for a long time," Mrs. Pao responded, simultaneously making a quick move of her tiles. Mini was always amazed at her mother's ability to speak to a third person and not miss a single movement of the game.

"I'm so sorry. I met Miss Chang for lunch," Mini said.

"A young girl meets another girl for lunch. Modern era now," Wu Ma commented acidly.

"I hadn't seen Miss Chang for a long time," Mini said to her mother, ignoring Wu Ma.

"Bang!" Mrs. Pao yelled and dropped her neatly lined Mahjong blocks. She had won the hand. Her game mates smacked their lips at the loss.

Smiling, Mrs. Pao turned to Mini: "Go to the living room. Tailor Chung is there. Now, don't pick material that's too expensive. I don't want to spend too much." She shook her head at her friends. "A new dress for a party with foreigners. Extra expense." Her friends nodded sympathetically.

Mini ignored all of this and headed to the living room, where a fat man sat rigidly in a straight-backed chair, waiting for her. A soft measuring tape hung around his sweaty neck. By his feet sat an open case with many fabric samples sticking out. A cup of cold green tea sat on the side table next to him. He bolted up as Mini entered the room. Smiling broadly, he clapped his hands in front of him and bowed.

"Miss Pao, did you have a good lunch?" the man asked.

"Sorry I made you wait so long," Mini replied. "Let's see what you have."

Not in the mood for small talk, Mini took the materials from his open case and fanned them out on the couch in a rainbow. Her eyes scanned them as her mind calculated prices.

"Your mother said the party will be outdoors," the tailor remarked. "It is already October, so I brought more wool than silk. I think wool suits the situation better."

"How much is this?" Mini fingered a piece of wool.

She envisioned herself in a qipao made of the dark blue fabric under a white cardigan, wearing a pair of black leather shoes and walking arm in arm with Kung Yi. She smiled shyly at the fantasy. *Pearls will look nice with the dress. I'll borrow Ling's pearl necklace for the party.*

"Five yuan a yard."

"Oh?" Mini asked demurely. "I went to a fabric store today. I saw they charge three and a half a yard."

"Miss Pao, times are hard," the tailor wheedled. "I just try to make a living."

"Well, I must try to save for my parents. If you match the price, I will buy from you," Mini said coolly.

"All right, all right, I'll take it." The fat tailor shook his head vigorously, as if he were making a grand sacrifice. "Now, do you want to have no sleeves or a long-sleeve qipao, and how high do you want the slit?" he asked. "The fashion now is ankle length with a high slit."

"I will have the sleeves an inch below my elbow," Mini said decidedly. "It should be ankle length, with a slit up to my knee. I want to have a butterfly button made with the same fabric over my right chest."

"Miss Pao, you *really* know what's fashionable," the tailor said obsequiously.

"Now, I'll need to have a fitting next week. Please send the bill to my mother," Mini directed.

"Will do." The tailor bowed as he left.

Mini sat on the couch and thought of Kung Yi, what he would say to his parents, and whether he would be successful in getting his mother to send the matchmaker to her house. She sighed as her mind turned to what she would say to her own mother, should someone really show up to make an introduction to Kung Yi's family. Mini wasn't supposed to meet a young man on her own. Her mind still in disorder, Mini got up and went into the kitchen to help Ai May prepare dinner.

6

AN ENGLISH PICNIC IN SHANGHAI

It was a cloudless day. Mr. Pao stood on the curb as Mini stepped out of the rickshaw. They had arrived at the Bund, where the British consulate picnic was being held. Mr. Pao wore a carefully ironed cream-colored suit, a Panama hat, and two-toned leather shoes. Mini was equally elegant in her new dress, adorned with her sister's pearls. They walked up the short path to the gated park, and Mini stopped short before a large sign proclaiming in both English and Chinese:

CHINESE AND DOGS ARE NOT PERMITTED

Mr. Pao ignored the sign and signaled for Mini to continue. A Sikh policeman, wearing a red turban with a wooden staff slung from his waist, stopped them and asked to see Mr. Pao's invitation.

Red-head number three, Mini thought. In Shanghai, British police were number one; other white police were number two, because they took orders from the British police; and the Sikhs were number three.

They bent to both the British and other whites. Sadly, all three were above the local Chinese police force. Mr. Pao reluctantly pulled a piece of paper from his jacket pocket and offered it to the policeman, his face expressionless. He looked away as the Sikh read the paper closely.

Inside, about forty or fifty people were scattered around an open white tent covering a long table with many glasses, plates, and food, along with a few chairs. Waiters in black jackets and white pants threaded through the crowd, carrying trays of finger foods and champagne. Most men wore suits and hats—no ties—and a few young men were in their shirtsleeves with their collars jauntily open. The younger ladies, all in sporty outdoor dresses, grouped together near a few uniformed men. Mini paused to take in the strange scene. Although she hadn't known what to expect, Mini had imagined something more like a Chinese party, with people sitting under composed trees around big round banquet tables, eating languidly amid animated banter. This was altogether different.

As they walked toward the crowd, Mini noticed that her father slowed his pace, as if he felt just as uncomfortable as Mini. She observed only a few Asian faces—all of them men.

"I say, Pao, nice you're here." A red-faced man slapped Mr. Pao's shoulder.

"Mr. Robinson, how do you do?" Mr. Pao bowed slightly to the man before looking up. "This is my daughter, Zhi Fen. We call her Mini."

"Mini, what a curious name. How do you do?" Mr. Robinson extended his large hand to Mini. Mini shook it weakly, unsure of how to respond to this British gesture.

"Very well, sir," she replied in her best English.

Mr. Robinson spotted a few men passing. "Excuse me. I must speak with these gentlemen. Please enjoy yourself." He turned and left them alone.

Mr. Pao continued to introduce her to a handful of other British men who worked with him at the consulate before finally settling in with a group of Chinese men. Mini assumed they were employees of the British, just like her father. They teased her father about hiding a beautiful daughter at home, but otherwise ignored Mini entirely, becoming engrossed in discussing the latest news and rumors of the Japanese in the North. Mini quickly grew tired of hearing the men speculate about what the Americans and British would and would not do and drifted away toward the riverbank. She resented the fact that her father had brought her here, only to abandon her to a crowd of unfamiliar people.

Not knowing what to do, Mini stared at the busy waterway that lay before her. She could make out British and American gunboats docked at the quay. She recognized the British flag, with its pattern like the Chinese character for "rice," and the American one, its red and blue colors as bright as flowers—the "flower flag," as the locals called it. Ferryboats blasted their big horns and sped ahead, creating huge wakes that crashed against a fleet of flat-bottomed sampan boats along the bank. The sampans bounced up and down precariously, as if they were about to topple over. They were close enough that Mini could see through the thin sheets of bamboo arched over their cabins to the stacks of goods that were piled high inside, protected from the weather.

Goods these boatmen can't afford are given better protection than the people onboard, she thought. Mini watched dark, half-naked children with matted hair, covered in dry streaks of filth sitting exposed at the bow of a sampan in front of her, sucking their fingers and bouncing up and down with the wakes. Their equally dirty mother sat next to them, busily preparing the family meal. A thin, bent man in rags was rhythmically pushing and pulling the oars that reached into the river. Mini thought she could even see thick veins bulging on his brown legs as he rowed. He was shouting to the woman and children in a dialect Mini didn't recognize. *These are the boats Kung Yi's family uses to transport rice to Shanghai. These people don't have enough to eat, but here they are shipping tons and tons of freshly harvested rice they could never afford themselves*, she thought.

Mini's mind continued to wander, thinking of Kung Yi, and she wondered where he was at this moment. Before he had left her at the café, he said he would have to return with his family to their country home to oversee the preparation of the rice harvest for delivery to Shanghai. She hadn't seen him in the two weeks since he proposed sending the matchmaker to her home. *Is Kung Yi talking to his parents about me now?*

"Nice view, isn't it?" A cheery voice broke Mini's train of thought.

Not sure if the voice was addressing her, Mini turned around to see a young girl about her age. She had long, curly brown hair that was casually tied to dangle down her back. She looked at Mini with a pair of deep-blue eyes. The Westerner smiled at Mini and extended her hand.

"I'm often mesmerized by this view too. My name is Mary. Mary Hayworth."

Mini shook her hand. "My name is Mini. Mini Pao."

"Mini, interesting name. You are *not* mini," Mary observed. "You're quite tall for a Chinese girl. How do you do?"

"Very well. Thank you," Mini said. Unsure how else to respond, she simply smiled.

"Did you come here alone?" Mary asked.

"No, I came with my father." Mini pointed out Mr. Pao, who stood another ten feet away with a group of men. "He works for the British consulate."

"I see. My father works there too. He must know your father." Mary drained her champagne glass and noticed that Mini had neither drink nor food. "Why don't you join me, and we'll get something to drink?"

"All right," Mini agreed, realizing she was thirsty. She followed Mary to the tent-covered table.

Mini poured herself a glass of fruit punch and joined Mary outside the tent with a group of young girls talking about a new American film Mini hadn't seen. She stood quietly as Mary introduced her to everyone. The girls nodded politely to Mini as introductions were made, but swiftly resumed their conversation. Mini tried to follow the rapid exchange, but her English wasn't good enough, so she stood there quietly, drink in hand, alone in a crowd again. Eventually she slipped away from the circle of girls and slowly walked back to the riverbank. No one noticed, except for Mary, who followed her.

"Are they talking too fast for you? I'm sorry," Mary apologized.

"It's all right," Mini said softly. *I really don't belong here. I will never go to another party full of foreigners again.*

"You aren't missing anything," Mary replied quickly. "I saw the movie, but I just can't get excited about Clark Gable. I know, you'll say I'm odd that way."

They continued chatting like that, Mini with her rudimentary English and a very patient Mary. Mini learned that Mary's mother was an American whose family lived in San Francisco—the Old Golden Mountain, as the Chinese called it. Mary was born in Shanghai but had little opportunity to meet any locals or eat Chinese food. Her "Amah"—to Mary's surprise, Mini explained that the word used by Westerners for a nanny was in fact not a Chinese word—made the only Chinese food Mary had ever eaten, and that was only when she had been little. Mary had liked it, she was quick to add.

From time to time, Mini glanced over to look for her father. She had thought he would mingle with the British, but mostly he stayed with the other Chinese employees. On occasion she saw him speak with one of the British, and each time the man patted her father's shoulder in a friendly manner before moving on to one of his own groups.

"Who is Mr. Robinson?" Mini asked her father on the ride home.

"He's my boss. He invited me to the party," Mr. Pao replied.

"Do you know Mr. Hayworth?" she asked.

"Yes, he is a very important figure at the consulate. I don't speak to him often," her father said.

"But you are an important employee there," she said.

"Mini, I am only a Chinese employee," Mr. Pao replied.

They rode quietly the rest of way, and Mini was glad when they finally reached home to find the dining table covered with steamy dim sum and the familiar sound of Mahjong tiles clicking in the drawing room.

7

AMERICAN SPY

TING, SHANGHAI, 1975

I sat on my bed brooding in my windowless room without bothering with the light. I should get dressed and be ready for school, but I wished I were sick so I wouldn't have to go. My thoughts oscillated between hating Grandma for leaving us and wanting to be far away, in Hawaii with her.

She could have stayed longer. We have enough room. Mien's grandma lives with her, and her home is even smaller. Grandma said she would return again, but then what? She'll just go back to her real family in America. If only I was part of her real family, her Hawaiian family.

"Ting, hurry up. You will be late," Mother shouted impatiently outside my room.

"Okay. I'm getting up."

Grandma had left me weeks before, as did the respect my neighbors and schoolmates had shown me, fueled by curiosity. Everyone knew when she left, and that day, I had walked into the school bathroom only to notice big, bold graffiti scrawled on the wall: "American Spy!!!"

I knew those words were meant for me. Maybe I should have expected it, but I hadn't. I thought the special treatment we had received during Grandma's stay would last forever. I tried hard to erase the words, but my efforts only left a big smudge on the wall. I wanted to hide in the bathroom and cry. I held back my tears. I knew they would find me there, and I didn't want the other kids to know I cared.

Each day after that, the smudge was a reminder. Not that I needed reminding. Grandma was gone. The time she was with us was just a bright but fading memory. The taunts grew each day after she left. As the weeks wore on, I didn't know if it was for better or worse that she had come to visit. I *knew* it was better, but somehow it was worse, too, because they had witnessed the glamour of my grandma, and their uncontrollable envy had turned into spite. Life before and after had merged together, and I dreaded school, even though there was only a month left. I longed for the summer to come so I could have some respite.

The changes started out as annoyances, mostly just at home with the neighbors. Tai Pao had become my protector at school when Grandma was visiting, and for a while after she left. He was no better than his ugly parents, but he knew I still had some foreign candies I was willing to share. His parents had gone back to lording it over us after Grandma left—over me most of all.

Mother and Father were no longer allowed to miss work, and things returned back to normal, both of them never at home. If they didn't come home late at night—held over for hours at work for political education—then they would return for a quick dinner, only to head back to work for more political study. The Yungs never had to go for study, because they were also the neighborhood leaders responsible for reporting about our apartment block to the party.

Our family had lost our kitchen and bathroom privileges the moment Grandma left. If we weren't early enough, then whichever neighbor was already in the communal area would slow down and occupy the space a little longer just to inconvenience us. It was obvious. When they saw one of us entering, their normal rapid movements shifted into slow motion. Usually it was just me, especially when Mother and Father came home at a normal time with plans to return to their work-study after dinner. They left me with the job of cleaning the dirty pots and dishes in the communal sink. Each night it felt like I had to wait even longer than the night before.

Tai Pao continued to be nice at first, and Lily too, but Lily only because she was afraid of her older brother. He was clear that he would only protect me at school as long as I still had candies or cookies for him. Goodies can only last so long, no matter how strict my mother's rationing. I didn't really give that much thought to what I would do when the butter cookies and candies from Hong Kong ran out—as it turned out I should've. I made the ill-considered decision to wear my new shoes on the same day the goodies ran out.

The shoes were the last gift Grandma had given me before leaving. I rarely got to wear them, and not at all since Grandma left. Instead, it was either the plastic sandals everyone wore for the unexpected, frequent thunderstorms or the basic black homemade cotton shoes we wore when it was dry.

I loved my new bright red leather shoes with their shiny buckles on the side. I missed showing them off. Each day I had asked Mother if I could wear the shoes and each day Mother said no. Maybe on this day she knew I had run out of candies, but for whatever reason she said yes. I rushed to change into my whitest shirt and matching white socks to go with my beautiful red shoes. It felt as good as putting on my new lace-trimmed jacket when Grandma had first arrived.

I didn't think how much my red shoes stood out, especially against the white socks and my drab blue pants. It hadn't been something I cared about before, when Grandma was still around. In fact, I was proud of how much my shoes stood out—surrounded in the school hallway by my classmates uniformly dressed in their simple black shoes or plastic sandals. The joy I found in dressing up again drove away the dread I felt in going to school, and the stark contrast between my leather shoes and my classmates' drab clothing was the furthest thing from my mind when I reached school. At least, it was until I entered the schoolyard, when everyone looked my way as I walked up to the door leading to our classrooms.

Then it began.

Several girls from my class fell in behind me as I walked the hallway.

"Old American Woman in red shoes," someone taunted. I didn't look back.

A few voices repeated in unison: "Old American Woman in red shoes."

First it was a handful of girls. More girls joined in, their singsong chant getting louder and harsher as they closed in.

"Old American Woman!"

"American Spy!"

"Old American Woman!"

"American Spy!"

I clung to the wall and tried to make myself invisible. I was at the door to my classroom when my neighbor and classmate Lily ran up and grabbed me, spinning me around. I braced myself: I had seen enough of that in school and in the streets, of the older kids who would drag a teacher or some other older person out and beat them for being counterrevolutionary. Instead, Lily spat on the floor. I stood frozen, watching as she ground her foot in her spit and stomped it onto my shoes, first left and then right.

Somehow, I had expected worse and her move caught me by complete surprise. I stood stunned. The girls encircling me burst out laughing. There was no more jeering. Maybe if they had continued doing so I wouldn't have lost control. The classroom was just behind me, but it could have been the entire length of the hallway away at that moment. I couldn't move and simply cried, my tears swiftly turning into an inconsolable sob. Only Mien came to my side: my best friend, one of my only friends.

She grabbed my arm, pulling me into the classroom. "Ting, let's sit down."

I was still crying when Teacher Ni came in. She scanned the classroom and quickly assessed the situation. "Can anyone tell me what happened?"

A girl raised her hand. "Lily stepped on Ting's shoe so Ting is crying."

Teacher Ni looked at me: "Accidents happen. No need to cry like that. Lily, please apologize to Ting."

Lily stood up and turned to me. "I am sorry," she said with a wink and hopped back into her seat, the classroom bursting into laughter once more.

"Quiet!" Teacher Ni paused, drumming her fingers on the podium before continuing. "Today, we are going to study Mao's Old Three Pieces. I hope you all have Mao's Red Book."

I kept to myself the rest of the day and was relieved to get home without anything more than some sneering. After school was always a better time and I looked forward to going home. We never had any homework and could do what we pleased because, with few exceptions, nobody's parents were home.

Mien walked home with me that day. I had shown her my Barbie earlier and told her stories about Grandma's life in America, most of them made up since I knew nothing of her life in Hawaii or how Americans lived. Still, Mien loved my stories.

Even though Barbie had a bigger wardrobe to work with than we did, we had tired of mixing and matching her clothes. Probably to lighten my mood, Mien suggested we try making Barbie new clothes ourselves. We were measuring the doll and cutting scrap fabric from Mother's sewing box when we were interrupted by a knock on the apartment door. I opened the door and found Lily standing outside, alone.

"Can I come in to play with you?" she asked.

"We are busy now," I replied, and tried to close the door. Lily stuck her foot between the door frame and the door.

"Please. I know you're playing with your doll," she said. "I want to see it. If you let me play with you today, I'll tell everyone not to insult you tomorrow."

I'm sure I frowned, giving her a suspicious look. I was still hurt from the morning. I looked down at her foot blocking the door. Compared with her brother Tai Pao, she was mostly a nuisance. Well, at least until today she had been. I didn't like Lily, but I couldn't think of anything to say that would stop her. If it meant a whole school day in peace tomorrow, I could put up with her.

"You can come in," I said finally.

Lily walked past me to Mien. "What are you doing?" she asked.

"We're trying to design a new dress for Barbie," Mien replied. "See, we're trying to copy the dress Ting's grandma was wearing in this picture." Mien pointed to a color photo on the table, in which Grandma was wearing a simple sky-blue dress and a string of pearls, sitting by the pool. Barbie was laid out next to the picture, stripped of her clothes.

Lily picked up the photo and looked at it intensely. It seemed as if she were studying every detail. Abruptly, she threw it back on the table.

"Rotten Capitalist and American Spy. Ting is from a black family, but Mien, you should be ashamed, you two thinking bad thoughts." Lily swiped the naked Barbie up off the table and ripped her arm off.

All I could think of for some reason were her grimy hands tearing at Barbie as Lily threw my doll at the table and stormed out, leaving Mien and me staring at the mutilated Barbie. I didn't cry then. I didn't say anything after that. Mien hung around for a little bit, also quiet. Some time passed before Mien said something about getting home to her grandma.

I didn't say anything later at dinner either, but Father must have noticed. He was the kind of father who always guessed when something was wrong and he'd figure it out even without asking me. I went to my room after dinner. The sun had long gone down, but even during the day, my windowless room was dark. I sat by the desk without switching on the lamp, my head hanging low.

Father walked into my room without saying anything and put Barbie in my hands. He didn't turn on the light either, just walked back out. After dinner, he must have found Barbie and glued her arm back into place. I turned the light on after he left. Looking at Barbie's wounded arm, I felt hatred welling up. There was no ignoring Barbie's scarred, twisted arm. No matter Father's best effort at gluing it back on, Barbie wasn't the same, and she never would be.

I was no longer hurt, I was angry. I wanted revenge. Until then, my thoughts were confused, dark, and cloudy. Holding Barbie made it clearer. I realized I didn't hate Grandma for leaving us; I hated Lily. I wanted to make Lily *cry* like she made me cry.

For days and nights afterward, that one thought consumed me until, one day, I found a pretty candy wrapper as I was thumbing through my book on Chairman Mao's thoughts in class. The wrapper had an image on it, depicting a fresh orange surrounded by chocolate. I thought back to Grandma's candies and remembered how frustrated Lily was, looking on greedily when her brother made me share my candies, knowing she wouldn't taste any. Suddenly, the idea came to me and I pocketed the wrapper until class ended.

After school, I walked to the field and pinched a small lump of dirt. Once home, I found some of Mother's flour and sugar and mixed it all together with water until I had what was as close as I could get to chocolate. I shaped the mixture into a square, like a piece of candy, and wrapped it with the orange candy wrapper. It didn't look at all like candy, but I didn't care.

I waited for the next day.

"Hey, Lily, guess what I have," I said as we walked to school. I pulled the fake candy from my pocket and turned away to tease her. Lily moved closer.

"Give it to me before my brother sees it," she demanded. Lily looked at her brother, walking ahead of us.

"Why should I?" I asked.

"I want to try it," Lily said.

"At least if I give it to Tai Pao, nobody will bother me," I said. I picked up my pace as if to catch up with her brother.

She kept pace with me, not moving from my side.

"I won't spit on you," she finally whispered.

This is better, I thought. It was still about revenge, and I was going to give the fake candy to Lily anyway, but maybe I could get her to also lay off.

"You will keep your word like your brother?"

"Of course, you idiot. Give it to me now," she snapped.

"You called me an idiot. You aren't nice," I replied.

"I am sorry, okay? Now, give it to me," she demanded again.

"After school," I told her.

In the school courtyard later that day, after we swarmed out of our classroom, I figured the day wasn't as bad as yesterday. Lily had left me alone. She was with her friends when I called her over.

"You really want to try it? I'll give it to you." I said. "But you have to leave me alone. If you don't, then I won't let you have any more when my grandma comes back. I'll give them to Tai Pao, but I won't let you have any."

Lily didn't say anything. She just stuck her hand out, her face expressionless. I gave it to her and skipped off. Hiding behind the gate to the school, I watched as Lily quickly and secretively put the fake candy in her mouth. *She's not spitting it out?* I wondered why as she continued to chew at it with a confused look, as if trying to figure out what was in her mouth. Her face pinched up and she turned her head as if in disgust. My heart soared. *Lily ate it!* I ran off before she looked over and saw me watching her.

I was still on a high the next morning. I expected Lily to say something nasty, maybe worse. But, while cautious of her, I no longer cared what Lily would say, because I had made her *eat dirt*! To my surprise, Lily even talked to me the next morning as we walked to school.

"That candy tasted real bad. So much for Hong Kong candies," she told me.

"Sorry, it was old. My grandma left a long time ago," I said apologetically.

"If you have any others, one of those cookies maybe, let me try one."

After that, things improved a bit. Lily at least seemed to back off a bit. She'd still sneer and mock me, especially when our teacher lectured us about capitalists, reactionaries, and foreign imperialists. But America came up a lot less those days. You could feel it, like it was no longer proper to criticize America, even if it was never said out loud.

8

PLANTING WRONG IDEAS

What was left of the school year came and went, as did summer after that. Autumn arrived and the start of the school year brought little if any change to my usual routine of being taunted mixed with reciting Chairman Mao's thoughts and drawing big character posters condemning some reactionary or enemy of the people.

As time passed, so, too, did my thoughts of Grandma's visit and her story. Winter crept up as the wind became colder and the trees became bare, and 1975 turned into 1976 with the same monotony. Eventually, the Chinese New Year break gave me welcome time off from the bullies at school and, besides helping my parents with chores, I had a lot of time to myself. Standing in the various lines to fill out our rations prompted memories of the year before. It wasn't intentional at first, but one thought led to another until daydreaming about Grandma's life in Hawaii seemed to provide the only distraction from the cold that penetrated my bones at five o'clock each morning. Huddled over, with my head down, hands stuck in my sleeves, and feet stomping constantly, I imagined sitting with Grandma by her pool in the bright Hawaiian sunshine, or exploring the beach near her house. I'd wonder what Grandma was doing, and whether, like us, she was with her family waiting in various lines to purchase her New Year's rations. I tried to imagine her in line, but somehow, she didn't fit into the picture in my mind. Her elegance in contrast with the people around me automatically excluded her from such unglamorous drudgery. I thought about the image of her husband, Bob, and of the family she had in America, smiling at the camera in front of a tree decorated by shiny objects. *Maybe they don't even have Chinese New Year in Hawaii*, I thought. *It's America, after all.* I recalled her saying that she would cook two meals each night, one for them and one for her.

On these occasions, my mind kept returning to the picture I had seen of her lying back in the chair by her pool. *What did she do each day other than sit by the pool? What did her family eat in America if they didn't eat Chinese food?* I realized I didn't really know what she did or how she lived. I tried to imagine the Western-styled house where she lived with her parents and sister in Shanghai, but I thought of the buildings around me and I just couldn't visualize how only one family could occupy a whole house. She had even pointed the house out to me. It was still standing. The exterior wall had faded to a colorless gray and six families now lived there. The fact that she had lived in Shanghai, the very same city I lived in, was as foreign to me as the home she had made for herself in America. Grandma's Shanghai and mine seemed worlds apart. I found myself looking for the Shanghai in Grandma's eyes as I walked with Mother and Father to and from the markets to fill out our rations. Yet, it remained distant and foreign to everything I knew or saw around me. I'd look at the intersections and imagine the Sikh policemen from India directing streets full of cars and coolies, and puzzled over what Grandma called them, *Red-heads number three*, and where they had all gone to. There were no cars in our neighborhood—only crowded buses that lumbered along—and no coolies carrying fancy-dressed men or women to restaurants or hotels on the Bund. I struggled to conjure made-up images of these foreigners in the former international sections of Shanghai, but when I looked around me, I could see nothing but thousands of people, all of them more or less dressed in the same blue Mao suit, walking or bicycling along.

I went to the park on the Bund where I knew she had gone for the picnic held by the British consulate. There were no more gates or signs. People strolled in the park, bundled up against the cold air. I figured a cold park was still better than a crammed, cold apartment, because there was no indoor heating anyway. It must have been a different Bund than I knew. I wondered what the park in Grandma's story could have been, a park where only foreigners could play and have parties.

Standing by the river, I remembered Grandma said she spoke to Mary and other foreign girls at the party. It dawned on me: *Grandma spoke English*! I realized I had never heard her say anything in English. *Why didn't I ask her to say something?* I had never heard *anyone* speak English, so that Grandma not only spoke it but also had learned it in school was both impressive and unbelievable to me. It only inspired more questions about Grandma and her past. *What was this missionary school that Grandma went to, and how come I never heard about it until Grandma mentioned it?* I wondered.

Rumor had it an old man who swept streets in the morning spoke English. He kept to himself. Rarely had anyone spoken to him as long as I could remember. He was a bad guy, an engineer educated in England long ago. I was told he was allowed to live in the neighborhood as an example of the public enemies who secretly surround us. Despite knowing this, I felt a little sorry for him when he was paraded through the streets as a reminder to remain vigilant for the reactionaries in our midst. Bent and bedraggled, he looked more like someone's grandpa than the capitalists we would draw at school. I wondered whether he had known my grandma.

One morning shortly before the New Year's holiday I was pounding sesame seeds in the kitchen to make the sesame paste that would go into Mother's dumplings, when the postman arrived.

"Certified mail for your mother. Go get her seal," he called from the hallway leading to the communal kitchen and our apartments.

I wiped my hands on a towel and ran past him into our apartment to fetch the seal. With the New Year's break, I had decided to read her letters again, and I knew this must also be from Grandma. I had been longing for her letter.

The mailman handed me an envelope with a red-and-blue pattern around the border and a blue plane on the top right under the words "Air Mail." I lifted the envelope to the light, trying to see inside. Nothing revealed itself, so I put it on the dining table, in the center where no one could miss it. I went back to the kitchen, returning to my task. An hour went by, but I couldn't forget the letter. I went into the apartment and picked up the envelope again. Looking front and back, I hoped to pick out some words through the envelope or find a little unsealed space where I could peek. But no, the envelope was sealed tight, and I put it back down again.

Hours had passed by the time I heard Mother's footsteps in the hallway. I was still in the kitchen, having begun cooking rice for dinner. I ran out and shouted, "Ma, Grandma sent a letter!"

"Okay" is all she said.

Forgetting the rice, I followed behind as she went inside the apartment. She took her time putting down her handbag and taking off her overcoat. She sat down and opened the letter slowly while I held my breath. A small piece of colorful paper fell out, and I caught it.

"What is it?" I asked eagerly.

Mother took it from me: "Oh! A check for fifty US dollars! Your grandma sent fifty dollars to help us with the New Year!" she exclaimed, her tired voice transformed.

"What is fifty dollars?" I had never seen any kind of foreign money.

"It's like our yuan, only it is American money. Father will have to take it and have the bank give us yuan," she explained.

"Why didn't Grandma just send us fifty yuan?" I asked, confused.

"Oh, this is much more than fifty yuan—more like three hundred yuan, I don't know. Your father will find out when he goes to the bank. But, we will be able to buy extra fish, maybe even cakes if we can get them." *Cakes with fresh cream on top!* I thought. *Wow, I don't even remember the last time we had them, maybe when Grandma was here!*

I watched my mother put it carefully on the table and pause before picking the letter back up. I looked at that fifty-US-dollar check, worth more than four months of my mother's salary. She wouldn't have to ask for an advance to buy more on the black market than our rations allowed. *This will be our best New Year*, I thought.

"Here, your grandma sent you a separate letter," she said as she handed a sheet of paper to me.

I read it eagerly.

> *Dear Ting,*
> *I was very happy to read your letter and was very proud of your good grades. I know you are a smart girl—never doubt it! Ask your mother to buy some candy for you from the money I sent to her. You deserve a reward for all your hard work. Keep it up. Study hard. When you grow up, I hope you will study at college here in America.*
> *Love,*
> *Grandma*

I stared at Grandma's letter. *Study in America?*

"Aiee! Someone's burning rice!" a neighbor's cry broke into my reverie.

"Ting!" Mother snapped. "What's wrong with you?"

I rushed back to the kitchen to find the pungent smell of burning rice. Fortunately, the neighbor came in early enough that the bottom layer of rice had just begun to singe. It would be hard after stirring, but we could still eat it. After adding a little more water, I read

Grandma's letter again as I stirred. Her words sank in, and I stirred as if on autopilot, trying to fathom the idea of studying in America. I remembered what Mother said about not planting wrong ideas in my head. Grandma did it again.

I folded the letter neatly and put it into my pocket. I didn't want to upset Mother. I wanted to go to college like my great-grandpa had, but that was a long time ago and colleges had been closed since the Cultural Revolution. If I wanted to go to college, I would have to go to America. But going to America was like going to the moon, Father said once. Like everything else about Grandma, I had more questions, but they were muddled questions as my mind tried to give form to things I had never seen and could not grasp. I knew though that if going to the moon was somehow possible, then Grandma would find a way for me to go to college in America.

In the week since receiving Grandma's letter and leading up to our New Year holiday, I went back over the old letters she sent us and arranged all of them by date, reading each letter closely. Each day I would reread them—out loud when I was home alone—digesting every sentence and filling in the holes with my imagination, trying to grasp meanings beyond the words she wrote as a way to answer all the questions I had about Grandma, her sister, and how she came to be in America without Mother or my grandfather. I started weaving stories in my head, mixing reality with fantasy.

I contrived images of Grandma's secret rendezvous with my grandpa, only to recycle questions and wonder anew about this family I never knew: *What happened to them? Did Grandpa send the matchmaker to Grandma's house? He must have, because Grandma had my mother. She had to be married to have a child—it was impossible otherwise. But why was Grandma now married to Bob?*

Thinking back to her story, I remembered Grandma's low and quiet voice, most of all, and the calmness in her voice while I lay motionless, listening intently to her every word. Those stories were a secret between Grandma and me. I would tell no one.

Finally, the morning of New Year's Eve arrived. Woks were firing away on the four stoves in the communal kitchen: vegetables, meats, egg rolls, and hot chicken soup bubbling with dried ham and egg dumplings. The kitchen smells lingered long after each family had cooked for the day. Building up to the day, the neighbors were festive and harassed us less and less or were at least too caught up with their own preparations to give us any mind. Even Tai Pao and Lily were caught up in the mood and left me alone. They hovered around the kitchen and dipped their fingers into the dishes to sample the food, only to have their mother or father slap their fingers back.

My grandaunt Ai May came to visit from her village in the countryside. She arrived a few days before New Year's Eve, bringing fresh bamboo shoots, fish, and chicken to add to what we already had. Word spread quickly that we had a live chicken that would be slaughtered on New Year's Eve. By ten o'clock in the morning the kitchen was full of children from our apartment and neighboring ones, all of them gawking and circling as we watched Grandaunt grab the chicken by its wings. She carried it to the sink in one hand, and carried a bowl and knife in the other. The chicken let out sharp cooing sounds, its bound legs kicking desperately. She set the bowl and knife on the rim of the sink and snapped the chicken's neck back against its wings, pressing neck and wings together in one hand. But for the thrashing of the chicken's feet as it continued to kick uselessly—the kitchen went quiet. The children went as mute as the chicken, no longer able to protest with its neck bent back. Grandaunt plucked a few exposed neck feathers, two, then three, and lifted the knife, a quick slice. I was so focused on the feathers I wasn't prepared for the deft, quick movement. She shifted her weight to one leg and motioned for me to come closer as she drained out the blood into the bowl.

"Take the bowl to the table there, and try not to spill any. This will be good for the soup," she instructed.

I removed the warm and bloody bowl from the sink, and Grandaunt switched to the adjacent basin and poured in boiling-hot water to soak the chicken in before plucking the remaining feathers and gutting it. Kids left satisfied with a few feathers in hand. Grandaunt made sure everyone had some. When she was finished cleaning the chicken, she moved on to washing vegetables and rice.

I would normally help Mother as she moved from dish to dish, but Grandaunt insisted on doing all the washing. I loved having her with us. She relieved me from washing dishes in the icy-cold water, and I got to hang around and listen to her tell Mother stories from the countryside. I had visited Mother once when she was sent off to live like a peasant in a village on the Pudong side of the Huangpu River that was Shanghai's border. But where Mother refused to speak of her time in the Pudong commune, Grandaunt would tell us endless stories about her village and family. I imagined Grandaunt in a village similar to where Mother was sent, although hers seemed to be much larger and was more than a day's ride by train. I enjoyed listening to her mix in words from her Anhui dialect with the fluent singsong of Shanghainese that we spoke at home.

An old woman in her sixties, her face was dark and wrinkled. With deep lines under her eyes and mouth, dry skin, and thin hair, she looked very much the peasant woman who had spent her entire life exposed to the elements. When she talked about digging for wild roots to supplement their food when the crops weren't enough, I would look at her hands thick and full of calluses and imagine her pulling up the roots around the trees that lined our street.

That New Year's Eve dinner was delicious. I had stuffed myself so much that I couldn't lie down. I fell asleep in a half-sitting position in the bed I would share with Grandaunt—the same big bed I shared when Grandma had come to stay with us. In my sleep, I only vaguely heard Mother and Grandaunt speaking. Mother mentioned money and a letter, the letter from Grandma, I realized. As I struggled to listen in my slumber, I could hear Grandaunt crying and Mother telling her to take the money—that it did not matter what had happened.

Although they argued, Mother wasn't using the sharp tone she would use when she and Father fought. It seemed like she was concerned about something, though what I couldn't tell as I drifted in and out. I was a little more aware when Mother scolded Grandaunt for not being in Shanghai when Grandma visited and asked to see her. Grandaunt only cried harder and said she was too ashamed to face Grandma because she lost her precious thing. I tried to make out what the precious thing was, but then I was too sleepy to concentrate. At some point their conversation and my dreams merged, and I awoke wanting to ask Grandaunt but found she had left early to walk to the train station and return to her home in Anhui.

"Why does she leave on New Year's Day?" I asked, disappointed.

"Because that way she will get a seat on the train," Father explained. "Very few people travel on New Year's Day. She is not young anymore. Standing on the train for more than ten hours is just too much for her."

"Still, I don't think it's a good idea. Likely, she won't get a seat anyway. We have no back door to knock to secure a seat for Aunt," Mother added incredulously. "A seat is a privilege only for people who are connected. Nobody cares about an old woman from the country."

"But she's a peasant, and everyone is learning from peasants," I protested.

I was *sure* that being a peasant granted one privilege automatically. Doesn't Mao's "Learning from Peasant, Factory Worker, and Soldiers" movement say so?

Father shot Mother a look. "Getting a seat on a train is extremely difficult, even for a real peasant. Your mother is right."

Though I felt bad for Grandaunt and understood that traveling by train wasn't easy, I was more frustrated that I missed an opportunity to ask Grandaunt what she and Mother were talking about. I dared not ask Mother about the conversation. I was supposed to be asleep and shouldn't have been listening. I had only a vague guess that the precious thing was maybe Grandma's jewelry or some other heirloom, because I had heard many stories of wealthy families burying such things after the Civil War. While I wondered what and where it could be, I realized I had heard one thing clearly: She kept referring to Grandma as Young Mistress.

She is the maid in Grandma's story! Not mother's real aunt! I was very pleased with myself. I had figured that out.

Later that morning, Mother went out for an errand and Father reminded me not to repeat conversations from home to anyone, a warning he repeated to me often. I knew better by then. I may have said more than I should about Grandma when she was visiting, but my stories of Grandma had only led to the constant ribbing and mocking when she left. Something changed that day in school when Lily led the girls in mocking me. The New Year's break had reawakened my curiosity, and Grandaunt's visit only seemed to fan it. But I would keep it to myself.

9

CHANGES COME TO SHANGHAI

"Enough is enough. Please turn it off. We don't need the radio anyway," Mother said. "You can hear it blaring up from the street. It comes through the walls."

It was early September 1976, still too hot to sleep with windows closed at night, so we can hear every noise on the street. We hear mourning music from early morning to late at night. The music permeates every corner of Shanghai: It was in every school, every market, and even in the streets. Every radio was set to the state-run radio broadcast, which alternated between mourning music and Mao's famous "Chinese People Stood Up" speech. I knew his rousing 1949 speech by heart, as did every other Chinese citizen, but that September it was our anthem. At once, its ubiquity ruined it for me.

"You would think I could at least escape it at home," Mother added after Father turned the radio off.

Mother was right: I would hear it through the walls of my internal bedroom, so that I woke to it early in the morning and when I went to sleep late at night.

I longed to hear something else. It's not like we had great variety before Mao's death, but in those weeks, I would have cheered to hear the revolutionary songs that were broadcast on most days.

Now the radio had halted these already limited programs. The constant reminders of Mao's passing were depressing. It made me feel like the world was going to stop. I worried how the revolution was going to continue without our great leader.

There was no class on the day he died. We arrived at school and were directed to the school auditorium. I thought we were going to watch another purging of some teacher or administrator who was discovered to be a Black Reactionary, but the air was different this time. It was still and uneasy, not the kind of unease when you don't know who is going to be targeted, dragged out with a dunce cap, and forced to kneel with arms strung up in the flying pose to be denounced—but something else.

This time, the atmosphere was much more somber, and we knew we weren't there for denouncing or to cheer at some speech. Sitting in the auditorium, my eyes naturally settled on the big portrait of Chairman Mao on the wall above the stage. His kind gaze was adorned with long black mourning silk. We stood up for a moment of silence. I bowed my head low. Peeking, I could see several teachers crying, tears rolling down their cheeks. I tried to act sad, but all I felt was guilt at being unable to squeeze any tears from my eyes, even though I was still unclear why we were crying. This seemed to last for several minutes and, looking around me, I could see that other kids also had scrunched up their dry, tearless faces, and I felt better knowing they were pretending, too.

Over dinner that night I told my parents that all of mankind mourned Mao's death and that the Chairman had made China the envy of the proletariat the world over. He changed everyone's lives, our principal had told us that day as he and then the teachers had all told stories about how Mao had changed their lives.

I felt Mother's disapproval with her caustic "humph" when I finished retelling the principal's story during dinner. Father quietly continued to eat.

"How does the revolution continue now that Chairman Mao has died?" I finally asked the question I was supposed to ask, while realizing it wasn't the question I really wanted an answer to.

"It's not something that concerns you," Mother brushed me off.

"There will be a new leader," Father said casually, wanting to change the subject.

"Who? His wife?" I asked, relentlessly.

"That's not for us to discuss and don't you go saying anything. Keep your mouth shut and that way you won't get anyone in trouble," Mother snapped.

"Mother is right. The central government will find a capable one. Everything will be fine, but it's best we don't try to guess these things. We will be okay," Father added, sensing my unease. "So, you needn't worry."

It was such a simple comment, but the weight I couldn't place seemed to lift instantly.

"Chairman Mao's body is going to be preserved in a temple. Did you know that?" I asked, proudly repeating the rumor I overheard from a classmate. Father patiently nodded. Mother ignored me.

"How do they do it?" Mother asked, turning to Father, which surprised me because she rarely demonstrated any curiosity in these matters.

"I don't know for sure. There are some chemicals that the Russians used when Lenin died. I imagine that's what will be used," Father answered.

Mother looked away with a pinched face and shake of her head.

"I doubt very much that he will be laid to rest in a temple, but the rumor is he will be at Tiananmen Square," Father continued. Obviously, he had heard rumors too.

"Will you go see him? Can we go? Can we see him?" I asked

excitedly, thinking surely my parents wouldn't object to visiting Chairman Mao—the ultimate wish for all Chinese.

"Who wants to see his dead flesh preserved in soy sauce like a piece of meat?" Mother asked sharply. She looked around quickly, even though nobody was with us. The door was closed to the common area in the apartment.

My mouth hung open. I couldn't find my voice. Father put his hand on Mother's arm but looked at me: "Don't you ever repeat what your mother said." I nodded. He didn't need to say it. The alarm in his eyes made that perfectly clear.

The months that followed were a confusing time that undermined Father's effort at reassurance. It seemed like we were gearing up at school for a new anti-reactionary movement. Mother and Father were extra tense in the few hours when I saw them at home. I sensed their fear that something was coming, until the news came over the radio one morning extolling the leadership of Chairman Hua, now the leader of China.

Our new chairman came on the radio later that day. He declared the end of the Great Proletarian Cultural Revolution and the arrest of the "Gang of Four." Mother was circumspect. It was Father's manner that gave me comfort that things would be all right. I had never heard of Chairman Hua before, and except for Mao's wife, Madame Jiang, I had never heard of the other members of the Gang of Four. I didn't know what to think really but learned in the days after his speech that they had been responsible for bringing about the excesses during the Cultural Revolution and had corrupted Mao's teachings. At school, we studied Chairman Hua's fierce loyalty to Chairman Mao and the crimes of the Gang of Four. I learned that the Gang of Four was behind all the bad things that happened to China. This was the first time someone had used the word "bad" to describe someone or something other than a reactionary.

"What bad things?" we asked when our teacher first tried to explain their crimes and how they had corrupted Mao's great revolution.

"Um," she said weakly, "lots of them."

I didn't understand any of this, but we had a purpose again and I enjoyed making new posters about the Gang of Four instead of the same old political enemies we had drawn before. Each day I would draw up a big poster in class, mostly of the same theme with four shrinking little people who were swept away by a huge broom held by a girl, which I'd then paste in the hallway or outside around the school.

Otherwise, little seemed to change at school, at least until the next fall. A new chairman replaced Chairman Hua after our summer break. I came back to school to hear my teacher try to explain that China was a backward country and we were poor. Our teachers told us we needed to catch up, to be strong, and to achieve the four modernizations so we could compete with the rest of the world. There were similar comments I picked up from the radio in the summer, but who Chairman Deng was and what this new leader had planned for me was removed from my world until now. To hear that we were going to compete with other countries, and that we would do this with science, was a surprise.

"To catch up with Russia?" a boy asked.

"We need to be stronger than all other countries, stronger than Russia, stronger than America and Britain," my teacher answered.

He continued to read on from a speech about succeeding because of the strength of the people, and as students we were the vanguard in this constant struggle to build a socialist society. I struggled to understand what I was supposed to struggle *against*.

"What are the four modernizations?" a boy eventually asked, repeating a phrase the teacher had used.

"To modernize in the fields of Agriculture, Industry, National Defense, and Science and Technology," the teacher answered patiently. Since he had repeated this line directly from his speech, it didn't help me any more than the original speech had, which was little.

"Will we be drawing posters?" a girl asked, clearly as perplexed as I felt in trying to visualize what I would be drawing.

"We won't be doing any big posters today."

We looked around at each other, unsure of what would come next. Instead of posters, I was told we would study to make China as rich as America. *How would studying make China rich?* I wanted to ask, but looking at the sea of raised hands, I gave up.

"We will be rich after we achieve the four modernizations?" another classmate asked.

"Yes, we will be rich, and you can eat meat every day, and you won't have to stand in long lines to get food and everything else," my teacher answered with renewed enthusiasm.

It didn't matter that we didn't know what any of this meant, his answer was like music to our young ears. I'll admit I didn't understand anything my teacher said that afternoon, but during break we all offered our own theories, mostly thoughts of arriving home that day to a big feast like we have every New Year's.

I was greatly disappointed when I returned home and didn't find Mother, or any of our neighbors, cooking in the kitchen. The apartment was just as empty as it usually was, except for the Yungs, who sat out on the stoop and watched the neighborhood. For months afterward, we continued to read Mao's poems, the story of the Long March and of revolutionary heroes, largely forgetting the rich promise of the four modernizations.

It wasn't until the following spring, when we returned to school from New Year's break with our Mao's little red book, that our teacher told us to put the book back in our knapsacks and handed out textbooks. These were old, used textbooks. To my surprise, none of them were of Mao's quotes—the poems instead were from the Tang and Song dynasties. Some famous excerpts from the Chinese classics also found their way in.

We would be learning math, science, and subjects appropriate for the advancement of China, our teacher said on our first day back. We would be responsible for achieving the four modernizations, and it was our duty to read our textbooks carefully and complete our homework every day. I now had several teachers, each one teaching a different subject. For the first time, I was exhorted to study hard, to master math, the sciences, and practical skills instead of to kill the poisonous weeds of anti-socialism, to destroy old and feudal ways of thinking, or to smash reactionaries.

Other things were changing, too. The differences seemed random, such as one day when Mother brought home a few yards of flowery patterned cotton.

"Tomorrow we will go to People's Square and have a new blouse made for you," she told me excitedly. *Making a blouse in People's Square?* I thought that was odd but knew better than to question her.

The next morning, she roused me up early and took me to a small area near the People's Square. "What is all this?" I asked, upon seeing the various people who had set up folding tables, many of them covered with various objects and tools.

"It's like a market," she told me.

This was unlike any market I had been to. It was a disorderly mess of people looking for trades, but without any lines. The tables were set out randomly along the sides and clustered in a confined area. Most of them were tailor stands, shoe repair stands, and bike repair stands.

Mother approached the first of many tailor stands. Her enthusiasm in coming to the square seemed to have ebbed a little as she approached tentatively.

"I want a blouse made for my daughter. I have this here," she pointed to the material in her bag.

"Five yuan."

Mother didn't respond, simply moved on to the next table as the vendor there yelled out at us. "Four and a half!" the first tailor called her back. More determined, Mother walked up to the adjacent table. The woman there had been eyeing the prior exchange.

"How much for a blouse? I have the material," my mother said.

"I will do it for three yuan, thirty cents. I will add lace for the collar, no charge," she offered. "My thread is strong, the seams will be strong, you see. It will last."

Mother wasn't satisfied and moved on confidently to the next stall, checking each one until she found the cheapest, and she haggled the vendor there down to one and a half yuan. On the way out, a shoe repair stand owner chased after us to tell us that for less than one yuan, he could fix the broken shoe buckle that held on to my shoe by a string. Mother bargained him down to fifty cents.

"Ting, I like this," she said happily. "This is how I remember it before—" She caught herself, looking around at who might be listening.

"It is so good now we don't have to trouble your Aunt Fong anymore," she continued after we had walked further away.

"Where are these people from?" I looked at the hundreds of stands and the people who swarmed around them.

"They are recently returned from the countryside."

"Like Grandaunt?" I asked.

"No, these are mostly Shanghainese, like us," she told me. "All the young people in the city were sent to the countryside as part of Mao's 'Learning from Peasants' movement. Now they are home."

"Why don't they go back to school?" I asked.

"After so many years away, they are too old for school. Even the younger ones, they haven't been in school for five, six years," she said. "What are they going to do in school?"

I was confused as to why they couldn't return to school, and as I thought back to our neighbor's son who left for the countryside, I was even more confused. I barely remembered him. I guessed he was in middle school when he left, so he must be in his late teens or early twenties now. *Yes, too old for school*, as Mother said. Kids *would* laugh at him if he were in the same classroom with us. I imagined him among the adults here.

"But they don't look that young," I said.

"It's hard in the countryside. It changes a city person," she replied, and I could see cloudy thoughts overtake her.

"But, why are they in People's Square?"

"There aren't jobs for them in the city," she explained. "The government announced it had changed the laws to allow them to make a living on their own. People's Square is the place."

"So, they will be here every day?"

"Yes, for now at least." Mother squeezed my hand. "I don't know how long it will last, but I have a feeling that things are going to be better from now on."

Former students sent to the countryside weren't the only ones returning home, I soon learned. Not long after our visit to People's Square, my friend Mien confided that her father was coming home.

"Ting, I need to do something tomorrow. Will you help me?" she asked.

I was made curious by her hushed voice, but of course I would do it. I would do anything for Mien. She was the only girl in my class to ever stick up for me.

"Can I ask you also, please don't tell anyone," she added.

"Of course! We are friends, aren't we?" I asked.

"Really, please, I haven't told you or anyone else. I didn't know how," she said.

The added intensity in the way she said this made me feel uneasy. She was my best, and really my only, friend, but I was unsure what I had just agreed to do.

"Will you accompany me to my father's work unit tomorrow after school? I'm afraid to go alone," Mien confessed.

"Your father? For what?" I was surprised by the mention of her father. I didn't know she *had* a father.

My asking seemed to make Mien even more nervous, and now I felt more awkward at making her feel bad. She paused, wringing her hands until the whites of her knuckles showed.

"My father has been released from prison. He wants to see me," she admitted nervously. "You see, he's all cleared. He's no longer an anti-revolutionist."

"He was an anti-revolutionist?" I asked, more loudly than I intended.

"Be quiet!" Mien glanced around to make sure no one heard us.

"He was, but not anymore. They told me he said something bad about the Gang of Four, who had him put in prison. He is a hero now for criticizing them, really."

"Wow." I had heard the rumors that people were being released from prison, but I didn't know any of them and I was actually afraid. *What if I run into one on the street? Aren't they dangerous? Mien's father, a criminal . . .* I never expected that. For as long as I knew her, I had only seen her mother a few times around the holidays. Her father was never in the picture, but I never thought to ask why. This was all so confusing. "But, when did he go to prison?"

"When I was about two," she said. "I don't remember him anymore."

"What about your mother? Why doesn't she go with you?"

"My mother divorced my father. My father suggested the divorce because he thought it would be good for me. And . . . and . . ." She faltered. "My uncle and my grandparents don't want to see him. They think he ruined my mother's life."

My mouth dropped open. I had no idea. I had been her friend for so long and I never knew. Mien had been living with her grandparents from her mother's side because her mother was working in Huzhou. Now I knew why.

"Where is he now?" I asked.

"He's out of prison. He was released to his work unit. That's where I'm to go tomorrow. I know it's not prison, but I'm scared. I don't know," she said.

"Mien, I'll be with you tomorrow," I reassured her. "Don't worry. Everything will be fine."

Rumors were truer than the news in the state-run newspaper, Father often told me. He also said we lived in a time when we had to interpret news in creative ways. I couldn't figure out what he meant by that. Sometimes I pressed Father to explain, but he refused to say any more.

"You will understand when you are older and more mature," was all he'd say.

It was frustrating, and this was one of those times. People had been gossiping for weeks about this person or that being released from prison, but I didn't know their names. They always seemed to be someone related to someone who knew someone. Now, to actually *know* someone—my best friend even—with a father in jail. And now she was asking me to see him. I didn't know what to think. I had just said I would go, but I wasn't so sure. I had so many more questions, but looking at Mien's nervous face I felt asking more would only make Mien more upset than she already was.

The next day after school, Mien and I went to the bus stop without dropping our book bags off at home. It felt like the adults were staring at us for most of the ride, knowing that we were going somewhere we didn't belong. Mien had never been to her father's work unit, and we stayed close to the bus door to get off quickly once we saw the sign for the Shanghai Biology Research Institute.

Once we got off, Mien led the way only to stop in front of the intimidating-looking big door of the building. I felt small and unsure standing there and I guessed that Mien felt the same. It was a cold and gray winter day, and I wanted more to get out of the cold dampness that was seeping into my bones.

"Let's go inside," I said. "It is too cold outside."

I pushed Mien to the front so she would be the one to knock. To our surprise, the door opened automatically under her hands. We walked down a long hallway, still shivering. It was just as cold as it was outside. A small window on one side of the hallway opened up and a man stuck his face out.

"Who are you?" he asked in a stern voice. "This isn't a playground."

We stopped and I pushed Mien toward the man in the window.

"This is Mien Wong. She is here to see her father," I said by way of explanation.

He glanced at Mien. "What's your father's name?"

"Gong Wei Wong."

"Oh, why didn't you tell me earlier?" He was suddenly all smiles. "Stay there."

He disappeared from the window and came out from the door a few more steps up the hallway. Grabbing Mien's hands into his, he continued.

"Lei, come, he is inside and has been waiting for you for a while."

He led Mien inside, the two of them seeming to forget I was there. I thought about going back outside, but it was too cold—plus, I didn't know how long I had to wait. So I hurried along behind and didn't say a word.

There were many offices inside. Some of the rooms looked like they were once labs. Now they were like labs without equipment. The man tapped on the door to one of these rooms until a hoarse voice called out, "Come in."

The man pushed the door open. I saw a small old man sitting behind a large wooden table. His face was very dark and his skin wrinkled. The lines on his face were deep, as if they were carved into his face. He wore a dark gray, ragged jacket and the gray army hat that everyone wore—only his was as worn and colorless as the hair on his head. He looked like a person who had herded sheep in the sun and rain all his life.

He looked up and saw Mien. She saw him as well, but she didn't move an inch. She just stood there expressionless, like a stone. This peasant man stood up, knocking down a glass of hot water in front of him. He didn't seem to even notice as he came forward and wrapped his arms around Mien. He held her and began crying silently. I couldn't see her face from behind, but I saw her father's hands, thick and covered with calluses, on her shoulders. Tears streamed down his face. Mien stood there, letting this man hold her. Her body was rigid, her arms hanging at her sides. I didn't know what to do. I was embarrassed to watch this stranger cry and hold Mien so intensely. I stared at his callused fingers until the man who led us into the room tugged me, pulling me outside.

"Young girl, you should wait outside," he told me.

I followed him back to his little room along the hallway and I sat on a bench to wait. He was very nice and gave me a glass of warm water to drink and warm my hands. It was a long time until Mien showed up with red eyes and puffed face. We quietly went home. I wanted to ask what they talked about and where her father was going to live, but I didn't dare, because her eyes seemed distant, staring at things but not seeing them, like a ghost.

Later, only after Mien's father was returned to his title of Senior Scientist and moved into a new apartment along with Mien, did she start telling me his story. He wasn't that old—he was in his forties, just like my father. He had been an accomplished scientist working on some important state projects until he'd been arrested for slandering Mao's wife at a dinner party. He had been sent to Qinghai, a place out west where nothing grows. He languished there for ten years and was almost beaten to death several times. One time they hung him from a tree and used a belt to beat him. He didn't die, he told Mien, because he was determined to see his daughter again.

10

GRANDMA RETURNS

When a letter from Grandma announced she was coming for another visit, it was a surprise, but somehow less extraordinary after all that had happened. Even the letter announcing her visit was just an ordinary letter, delivered by a postman from the post office. Mother's biggest concern last time was managing the food rations. That was no longer a worry with peasants coming to sell food to city folk at People's Square and the other local gray markets. My parents were more relaxed this time and, with all the other changes overtaking us, there was less excitement in her visit.

My memory of her last visit and her stories had receded and, more than the anticipation of her return, I was most excited by the idea that she would come to Shanghai by plane. I didn't even know Shanghai had an airport, let alone where it was. I had never heard of ordinary people flying in planes before then. I had seen pictures of famous people arrive, like Sukarno from Indonesia, America's president, and leaders from Africa, and I imagined Grandma standing at the door of the plane waving to us. *It will be a big place just for her. There will be a special carpet for her to walk on so she won't have to walk on the regular ground.* The first thing I did when I got to school the day after Grandma's letter came was boast that I was going to the airport to pick up my grandma. Like me, my friends were only interested in the imagined flight, not so much my grandma's return.

"Is she flying on an American plane?"

"Yes, of course," I said proudly. "The American president came on an American plane, didn't he? Hers will be a big plane just like his. I bet it's the same plane he flew on when he came to China."

They all murmured their agreement.

"Will someone from the government be there to greet her?" someone asked.

"Of course, they always have an official," another said, knowingly.

"Yes, and the army will be there, too," added someone else. "They will be lined up to welcome her, like in the news pictures."

I hadn't thought of that, and I wasn't sure Mother would be happy if she knew the army would be there to pick up Grandma.

"Where is the airport? How do you get there?" someone asked—practical questions that I hadn't given a thought to. I stumbled for an answer.

"I bet you'll go in a government car," someone answered for me.

"No. I think Father will get a van," I offered.

Father and Mother had talked the night before about the problem of transportation. The distance between our home and the airport was far, at least an hour, if they could borrow the van.

"A van? Your Father drives a van? Wow!"

"No, but he can get one easy," I boasted, even though I knew it wouldn't be so easy.

My parents had spent half the night trying to figure out how to pick up Grandma, until Mother told him to ask a friend to ask for a favor of another friend who had access to one at his work unit.

"In fact, Father won't even have to drive," I said. "He will get someone to drive for him." I didn't add that the price for this trouble was likely to be a carton or more of foreign cigarettes. Once Father confirmed the price, Mother would write Grandma and ask for it.

My classmates were so impressed. They couldn't stop talking about it during recess and lunch break for days.

The day finally arrived. We set out to the airport early to avoid traffic, and we ended up sitting in a large waiting room for many hours. The room was furnished with rows of hard benches and big windows shut tight on the sides. Faint cool air from an air conditioner made the place comfortable. The coolness made up for the boredom of waiting. Summer in Shanghai was very unpleasant, and it was the height of summer. It was perpetually muggy and hot, inside and out. I had no complaint sitting in this air-conditioned space and entertained myself by watching people in the room.

Unlike the train station where Grandma arrived the first time, this airport waiting area was crowded. We wore our Sunday best; everyone did. Even with a Mao suit you could tell when one was new, or had been kept fresh, from those worn every day. Mixed in with the blue-gray were spots of color that enlivened the cavernous waiting room, from two young girls in starched dresses, who danced on the floor while their family cheered them on, to young boys parading proudly in white shirts and navy blue shorts, their ironed red "Young Pioneer" scarves neatly tied at the collar.

I zoned out until I spotted a large group of people with dark complexions wearing homemade, ill-fitting cotton shirts and pants that I remembered from when I visited Mother in the countryside. They talked loudly in a dialect I didn't understand, with no consideration for us or the other people waiting, as if they were the only ones there. Mao's "Learning from Peasants" movement hadn't changed my Shanghai superiority. I stared at them, frowning my displeasure, hoping they would lower their voices. They carried on just the same.

I muttered: "Stupid people. Peasants."

Father turned to me. "What are you complaining about?" he asked.

I pointed at the group. "Look, these people. They are so loud, and they're dressed like peasants."

"I bet they are," he replied. "Look, my family was from the countryside. Being a peasant is not a bad thing. For one thing, they have no choice. You're lucky you were born in Shanghai."

I didn't like the tone of my father's voice, but I didn't argue. *Yes, I'm lucky I was born in Shanghai, but what about people in Hong Kong? They're so much luckier than me! Oh, well . . .* I decided not to pay attention to these people anymore. I focused my attention on the translucent glass doors leading to Customs. The doors were shut and despite the glass, there was nothing to see beyond, not even the shadows of people moving about. Another couple hours passed before the doors finally swung open without any announcement or sound. People in the waiting room all stood up and crowded the doors, pushing each other to land the best position, on their toes with craned necks, everyone hoping to spot their relatives inside.

Men and women started trickling out in colorful tight shirts and bell-bottoms. They were mostly Asians, but a few yellow-haired and blue-eyed foreigners as well.

I saw Grandma coming from inside. She was with a tall brown-haired man, who walked slightly behind. He pushed a luggage cart piled high with suitcases ahead of them and laughed at something she said. She walked tall, wrapped in a red-and-black flowery T-shirt and a pair of navy blue pants. Her hair was cut short but stylish. She didn't look like she had aged at all. Was that Bob? The man looked much too young to be the Bob in her photos.

As they came through the open door she saw us. She walked quickly to us as the man trailed behind with the luggage cart. She gave me a hug and told me to take over the cart: "This young man is very nice. He helped me with the luggage."

I felt awkward to be near the foreign man. I put one of my hands on the handlebar of the luggage cart without saying a word. The young man sensed my discomfort. He took one small suitcase from the cart and, nodding to me slightly, left.

"Ting, you can at least say thank you to the man," Grandma said.

"Sorry, I just don't know how to talk to foreigners," I replied.

Before she had a chance to say more, Mother stepped up and hugged Grandma tight.

Grandma sat next to me in the van on the way back. She held my hand. "You are much taller than I remembered," she said.

I smiled at her. *Of course, I'm twelve now*, I thought, saying nothing. I was happy to see her, to sit next to her, but I didn't know what to say to her. It was so strange. I thought I had a lot to tell her, but now everything I had prepared vanished from my brain. I couldn't find a single word.

We had the same sleeping arrangement as we did during her last visit. Grandma and I shared my parents' bed in the front room. And that night, she resumed her story.

11

YOU ARE
A DRAGON,
I AM A SHEEP

Mr. Pao lifted a small porcelain cup, tilted his head back slightly, and drew the last drop of rice wine. He sighed with satisfaction.

"Old Master, do you want more wine?" Mrs. Pao asked attentively.

"No," he replied kindly. "This is just enough to warm me up. I think I am ready for rice and soup."

Ai May dumped clear noodles and egg dumplings into the chicken soup that simmered in the clay pot on the portable stove, which she had set up in the dining room to keep them all warm. The scent of the steamy broth added warmth to the room. Ai May opened the small gate at the bottom of the stove, and a flame shot up. She brought the soup to a boil, closed the gate to reduce the flame, lifted the clay pot, and carried it to the dining table. She gently placed the bubbling soup down.

"Careful, it's hot," Ai May said as she moved to serve the family.

"Ai May, I'll serve the rice and soup," Mini said. "You can go back to the kitchen and have dinner." Mini ladled hot soup into a big bowl and handed it to Ai May.

"Thank you." Ai May took the soup with a barely perceptible bow and retired to the kitchen.

Dinner was much quieter without Ling. Mini never thought she'd miss her sister so much. Ling's bubbly laugh and silly stories always added life to the dinner table. Ling visited during the day, but she couldn't stay for dinner. She had to be home for her husband.

"Pa, Ling was here today," Mini said.

"What? How irresponsible," he replied. "She shouldn't go about town with a seven-month baby in her belly. Mrs. Pao, tell her to stay home."

"I did just that, Old Master," Mother said. "I told her she needs to be careful and rest all the time. But you know Ling—she cannot stay confined for long. I told her that instead of shopping in crowded streets, she should come here and keep me company."

"You spoil Ling, as always," he said disapprovingly. "What if she were to slip and fall? On these cold January days, you can't be too careful."

"But Pa, it was good that Ling was here today. Wu Ma wasn't able to play Mahjong. Ling took her place and lost a lot of money to Ma," Mini interjected cheerfully.

"No wonder your mother is in such a good mood today," Mr. Pao remarked.

Mrs. Pao watched him take several sips of his soup before changing the subject: "Ling came today with something serious. She was thinking of her sister. Ling mentioned that Jie Xing found a potential match for Mini."

Mrs. Pao glanced at Mini, who rolled her eyes but stayed quiet, knowing better than to interrupt.

"Mini is almost twenty-two now," Mrs. Pao continued. "If she doesn't find a suitor and marry soon, people will think there is something wrong with her. You know, Old Master, daughters belong to other families."

"Oh? Who is the suitor?" Mr. Pao asked.

"Ling said it's a business associate who'd like to take a second wife from a decent family."

Mr. Pao slammed his soup bowl down with a violent bang. Soup splashed onto the table.

"Woman!" he scolded. "One daughter married as a second wife is enough for our family. Mini can do much better than this. I won't discuss it further."

Mrs. Pao bowed her head, but spoke again: "Ling is a second wife, but she is the second wife of a powerful man. She'll be the rightful one once she gives birth to her boy. I can tell from the way she is carrying that it will be a boy. I don't worry about Ling, but Mini, yes. Instead of marrying into some family, she's running about the whole of Shanghai every day. It's a turbulent time, and I don't want Mini to miss her opportunities."

Mr. Pao calmed down. He reached out and patted his wife's shoulder, as if to make up for his outburst.

"I know, I know," he said soothingly. "I will call on my friends tomorrow. I want to find someone who will be compatible with Mini. She's my daughter, too."

After the initial shock of hearing the real purpose of her sister's visit, Mini had fixed her eyes on a water and ink painting of the Yellow Mountain hanging on the wall opposite her, so as not to reveal her racing thoughts. She sat silently through their conversation. *Mother is right. We are in turbulent times. Who knows what's going to happen? Father told me of students and workers demonstrating for unification of all the warlords. But is it always so bloody, or is it getting worse? Those students said a Japanese invasion is inevitable.*

"Mini, what are you thinking?" her father interrupted Mini's train of thought. "Your mother and I were carried away."

Mini looked up and caught her father's eyes. "Pa, what is really going on? I saw another student demonstration today. Lots of students were protesting, and many of them were beaten by the police. They filled up all of Nanking Road. They said our government only focuses on eliminating the Communists and not on fighting the Japanese. Have we lost our land in the North? They're saying if we don't fight, we'll lose the entire *country*."

Mr. Pao was caught up short by Mini's change of subject and paused for a long moment before responding.

"Mini, the students are right, but their methods are wrong," he explained. "Things aren't so simple. The KMT government's weak response has fueled Japanese aggression. But I don't think the Japanese would dare invade Shanghai. The KMT, I believe, is biding its time to strengthen our forces and build coalitions with the warlords that have power in the north and west. Without them, the KMT is a divided government. We have the British and American forces here, not to mention the French and Germans. The Japanese have to be careful not to go too far or they risk fighting them, and they know they can't defeat the Western powers. I'd like to think we are safe living in Shanghai." Mr. Pao gently touched Mini's hand. "Mini, I will find a good husband for you—don't worry." He winked at her.

Mini blushed. *I don't want to marry anyone but Kung Yi. Oh, but am I dreaming?*

She thought back over the last several weeks. Mini and Kung Yi had been holding hands in the dark theater where the latest Hollywood movies were showing. Lately, he had started wrapping his arm around her shoulder at the first scene of someone kissing on screen. She couldn't help but notice that her heart raced each time he touched her. She wanted to fall into his embrace. One time—perhaps sensing her desire—he even tried to kiss her earlobe, but she playfully pushed him away with the tips of her fingers. She had waited until the very last moment, letting his warm breath caress her neck before she turned him away.

"Mini, why is your face so red?" Mrs. Pao asked.

Mini startled, realizing she was thinking inappropriate thoughts in front of her parents.

"The soup made me hot," she said, and fanned herself with her hand.

Time is running short, Mini thought to herself. *Jie Xing will convince Ma eventually and Ma will convince Pa. What happened to Ling will happen to me. I must mention my feelings to Kung Yi tomorrow. I have to be bold. I have no choice.*

The market was more subdued than usual when Mini and Ai May arrived the next morning. Customers and merchants alike were bundled up in layers, going about their business more abruptly than seemed normal. Was it the January cold or the rising tension, which only seemed to feed and be fed by the rumor trade? Mini and Ai May also didn't want to expose themselves to the biting cold for a minute more than necessary and finished up their routine shopping quickly before they turned back to meet Mr. Shi at the market entrance.

He stood there looking handsome in a long black wool coat and a fur hat. A burgundy wool scarf protected his neck and partially covered his mouth. He raised a hand to greet Mini, pulling the scarf down from around his mouth as he did so. His broad smile was sunlight to her, breaking through the cloudy morning.

Kung Yi turned and whistled to a passing rickshaw. His movements by now were more certain, and he wasted no time helping Mini into the rickshaw as she reached him. They had been dating twice a week—at least—since September. Mini had long since stopped making excuses at home. It seemed her mother hardly noticed. They settled into the rickshaw and he took down the curtain to shield them from the wind, shamelessly wrapping his arms around her. She didn't push back, instead leaning into him. The moments passed quickly as their rickshaw passed through the busy streets. Returning to her senses, Mini pulled herself from his embrace, as her thoughts returned to the dinner conversation of the night before.

"Kung Yi, we shouldn't be doing this. We have no future together," she said calmly.

He opened his mouth to protest, but no sound came out. Kung Yi reached out and took her hand. His hand was warm against hers.

They continued the rest of the way quietly, hand in hand. When they reached their usual café on the Bund, the waiter took their coats and showed them to their booth. The café was mostly empty. Mini was only vaguely aware of Kung Yi studying her until the coffee and tea arrived. She glanced up at him, still watching her intently, and she turned to her coffee rather than return his gaze. She sipped it slowly in the semi-darkness, struggling over how to approach the subject of marriage. *Why do I have to force the issue?* Mini thought. *He should know better than to—*

"Kung Yi, what happened to the matchmaker you said you were going to send?" she finally asked.

Kung Yi paused, looking as if he was searching for the right words. "I told my mother your address and birthday. She said she would do it, but first she consulted the family fortune teller." Now he was the one avoiding her eyes.

"Why? When?" Mini put her coffee cup down quickly.

"You are a dragon and I am a sheep," he explained. "She said you are too strong for me."

Mini sat up straight. "You don't believe this, do you?"

"No, I'm not superstitious. But my mother is. She's very traditional. And she's the one who controls my marriage." He looked down at his cup. Kung Yi's broad shoulders slumped.

"Tell me, what kind of wife does your mother want you to have?"

"Someone from a family like us, from the land," he said. "No

Western education. Mother believes it spoils young girls. She expects her daughter-in-law to obey her absolutely."

No Western education! Well, that eliminates me. But I only had a few years of missionary school. And most of my teachers were Chinese anyway. Maybe she wouldn't hold this against me?

"But why are you still not married? You are twenty-nine. Most men at your age are married," Mini said.

"Most girls at your age are married too, Mini." Kung Yi looked at her.

Mini blushed. "True. I'm going to be an old maid, as my mother said."

"A very pretty old maid," Kung Yi teased.

Mini laughed, her rising anger collapsing. "Who does your mother want for you? What do they look like?"

Kung Yi was silent.

"Did you ever meet any of the girls your mother likes?" Mini tried again.

"No, I didn't. I saw photos."

"How did you avoid marrying one of them?"

"Oh Mini, I have my ways," he said. "I told her I'd leave home if she forced me. I am her only son and she expects to live with me the rest of her life. But she's been on my back lately."

A waiter brought their cakes to the table. "Will this be all, sir?"

"Yes, thank you," Kung Yi answered.

They dug into their cakes as Mini gathered up her thoughts and what this meant for her future.

"Did you mention us?" Mini asked abruptly.

"No I didn't," he said. "Not directly anyway. Mother's a very strong-willed person. She's the one who really runs the family's business. Father prefers Chinese opera and the teahouses. He spends his days singing opera with his friends. She meets the manager from each rice store and the overseer from our home village and she checks the accounts. She's really very good at it, and none dares to cheat her."

Mini picked up her cup and took another sip. *I don't care about that.*

But how to get around the problem? Maybe Mrs. Shi would like me if she actually met me?

"What would you say if I met your mother? Do you think she would change her mind?" *Am I too forward?* she thought. *He'll think me shameless.*

He was silent and stared at Mini intensely, as if measuring her up.

"Maybe," Kung Yi said finally. "I will try to invite you over for lunch. She can see for herself. I will tell her that unless she gives me one chance, I will not agree to any marriage proposal."

Oh, he really does want the same thing! Mini rejoiced silently. *He wants to marry me, too! At least it's not one-sided.*

"Really, you think she will agree?" Mini mumbled, trying to mask her eagerness at the possibility it could work out between them.

"She'll have to," he said confidently.

With that, he straightened up and looked into Mini's eyes. The happy warmth returned to his eyes, which radiated hope and a confidence that maybe what he had envisioned as impossible was possible after all.

"When?" Mini asked, though she regretted it immediately. *I act like I'm desperate*, she thought.

Kung Yi didn't seem to mind. He smiled at Mini.

"Next week," he said. "I think next Friday will be good. I've got an idea. My sister is getting married in less than five months. My mother is preparing her dowry. She'd like a city girl to give her some ideas on the latest fashions because she doesn't want to appear out of touch with the times. You'll be perfect."

He got up and sat down next to Mini. He leaned into her closely. Mini felt his hot breath on her cheek. He whispered playfully into her ear: "See, I'm brilliant."

Mini giggled and pushed him away.

True to his word this time, a boy delivered a note to Mini the very next day. It was an invitation for a causal lunch on Friday from the Shi family—no parents to be invited, because this was not a marriage arrangement. As Kung Yi explained, Mini would be introduced to Mrs. Shi as a friend of Kung Yi, someone who understood the latest fashions and would help with her daughter's dowry.

Mini got up early Friday morning. She stood in front of her open wardrobe, staring at her assorted qipao.

I can't be too flashy. I've got to be modest but stylish.

As she flipped through a row of hangers, her eyes rested on the navy blue wool qipao she had worn to the picnic at the British consulate.

She took it out, along with a long black coat and a light-blue woolen scarf. She put the coat over her qipao and placed the scarf at the collar, laying them flat on the bed. She switched to a red scarf but had second thoughts. *Too colorful.* She put the blue one back.

Satisfied, she opened the bottom of the wardrobe and considered her shoes, all in a neat row, just as Mrs. Pao called her downstairs for breakfast. She took out a pair of low-heeled Mary Janes and set them out at the foot of her bed before going downstairs. *I don't want to tower over anyone*, she thought, conscious of her height.

Mini was so excited that she almost let slip her planned lunch meeting during breakfast, but she caught herself. *Better wait. I don't even know what will come of it. I am sure Mother would approve and Father would, too. After all, Kung Yi is from a prominent family, and I won't be a concubine.* She smiled to herself as she ate, preoccupied in her reverie. Fortunately, neither her mother nor father seemed to notice.

Shortly after breakfast, with her father off to work and her mother getting ready for her daily game, Mini returned to her room to get ready. She touched a light layer of makeup to her face and gingerly sprayed on a little bit of perfume. *Not too much . . . but what to do with my hair?*

Mini sat before her vanity and studied her newly curled hair. She first twisted it into a bun and paused to look at herself. *No, that makes me look older than I am. The last thing I need is to look like an old maid.* Pinning it back, she reached for a hat. *Too Western. That will surely put her off.* Tossing the hat on the bed, she let her hair rest on her shoulder, combing it out a bit with some water. *Too plain, but it's probably right for Mrs. Shi. This mother-of-pearl will be perfect over my ear and will hold everything in place.* Mini's wavy black hair hovered just above her shoulder, pinned in place with the comb. She looked her age, but sophisticated, and not so stylish that Mrs. Shi would dismiss her out of hand as some spirited flapper.

Finally, she dressed and went downstairs.

"Where are you going dressed so fancy?" Mrs. Pao gave Mini an assessing look.

"I'm going to lunch with a friend," she replied casually.

"Who's your friend?" Mrs. Pao asked.

"You don't know him."

"Him?" Mrs. Pao asked, alarmed.

"Yeah, Ma, he is the son of the Shi Rice Store, you know, the one where we buy our rice? His sister is getting married and his parents want me to help with the dowry."

"Aya, why didn't you tell me earlier?" her mother crowed. "The Shi family is a big family. They own at least fifteen rice stores in Shanghai. I didn't know you were friends with the son. You should invite him over sometime." Mini's mother was all smiles now: "Go and do a good job. I hope something good will follow."

Mrs. Pao wobbled on her lily feet, following Mini to the front door. Mini caught the first rickshaw, stepping in before Mrs. Pao could offer any more advice.

The Shi family mansion was situated in the Old Chinese quarter, quite a distance from Mini's house in the British Concession. The paved streets gave way to cobblestones, narrowing with the shrinking houses. As they made their way deeper into the Chinese quarter, small houses crowded the streets and the rickshaw slowed to navigate the people on foot, in rickshaws, and pulling carts—a discordant array of Chinese people in Western dress, Chinese robes, and the cotton tunics of coolies and peasants.

The narrow street leading to the Shi mansion was pressed on each side by stores overflowing with their wares, and food and clothing hanging out to dry from the upper stories. Old men sat at an open teahouse, likely playing Chinese chess. Roast duck hung upside down in the glass window of the deli next door. As the crowded street slowed the rickshaw down even further, the coolie shouted at the people and forced his way through.

Eventually, the rickshaw left the commercial area and stopped in front of a Chinese-style mansion. She got out and stood in front of a massive black wooden gate. A metal plate—a lion's face—hung in the center. An iron hoop through the lion's nose served as a giant door-knocker. Two giant carved stone lions stood at each side, guarding the gate and glaring at her as she waited. Mini didn't know what to do. She had expected Kung Yi to be there, waiting for her at the door, but he was nowhere in sight. Her expectation had been silly, sure, but the weight of the moment, like the gate before her, filled her with a sense of trepidation that she hadn't realized was in her until then. Gathering all her courage, Mini grabbed the doorknocker and knocked. A moment passed and a servant opened the door, with Kung Yi trailing behind.

He smiled broadly and was about to put his arm around her shoulder but caught himself. "Come in. Mother and Father are wait-ing for you."

He led her into a deep courtyard garden, open except for the art-fully placed bonsai trees, framed by oddly shaped rocks. A stone walkway led to a house with an arched roof, graced by a stone-carved dragon extending the length of the roofline. A small rising phoenix stood watching behind the dragon's powerful tail. Kung Yi pushed the door open and showed Mini in.

Mini passed through and into a massive room. A maid took Mini's coat.

"Mother likes to call it the Great Hall," Kung Yi whispered close to Mini's ear.

A six-foot-long and three-foot-wide black-and-white ink painting of bamboo trees filled Mini's view. Two long, narrow scrolls of calligraphy flanked the painting. One scroll read: "Success upon arrival of a horse." The other: "Reach success and gain recognition." *An ambitious family,* Mini thought. *They must have high expectations for their only son.*

Reading down the second scroll, her eyes fell upon a woman sitting in a high-backed, ornately carved rosewood chair just under the scrolls—Mini hadn't noticed her before. The stout middle-aged woman was dressed in black from head to toe. A satin tunic and a long skirt of the same material covered most of her tiny feet, except the pointy tips. Her hair was pulled back into a bun. Separated from her by a carved redwood tea table sat an old man in a long brown satin robe, drinking tea from a tiny brown teacup. He was much older and smaller. His skin was withered and dark, like a dried prune. They watched Mini and Kung Yi coolly, without acknowledging them. Mini resisted the urge to turn back and flee the house. She forced herself forward with a smile on her face and bowed deeply.

"Mother and Father, this is Miss Pao, my friend," Kung Yi said and bowed slightly.

"Please sit down and have a cup of tea, Miss Pao." Mrs. Shi pointed to a smaller set of chairs and table just to the side. Her thin lips curled into a smile, but her sharp eyes didn't hold a hint of warmth.

Mini sat down. A maid came with a small pot of tea and two cups for her and Kung Yi. *Yi Xing tea sets,* Mini thought. *The ones used by emperors in the past.* She noticed a young girl dressed in a loose-fitting qipao embroidered in pink and a pair of homemade shoes. The girl sat quietly opposite them in an identical set of chairs. She looked about seventeen or eighteen years old, and very skinny. On her pale oval face, two large dark eyes scanned Mini from head to toe while her hands played with the bushy ends of her thick braids. She stood up and gave a slight nod to Mini when Kung Yi introduced her: "Shiao Hui, my younger sister."

Mini nodded back with a bright smile. To relax herself, she picked up the hot tea and blew on it. Taking a sip, she held it a moment to warm her hands, but only briefly. She sensed holding on to the cup too long would quickly become awkward and would in some way reflect poorly on Kung Yi. Mini couldn't quite explain to herself why she felt this way, but she put down the cup and sat upright, hands on her lap, like a schoolgirl in class. She dared not look at Mr. and Mrs. Shi, though she was aware of them observing her.

"Miss Pao, I thank you for taking the trouble to visit us," Mrs. Shi said. "Shiao Hui's wedding is approaching. She'd like to have a wardrobe that is up-to-date before her big day. I am not much help. I am an old-fashioned woman. Kung Yi suggested you could help my daughter." Contrary to her pudgy body, Mrs. Shi's voice was high and thin, almost metallic.

"Mrs. Shi, it is no trouble at all," Mini said respectfully. "I am more than happy to help." She twisted in the chair self-consciously, trying to sit straight while at the same time turning to face the Shis. Mini made eye contact with Mrs. Shi.

The corners of Mrs. Shi's mouth drew upwards away from her double chin. She was smiling again, but her eyes were still icy: "I don't know how much Kung Yi told you. Shiao Hui is marrying into a big family and I don't want to be shabby on the dowry. She will have ten trunks of clothing. We took care of the furs and winter coats already. We need to pay attention to her spring, summer, and fall dresses."

Mrs. Shi glanced at her daughter, the ice in her eyes disappearing. "Of course, Shiao Hui doesn't know much about what's fashionable these days," she continued, turning once more to face Mini. "She was brought up in the traditional way and has hardly ever left this house. I will have to rely on you, Miss Pao, to accomplish this task. Everything has to be done by the end of April. We will have to transport the dowry in May."

"I suppose the wedding won't be in Shanghai then," Mini said.

"No, it will be in Cheng Zhou, our home village," Mrs. Shi replied. "Shiao Hui's future husband is the elder son of the Jian family, who owns the village next to ours, as well as many lumberyards in Shanghai."

"Shiao Hui is most fortunate." Mini smiled at Shiao Hui again. "I will come as often as you need me," Mini added, earnestly.

Shiao Hui lowed her head and nodded.

"Mrs. Shi, I am certain you have the most gifted tailors. But if your purpose is to provide a dowry with dresses that more reflect today's fashion, then may I propose to introduce our family's tailor?" Mini asked as diplomatically as she knew how. "He knows what's fashionable because he makes dresses for many young ladies in Shanghai. Shiao Hui will need many dresses if you still need clothing for the other three seasons. It would be easier to bargain with him. And he would also provide the fabric, so Mrs. Shi, you could save much of your precious time, as there would be no need to go to the fabric store."

Mrs. Shi looked at her husband. "What do you think, Master?"

He sipped his tea before replying simply, "Wife, it's up to you."

"Thank you, Master." Turning to Mini, Mrs. Shi said: "Let's settle it then. Miss Pao, please bring your tailor tomorrow if you can."

"Yes, Mrs. Shi," Mini replied dutifully.

As if prearranged to leave no awkward silence, a maid then announced that lunch was ready. Kung Yi jumped up, perhaps too eagerly. He hadn't said a word the entire time.

Mr. and Mrs. Shi each stood, and Mini was surprised to notice Kung Yi's father was a head shorter than his wife. Unlike his wife, he was thin. He walked energetically out of the room without a word, as if he couldn't wait another minute for his lunch. His enormous wife could hardly keep up on her three-inch feet. She struggled to keep her balance as she stepped forward. Shiao Hui hastened to lend her mother a helping hand.

Kung Yi followed behind, whispering to Mini as they filed into a dining room dominated by a round, carved rosewood table: "How are you holding up?"

Mini nodded her head in reply. *You were quiet the whole time*, she thought, even though she couldn't help but smile at him.

Lunch was delicious, though Mini was too nervous to do more than taste a few bites of the numerous small dishes. She left shortly after. Kung Yi walked her out to the gate and squeezed her hand tightly after the gate closed behind them. He insisted on seeing her home.

Conscious of the Chinese quarter's prying eyes, Mini began to relax only after the rickshaw had left the vicinity of the mansion entirely, with Kung Yi taking the opportunity to cuddle up next to her.

"You were very brave," he said to her.

"Do you think your parents like me?" she asked.

"They're impressed by your manners and your modern dress, I'm sure," he replied.

"How about your sister?"

"My sister is a little slow in the head," he said. "She wants to be a modern girl, but I don't think she knows how. She'll appreciate your help."

The rickshaw stopped.

"Will you come in for a cup of tea?" Mini asked.

"No, I have to get home," Kung Yi demurred. "Mother is expecting me."

"I'll see you tomorrow, then," Mini gave him a longing glance.

"Definitely!" he grinned ear to ear.

With Mrs. Pao's approval, Mini dutifully made herself available to Shiao Hui whenever she was needed over the next two months. She sent over her family tailor, negotiated prices, collected samples of new styles, chose fabric, and did it all in a way that made everything look like it was Shiao Hui's idea. But in all the time that passed, she didn't see the Shis once.

12

LING'S LITTLE PRECIOUS

A telephone ring pierced the late-night quiet of the house. Mini bolted upright in her bed in the dark at the disturbance. She listened vaguely, wondering what the phone call could've been. Silence met her, followed minutes later by the chaotic sound of footsteps and her mother's voice calling out, high-pitched and out of breath:

"Ai May, Ai May, wake up! Hurry up and help me dress. Master, Master, I need to leave at once. Oh, Ai May, go wake up Mini. I want her with me. Master, I apologize for having to leave you to eat breakfast alone."

Mini then heard Ai May run up the stairs, probably two at time, yelling: "Young Mistress, wake up, wake up!"

By then Mini was already up, her feet hunting for slippers in the still darkness.

"I'm awake. Go downstairs to help my mother."

The rumble from Ai May's footsteps receded down the stairs.

Her father called out: "Calm down, woman. It will be all right. Ai May, don't be so clumsy!" He sounded more annoyed than calm.

Mini went downstairs, pulling on a heavy sweater as she went.

"Oh Mini!" Mrs. Pao called out to her. "Ling is having her baby. Jie Xing just called. Ling went into labor an hour ago. She's crying for the two of us. We have to go now. Go, get ready."

"Yes, Ma. It will take me a few minutes to get ready. Ai May, put on a coat, go outside to the big road, and get us a taxi. Make sure it's a *taxi*, not a rickshaw."

"Yes, Young Mistress!" Ai May yelled back and ran out the front door.

The sky was still dark and full of stars when they arrived at Ling's house. A pale, fuzzy moon hung over their heads. Mini had no idea what hour it was. She helped her mother out of the taxi and paid for it. She had the urge to rush into the house, to see Ling, but slowed herself down, realizing her mother was struggling to keep up. Mini slid her hand under her mother's arm and carefully guided her through the dark to the front door.

The door opened swiftly as if by itself; a maid had been waiting at the door. She must have been there a while. They stepped inside, and the maid led them to the downstairs living room. The heat and noise overwhelmed Mini. The house felt stuffy, and a fire was raging in the fireplace. Jie Xing was pacing back and forth in white silk pajamas and slippers. A servant came from the kitchen carrying hot towels in a washbasin and ran upstairs.

Mini heard many footsteps in the kitchen, as if the entire house staff were in there. She heard a crash followed by an elder voice scolding. Someone had spilled water. After a moment, a young maid came out carrying a basin freshly filled with hot water and went upstairs.

Jie Xing was relieved when he saw Mrs. Pao and Mini. He held Mrs. Pao's hand for a long time.

"Where is Ling?" Mrs. Pao asked impatiently.

"More hot water, more hot water!"

The command coming from upstairs pulled Mini's attention back to the moment. Mini saw that her mother was already making her way toward the voice, wobbling to the stairs—pulling herself up with both hands on the banister. Mini hurried to help her mother climb the stairs.

"She's upstairs in the master bedroom," Jie Xing answered behind them. "The midwife is with her, and two other old women." The door to their bedroom was half open. Mini arrived to the sound of heaving breaths from three women she had never seen before, and a scream from Ling. Mrs. Pao pushed the door open further. Ling lay naked in wet sheets soiled by her own sweat. Her nipples were dark and hard; her legs spread wide open, and bent at the knee. Two old servants stood on each side holding onto her legs. The midwife massaged her protruding belly. Ling's eyes were hollow and her hair a knotted, soaking mess on the pillow. A strong sour smell filled the air. Mini closed her eyes and took a deep breath.

Mrs. Pao walked in and put her hands gently on Ling's face. Ling's body visibly relaxed. She murmured, "Ma, Ma."

Mini was about to follow her mother into the room, only to be stopped by an old servant arriving with yet more hot water: "Young Mistress, you are a virgin. You don't need to see this." She closed the door behind her.

Ousted from the birthing chamber, Mini went downstairs and sat rigidly on the sofa, jumping nervously with each scream from Ling. She couldn't imagine the pain her sister was going through. Jie Xing paced the room, but Mini ignored him—the searing image of Ling in labor filled her mind.

So Mini and Jie Xing waited, exchanging no words. There was no offer of tea and no one asked Mini whether she was hungry. She listened to her sister's low moaning as it built into a scream, followed by a quiet calm. Each scream came more intensely, more harshly it seemed, than the last. Hours went by like this when finally, instead of a scream, Mini heard a baby's angry cry.

Mini and Jie Xing both took off for upstairs instantly, bumping into each other in their eagerness, running up the narrow stairs. He opened the bedroom door to find Mrs. Pao.

"It's a boy. It's a boy."

Mrs. Pao was crying, holding a bloody, wrinkly baby in her arms. The baby waved his tiny fists, protesting his expulsion from his once-cozy womb. A servant tenderly wiped blood from the baby in Mrs. Pao's arms.

Jie Xing, radiant, reached out for his son.

Ling lay in bed, heaving her own tired, relieved cry.

The servants and midwife were all sweating, their shirts stuck to their backs. They were tending to Ling, wiping her legs with warm, wet towels. One towel had been thrown to rest on the floor, next to a basinful of pink bloody water and a pair of bloody scissors that Mini assumed had been used to cut the umbilical cord.

Mini stood there, this scene playing out around her, no one paying her any mind. She thought her eyes were stinging and touched them only to realize that tears were trickling down her cheeks. They were happy tears, Mini knew. Looking at the tiny boy, she was happy for Ling. She went downstairs silently.

The living room was bathed in the bright sunlight of day. Only then did Mini realize that morning had long come and gone. *Father will be at work*, she thought. She found Jie Xing's office and phoned her father. He was almost shouting at the other end of the line.

"Yes, yes, it is good news! Yes, yes, I am very happy. I will be there as soon as I can!" he exclaimed.

It seemed strange to her that he was so excited. *He has been so indifferent about Ling's marriage. But who wouldn't be excited? It's his grandchild. His first and only grandchild, his grandson.*

She returned upstairs to find her mother scolding Jie Xing.

"*What* did you say?" Mrs. Pao asked incredulously. "You don't have a wet nurse in the house? Your son needs to be fed right away, Mister! Now Ling will have to feed the baby. My poor Ling, she's already suffered enough."

The midwife handed the freshly clean baby over to Mrs. Pao, who laid him gently on Ling's bare chest, the exhausted mother only half-conscious. Ling took the baby and held him to her breast like a sleep-walker until she cried out, "Oh, it hurts!" Ling frowned in confusion.

"Of course it hurts," her mother echoed. Mrs. Pao turned to Jie Xing: "When will the wet nurse come to the house?"

Jie Xing turned to the midwife and repeated her question.

"She lives by Suzhou Creek," the midwife replied. "Send a messenger to fetch her. There is no address but tell the driver it is the third shed by the creek after the temple. She's in her thirties but still young and vital. She bore a girl last week and the baby died a few days ago. She has plenty of milk for Little Master."

"Died! How?" Mini cried out.

"Smothered by the father," the midwife reported.

"*How*?" Mini asked, shocked. "His own daughter?"

"Too many mouths to feed. Can't afford it."

"Jie Xing, please, send a car right away," Mrs. Pao interrupted. "I don't want to see Ling hurt anymore." She turned to a servant: "Feed some thin rice gruel to the baby now. One hour wait should be fine for him."

Feeling useless, Mini went downstairs again. She went to the kitchen. A young maid was filling a milk bottle with rice gruel. There was no food in sight. She backed out and found a sunny spot on the sofa in the living room, where she pulled her coat over herself and gradually dozed off.

By the time she woke, the wet nurse was there and already nursing the baby. She looked nothing like the young, vital woman the midwife had described—more like a tired woman in her fifties. Her hair was already thinning such that it barely covered her scalp. Wrinkles lined her dark face. The wet nurse was smiling at the baby. Mini could find no hint of sadness for her own child in the woman's eyes.

A fully dressed Jie Xing was talking to Mr. Pao, who sat next to Mini on the sofa. Fragrant cooking odors filled the room. Teacups and a teapot, along with some rice dumplings, sat on the table. Two bottles of gift wrapped rice wine stood on the side table. It was already dark outside.

"I must have slept for a long time." She rubbed her eyes.

"Since three o'clock this afternoon, the maid told me," her father responded.

"I am sorry," Mini said. "I was tired. Ling had a long birth. I think we were here before dawn." She reached for a dumpling.

"It's okay, Mini," Mr. Pao reassured her. "You were with Ling for a long time, but it's all over now. The little fellow looks healthy. I'm a grandpa!" He smiled broadly. "Let's celebrate, Jie Xing. Open the wine."

"Where is Ling? How is she? I should go see her," Mini said.

"Ling has already moved to a clean, spare bedroom for her resting month," her mother answered. "Let her be. She's sleeping soundly."

A month when she will not share a bed with her husband.

Jie Xing interrupted her thoughts. "Let's share a toast," he said. "Ling has graced me with a boy who will carry my family into the future. I cannot thank you, my in-laws, enough."

They toasted, and even Mrs. Pao, who usually wouldn't touch alcohol, joined in.

Jie Xing phoned his parents from his study. He stayed there for a long time, until a maid went in to call him for dinner. He came out with a theatrical flourish, humming a line from the Peking opera *A Red Maid*: "Graceful as she is, a mistress born is as a treasure for the family."

After dinner, Mrs. Pao gave instructions to the kitchen servant: "Ling must stay in bed for a whole month. Feed her broth daily." Mrs. Pao ordered a long list of food to buy for Ling.

Mrs. Pao spent most of the following month at Ling's house, doting on her new grandbaby and her daughter. Mini visited often. Jie Xing was happy beyond reason whenever Mini saw him at home, though these occasions were rare, as his late-night business engagements seemed to have picked up around the same time as his son's birth. Mini also noticed that a bigger diamond ring appeared on Ling's finger soon after.

"From my mother-in-law," Ling told Mini when she noticed the bauble, taking it off for Mini to try on. "My gift for having a son." She was so proud.

Jie Xing's parents, who hadn't bothered with the Paos before the wedding, came all the way from Suzhou to Shanghai for a visit. They heaped lavish praise on Ling to her parents.

Ling was floating in the clouds and couldn't find a way down.

The Wangs had longed for this banquet for years and years, and now they were finally able to put it on. Today was the one-month birthday of Ling's son, Xiao Bao, "little precious." More than two hundred relatives, friends, and business associates packed both floors of an elegant restaurant on the Bund—one appropriate to the family's standing and fit for a celebration of the first male child born to the family. Even Jie Xing's first wife and daughters joined in the merriment. Birth announcements ran in the major newspapers. Mrs. Pao was vindicated.

When Mini helped Ling with the invitations during her convalescence, she confided in her sister that she was seeing Kung Yi. Ling made a point of inviting him to the banquet, too. Mini was with Ling and Jie Xing at the gift table when he arrived in a crisp blue suit and red tie with his hair combed back, mimicking the hairstyle of a famous movie actor. He waved at Mini and then wriggled through the crowd towards them.

"Congratulations! You must be Mr. Wang, the famous silk tycoon. I'm Shi Kung Yi, your sister-in-law's friend," he said as he shook hands with Jie Xing.

"You are exaggerating—I am no tycoon, Mr. Shi. Thank you for coming." Jie Xing tried to be humble though he was visibly flattered.

Kung Yi took a large red envelope from his breast pocket. "A little token for your precious son."

"Thank you, thank you. You are very generous." Jie Xing took the envelope with both hands and handed it to Ling, who handed it to Mini, who put it into a large bag.

A Japanese couple appeared at the top of the staircase. The lady's pink kimono stood out in a sea of multi colored qipao. Jie Xing spotted them right away. "Sorry, Mr. and Mrs. Sato are here," he said. "I must go. You enjoy yourself. Ling, make sure Mr. Shi is comfortable."

Mini introduced Kung Yi to Ling, and they shook hands.

"Mrs. Wang, what a pretty diamond ring you have," he said as he took her hand.

"Thank you. Now, when is my sister going to get a diamond ring?"

Mini flushed. She pinched Ling on her arm. "Ling, stop this nonsense."

Ling cried out, "All right, I'm joking!"

Kung Yi smiled at the playfulness of the sisters and added coyly, "We'll see."

Ling had placed Kung Yi at the same table as the rest of the Pao family.

"To the lucky grandpa and grandma!" he toasted when they were all seated. He then talked to Mr. Pao during the entire twelve-course, four-hour-long meal, regaling him with stories of the countryside and his family's rice operations, and eagerly asking for Mr. Pao's views on the British interests and their commitment to China. He insisted that Mrs. Pao be served first when each course arrived.

After dinner ended, Kung Yi said goodbye, but only after hailing a taxi for the family and insisting he see them off first.

"That friend of yours, he is a pleasant young man," Mr. Pao said to Mini on the way back. Mrs. Pao, still beaming from the celebration, smiled her agreement.

13

A TEN-LI DOWRY

May brought a warm spring air filled with birdsong—but also spring cleaning. Furs, winter coats, and winter bedding were hung out in the sun, beaten, and put away. Light cotton and silk dresses were taken out from the bottom of trunks and readied for summer. In the midst of all the housework, Mini managed to help Shiao Hui pack her dowry, and Shaio Hui invited Mini to her wedding in June as an expression of her gratitude. Mini gladly accepted after receiving her parents' blessing.

When the time came for the wedding, Mini rode the train to Cheng Zhou. The trip was a lovely respite from all the hard work that spring.

She arrived at a station—really a small hut that served as a ticket booth—where a servant whose name Mini didn't know, but whom she had seen at the Shis' Shanghai mansion, met her and escorted her to the Shi estate. The estate was a large compound surrounded by miles of rice paddies, fields, and small mud huts where peasants lived. As they drew closer, Mini noticed that the compound rising above the fields was actually composed of two L-shaped buildings. A covered veranda wrapped around, connecting the buildings with a central courtyard.

Though much larger than the mansion in Shanghai, the Shis' compound was less intimidating. Mini was given a room in the west wing, a space reserved for guests. Kung Yi was already in her room waiting for her when she arrived. Mini coolly acknowledged him and took in the room as the servant set down Mini's suitcase next to a hand-carved wardrobe. The room was simply furnished with a four-poster bed covered with a mosquito net, a washstand at the corner with a clean towel hanging beside it, two chairs on either side of a small tea table, a wardrobe, and a dresser with a mirror.

"Thank you. You can return later and if I need help, I'll call for you," Mini said when the servant began to open Mini's luggage.

Kung Yi embraced her as soon as the servant left.

"I missed you so much!" he exclaimed. He rubbed Mini's back gently with his hand.

"I missed you too," she replied. "It's been over a month since you left Shanghai."

"Mother wanted me to stay put," Kung Yi said. "This wedding is a big deal for her. She wants to make sure every detail is in order, so she won't lose face. How was the journey?"

"It was fine. The train was comfortable. I wouldn't mind a cup of tea."

Kung Yi rang the bell and a young maid came in.

"Go get some dim sum and tea for Miss Pao," Kung Yi instructed.

The maid bowed. A few minutes later, a tray with a pot of tea and two cups arrived, along with a few small dishes of dim sum. They sat in the room for a while, catching up until Kung Yi was called away by his mother. Left to herself, Mini took out her qipao and gowns and hung them in the wardrobe and took a nap until a servant came to announce dinner in the grand banquet room.

The noise woke her early the next morning. Mini peeked out her window and witnessed the most spectacular wedding procession she had ever seen. There were men in the courtyard moving trunks of dowries from a large room opposite the yard. Silk bedding was piled up and wrapped in large red sheets, then loaded onto donkey carts alongside the trunks. Once one cart was full, a man led the donkey and cart outside and an empty one came in, the process repeating itself. It took hours to load the entire dowry.

Breakfast was a quiet affair, with neither Mr. Shi nor Mrs. Shi nor their adult children speaking. The other guests made small talk until breakfast concluded and Mrs. Shi summoned Mini.

"Would you be kind enough to help Shiao Hui dress?" she asked.

"Of course," Mini replied.

"Thank you," she said and walked off, leaving a sheepish Shiao Hui with Mini.

In the bride's room, maids were already busy laying out her dress for the wedding ceremony: a bright red silk dress along with a veil, a headdress, and a pair of red satin shoes. Then they carefully put the pink, blue, and purple silk qipao for the wedding banquet onto the hangers, the matching shoes into boxes, and carried them all out. Mini closed the door after the maids.

Shiao Hui sat in front of the mirror in her dressing gown. Her straight black hair fell like a waterfall onto her shoulders. Mini picked up a comb and started combing her hair.

"Are you happy to be getting married?" Mini asked.

"I don't know," Shiao Hui blushed.

"Do you know the groom?" Mini asked while continuing to comb her hair.

"I met him once when I was little. He's from the Jian family. They own lots of land here," the girl explained. "His father is a friend of my father's. My parents arranged my marriage when I was five."

"You don't mind?" Mini asked as she began applying white powder to her face.

"No. I trust my parents." Shiao Hui blinked as the brush touched her forehead.

"And you're ready now?" Mini asked.

"Mother says eighteen is old enough."

Whoever it is, I hope he's a decent man who won't take advantage of her innocence. Mini had grown fond of Shiao Hui after having spent months with her. She was not the dim-witted girl Kung Yi thought she was. She was just naïve. Raised in an enclosed environment, she had no choice but to see the world through her mother's eyes.

"I am sure your parents chose a nice young man for you," Mini said, carefully twisting Shiao Hui's hair into a bun and pinning it up.

After her hair was done, Shiao Hui took off her dressing gown and stood naked, waiting. Mini glanced at her, a slim girl with a flat chest, smiling shyly.

Mini helped her into her underclothes and the wedding dress.

"You look lovely!" Mini proclaimed. "Do you want to have the headpiece on now or later?"

"Later. It's so heavy. I can put it on before we leave."

"That's smart."

Someone rapped on the door with fierce urgency. Mini opened the door a crack and peeked outside. Kung Yi was there.

"Is Shiao Hui ready? The wedding sedan is waiting for her," he said.

"We're almost ready." Mini stuck her head out to look down at the courtyard. It was empty of all the donkey carts, with nothing left but a red carriage in the center. The carriage looked like an overly decorated Chinese chest drawer, with bamboo yoke sticking out at four sides. The curtains were pulled halfway down the two small windows on each side. One big, heavily muscled man stood at each corner of the sedan, waiting to carry Shiao Hui to her in-laws' house.

Mini closed the door. She put the headpiece on Shiao Hui, adjusting the veil to cover her entire face. Holding her hand, Mini carefully guided Shiao Hui out of the room and to the carriage.

Shiao Hui's carriage went first, then the carriage of Mr. and Mrs. Shi. Mini joined Kung Yi, following in a horse-drawn carriage, along with a long line of carriages holding guests and dowry. Firecrackers exploded around them, filling the courtyard air with a pungent burning smell. Once they were on the road, Mini looked out the window to see how long the dowry line was. She couldn't see the end. *Must be three miles—ten li!* "A ten-li red dowry ensures a happy marriage," goes the saying.

Mini swayed right and left as the carriage traveled along the bumpy, muddy road. It was lush country. Rows of weeping willows on each side separated the dirt road from miles of rice paddies. Long, willowy branches dipped into the water flowing down the irrigation trench. The vast unending shades of green contrasted with the pale blue sky, where motionless clouds hung in the horizon. Half-naked men in large straw hats and muddy pants abandoned their buffalo plows in the field and gathered at the side of the road to watch the wedding procession. Women and children followed the dowry line, the kids counting the number of donkey carts. The men of the Shi household broke up the crowd of onlookers as they ran alongside the family caravan, lighting firecrackers the length of the ride. Birds scattered, frightened by the noise.

Finally, they stopped in front of a compound similar to the Shis'. A crowd of at least twenty people greeted them. A maid took Shiao Hui's hand and guided her out from her carriage and into the building, along with the other female relatives. Small children ran around the bride, trying to catch a glimpse of her face from beneath her veil, the adults cheering as she walked by. Mini stayed close to Kung Yi, unsure whether she was counted as a relative. A dark-robed old man with a long white beard came forward and greeted Mr. Shi. They bowed to each other.

"This is the elder Jian," Kung Yi told Mini under his breath.

When it was her turn, Mini bowed to the old man like everyone else. He bowed back.

"Welcome," he announced. "This is a happy day for both of our families. I hope one year from now, we will celebrate again here, with the birth of my grandson."

"Merciful Kwan Yin blesses the Jian family," Mrs. Shi said.

The old man gave out a laugh. "Come, come, everyone. Please come inside to have a cup of tea. It was a long journey. You all must be tired."

It was a hot June day, and Mini realized she was very thirsty after three hours in the hot sun.

The group walked into the great hall. Mrs. Shi found a chair next to a small woman in a brown satin tunic and skirt, whose pale fingers were covered in jade and emerald rings.

"This is Mrs. Jian," Kung Yi whispered into Mini's ear.

Mini overheard Mrs. Shi tell her: "We are family now. This is one of my happiest days."

"Wait until we hold our grandson," Mrs. Jian replied, and they both covered their mouths with silk handkerchiefs, giggling like young girls.

The wedding ceremony was held in the great hall. The elder Shis and Jians were seated in the high chairs. A maid led the veiled bride out, who then stood before the elders. The groom, who looked more like a boy than a young man, emerged from the other side of the hall in a brown robe and small brown hat with a red knob on top. A red silk flower was pinned to his chest. He, too, took his place in front of the elders.

"Kneel to the elders," the uncle of the groom instructed.

Bride and groom knelt down.

"Kowtow to the elders once."

They did, foreheads touching the ground.

"Kowtow twice."

They did again.

"Kowtow three times."

They complied a third time.

"Stand up and bow to each other!"

They stood up. A maid helped Shiao Hui turn to face her groom. They bowed to each other.

"Now, uncover the bride."

The groom stepped forward and raised up the veil to reveal Shiao Hui's face. Her face was flushed, and her eyes cast down.

"Beautiful bride. I announce Shi Shiao Hui and Jian Xing Lin are husband and wife. Now, you may retire to your own suite and consummate the marriage."

Shiao Hui blushed a deep crimson. Everyone in the room laughed. A maid helped Shiao Hui up and out of the room, following her groom. Quiet chatter from small groups filled the hall while they waited. Not long after, the maid brought out a red-stained sheet and the banquet was announced, the union official now that Shiao Hui's virginity had been confirmed.

Mini didn't remember the rest of the wedding very well—she drank a few too many cups of rice wine. The bride and groom went around the banquet hall several times. Each time they stopped at a table, guests at the table would beat their cups with their chopsticks, insisting the bride and groom share a piece of candy that was tied to a chopstick and held aloft by a male guest standing on a chair. As the new couple went to bite the candy—reaching for it not with their hands, but with their mouths as the game dictated—the man moved the candy left and right so that the bride and groom would repeatedly miss it only to catch each other's lips instead. Each time the couple touched lips, the guests laughed and a toast was proposed. Each time, Mini would down a cup of rice wine. By the time the acrobat troupe performed in the yard, Mini was already very drunk and had almost passed out. She leaned on Kung Yi the whole time.

It was three in the morning when the Shis returned to their own home. Kung Yi sent Mini to her room. Mini closed the door behind her, undressed quickly, and was asleep within minutes.

A faint knock broke into her dream. Mini didn't stir. Then it happened again, a little louder. She dragged herself up and went to the door, half conscious.

Kung Yi was there. He forced his way into the room unsteadily. Just like Mini, he was drunk. He closed the door behind him and locked it tight. He pulled Mini closer to him.

"You are so beautiful," he said.

Only then did Mini realize she was exposed to him in her night-gown. She tried to break free from his embrace, to go find a robe. Kung Yi wouldn't let her go. His hands touched her naked shoulders, reached down to her back, and further down to her hips. His body pressed against hers, hard as a rock and hot to the touch.

Oh, Merciful Kwan Yin. Please help me to resist this temptation.

Mini wanted to pull herself away, but her attempt was weak. She felt that her bones were melting. She leaned into him, heart racing and blood pumping. She felt the desire, the desire to be held tight, to be possessed.

Kung Yi kissed her, and she kissed back. Her rationality was borne away, helplessly, by her passion. He backed toward the bed, holding her tightly until they both fell onto the bed. Mini unbuttoned his shirt and they became one.

14

A SMALL DINNER FOR MINI

Mini sat on her unmade bed in her rumpled housedress and slippers, passively watching the few stubborn yellow leaves that shriveled on the tree outside her window. *They are hopeless like me. The November wind is too strong for them to survive long*. She had been counting the number of leaves on the tree each day, and each day the number decreased. She sighed and covered her face with her hands. She wasn't in the mood to carry on her daily routine today and had decided to stay home, to watch time pass by, as she had spent many days lately.

It had been several months since she had succumbed to her desire for Kung Yi, and now the cruel consequences had become clear in her mind. Her father had brought a few marriage proposals to her in the time since then, but she had refused them all without so much as asking for details. She was no longer in the marriage market as far as she was concerned and no longer entitled to a decent man, because she was no longer a virgin.

Kung Yi had stopped showing up at the market since they had

returned from the wedding. Though embarrassed, Mini had been anxious to see him. She wanted to know her fate.

He reappeared at the market three weeks later. He blushed when he saw Mini and Ai May. Mini blushed too. Both of them stood silent, staring at each other, too embarrassed to speak until Ai May broke the silence.

"Young Mistress, will you go to lunch with Mr. Shi?" she asked.

"No. Not today. We will go home," Mini responded, her eyes still focused on Kung Yi.

"Maybe tomorrow then," Kung Yi replied sheepishly.

He didn't show up the next day, or the following day.

As time wore on, she despaired, her hope diminishing with each passing day.

What am I going to do? She asked herself again and again, coming back to just two options: stay home and become an old maid, or marry Kung Yi. She would have liked the second option, but it wasn't her choice to make.

What I did was shameful, but why should I be the only one to shoulder the consequences? Kung Yi's been with women before. He must have discarded these women and now he will discard me. He can go on and have a family, but I won't have a chance anymore, unless . . . Unless what, she didn't know. *It's so unfair. Women always have to carry the burden.*

One afternoon, Ai May's footsteps on the stairs interrupted her brooding.

"Ai May, don't bother me. I want to lie down quietly for a while," she called out without moving from her bed.

"But, Young Mistress, Mr. Shi is here. He wants to see you. Mistress said that you are home and you will see him."

It had been months now since she had been with Kung Yi—five months actually. They had seen each other only a handful of times. He had been very attentive to Mini each time they met, but Kung Yi never uttered a word of apology, never said a word about marriage. Mini opened the door, about to step down the stairs, but she caught herself and went back into her room to check her reflection in the mirror. She saw dark rings under her eyes and pale, sunken cheeks. Her face was puffy from lack of sleep. She rubbed her face a little to bring some color to her cheeks. She combed her hair and, having done the best she could, headed downstairs to face him.

From the stairs Mini could see Kung Yi chatting with Mrs. Pao in the sitting room. He was smiling, his dapper gray suit clinging to his body without a single crease. She paused. Some of her brooding lifted as she watched him bantering with her mother. He looked as smart as ever. He stood up as Mini continued down the stairs and walked into the room. Refusing to betray her mixed emotions, Mini gave him a slight nod, smiled a half smile, and sat down on the chair furthest away from him.

Sitting back down next to Mrs. Pao, Kung Yi took a sip of tea and said to Mini, "I asked your mother's permission to take you out for some dim sum. Would you mind?"

Mini slowly turned her head to her mother. Mrs. Pao smiled encouragingly and vigorously nodded her head.

"As you wish," Mini replied dispassionately. "Only give me a minute. It's cold outside. I'll get my coat."

She went upstairs again, changed out of her housedress, and put on a coat. She powdered her face a little to cover the dark rings under her eyes, all the while wondering what was on Kung Yi's mind. *How dare he show his face in my house! He will tell me that he won't be able to see me again, talk sweet talk as he always does, then throw me away like others, I am sure.* She sat there for a while, took a deep breath, and decided it was time to face her fate.

Kung Yi was waiting at the bottom of the stairs. As she descended the stairs to stand next to him, he put his hand under her arm. She stepped away, not wanting to be touched by him.

They went to their usual café and sat in a quiet corner. Kung Yi had stopped pretending to like coffee after their third date. From that point on, he took tea while Mini drank coffee. This time their tea and coffee sat getting cold on the table, their cakes untouched, as the two sat facing each other in silence.

"Mini, would you like to marry me?" Kung Yi asked, finally breaking the silence.

Mini looked into his eyes suspiciously. "Are you mocking me?"

Kung Yi took a moment to respond. "Mini, no, I'm not mocking you. I'm serious."

"Of course I want to marry you. We already did the married couple thing." She paused a second, looking down, before continuing angrily, "Marrying you is my only option. Or live as an old maid."

"I am so sorry for what I did. I was, I was . . ." Kung Yi's head hung low. He couldn't finish his sentence.

Mini waited patiently for him to continue.

"I was . . . I couldn't control myself," he said. "But I have been determined to marry you after that. I had to work on my parents for a while."

"How did you get your parents' permission?" Mini's interest was piqued, but she didn't dare risk eye contact.

"They didn't really give formal permission," Kung Yi said. "I gave them an ultimatum. I told them I would only marry you. If they want to have a grandson, they will have to agree to my proposal."

"And your mother gave in? She's not the type to give in easily."

"Well, timing works for me. My sister is possibly pregnant. It reminded Mother that she still has no grandson to her name. She resisted . . . and she's still resisting now, but my father agreed. He said you are just as good as any other girl if you can give him a grandson."

"I didn't know your father had a say in the matter," Mini said.

"Oh, he does. When he speaks up, my mother listens. He is the man of the house, after all." Kung Yi took a bite of his cake.

"Thank you for being so persistent." Mini lifted her head and smiled gratefully.

"I have to marry you. You're the only one I want to marry. You are beautiful and unique. I've never met a girl like you before."

Mini didn't say anything. She couldn't. Her eyes were tearing up.

Kung Yi handed her the handkerchief from his breast pocket.

"Now, don't cry. I will send you home and ask for your hand from your father," he said. "I want to wed you as soon as possible, before my parents change their minds."

He took her hands and kissed them tenderly. Mini was so happy. Tears were rolling down her cheeks. The heaviness in her heart had been lifted altogether. From the corner of her eyes, she noticed a ray of sunlight beaming through a window dancing on the opposite wall. As she watched it, she knew in her heart that she loved Kung Yi deeply. That was the reason she had given herself to him. It was not entirely his fault; she had been willing, too. They had simply given in to their passion.

The tense mood between them changed and they began to relax. Mini calmed down as Kung Yi continued to hold her hands. They sat silently in the café for a while. The hours passed as happy silence turned to thoughts, and then words about their future, their wedding, and their imagined life after that. They left the café only after it had long been dark outside.

The dinner table was already set for three when Mini and Kung Yi walked quietly into the living room. Mr. Pao was reading the evening newspaper and Mrs. Pao was sewing. There was no sound other than the rustle of Mr. Pao's newspaper. The rush of cold autumn air they brought in with them stirred Mr. and Mrs. Pao, both looking up at once.

"Well, well, Mini, where have you been?" Mr. Pao asked Mini anxiously before realizing Kung Yi was with her.

"I went to have a cup of tea with Mr. Shi," Mini replied. "Pa, Mr. Shi has an important matter to discuss with you." Mr. Pao stood up and shook hands with Kung Yi.

Mrs. Pao stood up, too. "Welcome to our humble home. Please join us for a simple dinner, Mr. Shi. You can discuss your matter with my husband after dinner. Mini and I will leave you two alone," Mrs. Pao said to Kung Yi.

She then rang the bell and Ai May appeared instantly, as she had clearly been waiting behind the door.

"Ai May, please arrange an extra setting at the table."

"Yes, Mistress."

"Oh, and add a few dishes," Mrs. Pao added quickly, betraying her excitement. "What do we have?"

"No worries," Kung Yi interjected. "Whatever you have is fine with me; I'm not picky. Please sit down." Kung Yi smiled at Mrs. Pao.

"I'll go help Ai May," Mini announced.

Dinner was a simple affair with four dishes and a soup. After dinner, Mr. Pao and Kung Yi disappeared into Mr. Pao's study down the hall as Mini and Mrs. Pao waited anxiously in the living room. Ai May lingered in the dining room, cleaning the table slowly, all the while peering into the living room with curiosity.

"What's he discussing with your father?" Mrs. Pao whispered to Mini.

"I don't know," Mini lied. She didn't want to spoil the moment. She wanted her father to deliver the news.

"Is it possible he is asking your father for your hand?" Mrs. Pao guessed.

"I don't know, Ma," Mini replied.

"It's about time he does it. But it's odd. The Shi family is well known to be a very traditional family. They would send a matchmaker with a marriage proposal," Mrs. Pao said quietly, as if to herself. "What he does now is like what the foreigners do in the moving picture shows, if that's what he's doing."

She leaned forward and looked at the closed study door, as if to will it open or see through to the two men inside. Mini picked up the newspaper her father had left behind and pretended to read it, though she couldn't make sense of a single word.

Finally, a happy Mr. Pao emerged with Kung Yi.

"Congratulations, Mini!" he shouted. "I just gave my permission to Mr. Shi. Now it is up to you whether you want to be Mrs. Shi."

Mini blushed and didn't know what to say.

Mrs. Pao steadied herself by holding onto the tea table next to her. "Of course Mini will agree. Great news! Great news! Congratulations to you both! You two make a good couple."

Kung Yi bowed to Mrs. Pao. "Ma—I hope you don't mind me calling you Ma—I wish to wed Mini as soon as possible. As I mentioned to Mr. Pao—I mean Pa—earlier, the situation with the Japanese isn't good. I suspect something serious will happen at any moment. I don't want anything to delay our wedding. I propose to have it in January. I know it's a bit hasty, but I hope you can understand."

"January?" Mrs. Pao replied. "It's only two months away. I'm afraid I can't get ready so fast."

"You don't need to go through all the formalities. No need to prepare much of a dowry. We have everything we need, since we will live with my parents. I hope you understand."

Mrs. Pao opened her mouth, vexed. "But still, I don't want to lose face before all your prominent friends."

"Woman, please let the young couple decide what they want," Mr. Pao chided her. "I agree with Mr. Shi: The Japanese are up to no good and they may invade Shanghai, though I doubt they will be so reckless as to ignore the British and American militaries here. We shouldn't gamble on it. It is sensible to have the wedding as soon as possible. Let's say January is the month. We can set a date later."

He turned to the dining room and saw Ai May still there. "Ai May, warm up some rice wine. We'll have a drink to celebrate."

A brief meeting between the Paos and the Shis took place at the Shi residence. Mini waited at home, the whole time absentmindedly helping Ai May with the evening meal. Ai May tried small talk here and there, projecting her own ideas of the happy married life that Mini would have until Mini finally told her to stop. Mini preferred silence. She was busy praying that the Shis were giving her parents the respect they deserved.

At last, she heard the rickshaw stop outside. Running to the door, Mini opened it quickly, and watched as her father helped her mother down. They entered the yard and walked to the living room without giving anything away. Mini followed nervously. She closed the never-closed living room door behind her.

"How was it? Pa? Ma?" she asked.

"Not eventful," Mr. Pao said. "We settled on the date. The wedding will be on January 20th. Mrs. Shi consulted her family fortune-teller and decided January 20, 1937, is not an auspicious date, but it's not bad either. Mini, if you'll excuse me, I need to write a letter. Why don't you bring a cup of tea into my study?"

He turned to his study and closed the door behind him.

Her father looked calm. He didn't seem in a bad mood. But Mini knew that in the past, he had only called her into his study when she was in trouble. Mini didn't know what to think. She told Ai May to prepare a pot of tea. Then, she went to Mrs. Pao in the living room, busy mending one of her father's shirts.

"Ma, what did you talk about with Kung Yi's parents?"

"Not much. They said they don't need much from us. In return, they will not give a big wedding either. No formalities, just a simple nuptial dinner." She broke the thread with a snip of her scissors.

"What did you think of Kung Yi's mother?"

"A very intimidating woman, Mini. I hope your life under her watch won't be too difficult." She picked up the shirt and looked at it in the lamplight, satisfied.

Unsure what to say or ask her mother, Mini was relieved when Ai May came in with a tray of tea and two cups. Mini took it and walked into her father's study.

The study was Mr. Pao's world; the ladies in the house hardly ever set foot inside. Mini looked around. The room was very warm from the coal stove in the room that Ai May had set before Mr. Shi's return. A pile of paper and an open bottle of ink were pushed to the corner. Old newspapers were scattered on a sofa, and books lined the shelves against the wall. Mini set the tray on the desk, poured two cups of tea, and sat down on the sofa facing her father, who sat in the chair behind his desk. Mr. Pao was engrossed in his letter writing and didn't say anything as Mini entered.

"Pa, is there something wrong?" Mini asked, unnerved by her father's distance.

"No. Mini, give me just a few minutes. Let me finish this sentence." Mr. Pao didn't lift his head.

Mini sat there, waiting. After a few minutes, Mr. Pao pushed the letter aside.

"Mini, I want to ask you how sure you are about your marriage to Kung Yi."

"Why? Was something wrong with the visit?" Mini fidgeted, feeling uneasy.

"No, don't always assume there is something wrong. But after visiting the family, I do see differences between us. Mini, I told them I don't wish to have a formal wedding ceremony that requires validating your virginity. I always thought that vulgar." He picked up his teacup and took a long sip without looking at her.

Mini's face flushed so red that she was glad he wasn't looking at her. She wished her father wouldn't say such things to her.

"Thank heaven Ling didn't have to go through that," he continued. "I argued with them for a while. Finally, they backed down. We will have a small wedding, nothing fancy, just an informal dinner like your sister's. That's all. Mini, I hope you won't be too disappointed."

"No, Pa. What you decided suits me," Mini said quietly. *Thank god, I won't have to do what Shiao Hui did. I could never face Father or anyone again if it became known that I'm no longer a virgin.*

Mr. Pao finally looked at Mini. "Are you ready to marry into the Shi family?"

"I think so," she replied.

"You realize that the Shi family are very different from our family?"

"Yes, I know."

"You like Kung Yi, I know. Are you prepared to give up your freedom? That's what comes with marrying into a family such as theirs."

Mini hesitated before nodding her head. "Yes, Pa. I think I know what you mean. I think I'm prepared. Kung Yi has been very kind to me."

Mr. Pao sighed. "Mini, Kung Yi has been kind to you, but marrying him also means that you have to live with his family. You have good judgment. I hope you use it. I just don't want you to be naïve."

"Yes, Father. You don't need to worry about me. Everything will be fine. Mr. and Mrs. Shi respect Kung Yi's choice."

"I hope so, Mini. I want to make sure you are happy with your choice. Just remember, the door to our home is always open to you."

"Thank you, Pa. I'm so glad you don't sound like Ma. Ma often says a married daughter is like thrown out water; there's no way to retrieve it," Mini joked, trying to soften the sober atmosphere.

"Don't mind her. She's an old-fashioned lady, but she means well. Mini, please promise me you will visit home often. Your mother relies on you for many things, though she may not realize it. You are very important to your mother—and to me, too." His voice trailed off.

"I promise I will visit whenever I can." Tears welled up in Mini's eyes.

"Now, please, no need to cry," Mr. Pao walked over and sat down next to Mini. "Let me quiz you on some new English words." He smiled at Mini.

Just as in the days before Ling's wedding, Mrs. Pao gave up her daily Mahjong game and set up a tailor shop in her drawing room. Mother and daughter agreed that this wedding dowry wouldn't be lavish. The only item that Mrs. Pao insisted on was a hundred-child design for one of the six sets of satin bedding to be made. It would be embroidered with a hundred playing children in colorful outfits.

"It will bring you luck. You will have many children," she told Mini, matter-of-factly. "Of course, you will have the requisite dragon and phoenix pattern made, too."

A small wedding announcement in the local newspaper was the only formality. When the wedding day arrived, Mrs. Pao went up to Mini's room and knocked on the door. Mini could tell from the tentative wobbling steps it was her mother. She didn't get up, though.

"The door is open. Come in," Mini said.

Mrs. Pao entered the room with a small black velvet box in hand and paused to survey her daughter's arrangements. A sleeveless red wool qipao lay on the neatly made bed. Next to it was a long fur coat. A pair of red leather shoes peeked out from under the bed. Mini was sitting in front of her vanity mirror, applying makeup. A pair of tiny diamond earrings and a small diamond ring were displayed to her left—the Shis' wedding gift to the bride. Kung Yi had been so embarrassed by the size of the gift when he presented it to the Paos that he couldn't look Mrs. Pao in the eye. He later explained to Mini that he had hoped to upgrade the size of the diamond himself, but realized he had nothing to his own name. Mini received the gift graciously. It was an unspoken rule that the bride would wear the gift for the wedding; Mini would wear them tonight.

"Everything is gone now. Only your house dresses are left." Mrs. Pao opened the dresser and looked inside.

"Yeah, I'll leave them here so I can have something to change into and be comfortable when I'm home," Mini said cheerfully.

"Good idea, Mini, only your home is with the Shis now." Mrs. Pao smiled, but Mini could also see tears well up in her eyes. She turned from the mirror to her mother.

"Please visit me and your father often," Mrs. Pao said. "It will feel so empty in the house without both you and Ling."

"Ling visits often with Xiao Bao, and I'll visit often too, Ma—don't worry." She stood up and hugged her mother.

Mrs. Pao put down the little box on Mini's vanity, pulled a chair over, and sat down next to Mini.

"Mini, this is something I want you to have," she said, opening the box. "It's nothing of value, but it has been in our family for a long time."

Mrs. Pao took a gold bracelet from the box and handed it to her daughter. Mini laid it flat on her palm and studied it in the sunlight by the window. The bracelet was made of thin, intricate golden leaves that interlocked together.

"How pretty, Ma. Thank you!" She turned and hugged her mother again, holding on a little longer this time.

Mrs. Pao clasped the bracelet around Mini's left wrist. "It has been passed down through three generations of my family. My mother gave it to me before I was married to your father. It came with a pair of earrings. I gave the earrings to Ling when she was married."

"I will take good care of it, Ma. I promise. I will pass it down to my children."

"Of course." Mrs. Pao stood up and picked a comb up from the vanity and started combing Mini's hair. They stayed like this, Mrs. Pao combing Mini's hair and watching Mini's reflection, for a long time. She then carefully twisted the hair into a bun and secured it with a handful of hairpins.

"Ma, I can do it myself. You've been on your feet too long. You must be tired," Mini finally said.

"I'm fine, Mini. Let me do your hair. I may not have the opportunity after today. I used to do both yours and Ling's hair every day. Remember?"

"I do, Ma."

Mrs. Pao didn't say any more. She redid Mini's hair several times even though it looked perfect the first time, and each time after that. Mini watched her mother's wrinkled face in the mirror, hands still working through Mini's hair. She knew her mother only wanted to prolong the moment as much as she could. She bit her lower lip to suppress a surge of tears.

A long time went by. Eventually the sight of a black Ford gliding through the narrow lane and parking in front of the house broke their reverie. Her mother finally finished with her hair as they heard the doorbell ring, followed by Ai May's voice telling the chauffeur to wait, and then her rapid footsteps as she skipped up the stairs toward them.

"Mistress, the car is here."

"Tell him to wait a little while. I need to help Mini dress," Mrs. Pao replied through the door.

"Yes." Rapid footsteps retreated down the stairs.

"Ai May, wait, are you ready?" Mrs. Pao shouted.

"Yes, Mistress," Ai May came back up and pushed the door open a little. "See." She was in one of Ling's old dresses. She smiled shyly, looked down at her feet, which were in Ling's old leather shoes. Mini had invited her to attend the wedding as a guest.

"Ai May, you look lovely! Now, I'll be ready in five minutes. Please make sure my father is ready," Mini said.

"I'll go check on Master." Ai May ran downstairs.

Mini changed into her red qipao and red shoes. She slid on her diamond ring and put on the earrings. She wore no veil. She had tried one on but didn't like the feeling of not being able to see what was going on around her.

"Daughter, take care of yourself. Be a good wife to Kung Yi and a good daughter-in-law to his parents. Give them a grandson," Mrs. Pao said to Mini's reflection in the mirror.

Mini nodded, her emotions welling up once more.

"Don't cry, Mini. Today is your happy day. We shouldn't cry. Crying is bad luck. Let's go. The driver is waiting."

She wiped Mini's tears dry, then her own. Mrs. Pao put the fur coat on Mini. She took Mini in one last time and gave her a satisfied look. They went downstairs, Mini holding her mother's arm.

The wedding was at a small, reputable restaurant in the Chinese section of the city, close to the Shi mansion. There were not many guests; few outside of the immediate families had been invited. Ling, her baby, and her husband, along with a few relatives who lived in town attended. The guests filled four large round tables. Shiao Hui couldn't come. Her in-laws and husband had decided to leave her at home since she was pregnant. It would be too risky for Shiao Hui to travel from Cheng Zhou to Shanghai.

The wedding started with the banquet, as agreed. Ling, her baby, and her husband sat with Mr. and Mrs. Pao, while the elder Shis sat with Kung Yi and Mini, their son-in-law, and other relatives. All the firecrackers, shouts for the couple to kiss, the clinking of rice wine glasses, and determined laughter, however, couldn't mask Mini's somber mood. She didn't feel the ecstasy she thought she would feel. *This is my own wedding—after all the anticipation, something is missing. But what?* Mini looked at her husband. He wore a big grin, happy to oblige every demand from the guests that he kiss his bride.

Don't ruin the moment. Everything will be fine now that we're married. There is nothing to worry about, Mini told herself. Still, all the while she felt like she was watching someone else, an actress maybe, playing the bride at her wedding.

She watched as her mother came over to the Shis' table and leaned over to speak into Mrs. Shi's ear. Mrs. Shi smiled, glancing over at Mini and her son with cool eyes.

Don't be too sensitive. Don't think too much. It'll take time to win her over. Mini reassured herself as she and Kung Yi smiled at another set of rowdy guests wanting the couple to kiss so they could empty their wine glasses.

Mini finally forgot her misgivings when the car carried her and Kung Yi home after the banquet.

Their home was a suite of three rooms with big windows, situated in the back of the mansion, directly facing the tree-lined backyard. The curtains were drawn when they arrived. Teacups and a steaming teapot were already on the round rosewood table in the middle of the living room. It was late, past midnight. Mini didn't feel sleepy at all. She sat down by the table and took off her shoes, looked around the room, and felt nothing but pride. She was the one who had chosen the furniture and the wallpaper. Kung Yi had managed to negotiate a good budget from his parents, and he took Mini with him while he did the shopping. The wall was a light green, and the sofa was one shade darker than the wall. It was a cheery room. *Finally, I have a home of my own. I can spend as much time in bed with my husband as I want.* She was so happy. Kung Yi showed no interest in sitting down to tea. He reached out with both hands, pulled Mini up from her seat, and led her into their bedroom.

They stayed in their suite until the next afternoon. They declined both breakfast and lunch, asking for tea and dim sum to be brought into their room. When they finally emerged and went into the family living room, hand in hand and happy, they were greeted by a cold stare from Mrs. Shi.

"Mini, it is a Shi family rule that the younger generation greets the elders each morning before breakfast."

Mini looked at Kung Yi. He hadn't mentioned the rule. "I am sorry, Mrs.—Ma, I promise it won't happen again."

Kung Yi glanced between his mother and Mini without a sound, as if the chilled air in the room had frozen his tongue.

"Sit down and join us for a cup of tea. I will go over the family rules with you. Kung Yi, you don't need to be around for this," Mrs. Shi added, dismissing her son.

15

CLASS ENEMY

I thought of Grandma then as I sat watching her apply makeup in the mirror of Mother's vanity. It was the second Sunday since she had arrived, and the second time I observed her routine in detail—the contents of the little tubes and jars and what they did to a woman. They could transform Grandma from looking tired and sad to spirited and glowing. It was like putting on a shield to cover what was underneath.

As I sat studying Grandma, Mother came in carrying bowls stacked high in one hand and spoons and chopsticks in the other.

"Oh, Mother, you're showing her useless things," she snapped. "Ting, if you have nothing better to do, then help your father in the kitchen."

I had noticed a change in Mother. She'd acidly chide Grandma one moment, and then apologize for it later. It was as if she couldn't help it. I first noticed this change when, just a few days after Grandma settled into life in Shanghai, she joked she could move back permanently because Mother took such good care of her.

Mother was quick to reply with a severe face and no hint of irony: "Yeah, no problem. I will wait on you. It is my responsibility to take care of my aging mother, as a mother should do for her children when they are young."

I didn't think twice about Mother embracing the adage that every child hears from an early age, but Father swallowed hard, even though he was neither drinking nor eating. And with that, the easy mood left the room and was replaced with silence. Grandma stared sadly down into her lap for a while and then left to clean up in the kitchen.

Later that night, after I was asleep—or they thought I was asleep—Mother came out from the back room, crying as she apologized to her own mother.

Grandma answered her calmly, "I understand your feelings. I feel just as bad as you do."

"It wasn't your fault. I was unfair to you," Mother said.

"No, it wasn't, but it doesn't make it any less painful." Grandma stood up and gave Mother a tight hug.

Most of the time Mother was still careful and tender to Grandma. But on this morning, I again sensed the sharpness in Mother's voice, though I was unsure whether it was directed more at Grandma or me. I got up silently and went to the kitchen to fetch breakfast and promptly returned with the steamed buns, pickles, and porridge Mother had prepared. As I set these on the table, Father followed with hot scallion pancakes and savory fried donuts, fresh from the street vendor at the corner of our building. The room was quiet, with neither Mother nor Grandma speaking, and the only sound coming from a standing fan that whirled in the corner.

Grandma managed to finish her makeup within the few minutes it took us to set the table.

"Ma, do you want some porridge?" Mother asked once we had sat down.

"Yes, please," Grandma answered politely.

Father gave me a bowl of porridge and then turned to Grandma, serving her. "What would you fancy eating today? I'll go to the market after breakfast," he said.

"Oh, I only want something simple. Conserve your rations."

"Ah, that's no worry Ma. We only use ration tickets for basic things—like rice, sugar, meat, and oil. These donuts we can get fresh now. For fresh produce, eggs, fish, and other stuff, we go over a few blocks where the street vendors are allowed to sell what they grow back in the countryside. No need to wait in lines at dawn anymore," Mother explained. "I'll take you to see if you'd like," she added more cheerfully in an attempt to lift the mood in the room.

"I'd be happy to, but you decide. When is Ai May going to come?" she asked Father.

"Should be at one o'clock. I'll meet her at the station," he answered.

"Let's cook something special for her. She'll be tired and hungry when she arrives."

"You needn't worry about that," Mother snapped. "We always take care of Aunt Ai May, just like she used to take care of me."

"I know you are thoughtful. It's just that I haven't seen her for a very long time, and I am a little anxious. She used to take care of me, too," Grandma said softly.

Father stuffed the last of his scallion pancakes into his mouth, chewed, and swallowed fast.

"Done," he said to no one particular. "I'm off now. See you all in a while."

Grandma helped me clean the table over Mother's protests, joking that she had to move around. Otherwise, by the time she was to leave Shanghai, she would have forgotten how to do any housework and Bob wouldn't be happy about it. In the communal kitchen, she exchanged greetings with the neighbors as if she lived there. They smiled their rigid smiles and carried on with their business, all the while stealing glances at her from the corners of their eyes.

It wasn't just them. Grandma really stood out in our neighborhood—actually, she stood out everywhere in Shanghai. People would stare wherever we went, first at her, then at us. At first, I figured it was because she dressed more stylishly. Maybe it was the way she walked, erect and confident, or maybe the pleasant fragrance of her perfume. She seemed to stand out even when she was dressed more plainly—then again, her plain was altogether different from our plain. No matter what it was, I held my head high and felt proud walking with her.

I couldn't wait for our outing today. "When are we going for ice cream?" I whispered to her when Mother was out of earshot.

Somehow, Mother heard me. "You have to finish your homework before you can go out," she answered.

"Good idea," Grandma agreed, winking at me.

It was almost noon when I finished my homework. Sunday was the only day off from school, but it also guaranteed a heavier workload, as if the teachers enjoyed punishing us for having a day off. While I labored over my work, Grandma and Mother sat chatting across the room. I was so focused on my task that their conversation had become background noise, at least until I heard a sob, and then Mother exclaiming: "Oh, Aunt Ling. It was wretched how she died!"

Out of the corner of my eyes I watched as Mother rubbed her eyes with her handkerchief.

"Wretched? What do you mean?" Grandma asked with urgency.

"1967. It was in November," Mother said. "I was in the middle of steaming needles and syringes when my party leader told me to drop everything I was doing and to go to the jailhouse right away. When I got there, they told me Aunt Ling was dead. Suicide, they said. They wanted me to sign the death certificate and collect her body."

"Suicide? Ling wouldn't do that. And why would she be in jail? Ling was never someone to get mixed up in anything. How?" Grandma's voice was raised.

"Mother, you were lucky you left China. Otherwise you would have been in jail too, or worse. It didn't matter whether you broke the law or not." Mother's red eyes stared out the window into nothing. "Anyone not from a proletarian background is a class enemy. They condemned Aunt Ling as the concubine of a capitalist who collaborated with the Japanese, the daughter of a running dog of the British Empire, and a rotten person who exploited her servants and never worked a day in her life."

"This is not true. She didn't benefit at all from her husband. He was a good-for-nothing louse!"

I had never heard Grandma say such things.

"Doesn't change anything," Mother sighed.

"What about you? Were you affected?" Grandma asked, suddenly concerned.

"Of course. I'm always at the mercy of the party leader of my work unit. I had a landlord father and grandfather, an American spy for a mother. I was double-black," Mother explained. "I had to work really hard, took on the dirtiest jobs that no one would touch to prove myself. Luckily, I was deemed salvageable. I was more fortunate than others. I didn't go to jail. I went to a labor camp in the countryside several times . . . to be reformed. But I came back. Not everyone did."

Grandma looked at my mother in disbelief. Her lips trembled, but she couldn't speak. Finally, she murmured: "I had heard, but I didn't believe . . . It didn't make sense. I just . . . dismissed it. You know, I thought it was anti-communist hysteria. Why would they? But it was all true." She shook her head slowly.

"Enough of these sad stories. That's all behind us and things are improving. I am just glad everything is going to be better now. Ting will have a better life. Let's see if she finished her homework." Mother's voice suddenly sounded brighter as she mentioned me. She looked in my direction.

I lowered my head quickly, pretending to read my book. Up until now, they had been very careful not to mention family history in front of me, but I guessed that Grandma had so many questions on her mind that she dropped her guard today.

I wanted them to continue talking about this so much. So many things had happened in my family that I knew nothing about. Bits of information I had heard over time were like a colorful but incoherent collage in my mind—partly pretty but often not so pretty. I remembered Ling, though I had never met her. I remembered finding a small, yellowing snapshot of a pretty lady in Mother's shoebox of mementos.

Mother told me it was her Aunt Ling. She had died when I was just a year old. Mother said no more. That was all I knew of her. I hadn't thought of her since then and now I held my breath, hoping that if I didn't make any noise they would start talking again.

They didn't. Grandma came to me, a little more relaxed.

"Are you done? We can go for ice cream if you're finished."

"I'm finished." I jumped up, leaving the open book and my paper on the table.

"Ting, it's lunchtime. No ice cream before lunch," Mother ordered.

I stayed still, looking between Mother and Grandma.

"Jing Ling, lunch is going to be late today. We are waiting for Ai May, right?" Grandma asked. "She won't be here until, what time, two maybe? A little snack before a late lunch isn't going to do any harm to our girl, right?"

I nodded in agreement.

"Ok, then. You have to clean up the table before you go. Put those books into your book bag. You've got to be prepared. School starts early tomorrow."

I did what she told me as quickly as I could and left with Grandma.

Ai May was already in the apartment when we returned from our ice cream excursion. The pile of dried vegetables and salted fish on our kitchen table, plus two live chickens in a large basket on the floor, told us she was there before we even heard or saw her.

As it was summer, she hadn't brought any fresh treats, but I was happy regardless. Her presence always meant good eats, reduced chores, and lots of excitement. I saw the chickens in the kitchen and figured that we kids would all gather to watch her slaughter chickens again. I skipped to our door and pushed it wide open to find Grandaunt Ai May sitting by the table on a hardwood chair, sipping tea, and chatting with Father. For some reason she refused to sit on the sofa, even though my parents always insisted. She said she was more comfortable in a hard chair.

She stood up when I opened the door. A few strands of hair had pried themselves loose from her tight bun and fluttered in the breeze from the fan near the table. Her stooped body leaned in slightly and her clouded eyes searched anxiously beyond the door frame. I ran to her and held her hands, but she didn't acknowledge me. She looked beyond me to Grandma, who stood frozen at the door. I looked back at Ai May, watching as her lips trembled and tears slowly filled her eyes, only to roll down her leathery brown face full of deep lines. It was Grandma who snapped out of the trance first. She walked toward Ai May, pulled her close.

"Young Mistress, am I dreaming? Am I dreaming?" Ai May repeated.

"No, it's not a dream. Ai May, I am back," Grandma murmured.

They held each other, crying in each other's arms. Tears streaked down Mother's face too. Father and I stood in silence until I felt him tugging at me.

"Let's start the lunch, Ting," he whispered into my ear. I quietly followed him out to the kitchen.

"Why are they crying like that?" I asked my father.

"They haven't seen each other for more than thirty years. Also, there were many sad things that happened in your mother's family. Really sad things," Father said, matter-of-factly.

"Like what?"

"You wouldn't understand. You are too young."

"Tell me anyway. I want to know," I demanded indignantly. "I heard Ma tell Grandma about Grandaunt Ling. Tell me what happened to her!"

Father always said I was too young to understand things. But I knew more than they thought. To prove I was not a stupid child, I added defiantly: "I know Grandaunt Ai May is not my real grandaunt. No one told me, but I figured it out by myself."

"She is real as far as your mother and I are concerned. She raised your mother." He put the cold noodles and cucumber that Mother had prepared onto two big plates.

"What happened to Grandaunt Ling? Why did she go to jail? Was she an anti-revolutionist?" I asked again while mixing the peanut sauce for the cold noodles. I wouldn't give up.

"No, she wasn't. Ting, no one in our family is. She wasn't right in her head. She should've been in a mental hospital rather than in jail."

"Why didn't they send her to the hospital?" I stopped making sauce. It was quiet in the kitchen; our neighbors all finished lunch hours ago.

Father was silent for a while. He always paused for dramatic effect when he told stories, and I waited patiently, thinking that's what he was doing. Instead, he cleared his throat and said merely, "Let's get lunch ready, Ting. Is your sauce done?" He got out a bowl of barbeque pork he had bought at a deli down the street and transferred it to a plate.

"How did she die, exactly?" I insisted.

"She was tortured and starved in prison. She jumped out of the window one day when the guards weren't watching." His voice trailed off.

"So, she committed suicide?" I asked.

"That was what we were told, Ting, but don't tell your mother I told you this," he warned. "She doesn't like to talk about her family."

"I know, but . . ." Before I could figure out what I wanted to ask next, Father was carrying the dishes out. I finished the sauce and helped Father bring the rest of the food into our apartment.

That night, I was demoted to sleeping on the sofa in the big room. Grandaunt Ai May took over my side of the bed with Grandma. I had planned on eavesdropping, and so drank several cups of strong tea before I went to bed. I wanted to hear every word between them.

They were quiet in the big bed and, though I figured they were waiting for me to fall asleep, I couldn't manage to stay awake in the dark, quiet room. It was only after I had dozed off that I heard some crackling sound, as if someone was digging deep into a plastic bag. I opened an eye and saw Grandaunt Ai May searching through her plastic duffel bag. She took out something small, like a black box, and handed it to Grandma.

"Ling told me to give it to you. It was the last thing she had before she was swept out of her home." Her whispering was accompanied by quiet sobs.

"Swept?" Grandma asked as she turned on the bedside lamp. I closed my eyes quickly. I imagined her holding whatever it was under the light, and I opened my eyes a crack. Grandma's profile was enlarged as it was projected on the wall together with the shadow of a pair of leaf-shaped earrings, dangling slightly.

The light switch clicked, and it was dark again. I opened my eyes and stared, lying still on my belly, and lifted my head as I focused all my attention on the big bed.

"Oh, Ling!" Grandma's low voice sounded very sad yet controlled. "I am so sorry."

Ai May was sobbing harder now, her face buried in her hands. Grandma gave her a handkerchief to wipe her face. "Jing Ling told me Ling committed suicide. I don't believe it."

"It was 1966, three years after your mother passed on. Your house was confiscated by the workers at the silk factory that Jie Xing used to own. Ling didn't like the bad people who took her home. They trashed the house, so she tried to kick them out. She went to the party leader at the silk factory every day to tell him that the house was not Jie Xing's. It belonged to her parents, so it was illegal for these people to squat. She threatened the party leader, saying she would bring the matter to the Shanghai Municipal Party Unit. She called the leader a highway robber. The leader reported her to the Public Security Bureau soon after that for 'stirring up anti-revolutionary sentiment.' They arrested her and shaved her head. If that wasn't enough to humiliate her, they paraded her through the streets with a bench-sized wooden lock around her neck. She had to carry a big poster that called her a member of the Anti-Revolutionist Gang."

"Oh my poor sister. How? Why? How could they do that to such a gentle soul?"

"It was happening everywhere, to everyone who didn't listen to them, or came from a family like yours."

"Nobody helped her?"

"What could anyone do?"

"How long did this go on? When did she die?"

"A year later. It was already too long for her. She had lost a lot of weight. When she died, she was just skin and bones. Prison officials said she wouldn't eat—or at least that's they told me. But—" Ai May broke off sobbing again. Between sobs, she continued, "She was fed rotten rice and only allowed to bathe once a month. Each time I visited she begged me to bring some food and a bar of soap."

"Did you?" Grandma's voice was so low and dry.

"I tried. The guards took whatever I brought. They said she was a dirty landlord's concubine who lived off the peasants and deserved to eat and live like those she had oppressed. I tried to tell the guards she wasn't like that, but they called me a fool for having been deceived into defending a class enemy and that she had oppressed me. They laughed at me for visiting, but still allowed me to see her once a month. She looked like a skeleton toward the end, a ghost. She lost her teeth. Her gums were bleeding. She couldn't see very well. I thought she had gone mad."

Silence followed.

"So, it's true. Ling committed suicide?" Grandma finally asked.

"No," Ai May said gravely. "I never told anyone, but I cannot lie to you. She was thrown out a window. It was my visitation day, but by the time I got there, she was already dead. I saw her all tied up. They told me I was not kin so I couldn't take her body. I couldn't sign the death certificate because I can't read or write. I had to notify Jing Ling. They had cut off the rope by the time she got there and told me not to say a word. They said they trusted me since I was a peasant daughter. I should stand by them and condemn all the anti-revolutionists. I wanted to spare Jing Ling the truth. She had enough trouble of her own. But I cannot lie to you." Ai May broke down. She started hitting herself.

"I'm useless. I am a useless person. I let them kill Young Mistress. I can't face Master and Mistress in the underworld after I die."

Grandma patted Ai May's back gently. "Ai May, it wasn't your fault. No one could save her." She wiped her own face with her hand. I suppose she had teared up as well.

I was horrified. I had been taught that all the people who were crushed by revolutionists were bad. But I didn't believe Grandaunt Ling was bad. She didn't deserve to die like that. I felt angry but didn't know where to direct my anger. *Who are they? Who killed my aunt?* These people didn't have faces or names.

I fell asleep eventually. It wasn't a peaceful sleep and I woke up very tired. I sat up on the sofa feeling very heavy, too heavy to get up. I felt guilt knowing something Mother and Father didn't know. *Should I tell them?*

A warm hard hand touched the back of my head. I looked up to see Ai May there. Lost in my thoughts, I hadn't noticed her coming up. Her face was puffy. I supposed it was from crying the night before.

"Ting, I know you were listening last night. Are you going to tell your parents?"

I stared at her. I didn't want Mother to be sad. I looked into her eyes and shook my head: "No."

She held my hands, "You are a brave girl."

Brave girl? I questioned her statement then. I didn't understand until I was much older. Carrying such a horrible secret.

All through school that day I thought about their conversation and wondered what secrets I still didn't know. I couldn't wait to return home, thinking I could eavesdrop on their conversation while I did my homework, but Ai May was busy in the kitchen and had a crowd of children squeezed in around her, waiting to watch her slaughter one of the chickens she had brought.

Between the excitement of that afternoon and the delicious dinner that followed, there was little talk that night. Nor was there in the days that followed. Ai May had to hurry back home to the countryside to prepare for the fall harvest, and only stayed the week. But they spoke no more of the past, or of our family, and Ling's dark story receded into the back of my brain, as if banished to a corner.

Grandma insisted on taking Ai May to the train station the morning she was to leave, and I insisted on accompanying them as well. We hailed a taxi, a treat for Ai May.

"I rode a taxi before. I bet you never did, Grandaunt," I boasted as I climbed in.

"Little one, I did. Way before you were born. I lived in Shanghai then," she told me proudly, glancing at Grandma, who watched, amused.

"When?" Somehow, I couldn't imagine her being a city person. To me, she was always an old woman from the countryside.

"Oh, a long time ago. I sat in a nice car to go to your grandma's wedding."

"Really, Grandma?" I turned to face her.

"Yes. Ai May has known me since I was a little girl."

She changed the subject and asked if Ai May had enough food for the journey. Mother had said Ai May was too frugal to buy any food onboard and so had packed a dozen boiled eggs and some scallion pancakes before we left home. Ai May assured Grandma that she had enough, but Grandma bought a few pounds of candies at the train station anyway.

"Give them to your neighbors as a gift," she said.

"The kids will be so happy," Ai May said. "They never get treats. They'll be spoiled by Shanghai candy." Her wrinkles deepened when she smiled.

Grandma watched Ai May board the train. We stood waiting for the train to pull out, when Ai May came back down to the platform one more time. She held Grandma's hands tight.

"Young Mistress," she paused. "I am sorry. I tried, I wanted to tell you earlier." She stopped and looked away before continuing, "I couldn't find your treasure. I tried but I failed. I am very sorry."

Grandma almost lost her balance and leaned on my shoulder for support. She regained her composure and calmly said, "Ai May, I know you tried your hardest. But please keep looking."

"I will." Ai May nodded and returned to the train, her head down.

The ride home was somber, and I knew better than to ask questions while Grandma sat deep in thought, with none of her usual jokes or poking fun. Finally, I couldn't hold back.

"What is the treasure Grandaunt mentioned? Will it make us rich?" I asked.

"No. It won't make us rich." She smiled at me, but I noticed the corner of her mouth twitch as she said it.

Later that night I prodded Grandma to continue her story. She began by telling me of a dream that she had many times while she was pregnant with my mother.

16

MARCO POLO BRIDGE

Misty rain drizzled from a gray sky over a gray city. Only the flashing neon lights with their occasional eruptions of color broke the grayness. People were running, shielding themselves from the rain with newspapers and purses. Mini wanted to run but couldn't. She was rooted to the ground. She looked down, staring at her protruding mid-section, which obscured her view of her own feet.

She looked around again. The city had vanished. She was standing in the middle of a rice field, as if she had just teleported there. She heard music and saw a long wedding parade pass by her in the fog. Maybe it wasn't a wedding, but a funeral. The people were dressed in black and were somber, though no one was crying. She wanted to join in and follow them, but again, her feet rooted her to the ground.

"Wake up, please."

Her maid was shaking her gently. "Young Mistress, you're having nightmares again."

Mini opened her eyes, sat up slowly, and looked down at her belly. It was flat. Standing up, she looked down again—she could see her feet just fine. She exhaled with relief. It was only a dream.

It was two o'clock in the afternoon and she had been napping. These days, it seemed that was all she did. Her in-laws had become more lenient since Kung Yi had announced her pregnancy. She was allowed to stay in her own room whenever she wanted. Her pregnancy was difficult, and she thought of how Ling struggled to carry Xiao Bao. Mini's morning sickness would last the whole day, such that sleep seemed to give the only respite. She was in no mood to step outside their room. So she walked to a chair by the window and watched the still leaves on the trees outside. Kung Yi was gentle to her—so gentle that he had stopped touching her altogether. When she approached him, he'd push her away softly and said he didn't want her to miscarry their child. Often, they'd lie in bed in silence. There was a distance between them.

It's only temporary. Six more months. We'll be back to the way we were. Oh, merciful Buddha, let me have a boy. Mini comforted herself.

It had been six months since they married. In these months, she had gained an understanding of what her father told her. Life in the Shi mansion was completely different from life at home. She needed permission for just about anything. Each day began with greeting her in-laws and then waiting around until she was dismissed, usually when her mother-in-law took a nap or her father-in-law's opera group visited.

Mini was asked to learn to run the house. This in itself was not so complicated. And although Mini had capably managed her own house before, she soon realized the Shi household wasn't so easy. The servants didn't like her. Every time she gave an order, the servant would go to Mrs. Shi, who'd overrule her. Her pregnancy provided a nice break, but with it came the distance between her and Kung Yi, and that became unbearable.

If I give birth to a son, everything will improve. The servants will respect me. More importantly, my in-laws will respect me. I will have a solid position in this household. But is it a boy? What if I have a girl?

"Young Mistress, would you like a cup of tea?" The maid's voice distracted Mini from her thoughts.

I shouldn't worry—not about this, not now.

"No, thank you," she replied.

She stood up, waiting for the surging nausea to pass. It was early July and the hot and humid air blanketed her so heavily that it felt as if it were pulling her back into the chair. She sat down again. She and Kung Yi needed to visit home for dinner today. Her father had called that morning from his office and requested they come that evening. It was unlike her father, but she could think only of returning to the comfortable surroundings of her childhood home. Mini phoned Kung Yi at the rice store; he said it'd be fine. She had meant to ask Mrs. Shi for permission right away but was interrupted by nausea. Now, it was already late in the afternoon. She needed to get permission or she wouldn't be able to go. Finally, she gathered herself up and walked into her mother-in-law's drawing room.

Mrs. Shi surrounded herself with her account books when she was not accompanying Mr. Shi. She was unlike Mini's own mother, who constantly played Mahjong. It was quite amazing to see such a large woman with bound tiny feet sitting behind a large desk, a pair of glasses low on her nose as she read accounts and quickly moved her fingers over the abacus.

"Mother," Mini knocked on the door lightly.

"Come in."

Mini pushed the door open but didn't go inside.

"My father asked Kung Yi and I to dinner. Would you please give us permission?" She wanted to say it was urgent but caught herself. She didn't know what her father wanted to discuss. Mini had learned to be careful with her mother-in-law.

"You have my permission. Please send my regards to your parents." Mrs. Shi didn't even look up from her books.

Ling and Jie Xing were already there when Mini arrived. Ling's one-and-half-year-old son was in the yard. No longer a cute baby, Xiao Bao was a drooling fat toddler who walked like a drunken sailor through the yard, a wet nurse closely following behind to catch him before he fell. Mini usually picked up the boy whenever she saw him, but she couldn't this time. She was too tired to bend down. Kung Yi picked him up and carried him inside. Mini heard Ling's laughter and high-pitched voice before they entered the living room. She was recounting her recent shopping trip. Mini's mother was giving her approval of something when they walked in. Mini's father and Jie Xing sat listening to their animated banter.

"Mini, you don't look good!" Ling greeted Mini, pointing out her sister's deficit as usual.

"I am tired and sick all the time," Mini replied.

"How is business?" Kung Yi asked Jie Xing.

"Not bad at all. I have a few deals right now with the British on top of the Japanese. How about yours?"

"Busy. We are preparing for the unknown. My parents are very cautious. They are checking all of our inventories. Thefts are increasing and, well, we may possibly move them to safer places just in case." Kung Yi turned to Mr. Pao. "Pa, you have better access to recent news. What will the Japanese do? To Shanghai?"

"That's why I called all of you here. I want to work out a plan in case the worst happens." He paused when he saw Ai May walk in. She announced dinner was ready.

They left for the dining room and sat down at the table. Mini and Ling flanked their mother, while Kung Yi and Jie Xing flanked their father-in-law. The men leaned in, eager to hear the news.

"They've begun screening moving pictures with news from Britain and Europe, ones that aren't distributed locally," Mr. Pao said. "Ever since the British consulate started getting newsreels, they've been provoking hushed arguments over what the Brits should be doing and who is going to make the next move in Europe. Never before have the Brits been so focused on what's going on back there. War is raging in

Spain and the constant talk is whether Britain will stay neutral, and what Germany and Russia are up to. They're ignoring China. The Japanese know it. We Chinese employees pay more attention to what's happening here. But we have no influence and the government is not, well . . . you all know what happened yesterday, right? At the Marco Polo Bridge outside Beijing? It has to be taken seriously. I'm worried the Japanese are taking advantage because the Europeans talk only of the Communists and the war in Spain. But I believe Generalissimo Chiang will fight for real this time."

"What happened yesterday?" Mini asked.

"The Japanese fired on Chinese soldiers at Marco Polo Bridge, which leads into Beijing. It was a flagrant attack by the Japanese. They are marching toward Beijing now. The occupation of Beijing is imminent, and they won't stop there. They'll push south and Generalissimo Chiang will declare war."

Everyone stopped eating.

"You think so? He's a wimp. He hasn't stood up to the Japanese so far," Kung Yi said.

"No, this time he has too much to lose. He may have to be pushed into it, but he is the only one who can unite China against the Japanese. His political career will be ruined if he doesn't. But with the British distracted by Europe, I question how much he can do to push them back. And the north, well, it might be too late."

"What about Shanghai? And the surrounding areas? When do you think it will happen?" Jie Xing was uneasy.

A cry came from the living room. Ling got up to check on Xiao Bao and Mrs. Pao followed her.

"Yes, that is the question. Shanghai is ruled not only by the Chinese government, but also by many foreign governments. The Japanese have to worry about the Americans and the British, not to mention the French and German concessions. The Japanese know better than to offend the Westerners too much . . ." Mr. Pao trailed off, deep in thought.

"What if the Japanese attack Shanghai? What do we do?" Mini interjected. Her question drew the men's eyes.

"My guess is the Japanese won't dare for fear it would provoke the Westerners. That being said, if they get as far south as some fear they will, then they could encircle and enter the city," her father answered.

"What about the foreigners?" she asked.

"They'd leave the foreign concessions alone." He paused to look squarely at the two other men. "If this happens, I want you to move back home. Kung Yi, you live in the Chinese Quarter. I expect the Japanese will be harsh, just like they have been in Northern China. And Jie Xing, you may expect you're safe in the Japanese settlement, but they will not be so kind to Chinese. Our government is useless at stopping them. They know no honor. The Japanese are evil and our army, our police forces, they do nothing." His tone grew angry. Calming down, he continued: "Promise me you will move back once war breaks out. We should be together no matter what." He reached out to take Mini's hand.

Mini nodded her head. "I promise."

"Ling, did you hear anything I said?" Mr. Pao raised his voice to Ling, who had just returned to the table.

"Sorry Pa, I didn't hear at all. What were you talking about?"

"I was saying that if the war breaks out, you and your family should move back as soon as possible. It is relatively safe here, in the British Concession, compared to the Chinese territory. Mini promised," Mr. Pao said patiently.

"I promise too, Pa," Ling said. "But Pa, I think you worry too much. The Japanese wouldn't dare touch Shanghai. It's such an important city, plus they have large business interests here too. Jie Xing, am I right?" Jie Xing smiled at her.

"You will do what I said in case the worst happens, okay?" Mr. Pao responded before Jie Xing could say anything.

"Sure, sure. I will, Pa. You worry too much," she said as she rose to return to the living room, where Xiao Bao was having another fit.

They quietly finished their dessert, a sweet lotus seed soup that was in season, and the four of them said goodbye to Mr. and Mrs. Pao and caught rickshaws home.

As Mini and Kung Yi dressed for bed in their bedroom, Mini asked Kung Yi, "What do we need to prepare for the worst?"

"Let's put your jewelry and money in a small bag and pack some necessities in the suitcases. We should be ready to leave once we hear the first gunfire," he said.

"You agree then? It's that serious?"

"I don't know, but I'm afraid so. Your father's right to worry. We need to watch out for looters, as well."

"What will you do with your business?" she asked.

"I will talk to mother and father. We have already moved some inventory to stores in the foreign concessions. We need to buy some sandbags to fortify the stores. It won't do much, but at least it may provide some obstacles—for the looters at least, if not for others." He sighed. "I have run out of ideas."

"Don't worry, I will take care of the packing tomorrow."

"I trust you, Mini," he said. "Let's go to bed. I'm so tired."

Mini kept her eyes open for a long time, staring blankly into the dark. It was her fear that kept her wide awake. Each time she closed her eyes, she thought she saw a bloody baby. So, she kept her eyes open and made a mental list of what to pack, going over it, adding and subtracting what she thought they needed, and what they could carry, until she finally drifted off to sleep.

17

THE FIRST GUNSHOT IS AT BREAKFAST

The city remained on edge throughout July. Wild rumors circulated freely. Some even made their way to Mini, who remained shut up in her room at the Shi mansion. The nausea from her morning sickness hadn't eased up—or maybe it was made worse by the city's anxiety infecting her.

Each morning she sent her maid out to buy the daily newspaper and, seeing little in the way of real news, she would wait patiently to call her father after he returned from work at the British consulate. Generalissimo Chiang Kai-shek had immediately responded to the Marco Polo Bridge incident, much as her father predicted. The generalissimo promptly declared he would fight and drive the Japanese back. His words, though, fell short of a formal declaration of war, and his troops remained where they were. He even declared a victory when the Japanese didn't push farther south and agreed to an immediate ceasefire.

After the Mukden Incident six years earlier, Japan wasn't ready to take on the Western powers that competed for Chinese resources. Back then, they agreed to a truce at Tanggu and withdrew their troops to their puppet state of Manchuria, north of the Great Wall. With this latest ceasefire, Shanghai's papers celebrated the generalissimo.

Soon the euphoria of a stalemate turned to dread. The British and Americans had lodged feeble complaints with Japan. This time the Japanese remained well south of the wall and made no pretenses of retreating. Fresh rumors of an imminent invasion spread. *What were they doing?* Mini wondered.

The press began reporting appalling, unthinkable Japanese atrocities alongside reassurances from the government and Western officials that southern China was safe under the generalissimo's protection. Mini's calls to her father did not ease her fears. Her father had cautioned her that what news was government propaganda and what news was the truth was very hard to know. The Peace Preservation Corps, a Chinese police force created by the earlier Tanggu truce, continued to patrol and maintain peace south of the Great Wall, he explained. But Mini could hear the edge in his voice during their calls and she feared the worst.

Japan resumed their invasion just weeks later. The ceasefire proved to be nothing more than a final, deliberate test of the West's resolve.

Any hopes that Japan would merely occupy the north collapsed in August when a Peace Preservation Corps policeman shot and killed a Japanese soldier near the military airport in the Shanghai district of Hongqiao. Japan seized the opportunity to raise hell with the Chinese government, never once explaining why a Japanese soldier had been scouting the airport in the first place. Their demand that the Peace Preservation Corps withdraw from Shanghai heightened fears. News of looting and hoarding added to the tension.

The Shis began taking their own precautions when one day a maid returned from shopping with the news that Chinese soldiers were digging a trench several miles down the road from the Shi mansion. Kung

Yi and her in-laws spent the day behind the tightly closed door to their study. When Mini finally saw Kung Yi later that night, he told her they were trying to figure out the best way to preserve the inventory and stores.

"Every day, that's all we discuss. But we're running out of options and it's getting worse," he said. "Everyone needs rice, whether they're Japanese or Chinese. If we can keep the rice safe, we may have something to bargain with when war comes."

Later that night, past midnight, their room was sweltering. Not a single breeze came in from the open windows. The buzzing of an electric fan was the only sound in the room. The bed creaked, rousing Mini from her fitful sleep. Opening her eyes, she saw Kung Yi sitting up in bed. Apparently, he couldn't sleep either.

"What are you doing?" she asked.

"Mini, go back to sleep," Kung Yi said. He got up and went downstairs.

She waited until he was out of sight, then got up and tiptoed to the staircase, stopping when she heard hushed conversation below. She could bend down and crane her neck to look below, but there was little to see in the dark. She heard a door open. She moved down several steps and peered around the base of the staircase. Kung Yi was holding a candle and walking outside. His parents followed behind him and into the backyard.

Mini went back upstairs to a window facing the backyard. In the flickering candlelight, she saw Kung Yi digging in the ground by a large London plane tree. Her in-laws each held something in their hands. Kung Yi stopped digging. Her in-laws bent down, reached into the ground, and stood up, their hands empty. Kung Yi went back to digging. She quickly went back to bed, pretending to be asleep when she heard the door to their room creak.

When they woke the next morning, Kung Yi told her that his parents agreed that both of them should go to her parents' house in case war broke out. She didn't ask about that night. Mini figured her in-laws were preparing for the worst by burying valuables. *I shouldn't mention it. Kung Yi will tell me what they were doing when it's time,* she thought, but Kung Yi never told her.

On August 13, 1937, what she had feared finally came to be.

The first gunshot was fired as she was finishing breakfast. It sounded from a distance. At first, she thought it might be a firecracker. She sat still, listening intently as minutes passed. Then, the unmistakable rapid sound of machine gun fire made her jump. She hurried back to the bedroom. She pulled three suitcases from under the bed and stacked them by the door. She rang the maid.

"Where is Young Master?"

"He went out," the girl replied.

"Where did he go?"

"To a store."

"Which one?" Mini demanded.

"He didn't tell me."

Mini rushed downstairs to her mother-in-law's drawing room and pushed the door open without knocking.

"Ma, do you know where Kung Yi is?"

"He went to the rice store close to the Bund. So, you heard the gunshots too?" Mrs. Shi sat quietly, very calm and composed. There were several satin purses on the table.

"I'll phone the store."

"Hurry up. Ask Kung Yi to come home as quickly as possible. Tell—" Mrs. Shi stopped mid-sentence. They both turned to the sound of brisk footsteps in the hallway. Mini looked around to see a maid running toward them.

"Young Mistress, your father is on the phone."

Mini ran to the study and picked up the phone. Her father's voice was urgent and intense: "Mini, you and Kung Yi should come home right away. It's started—it started last night outside the city. The Chinese army is too poorly equipped. They can't resist for long."

"I'm waiting for Kung Yi. He's not here."

"Where is he? He shouldn't leave you alone. Not in a situation like this."

"Pa, that's not fair. He didn't know when the fighting would start," Mini defended her husband.

"Fair or not fair, I don't care. I want you two safe. Come home right away, with or without Kung Yi. I have to go now. I need to call Ling." He hung up.

Something must be terribly wrong. Father is never so brusque.

Mini dialed the store with a trembling finger. It rang and rang. It seemed like minutes. Finally, a clerk picked up. Kung Yi wasn't there. He never arrived. Mini sat down and buried her face in her hands. She wanted to cry.

Someone tapped her shoulder lightly. She looked up and leapt to her feet, but before she could say anything, Kung Yi spoke.

"Let's go, now."

Mrs. Shi and Mr. Shi were already at the gate, waiting to send them off in Mr. Shi's car.

"What about you and Father?" Kung Yi asked through the open window before the car pulled out of the gate.

"We're going to stay for a while. We'll retreat to the countryside when the situation gets worse. Here," she handed a satin purse to Kung Yi. "Please keep this close to you at all times. These are all the silver coins from our safe. I divided them in half. You take one purse and your father and I will take the other." She briefly looked at Mini before continuing, addressing Kung Yi. "Use the coins only in an emergency. Keep them and return them to me once you return home."

"Mother and Father, please join us. My father wouldn't mind at all," Mini said.

"Thank you, Mini. I will consider your offer. Please take good care of my grandson." She looked at Mini's belly. Mini cringed.

Mr. Shi nudged his wife aside. "Son, be safe. We will see you soon. Send the car right back after you get to the Paos." He signaled the driver.

The gunfire had paused only to restart on their drive through the city, though not as intense. Sporadic gunshots punctuated what were otherwise eerily quiet streets. It was as if the city itself was holding its breath.

They arrived safely, and Ai May took Mini's hand to navigate the dark and humid house. All the windows were closed and the curtains drawn. Mini and Kung Yi sat down next to Mrs. Pao in the living room. She didn't move. She was sitting alone, eyes shut tight, her lips moving silently as she nervously thumbed a string of worry beads that rotated on her fingers in time with the electric fan next to her.

Mr. Pao returned from work an hour later.

"Where is Ling?" he asked upon seeing Mini.

"I don't know. I phoned her several times. But the line isn't working," Mrs. Pao replied.

"I told her to leave right away. That was hours ago." Mr. Pao shook his head.

"Should I go find her?" Kung Yi offered.

"No, it's too dangerous. We don't know where they are. All we can do is wait." Mr. Pao sighed. "Jie Xing should know better."

"Ai May, do we have enough food in the house?" Mr. Pao turned to Ai May.

"Yes, Master. I bought some vegetables and we have some pickles, salted fish, and cured meats. It is too hot to store fresh meat or fish. We have enough rice to last for weeks."

"Do we have enough coal?"

"Yes, Master. I had our monthly supply delivered a few days ago."

"Very well. Now, fill the buckets with water in case the water supply is shut off. We'll be staying in for a while. I don't know for how long. Chiang Kai-shek just announced that he'll fight to the end. I fear the worst."

"How long do you think we can last?" Kung Yi asked.

"The Japanese say they will take Shanghai in three days. The British and Americans estimate it'll take a week. So . . ." Mr. Pao wiped his face with a white handkerchief.

Silence followed, heavy as death. Mini broke it: "I'm tired. Kung Yi, can you please help carry our suitcases up to my room? Ma, we'll use my room, right?"

"Yes, and Ling will use her room," Mrs. Pao confirmed.

Sporadic gunshots lasted through the late afternoon and well into the evening. Mrs. Pao refused her afternoon nap, and instead waited by the front door.

The planes flying over their house woke them early the next morning. The sound of the planes was followed by whistling, the sound of bombs dropping from the sky. Each explosion shook the house violently. The electricity went out shortly after. Mr. Pao insisted on going to work in the face of protests from Mini and his wife, only to return an hour later.

It was impossible to get to the consulate. Not a rickshaw to be seen in the streets. The bombing was too fierce, and the roads were blocked. He brought news that the bombing was in fact miles away and had destroyed much of the Chinese quarter. Between Ling's absence, the destruction, and his inability to get to work, he was despondent. It was the first time he had ever missed work. If only he could go to work, he would be doing something, contributing in some small way.

When the bombing picked up again it seemed to be closer. They moved to a small, windowless storage room next to the kitchen. They remained huddled in there the rest of the day, gasping at each explosion, whispering worries about Ling's fate. They could see nothing. They could hear only the sound of this modern war. They didn't know who was bombing whom. They waited in silence in the dark room, fanning themselves with straw fans. They were filled with an alternating fear that the next bomb would drop on their house and concern for Ling and her family. After months, years, of reading news about Japan's encroaching war effort, they had no access to the outside world, no radio, no news. They were someone else's news.

Hours passed. The air became stale, hot, and thick, but they dared not move to the big rooms and open the windows, as if huddling in their windowless storage room would shelter them from all the dangers outside. Ai May was the first to break from the room, when during a brief respite from the bombing she had dashed out to gather up pancakes and salty donuts from the kitchen, which they ate cold. Eventually, one by one they each ran out during a quiet interlude to use the bathroom.

At dusk the bombing became more intense. So did their worry. The mounting heat in that cramped room and the concern for Ling made breathing difficult for Mini. The pungent smell of sweat grew unbearable and, magnified by her sensitive nose, triggered her nausea. At first, she ran to the bathroom, despite the bombs violently shaking their house. But it was too much to bear and she vomited many times in a pot that sympathetic Ai May had retrieved from the kitchen for her.

Eventually, they heard a new sound—it seemed like a knock, a faint, distant knock in the middle of the bombing and gunfire.

"Someone is knocking on our door," Mini nervously said aloud.

As she said that, they heard someone violently pounding, followed by a desperate shout, "Open up. Open up, it's me. It's me."

"Ling!" Mrs. Pao exclaimed. Ai May rushed out, leaving the storage room door open.

"Lock the door once Ling is in," Mrs. Pao shouted after Ai May.

Finally, after what seemed like an eternal wait, Ling walked in, followed by Ai May carrying Xiao Bao. Mr. Pao lit a candle, their first light since they had cloistered themselves that morning. Ling's soot-covered face was marked with black, sweaty streaks. Her hair was a mess; her dress was torn at the hem. Ling went straight to Mrs. Pao and collapsed in her mother's outstretched arms and cried. Mini noticed Ling had just one shoe; her other foot was bare and covered with blood.

"What happened to your foot?" She bent down and wiped her sister's foot, only to jump back at the feel of Ling's raw flesh.

Between sobs, Ling told her story. The wet nurse left for home yesterday after she heard the gunfire. Ling had let her go because Xiao Bao was already on solid food. That was when their father called. She had been ready to leave. She even had her belongings, but their car was gone. Jie Xing took it the day before and hadn't returned. She tried to phone him at the office, but he wasn't there. His secretary was tight-lipped about his whereabouts. That was normal, so Ling didn't worry, but the gunfire got worse and she waited until this morning. She knew she had to leave once the bombing started up again. She phoned for a taxi, but no one answered. So, she packed a few buns in her handbag and picked up Xiao Bao, hoping to find a rickshaw along the way.

The streets were already filled with people escaping the neighborhood. There were no taxis, no rickshaws, nothing. Massive crowds of people fleeing filled the streets. She walked all the way, street after street, and across the Garden Bridge, joining thousands, it seemed. All of them refugees like her. Someone snatched her handbag and food. With Xiao Bao in her arms, she couldn't fight back. Someone else stepped on one of her shoes along the way and she lost it. The momentum was unstoppable. She was pushed forward and forward. It was all she could do to hold on to her son. He fussed the whole way. He got heavier and heavier. He was thirsty and hungry.

After hours of walking with no idea how long it would take, she began begging strangers to give her some food for the baby. No one would spare her anything. No one would even listen to her as she plodded forward with them. She pinched Xiao Bao in desperation each time he cried. It did nothing to keep him quiet. He cried for hours until he was too tired to continue and, exhausted, fell asleep. It had taken her more than six hours to journey home under the hot sun without food or drink.

"Where is Jie Xing? Why isn't he with you?" Mrs. Pao asked.

"I don't know. He stayed out last night."

"What? After the gunfire, he stayed out all night?" Mrs. Pao said.

"He was out before the gunfire. He didn't come home and didn't phone." Ling lowered her voice to cover her embarrassment.

"Since when has he started doing this?" Mrs. Pao continued.

"Woman, stop this interrogation. You can ask Ling after she settles down," Mr. Pao said to his wife.

"Yes, yes. Ling, you're here now." Mrs. Pao said. "Ai May, bring some cold porridge for Ling and Xiao Bao. Ling, wait here—I'll get a basin of water to wash your feet."

"Ma, I'll bring the water." Mini was already getting up, heading for the bathroom.

Ling was eating cold pancakes and porridge when Mini returned with the water. Ai May was feeding soymilk to Xiao Bao.

"Here, here's some water. Ling, you should soak your feet. It'll make you feel better," Mini said.

"Mistress, Xiao Bao is vomiting . . . ," Ai May interrupted everyone.

They all turned to Xiao Bao. He was lying on Ai May's lap, spitting soymilk. His eyes filled with tears. His filthy little hands pressed at his stomach. It was the first time Mini had looked at him closely. He looked like a withered plant, droopy and without any strength. His once-white shirt was a grayish black and there were scratch marks on his knees and elbows.

Kung Yi picked up the boy and carried him to the bathroom. Mini told the exhausted Ling to stay put and followed after them. Ai May joined after going to Ling's old room to get a set of Xiao Bao's pajamas and slippers.

Mini undressed the boy with Kung Yi's help. She had forgotten her nausea and efficiently wiped his sweat-soaked body with water from a bucket that Ai May had filled the day before. It wasn't quite cold, but it was all they had to cool him down. She cleaned his scratches with rubbing alcohol. His body trembled at her touch; he didn't even have the energy to cry out.

Mrs. Pao walked into the bathroom to check on Xiao Bao. Mini turned to her mother. "Ma, I hope he doesn't have heat stroke. Do we have any ice?" she asked.

"No, the ice wasn't delivered yesterday."

Mini continued to wipe the boy down with the cool water until the redness on his face subsided. He seemed to perk up a little after drinking some fresh water Ai May had brought in. Mrs. Pao fed him a spoonful of soymilk. This time he swallowed and kept it down.

Ling had also perked up a little by the time they returned to the storage room. She had finished her food, washed, and changed her clothes. Ai May put down a *tatami* in the corner and laid Xiao Bao down for a nap. Ling curled up next to her son and fell fast asleep as Mini fanned the boy with a large straw fan. In all the commotion, their thoughts of the fighting had receded as they passed the rest of the evening.

It was not to last. Bombs woke them again the next morning and continued throughout that day and the next. When the morning wave of bombs stopped, they could hear gunfire from the south where the Shi family lived. Kung Yi paced the room and then sat down in silence, only to soon get up again and resume pacing. Mini knew he was worried about his parents.

They were all anxious. Xiao Bao had started a high fever the night Ling and he arrived. Mr. Pao tried phoning the family doctor but couldn't connect. The fever would let up by afternoon, only to return at night. Mini, Ai May, Mrs. Pao, and Ling took turns wiping the child down with cool water and fanning him. It didn't break, and on the third day they woke to find him shivering constantly. He had stopped responding to their cooing and cuddling. Ling, Mini, and Ai May tended to the child, and Mrs. Pao spent the morning kneeling in the corner of the room, praying to Guan Yin, the merciful Buddha. Mr. Pao paced the room, back and forth, occasionally letting out heavy sighs. By the afternoon, white foam started gathering at the corner of the child's mouth. His little body started convulsing.

Mr. Pao and Kung Yi took advantage of a moment of calm in the fighting and whispered briefly before venturing out, only to return soon after the bombing resumed.

"What's going on?" Mini asked.

Kung Yi shook his head. "It's bad. All I saw were people everywhere, cramming the streets. They're not going anywhere. So, they must have all come from the Chinese quarter, hoping the Japanese wouldn't bomb them here."

"We have to go to the hospital," Mr. Pao announced. "We'll be able to get through."

"But the bombing—" Mrs. Pao said.

"The child is not going to make it if we stay here," Mr. Pao said.

"Pa, I'll go with Ling. You stay with Ma. Ling and I will go," Mini offered.

"No, Mini. It's too dangerous for women to be out alone," Kung Yi protested.

"It's no time to argue. Let's go," Mini insisted.

"I'll go with you two." Kung Yi picked up Xiao Bao and followed Ling and Mini out the front door.

The bombing and gunfire remained intense. It seemed to have gotten closer, or maybe Mini only thought that because it was her first time outside in days. The sky was black with smoke from all directions covering the sun. A thick burning stench filled their nostrils. Thousands of refugees swarmed the streets, each one holding their meager possessions tight, looking vaguely in the direction of the bombing and fires. Mini looked on at the crying children all around her, their lips cracked and their faces red. Some had parents who desperately tried to calm them.

Half running and half walking, Kung Yi, Mini, and Ling rushed Xiao Bao to the British hospital. It was roughly a mile away in the direction of the Bund, away from the fighting. Mini was hopeful, but Kung Yi questioned whether she should have left home, as she had to stop every few minutes to catch her breath.

The hospital felt like a war zone when they arrived. Wounded civilians and soldiers crowded the hallway, laying or sitting on the ground. Many were moaning, asking for anything to relieve their pain. Some were screaming but were given no mind by the stone-faced doctors and nurses who rushed about. The smell of blood attracted scores of flies.

Kung Yi got the attention of a nurse who took a look at Xiao Bao and rushed them into a room full of wounded. She put the child on a small table, moved the IV stand next to it, and started administering fluid. She took his temperature.

"How long has the child been running a fever?"

"I don't know. Two days?" Ling replied.

"Closer to three days by now," Mini corrected.

The nurse jotted down a note on a chart and left the room without a word. They waited an hour or more before a doctor and a nurse came in. The doctor touched the baby, checked his pulse, opened the boy's eyelids, and looked into his eyes. Ling stood next to them, her hands held tight in front of her chest, her eyes following the doctor's every movement. She was too scared to ask questions. Mini put her arm around her sister's shoulder. She wanted to tell her it would be okay, that the little fellow would be all right, but she didn't want to give Ling false hope.

"Is he going to be okay?" Kung Yi asked what Mini and Ling desperately wanted to know but were afraid to ask out loud. Ling and Mini looked at the doctor hopefully.

"I don't know yet. The IV should do the trick. We'll see in a few hours."

He tapped the fluid in the bag. It was nearly empty. He talked to the nurse in a low voice before they both left them alone in the room.

They waited by the table where little Xiao Bao lay, so focused on their own misery they completely ignored the agony around them. A different nurse returned shortly after with a fresh bag of liquid. A few hours like this passed before Xiao Bao started moving a little. His breathing was less labored. Kung Yi went out to get a nurse and returned with the doctor, who checked the baby again.

"How is he doing?" Kung Yi asked.

"He's going to make it. He's going to live."

Ling and Mini both let out a long sigh.

"But the fever ran too long. I am afraid it's going to affect him . . . in the long run."

"What do you mean?" Ling stepped forward.

"Usually, in a case like this, the brain is affected by a high fever. I can't know, not now."

"Do you mean? Do you mean he is going to be—" Ling broke off, unable to finish the sentence aloud.

"I can't tell anything for certain. He might be all right. As I said, I can't assess anything now. We'll have to wait. I'll look in on him tomorrow."

Ling broke down, sobbing. Mini hugged her sister tightly.

The fever finally broke in the wee hours of the next morning, but the doctor said the boy should stay at the hospital for another day and continue the fluids. Ling stayed at his side, and Mini and Kung Yi returned home. Mini was exhausted and couldn't stop weeping.

They returned to find Mrs. Pao joined by Mini's father kneeling down in front of the family's Guan Yin statue. Mr. Pao didn't believe in supernatural forces, but even he urged Mini to join in praying, kowtowing, and wishing the power of the Buddha would ensure Xiao Bao's full recovery.

Kung Yi and Ai May returned to the hospital the following morning and brought Ling and Xiao Bao home.

Ling was expressionless on the walk home, and even as she walked in the door to the relative safety and calm of her home. She passed her parents without acknowledging them. They looked at her in grave silence. Kung Yi directed her to the living room and helped her sit on the sofa. She did so mechanically, staring through the air with vacant eyes. Her lips were moving as if she was talking to someone, only without a sound. She was in another world.

Ai May tended to Xiao Bao, holding him in her arms. The feverish look was gone. His eyes were wide open, and his drooling mouth was half-open, smiling. But he was no longer the same child. He didn't recognize his grandparents, his aunt, his uncle, Ai May, or even his favorite toy horse. He, too, was in a different world.

18

IT GETS
VERY BAD

By the tenth day, the bombing subsided, but their fear kept them cooped up in the storage room until Mini's back pain grew excruciating in the stillness and forced her out and back to her bedroom. Stretching flat in a soft bed after spending all that time on a hard cement floor was a nice change. She instantly fell into a deep sleep.

Soon enough, her quiet stupor was shattered by a sudden, intense abdominal pain. She moaned softly, curled on the bed. Beads of sweat gathered on her forehead.

"Mini, what's the matter?" Kung Yi asked.

She closed her eyes. "Mother," she whispered.

Kung Yi hurried downstairs and returned with Mrs. Pao moments later. After one look at Mini, Mrs. Pao urged Kung Yi in a voice unusually stern:

"Kung Yi, take Mini to the hospital. You need to go *now*."

"What's happening?" Kung Yi asked.

"I'm afraid Mini is having a miscarriage."

He paused, speechless. Kung Yi then tried lifting her up from the bed; she was heavy as a stone slab. The pain had drained all her strength.

He let go and went downstairs to get Mr. Pao and Ai May. With their support, Mini managed to stand up, but her rubbery legs could hardly support her. Her body shook as she stood there, unmoving.

"Mini can't walk. She won't make it," Mr. Pao concluded. "You're going to need a car or rickshaw."

"What are we going to do? It's the middle of the night," Mrs. Pao said hopelessly.

"I'll find one," Kung Yi said and ran out.

Mini was back in her fetal position in bed, moaning like a wounded animal when Kung Yi returned empty-handed. There was no transportation, period.

Please let me keep my baby, Mini thought. *Please let me keep my boy.* It had been the only thing on Mini's mind, but until then she refused to acknowledge her fear. She closed her eyes, bit her lips tightly, and let out a desperate wail. It seemed an eternity until a large flow of blood rushed out. The pain disappeared like magic from her rapidly relaxing body. She stayed like that, as if in a trance, vaguely aware of the crying and sighs that blanketed the room. Mini opened her eyes. Her mother was crying, her father pacing the room in agitation. She heard Ling come and go, and Kung Yi's murmuring sorrowfully next to her, his face buried in his hands.

"Did I lose my baby?" she asked.

"Yes," Mrs. Pao said. She held Mini's hand. "My sweet girl, don't think about it now. Rest."

Mini closed her eyes again. She was too tired. All she wanted was sleep.

A violent commotion woke her. She struggled to get up, but it was all she could do to just sit up in bed. She heard Jie Xing's voice, angry and accusatory. Then came Ling's enraged response, followed by her parents' and Kung Yi's futile interventions. This went on for a while.

What is Jie Xing saying to Ling? How can he be so unfair? I need to explain! Mini tried once more to get up, but Ling was up the stairs before Mini could get out of the bed. She was crying.

"Goodbye, Mini. I have to go now. Jie Xing said I was a bad mother to Xiao Bao. He no longer trusts me to raise him. He's taking us back to Suzhou. He wants his parents to raise Xiao Bao and supervise me. We have to leave this minute."

"But, Ling . . . ," Mini began.

"I know what you're going to say. Whatever you say is useless. You can't convince him. Pa and Ma tried. Kung Yi tried too. Jie Xing is beside himself. You take care of yourself." Ling touched Mini's hand gently. "Thank you for staying with me and Xiao Bao these last few days. I know you were in pain." She turned and left, closing the door behind her.

Mini collapsed in bed. She stared at the ceiling; a sliver ray of light stole its way in past the covered window. Feeling her energy return, she slowly sat up and pulled her pajama top up. She looked at her bare stomach. She touched it and it felt incredibly empty. Any doubts about the child's gender gave way to absolute certainty now. It was a boy—she was sure.

My baby boy is dead.

Her tears flowed. She lamented her lost boy and wished she could turn back the clock. She wept—for her boy, for Ling, and for Xiao Bao. She was so deep in her misery that she wasn't even aware of Kung Yi appearing at her side. He came in, sat next to her, and held her tight, comforting her and whispering in her ear.

"It's okay. It's okay. You're young and healthy. We can have another one in no time." He kissed her head and rubbed her lower back as he held her. "We'll have a good time making our baby when you're ready."

Ai May put some cold rice and pickles on the table in the dining room, which was lit by a single candle.

"Master, we are low on coal. Also, there was nothing in the market today. I couldn't even find any eggs."

"This is fine, Ai May." Mr. Pao took a bowl of rice from her.

"Pa, you are the only one who knows what's going on. What did you hear today? Where is the fighting?" Kung Yi asked. Mr. Pao had returned to the consulate. The British concession had remained remarkably untouched.

"The fighting has been pushed outside of Shanghai proper now, but it's still going. The Japanese thought they'd take Shanghai in less than a week, but it's been more than a month and a half now and they still haven't managed to enter Shanghai," Mr. Pao said, putting down his rice bowl. He sounded hopeful.

"Do you think we'll win this battle?" Kung Yi asked.

"I wish that to be the case," the older man replied in a more careful tone. "The reports I read still project the Japanese defeating us. They say the Chinese army doesn't have the training and our decades-old weapons cannot rival the modern ones the Japanese have." Mr. Pao shook his head: "The situation is bleak."

"So, it's just a matter of time until the Japanese take over Shanghai?" Kung Yi's shoulders slumped. He, too, pushed his rice bowl away from him. "You said the Japanese would leave the foreign concessions alone. What about the Chinese territory?"

"No way of knowing. But they haven't been gentle in the North. Kung Yi, how are . . ." Mr. Pao looked at Kung Yi. "You must be worried about your parents."

"Yes, I haven't heard from them since we escaped, before the bombing. People say there was heavy bombing in the area. I can only hope they got out to our land." Kung Yi's voice became heavier: "But I can't bear not knowing whether they're alive or dead. I should have checked on our house; they might have gotten trapped like us."

Mini reached out and touched his hand. "Kung Yi, just wait a little longer. It's too dangerous to go to that part of the city now."

Kung Yi sat quietly but Mini could tell his mind was racing.

He was gone when Mini awoke the next morning. Nobody had seen him leave. Mini paced the house until he returned after sundown. She ran to him as he came in the door.

"How *dare* you leave without even saying a word to me! Where have you been all day?" Mini was so angry she could slap him.

"I went to see my parents." Kung Yi avoided Mini's eyes.

"What? Why didn't you tell me?" Mini shouted at him.

"Mini, please, don't be angry with me. They're my parents. You have to be reasonable," Kung Yi said in a low voice, calm and tired.

Just as quickly her anger turned to shame. *How selfish I must sound.* Mini's voice became softer: "Did you see them? Your parents?"

"Yes, they're holed up in the house just like us. I'm surprised they held out that long. There was a lot of bombing in the area. They didn't say so, but I think they're terrified. Who wouldn't be? Oh, I wish I had gone back sooner. They're thinking about leaving Shanghai to go to the country."

Mini tried to picture her in-laws frightened, hiding in a darkened pantry room full of year-old rice, surrounded by dried meats, mushrooms, and other goods. She couldn't—all she saw was a tall, intimidating old woman and a short, thin old man whose mind always seemed miles away. *Who would've thought? The war has made everyone equal. We're all frightened.*

Mini was calm now, no longer mad at Kung Yi. She put her hand under his elbow, and they walked to the living room.

"What did you see, outside the Concession?" Mini asked. Besides the brief trip to the hospital with Ling, Mini hadn't set foot outside the house since the war broke out.

"It's very bad. Refugees are everywhere. Many buildings are half-standing. So many charred houses. Children were crying alone in the streets with their hands out. Who knows whether their parents are still alive? Luckily our house is still there, but the surrounding area is badly destroyed. I think it's a good idea if Mother and Father leave as soon as possible." He sat down on the sofa and Mini snuggled up against him.

"I had so many horrible thoughts. Why did it take you so long to go home and get back? You scared me." Mini scolded as she squeezed Kung Yi's hand tight.

"I'm sorry. I didn't mean to make you worry. I thought if I left early enough . . . Well, it took me a while to find a rickshaw, and the roads are badly bombed. You really can't imagine it. There's rubble everywhere—still, after all these days. And some streets, entire blocks—they're hollowed out, like small craters. It took so much just to get through the refugees around the house to find my parents huddled up inside. I didn't want to turn and leave right away once I got there. Just being there with them seemed to calm their nerves. Mother and Father are both very concerned about the situation. They said they had been through many bad times, but none as bad as this. They are so worried about the stores, what will happen to the inventory and the buildings. They're afraid it's going to get worse. They're not ready to check anything out," Kung Yi sighed.

Ai May came to the living room, "Young Master, would you like a cup of tea?" she asked.

"You read my mind, Ai May. I am parched. Thank you," Kung Yi said, flashing his charming smile at Ai May. She flushed and left the room quickly.

"What did they say about my miscarriage?" Mini looked down at her toes.

"Nothing. I didn't mention it."

Mini felt her heart contract. "Why? You have to tell them—tell the truth."

It would be worse if they found out on their own. They had so much hope that I'd give them a grandson. I failed them. What are they going to think of me now? Why didn't Kung Yi make it easier for me? How am I going to face them?

"They are already disturbed as it is," Kung Yi replied. "I didn't want to add more bad news. I figured we would tell them together."

What a coward! He didn't dare face them alone!

Ai May came in with tea. She turned to Mini. "Master and Mistress are waiting for you two for dinner."

"What, you waited for me? You shouldn't have." Kung Yi was touched.

"Yes, Ma and Pa insisted on waiting," Mini responded. "They want to have dinner together."

19

BUDDHA'S
PUNISHMENT

Dead leaves swirled through the streets on the cold October wind. The war was still going on, though it was much quieter than just a month ago. Shanghai, the city that was said to never sleep, was now in a lifeless slumber, holding its breath in anticipation of defeat.

One evening, Mrs. Pao was knitting a sweater for her grandson in the flickering candlelight. Mini was sewing a white cotton shirt for Kung Yi, who now stayed home reading kung fu novels to pass the time, after he had taken advantage of a brief period of peace to sell his family's inventory. People still had to eat, and their inventory of rice sold out in less than a week. The new harvest—Kung Yi didn't even know if there *was* a harvest—was blocked from reaching Shanghai. With nowhere to go, he remained holed up in the house with the women each day as they waited for Mr. Pao to return from work.

"Mini, how do you like it?" Mrs. Pao held up the little sweater to show Mini its yellow star pattern. Before Mini could answer, they heard a knock on the front door. An old woman and a child had taken to knocking and begging for food every night at this time, like clockwork.

"Ai May, get some cold rice. Must be the beggars again," Mrs. Pao said.

Ai May filled a big bowl with rice and walked to the front door. She opened it a crack and stuck the bowl out without looking. A strong hand pushed the door open. Mr. Shi stepped across the threshold and announced in his booming voice, "Little Sister, this is Kung Yi's father and mother."

"I am sorry, Master and Mistress." Ai May bowed, backing into the room.

Kung Yi rose from his chair quickly upon hearing his father's voice, as did Mini. For a second, Mrs. Pao was confused as to why both Mini and Kung Yi had walked out, until she saw her in-laws marching inside. She tried to stand up but failed. She motioned to Ai May to give her a hand.

Mrs. Pao bowed as the in-laws walked into the living room: "Aiya, welcome, welcome! It is so nice to have you here in our humble house. Ai May, please bring tea."

Mrs. Shi walked forward unsteadily. Her tiny feet were so out of proportion to her large body that she always seemed awkward when she stood upright. Mini wanted to help her but dared not. She followed behind, slowly and patiently. Mr. Shi clasped his hands together in front of his chest and returned a bow to Mrs. Pao. Kung Yi held his mother's arm to steady her and guided her to a large chair. Once she sat down, Mrs. Shi's sharp eyes surveyed the room, stopping at Mini's body. Her smile went cold.

"How is my future grandson doing?"

Her words dropped like a bomb. Mini and Kung Yi looked at each other, and Mrs. Pao stood rigid, lips trembling. Nobody said a thing. Finally, Kung Yi cleared his throat loudly.

"Mother and Father, I am sorry that I didn't tell you earlier. I wanted to spare you the bad news: Mini lost our child. She had a miscarriage."

Mrs. Shi's face contorted at the word "lost." She burst our crying, as if she were a child who had lost control of her emotions.

"Aiya, Aiya, my grandson is gone! Buddha is punishing me, for I must have done something bad in my last life." She beat her chest.

Mini stood quietly. She didn't know what to do. Mrs. Pao kept apologizing to Mrs. Shi. Kung Yi stood behind his mother-in-law and his wife, his face ashen white.

"Stop it, woman. Enough already!" Mr. Shi shouted at his wife. "Kung Yi, we need a grandson for our family. You know it is your duty to us and to our family to have a son. We need an heir, especially at a time like this. Please don't disappoint us."

Mr. Shi made eye contact with Mini. Mini knew it was a warning. She felt sick. Resentment stirred in her. Kung Yi told them of the days and nights in the storage room during the bombardment and how Mini had lost their child. Mini was healthy, he promised. Mrs. Shi continued to wail as Kung Yi repeated his explanation. Eventually, Mrs. Shi regained her composure.

"Kung Yi, it's time to return," his father continued.

"Yes, father."

"There is nothing for you to do here. We need you."

Mr. Pao returned from work before Mr. Shi could continue. Rather surprised to see his in-laws in his living room, Mr. Pao bowed in greeting them.

"Mr. and Mrs. Shi. It's an honor. I didn't expect you. You're so kind to travel all this way. You must be tired. Please, join us for a simple dinner. Ai May, get our last bottle of rice wine."

After a round of rice wine, Mr. Shi cleared his throat: "In-laws, I thank you for taking care of our son and daughter-in-law for so long. It's time that they should go back to their own home."

"Home? I disagree. Forgive me for pointing it out, but your home is in a neighborhood the Japanese will strike first once they enter the city, as it falls under Chinese jurisdiction," Mr. Pao said indignantly. "I'm afraid to say, it is only a matter of time. This is but a temporary respite."

The elder Shi shook his head vigorously. "No, in-law, I mean they should leave Shanghai with us. We can stay in our country home for a while until this wind blows over."

"I think it's safer to stay here until the wind blows over," Mr. Pao responded. "You see, the Japanese were quite brutal to the peasants in the North. They don't think much of killing Chinese peasants, but they won't do such a thing here in the city. The British government protects the people here. I hate to say that we need the British, but it's a fact. We cannot deny it."

Mr. Shi was about to respond, but paused and looked at his wife, as if seeking her opinion. She nodded slightly. He turned to study Mr. Pao.

"Of course. Your position grants you access to information that is not available to us *common people*. I'd like to think you care about them just as much as we do. In this case, I will trouble you a little longer."

"No trouble at all. Mini is my daughter, my flesh and blood. Kung Yi is just like my son. I will return them to you safe and sound once you are back to Shanghai." He raised his wine cup. "Cheers!"

They all raised their cups.

The Shis left after dinner, though the Paos offered to put them up for the night.

"When will you be back, Mother and Father?" Kung Yi asked, choking up a little as he spoke.

"I don't know, son. When the situation is better," Mr. Shi said.

"What should I do with our house?"

"Old Wei is watching the house along with a few strong guards. Old Wei's wife is to cook and wash for them. He's been your father's servant since he was a child," Mrs. Shi answered. "He's trustworthy and loyal. Please keep an eye on our property when you think it is safe to go," Mrs. Shi added, waiting for his response.

When Kung Yi nodded, she continued: "You needn't stay at home overnight, because the area is full of debris and beggars. It can be violent after nightfall. Be careful." She moved forward and touched Kung Yi's arm. It was the first time Mini saw her display any affection toward her son—or anyone.

20

BLISS AMID
THE MADNESS

On November 26th, the Japanese army marched into and occupied the Chinese section of Shanghai. They set up checkpoints encircling the Concessions. The paper told of the Japanese who were searching everyone going in or out of these so-called "isolated islands," no matter whether they were Chinese or fair-haired Westerners. That was the least of the indignities. Each day, the paper reported the rape and execution of Chinese women and men. And to think they would do this in public, in broad daylight! The Japanese army avenged their losses by committing atrocity after atrocity. Mini grew weary and feared that she would recognize someone in the newspaper pictures depicting the corpses lying in the streets.

The news only increased the tension between Mini and Kung Yi. He was anxious about his home, often wondering aloud: "Maybe I should make a trip soon—"

"You're out of your mind," Mini would say, always cutting him off before he could finish giving voice to his thoughts.

Kung Yi put off going home for another month. By then the news was mixed, the more gruesome stories now the subject of rumor and no longer a staple in the local papers. After reading the puppet government's propaganda encouraging people to return to their normal trade, he announced: "Mini, it's time I go and check on our home. It's been too long since anyone has been there. According to the papers, the situation has calmed down. I must check. I promised Mother and Father. I will go after lunch."

Mini stopped her needlework. "But you don't know for sure, Kung Yi?"

"The newspaper said it's better. I have to go."

"Please, Kung Yi," Mini pleaded. "Father says it's still too dangerous. You can wait a little longer."

"How long? We don't know how long. I don't want to go either, but it's our home." Kung Yi pulled Mini close to him and kissed her cheek.

"Please don't go!" Mini insisted.

"I'm sorry, Mini. I have no choice. I'll return home as soon as I can."

"Then let me go with you." She was nearly begging.

"No," Kung Yi said firmly. He went upstairs and changed into his street clothes. Mini walked him to the front door and watched him leave with a heavy heart.

Please let him return safely to me, merciful Buddha!

Mini couldn't stop pacing the entire time he was gone.

Where is Kung Yi now? Did he get through the checkpoints safely? What if the house is occupied? What would the Japanese do to him?

The chilly air in the house made her shiver even after she put on a heavy sweater. Mrs. Pao understood her daughter's anxiety and chatted about this and that in an attempt to distract her. Hours passed and Kung Yi didn't return. Mini moved a wooden stool to the atrium and sat waiting by the front door in her mother's heavy winter coat. She had left most of her own winter clothing behind when she fled the Shis' house in the summer.

"Young Mistress, can you help me with dinner?" Ai May asked, trying to interrupt Mini's thoughts as it turned to dusk. "I was lucky today. I bought some greens and a half duck, but the coal stove is not working properly. I need to tend to it. Can you please chop the vegetables?"

Supplies were scarce. Mini couldn't even imagine what Ai May could have done to get a half duck. She nodded, stood up, and followed Ai May to the kitchen. Mini knew Ai May didn't need the help—she had cooked ten-course meals single-handedly—but Mini was grateful for the distraction. She set up the chopping board on the kitchen table and mechanically chopped greens as her mind wandered.

Oh, please, let Kung Yi come home soon. Where is he? How dangerous is it for him to go through the checkpoints? Please . . .

Mini felt pain and cried out. The knife had cut into her thumb. Ai May stopped cooking and looked at the wound. "Lucky, it's just a flesh wound." She cleaned and dressed the cut with a clean cloth.

"You should go rest," Ai May urged. "I'll finish here."

Mini retreated to the living room and resumed her pacing.

Shortly after the clock struck eight, she heard the knock on the door. *It's only Pa, back from work.* Her father had been staying at work later recently. She went to open the door. To her surprise, Kung Yi stood behind her father, smiling. Joy washed over her. Her heart lightened immediately.

"Ma," she cried out to her mother. "Kung Yi is back! And Pa is back too!"

"How was the journey? What did you do to go through the Japanese sentries?" Mrs. Pao asked Kung Yi at dinner.

"Bowed to them. I didn't even look at them. I just bowed and walked on."

Mr. Pao shook his head.

"How about the house?" Mini asked.

"It isn't occupied, thanks to Old Wei. He told the authorities that the owner of the house is still in Shanghai. I need to go there more often now. They may come to see the owner," Kung Yi said.

"You can't just go and leave me here alone. I was sick with worry," Mini protested. "I'll go with you next time."

"I don't think it's a good idea . . ." Kung Yi glanced at Mr. Pao.

"Pa," Mini turned to her father, looking to enlist support.

"No, Mini, I can't let you," Mr. Pao said firmly.

"Listen to your father," Mrs. Pao reasoned. "You don't need to go. Kung Yi is a man. Women shouldn't be out."

"We cannot hide all the time. I have to leave the house someday. Please let me go with Kung Yi. His home is my home, too," Mini pleaded.

"No, Mini, you aren't going to get your way this time," Mr. Pao said, shaking his head.

"Please, Pa," Mini continued. "I was so nervous when Kung Yi was gone. I'm his wife. I need to be with him."

"I understand. But you're my daughter and I've heard too many stories of the terrible things the Japanese do to Chinese women. It's too risky."

"Thousands and thousands of people go through the checkpoints unharmed every day. They cannot hurt everyone going through. Their army is not big enough," Mini argued.

Mr. Pao sighed. "Kung Yi, what do you say about this?"

"Let me go through the checkpoints a few more times and see how it is," Kung Yi said diplomatically. "The people I spoke to said if you go when it's busy, the Japanese usually don't do anything. It's when they're bored that they become vicious to civilians. However, Mini is your daughter, and so I leave it to you."

Kung Yi bowed to his father-in-law.

"I don't like it, but Mini cannot stay here forever," Mr. Pao conceded. "She will have to move back home one day. Mini, are you sure you want to go?" He sat down and looked at Mini across the room. As usual, she had worn him down.

"Yes, Pa." Mini held his eyes, even as they were beseeching her to stay home. But she had made up her mind.

"Can you at least wait a few more days? Just to be safe?"

"Yes, Pa."

"And please be careful," her father warned. "Turn back if you see any danger at all. Don't stay there long and call me once you are home—right away. I mean it."

Kung Yi returned to his family mansion in the Chinese section a few more times over that next week. Each time Mini paced while waiting for him. On his fifth trip, she insisted on joining him.

They left after lunch, carefully picking the busiest time of day so they could mix in with the hundreds of other people who would be going through the checkpoints. They huddled close to one another as they made their way to Nanking Road, the main road where they were more likely to find a rickshaw.

It was stop-and-go as they made their way to the old Chinese town. Streets remained blocked by debris. Mini saw a checkpoint manned by Japanese soldiers as they approached the old town. Kung Yi urged the coolie forward, and he gingerly pulled his rickshaw to a stop at the checkpoint. Kung Yi nodded for Mini to get off.

With her heart in her throat, Mini bowed 90 degrees to the soldiers, taking her cue from everyone else who was passing through. Kung Yi did the same. The soldiers regarded them with bored and uninterested stares, waving them through. The coolie followed, bowing also. Once through, they quickly climbed back onto the rickshaw, the coolie running from the checkpoint as if a devil were chasing him. It was a cold December day, yet Mini found that her forehead was wet with sweat.

They arrived at the Shi mansion at last. It stood tall amid rubble and charred houses. Little else around the mansion, it seemed, was salvageable. Still, months after the neighborhood's destruction, people were rummaging through the debris for anything of value. They watched resentfully as Kung Yi and Mini approached the still-intact mansion. Kung Yi unlocked the gate quickly. They stepped inside the front yard, once grand and tastefully manicured, now overgrown with grass that had turned yellow in the cold. Old Wei must have heard Kung Yi open the gate, because he met them at the front door. He carefully locked the door behind them before testing it to ensure the lock had taken. He looked around and then bowed.

"Someone tried to get through when you left last time, Master," Old Wei said. He looked at Mini. "I am surprised Young Mistress came along with you, Young Master. I welcome you both home. How was the journey?"

"It was smooth, but we saw too many children begging. Mini was caught by a bunch of them after she gave a few coins to a pretty little girl. It was sad, but we can't save everyone," Kung Yi said as he and Mini entered the house.

Old Wei's wife, Mama Wei, took their coats.

"So good to see you, Young Master and Young Mistress," she smiled, showing the gap from her missing front tooth.

"Mama Wei, I will trouble you to bring some tea and dim sum to our room. Mini is tired. She wants to rest for a while."

"Right away, Young Master. Though I must tell you we don't have much here. I only have a few plain buns," she said apologetically. "Would that be okay for you?"

"Yes, that's fine," Mini said. "Mama Wei, thank you for being here and for watching our home. We are grateful to you."

Mama Wei shook her head. "No, Young Mistress, this is home for me and my old man, too. You needn't thank us. I'll send tea upstairs to your room." She bowed again and disappeared in the direction of the kitchen.

"Mini, I'll check on the rest of the house. You go wash up and rest," Kung Yi directed. "I'll join you for tea in a few minutes."

Mini nodded. She climbed the stairs to their suite and inspected their abandoned rooms. The windows were shut tight and covered by thick curtains. The room smelled musty. Everything looked exactly as they had left it, except the furniture had been freshly dusted. Mini opened a window. Cold air rushed in and pushed the stale smell out. Mama Wei came in with a tray of tea and snacks, which she placed on the table in the suite's sitting room.

"Do you need anything else?" she asked.

"No, thank you. That's all," Mini said.

Mini went into their bedroom and sat on the soft four-poster bed. She looked at the light green satin chairs and matching bedspread, feeling a strange sense of serenity.

Finally, we're alone, away from the madness. How sweet life is, with just Kung Yi and me.

She heard Kung Yi's footsteps as he ran upstairs, as if taking them two at a time. She smiled, liking his eagerness. The door opened and closed as Kung Yi came in. He sat next to her and wrapped his right arm around her shoulder. Kung Yi looked into her eyes as he brushed his left hand over her breast and up, up. His hand continued until it found the top button of her qipao, just below Mini's left shoulder. He deftly unfastened the button, slid his hand inside her dress, and gently fondled her breast.

Mini's heart beat faster. This was their first opportunity for intimacy since they had fled. Burning at his touch, Mini responded almost violently. She hiked her qipao up above her waist, hastily kicking off her shoes. Then she grabbed at her stockings, legs in the air, until she pulled them off—first one leg, then the other.

Kung Yi gently pushed her back onto the bed. He kissed Mini deeply, the hand at her breast now pulling open the qipao to reveal her delicate flesh. Mini couldn't stand it any longer, pulling him down onto her. In that moment, their desire for one another seemed to melt the distance that had grown between them over the last year.

The large, empty house lulled both of them. Of course they weren't really alone—Old Wei and the guards were there, though they were mostly patrolling the yard, hardly in the house at all, and Mama Wei never set foot in their suite unless she was asked to bring tea or food. Without their families there to interfere, Mini and Kung Yi could live with abandon. The newfound freedom made their lovemaking feel so much sweeter. They didn't need to follow any rules. For once, they were the masters of their own lives.

They established a routine after that first day. They would arrive at the Shi mansion right after lunch and go straight to their bedroom to undress, staying in the room the entire afternoon to make love and enjoy each other in the most uninhibited ways they could think of. Nothing existed but their longing for one another. Her excitement and anticipation of each day's tryst was so great that it completely overcame Mini's fear of the checkpoints. Each evening, when they closed the door and left the mansion, she was already yearning for another day alone with Kung Yi. They rode back to her parents' home whispering to each other in the rickshaw, oblivious to everything around them, thinking only of exploring each other a little more the next day.

21

BUT A GIRL
IS A GIRL

Shanghai had regained some of its peacetime normalcy by the time Chinese New Year arrived. The puppet government continued encouraging businesses to reopen, as Shanghai and the surrounding area had escaped the worst. The Japanese army's seemingly gentle approach to the city in the last couple months led many to forget the early days of the occupation, and the atrocities still taking place elsewhere.

The Shis moved back to Shanghai and signed on to the rice distribution network established by the puppet government. This enabled them to ship rice into Shanghai once again. At the request of Mr. and Mrs. Shi, Mini and Kung Yi returned to live at the mansion. Their New Year's Eve banquet was subdued compared to prior years, but it was a happy one. It was as if, having gone through a life-and-death situation, the Shis found to their surprise that they weren't dead and saw fit to celebrate their good fortune. After she had a few rounds of rice wine running through her, Mini triumphantly announced her new pregnancy to her in-laws. The happy months that she and Kung Yi spent at the mansion had instilled in her a sense of invincibility. She was certain it was a boy.

The baby arrived in early October 1938.

During the labor, Mini's mother was with her. Mr. and Mrs. Shi stayed downstairs in the great hall, waiting patiently for the birth of their grandchild.

"They closed the gate today to all visitors, even to Mr. Shi's opera friends. They're waiting for their grandchild to arrive," Mrs. Pao told Mini.

She gave birth to a girl.

"Would you like to hold the baby?" the midwife asked, extending the little crying bundle to her.

Mini turned her head away. "No, I'm tired. Please send the baby to the wet nurse."

Betrayal stirred in Mini's chest, but she didn't know who or what had betrayed her. *I was so certain*, she thought ruefully. *Is it my fate? The gods? Oh, merciful Buddha, why did you have to . . . ? Why couldn't you give me another son after taking the first one from me? I just want to be alone to cry . . .*

Yet her eyes were dry and shed no tears. Mini was too tired to cry. She closed her eyes and felt her heart sink down into the pit of her stomach. With her eyes closed, she couldn't see anything or anyone. It made her feel safe. She wanted to disappear. Mini felt sorry for herself—she was angry at her fate and the hopelessness of it. These feelings churned inside her until she felt she would go mad.

Why? Why has my fate betrayed me? Why do I have such bad luck?

Eventually, a kitchen maid brought her a bowl of chicken broth, but Mini refused to drink it. Mrs. Pao sat on the side of the bed, holding the bowl in one hand and a spoonful of broth in the other, ready to feed her. Mini sensed all this, though she kept her eyes closed and her mouth shut tight.

"Mini, you need some broth after labor."

"No, I don't need anything," Mini murmured.

"You are young. This is your first child. You will have another chance. Now, listen to your mother and drink some broth," Mrs. Pao demanded, lifting the spoon and extending it to Mini's mouth.

Mini turned her head to the side, her eyes still closed.

Mrs. Pao sighed. She put the bowl and spoon down on the bedside table.

"I'll go next door to see the baby. You rest now," she said.

Mrs. Pao closed the door softly behind her, leaving Mini to wallow in her own sorrow, alone in a dark room full of the sour smell of sweat, blood, and bodily fluids.

Kung Yi didn't come to visit her until the awful smell had dissipated, the room was cleaned, and the bed remade. When he finally returned to her side, Mini sent the maids out. Tears streamed down her face.

"Kung Yi, I am so sorry!" she felt compelled to empty her heart to him. Her husband was the only one she could talk to without reservation. *He'll understand,* she thought. *After all, it's our baby. He had a part in all this, so he'll understand. We can try again! I am still young— no, we are still young!*

Finally, she gave voice to her thoughts. "I am still young, and we can try again to have a son."

"Mini, don't think about this now," Kung Yi said, giving her a wary smile. "I am glad everything went well for you. Rest now and we can talk about it later."

He doesn't want to talk about it. That only means he holds it against me like everyone else. I bet he's thinking about getting a second wife now. That's what these families do. When the wife doesn't give them a son, they take another woman. Ling was treated just like that—like a machine made to produce a son.

Mini felt a surge of anger.

"Why didn't you come to see me sooner? Where were you?" Mini asked accusingly.

"I've been outside all this time," Kung Yi replied, calm.

"So you didn't come in because I had a daughter?"

"No, Mini, I didn't come in because your mother advised against it," he explained. "She said that you were in no state to be seen by your husband."

Just as quickly as it had come, Mini's anger evaporated, replaced by self-pity. She sobbed aloud.

Kung Yi sat quietly, his lips pressed together in a thin line.

"You rest and rest well," he finally said. "You will feel better tomorrow. Ring the bell if you need anything. Your mother is going to stay with you. I told your maid to set up a bed outside in the sitting area."

"What about you? Where are you going to stay?" Mini blew her nose with a handkerchief.

"Downstairs, in the guest quarters."

"You should stay in the sitting area and my mother can stay in the guest quarters," Mini said hopefully.

"You know I cannot do this. It's not allowed. I have to stay away from you for a month, at least. I cannot break custom or the servants will talk."

"So, let them talk," Mini said stubbornly.

"Mother wouldn't allow it, even if I wanted to. You know I want to stay with you. I will come to see you and our baby often."

"No, you won't," Mini retorted. "You'll make up some excuse not to come, now that I have a daughter. You go, get out now. I don't want to see you!"

Mini was shouting at him, yet she still held his hands tightly, not letting him go. Anger filled her chest, burning through her heart. It was a feeling she had never experienced before. She felt alone, vulnerable, isolated, and so helpless.

Kung Yi moved closer, wrapping his arms around her, and he held her for a few seconds without a word. As Mini buried her face in his chest, a little peace and comfort came to her. Too soon, the moment was broken when Kung Yi stood up and walked to the door.

"Don't go, Kung Yi, please. I need you . . . ," Mini pleaded.

"I'm sorry, but I have to. Mother is expecting me to run some errands," Kung Yi said.

"You can say no," she insisted.

"You are being unreasonable, Mini," he replied. "You know I can't say no to her." He smiled at Mini—a forced smile—and turned. Her husband left the room without looking back.

Mr. Pao visited late the next day after returning from work at the consulate. He stopped in at the nursery before appearing in Mini's room, a big smile on his face.

"How is my girl doing?" he asked Mini.

"All right," she answered with a fake smile.

"What's the matter?"

"Nothing." Mini looked away.

"Must be something," her father replied. "I can tell, Mini."

"Just that I am so unlucky. I had a girl."

There was a moment of silence before her father spoke again.

"Mini, can you say I'm an unlucky person?"

Mini looked at her father. His radiant smile irritated her. She looked away again, saying nothing.

"I have two daughters. Two daughters *only*," Mr. Pao continued. "And I never once considered myself unlucky."

"But Father, you're different," Mini protested. "You didn't have family, and no one could give Ma a hard time because she had two girls."

"*I* could've," he said. "But I didn't."

"But Pa, how many men are like you in this world?" Mini cried out.

"Well, I can't comment on that," Mr. Pao said. "But the first step is for you to stop feeling sorry for yourself."

"That's easier said than done," Mini argued. "I feel sorry for myself and the whole household feels sorry for me. Ma said that she is sorry. See, I didn't marry into a family the same as mine and I have to fit in. Without a boy, I'll forever be an outsider. Worse, I might lose my husband."

Mr. Pao went to the window. He pulled up the curtain a little to let in some sunlight. "Mini, there is no guarantee that you'll have a boy, though I really hope so. You must learn to deal with it. Be strong, child."

Mini looked down, fighting back tears.

"Things aren't so bad," Mr. Pao consoled her. "Don't beat yourself up over something you can't change. Your baby is a lovely girl. Be kind to her and take good care of her. She's your daughter, Mini, your flesh and blood. You mother told me that you refused to see your baby. This is not right. She didn't do anything wrong." He walked back and sat next to her bed.

Mini turned her eyes to a ray of sunlight dancing on the wall. Mr. Pao sighed.

"Listen to me," he said. "Kung Yi is a decent man. I don't expect him to do anything drastic just because you had a girl." He swallowed hard before continuing. "Remember what I said, Mini, and don't dwell on it. You take care of yourself now. I will visit in a few days."

Later in the day, Mini had an early supper with her mother at her bedside. She drank only a bowl of broth, nothing else, insisting that she wasn't hungry.

"Mini, you have to eat. Come, have a piece of chicken leg," Mrs. Pao said in the tone she used to take when Mini was little.

"No, Ma, I'm not hungry," Mini insisted.

"Mini, stop. Stop tormenting yourself. Now you eat and after that, you're going to see your daughter. She is a lovely baby. She has your eyes."

"No, Ma, I don't want to. I just want to rest," Mini said. She closed her eyes, her sign that she was done talking.

Kung Yi visited that night. He stayed briefly with Mini and asked how she was doing but didn't say much. He went next door to the nursery, where Mini heard him ask the wet nurse how many times she had fed the baby and how well the baby was eating. Then, she heard his footsteps pass her door and move down the staircase. She sobbed softly, crying herself to sleep.

For the following days, Mini did nothing but sleep in the dark, curtained room, hardly eating. She spent her waking hours crying. Mini was in such a state that no one wanted to be in the room with her. Mrs. Pao repeatedly tried to persuade her to see the baby, but Mini refused.

One afternoon, Mini woke up from her nap to hear her mother's voice outside her bedroom: "Go on, take the baby to her room."

"But Young Mistress might not want that," Mini heard the wet nurse protest.

"Go anyway. I'll be with you," said Mrs. Pao firmly.

There was a tentative knock and then the door opened without her answering. The wet nurse came in with a bundle in her arms and Mrs. Pao in tow, walking timidly towards the bed.

"Would you like to see your pretty baby girl?" The wet nurse smiled rigidly, her eyes shifting between Mini and Mrs. Pao.

"The baby, Little Mistress, has a big stomach. She drinks my milk once an hour. Look, look," the wet nurse bent down to hold the baby under Mini's face. "She gained some weight already. Look."

Mini looked at the bundle. The child was wrapped in a tiny red cloth. Her tiny head was sticking out of the swaddle. A wrinkled pink face with a pair of shiny black eyes blinked back at Mini, once, twice, and then stared. Mini returned the stare. The wet nurse held the baby there for a moment without a word.

It felt like something heavy inside Mini's chest was dissolving. The weight that she had felt was lightening. It took Mini a moment to realize that she was crying. She took the bundle and unwrapped it until she reached the pink flesh of tiny arms, hands, legs, and feet. She saw ten perfect little toes and ten perfect little fingers. The baby kicked her legs rapidly, appreciating her freedom from the tight swaddling. Mini kissed the baby's fingers, arms, toes, and legs, rubbing her tear-soaked face into the tiny belly of her daughter.

Quickly, Mrs. Pao stepped forward and took the baby away from Mini, returning the child to her snug bundle.

"You've got to keep the baby swaddled—here, like this. She'll catch cold if you keep her exposed like that. Also, it's good for them in the long run. A baby's tiny legs and arms need to be confined so she'll learn to better follow the rules when she's older."

The baby cried, protesting her renewed confinement. The wet nurse unbuttoned her blouse stained with milk and took the baby back from Mrs. Pao, pressing the girl to one of her swollen breasts. The baby's little mouth quickly found the nipple and sucked happily.

"Did Kung Yi give her a name?" Mini asked.

"The elder Mr. Shi gave her a name," Mrs. Pao replied. "Your daughter's name is Jing Ling—Shi Jing Ling. Her cry was so loud and crisp that Mr. Shi thought she had a voice like a golden bell."

"Jing Ling, golden bell. My little golden bell." Mini looked at the tiny face.

From that point on, the cries of the baby and footsteps of the wet nurse created a pleasant cacophony to Mini's ears. She had come to forget about everything else, just as everyone else seemed to have forgotten her. Mini stopped thinking of Jing Ling as a girl, and when she did think about it, she shrugged it off, telling herself that her next baby would be a boy. No one had confronted her yet. She decided not to worry about it until she had to.

The day came soon enough. The sky was blue, and the afternoon sunshine penetrated the closed windows, spreading its warm glow into every corner of the room. Mini was busy changing Jing Ling's diaper when she heard a knock on the door. The wet nurse opened the door to find Mrs. Shi standing there, with her maid supporting her by one arm. Mrs. Shi dismissed the maid and walked with unsteady steps towards the nearest chair.

Mini was dumbfounded. She didn't expect her mother-in-law to visit her in her chambers. She hadn't seen either of her in-laws since the birth of her daughter two weeks earlier. Mini stood up and bowed quickly, her eyes downcast.

"Mother, welcome. Thank you for visiting, but you really needn't bother walking upstairs," Mini said deferentially. "You can send for me and the baby anytime."

"I have seen the baby all right. She is a good-looking child, like her father." Mrs. Shi turned to the wet nurse, "You don't need to be here now. Take the baby with you. I want to talk to Mini alone."

"Yes." The nurse bowed, gathered Jing Ling, and left.

"Congratulations for giving us a granddaughter," Mrs. Shi said.

Mini sat in a chair opposite to Mrs. Shi, unsure what to make out of what her mother-in-law had just said, her heart caught in her throat. Mini made brief eye contact with her mother-in-law, only to look down again. She struggled to stay calm, but her mind was racing, wondering why her mother-in-law would see fit to visit her.

"Here is a small token to show our appreciation." Mrs. Shi took out a thick red envelope and a small red satin purse, handing both to Mini.

Mini accepted them with both hands.

"Open them," her mother-in-law ordered.

Mini opened the envelope with shaking fingers: five thousand yuan. She opened the red purse and fingered a set of gold earrings and a tiny tiger pendant strung on a small gold necklace. Jing Ling had been born under the sign of the tiger. It was a strong sign, like her own—a dragon.

"Mother, thank you very much," Mini said.

"The money is for you and the jewelry is for your daughter."

"Yes, Mother, and thank you." Mini repeated, not knowing what else to say.

There was a heavy silence. Mini heard muffled footsteps outside the closed door and she imagined Lotus, her maid, putting her ear to the keyhole.

Mrs. Shi cleared her throat. "Mini, I have something important to discuss with you."

"Oh," Mini said, looking up from her lap to make brief eye contact again. When she caught Mrs. Shi's eyes staring back at her, she quickly looked away.

"I am happy that I have a granddaughter." Mrs. Shi picked up her teacup and took a sip. "But a girl is a girl. The Shi family is a prominent family. A family needs a son to carry the family name. Kung Yi is the only son in the family. So, all our hope is on him, and you, of course, being his wife." She took another sip of her tea.

Mini didn't interrupt. She steadied herself on the chair and sat upright. Though her back was weak and sore, she didn't want to betray any of her pain to Mrs. Shi. Mini listened attentively as her mother-in-law continued on.

Mrs. Shi's voice was very calm. "Mini, the Shi family wants to have an heir, and quickly. Considering that you just gave birth, it will take some time for you to recover and for Kung Yi to continue living in the same room with you again. Mr. Shi and I are thinking of persuading Kung Yi to take a second wife while you are recuperating."

"What?" Mini asked, hearing the shrillness in her voice.

"I am saying that Kung Yi can have a second wife now, while you are bed-resting," Mrs. Shi repeated, her calm unbroken. "The Shi family will always consider you as the first and proper wife of Kung Yi. The second wife will not have the same social standing as you. There won't be a formal ceremony, no wedding."

Mini's back was beginning to feel too weak to support her; she was sinking. Composing herself, Mini looked straight at her mother-in-law.

"I certainly do want the Shi family to have an heir, but I won't allow my husband to take a second wife. We are still young. We can have a son in the future, if you and Father will only give us a chance," Mini said, holding her mother-in-law's eyes steadily. "I don't think Kung Yi would like it either. We will have a son. Please give us some time."

"You are right," Mrs. Shi replied. "Kung Yi refused when I proposed it to him. I came here hoping you could help me to persuade your husband. I thought you were a sensible and virtuous girl. No doubt your father must have put some foreign ideas in your head. Don't get overly excited. You will be in bed at least another month, given the state you are in. Give my proposal some thought." Mrs. Shi held the arms of the chair she sat in, took a bracing breath, and pushed herself up. "I will come back in a few days. A virtuous woman puts her family's needs before anything else." She smiled at Mini, turned toward the door, and wobbled out.

Mini sank in her chair, shaking like a leaf. All her fears were coming true. She watched her mother-in-law struggle on her tiny feet but didn't rise to help her. Mini didn't care if her mother-in-law fell. She rang the bell for Lotus once the door closed behind her.

"Please find my husband right away," Mini directed.

"Yes," Lotus replied, giving Mini a sympathetic look. In all this time, she was the only servant who had been loyal to Mini.

"Go. Bring him here," Mini said in a weak voice, almost inaudible. Lotus darted from the room.

Mini waited in the chair, staring into space. Several times she heard footsteps, though she recognized each as those of the servants. Weeks of confinement since the birth of her daughter had taught her to recognize the sound of everyone's footsteps. Mini jumped up when she at last heard the familiar footsteps outside—the footsteps she looked forward to hearing every day, the footsteps that would instantly relieve her of her loneliness.

Kung Yi stood at the door. Rubbing his hands together, he smiled good-naturedly at Mini.

"Warm and cozy in here. It's freezing outside. I had to walk everywhere because there aren't enough cabs for such a cold day."

Mini glared at him, not saying a word. She paused for just a moment before picking up a cushion and hurling it at her husband with all her strength. "Already thinking about a concubine?"

"What?" Kung Yi asked innocently.

"You dirty bastard!" Mini replied. "I thought you were a decent man." Another cushion hit him squarely in the face.

"Calm down, Mini!" Kung Yi pleaded. "Did mother visit you?"

"Yes, she did!" Mini cried, about to pick up the empty teacup on the bedside table. But Kung Yi was quick this time. He moved fast, grabbing Mini's wrist before she could throw it.

Mini released the cup and broke down sobbing, covering her face with both hands. Her shoulders heaved and trembled.

Kung Yi tried to pull her hands away from her face. "Look at me. Mini, please look at me."

Mini refused, fighting his grip. She continued burying her face in her hands and cried harder.

"It was my parents' idea," Kung Yi explained. "I had nothing to do with it. I told them we're young and we will have a boy still."

"I thought you were different, but you are just as dirty as any other man," Mini shouted between sobs. "Am I not good enough for you? I'll tell you one thing: I will not allow you to have another wife. You'll have to do it over my dead body!"

"Listen, Mini. I refused. They already suggested it and I refused," Kung Yi repeated, shaking Mini's arm. He pulled her hands from her face and made her look at him.

When Mini stopped struggling, he held her tight. Her body relaxed.

Kung Yi caressed Mini's back gently. Slowly, he moved his hands down and his breathing became heavier.

"You are so soft," he whispered. "Mini, I miss you so much."

Mini blushed. "Stay here tonight, then," she whispered back.

"No, I cannot. I'm expected at dinner. I'd better be going now." He released Mini reluctantly and stood up. "I'll see you tomorrow."

As he left the room, Kung Yi could not see that Mini's head hung low, and she had begun crying again.

22

I WAS THE
ONE WHO LEFT

MINI, SHANGHAI, 1941

The hazy moonlight and soft breeze of this night reminded Mini bitterly of strolling with her family on a happy spring night. She pictured herself as she had been then: Laughing, holding Jing Ling in her arms. Kung Yi had hopped about, pretending he was a bunny to amuse their eighteen-month-old daughter. Kung Yi had been under pressure to take a concubine then, but the two of them had been a team. Their resistance to his parents' suggestion had miraculously extended a one-year deadline to eighteen months. They had thought they could put it off forever.

Who could have known that she would be here a year later, abandoned, her daughter taken from her?

Mini stood quietly behind a tree in the alleyway leading to the entrance of the grand New Asia Restaurant, taking pains to ensure she was completely out of sight. Wearing black from head to toe, Mini blended perfectly into the surrounding darkness. She looked in through the warm, inviting entrance of the restaurant.

Shanghai was back to its prewar normality. The Japanese military had done little to deter Shanghai's notorious nightlife. To the contrary,

it came roaring back into full swing, with many new businesses opening to serve the late-night crowd. Of these, the New Asia Restaurant
on Nanking Road was the most prominent. Its sensational new
Cantonese cuisine drew Chinese, British, and Japanese customers alike.
Though tonight it was closed for a private party: a wedding banquet.

Glowing red lanterns swayed gently in the breeze, their dancing red
light sweeping over the guests as they entered the restaurant. Mini held
her breath and listened to the giggles mixing with muffled conversation and Cantonese music, the mingled sounds growing louder and
sharper each time the door swung open for new guests. The restaurant
was only steps from Mini, but it seemed a world away. She rubbed her
eyes. They felt irritatingly dry. Maybe it was because she had cried so
much the last few days. Mini had no more tears now. She had nothing
left in her. She was numb and empty.

Earlier that evening, Mrs. Pao had locked Mini inside the house to
prevent her from leaving, but Ai May had let her out. Mini needed
to come. She needed to witness the betrayal with her own eyes. She
needed to witness the reality of her own misfortune in order to kill the
hope that lingered in her heart. Mini's life was finished. All her happiness was gone. She was alone, left with nothing.

The wedding announcement had appeared in the *Shanghai Daily News*
a few days earlier. Mr. Pao had gone to work and left the untouched
newspaper on the table. Mini flipped through the paper in silence as
she ate breakfast. Then she saw it.

> *The son of the prominent Shi family has married the*
> *daughter of the Yang family from Zhangzhou. The*
> *after-wedding party is to be held at the grand New Asia*
> *Restaurant at six p.m. on April 21, 1941.*

There were two tiny snapshots side-by-side, one of Kung Yi and the other of a young lady. Mini blinked several times and read it again. It was true. No mistaking it. She held the paper so tightly it shook. Mrs. Pao must have noticed, and she tiptoed around to look over Mini's shoulder at the smiling faces looking back at them.

"Which day?" she asked.

"Next Friday," Mini answered mechanically.

"Don't even think about going near there. You will stay home."

Mini didn't say a word. She left her breakfast untouched and went upstairs to her bedroom. Four and a half years since her own wedding, her life was back to where it had started, only worse. Now she had to live without her precious daughter.

Mini didn't come out of her room for days. She sat, weeping, unable or unwilling to sleep or eat. Ai May and her parents tried to comfort her, but quickly realized there was nothing they could do. They left her alone, and when Friday came around Mrs. Pao told Ai May to lock Mini's bedroom from the outside. Mini convinced her that it wasn't necessary to lock the door, that she wasn't interested in leaving the house. Then Mini had slipped out while Ai May was busy preparing dinner.

The New Asia Restaurant was still empty when she arrived. She waited patiently, watching the guests gradually trickle in until the noise began spilling out from within. She waited longer still, and soon a car with a large red silk flower decoration on the hood zoomed up, stopping sharply at the restaurant entrance.

"The bride and groom have arrived!" a woman's high-pitched voice called out.

Mini stood on her tiptoes, craning her neck to make out a pair of silhouettes standing near the entrance under the swaying red light. One was large and tall, the other skinny and short: Mrs. and Mr. Shi, waiting for their son and his new bride.

The chauffeur opened the car door on the right side. A man in a razor-sharp gray gabardine suit emerged. He looked down, smoothing out the invisible wrinkles on his suit before stepping around to the other side to open the door. A foot in a red high heel appeared first, followed by a leg wrapped in a fine silk stocking. Then, a fur-wrapped arm came into Mini's view. The limp white hand that came with it wore a sparkling diamond, which glittered as her hand found the outstretched hand of the man. He gave a gentle pull and a slim body emerged from the car: Kung Yi's new wife. She looked as small as a child. Her fur coat hung loose, like it would on a hanger.

She is a child. This child-woman is Mrs. Shi now, and this woman is going to raise my baby girl. This woman will tell my girl that her mother was a bad woman who abandoned her own daughter.

Mini's anger swelled in her chest. Her hands were shaking; she spread her fingers out and then balled them into fists. Her fingernails cut into her palms, but Mini didn't notice the pain. She wanted to raise her fists but forced her arms to remain tightly by her sides instead. She was afraid that she didn't possess the willpower needed to control her urge to slap this tiny woman.

This was Kung Yi's legitimate wedding, one blessed by his parents. He was marrying the daughter of a shoe manufacturer, who also owned land adjacent to Kung Yi's ancestral village. This was a proper marriage—the marriage the Shi family should have had before. Mini was sure of that.

As the happy couple approached their equally happy in-laws, Mini imagined she could hear what Mrs. Shi was surely telling her son: "We are so happy you have returned home from your wandering. Nothing is treasured more than a returned lost sheep. Forget about your marriage to Mini. It didn't really count. She was disrespectful to you and didn't know her place. We're glad you left her. The Pao family was never a proper match, and this girl from the Yang family is going to take care of you and your daughter. She will bear you many sons and daughters. She will do what you say and follow you forever, to heaven and to hell."

"I was the one who left," Mini said under her breath, though she knew she was arguing with a figment of her own imagination. "*I* left."

23

NIGHT OF SHANGHAI

After her failed attempt to enlist Mini's support in convincing Kung Yi to take a concubine, Mrs. Shi had left Mini alone. In fact, she had left Mini in peace for the rest of her postpartum confinement. When that was over, the Shi family graciously threw a banquet on their granddaughter's one-month birthday. Very few families would do such a thing for a baby girl, and Mini was extremely happy that morning. She couldn't stop humming "Scent at Night," a song from her all-time favorite singer and actress, Zhou Xuan.

Mini stopped her humming, though, when her new maid brought up breakfast and poured a cup of tea. Mini missed Lotus, who had been dismissed by Mrs. Shi for some slight or other. Mini was given Mai as a new maid, a young girl of about sixteen or seventeen. She looked at Mai with her pretty moon face. The girl seldom smiled and this morning was no different.

"Mai, you can sit down and have breakfast with me today," Mini said. "It's lonesome eating alone."

Mai bowed. "Young Mistress, thank you but I had breakfast already with the other servants."

"You're pretty, Mai. You'd look prettier if you smiled more." Mini looked her up and down. "You're about my size before I had Jing Ling. Tomorrow, you can help me sort my closet, and we'll find you some pretty dresses."

"Thank you, Young Mistress. If you don't need me, I'm going to leave. The kitchen needs me today," Mai responded with her usual expressionless face.

"You can go, Mai," Mini said. The maid was attentive, if distant and cold. *Maybe it's her upbringing. She was an orphan found in a rice field and brought up by the Shis as a maid. She probably never left their country manor until now, with nobody left to care for her, poor child.*

Mini spent hours putting on her makeup that day, and the great hall was already full of guests by the time she arrived. Each of them congratulated her for having such a beautiful girl.

It doesn't matter that I had a girl. Kung Yi's parents are so gracious to invite so many people to celebrate having a granddaughter. They forgave me, and they will give Kung Yi and me time.

The banquet was a success. Everyone was in a good mood; even Kung Yi's father smiled. His friend, a male Peking Opera singer who had perfected feminine gestures and refined singing, had performed for them. Mr. Shi had hardly taken his eyes off the performance, nodding his head in time to the music.

Kung Yi slept in his own bed that night, half drunk. He had been eager to join Mini, but she wasn't ready to resume their intimacy.

"What's the matter?" Kung Yi had asked his wife, frustrated.

"I'm sorry, Kung Yi. I don't think I am ready. Give me a little more time. I promise things will be normal again soon," Mini said gently.

"Mother was right then. She told me not to move back for another month. She said you wouldn't be ready to receive me," Kung Yi said bitterly. "I might as well go back to the guest quarters now."

"Please, Kung Yi, I only need a little more time," Mini replied, hoping to soothe him.

"I have been alone for more than three months now! First you were too big and didn't want me, then you needed to rest, and now you're not ready. I'm leaving. It's easier to sleep alone," Kung Yi said before getting up and storming out.

That next Saturday, Mini awoke early. It was her first trip to visit her parents with Jing Ling. She so wanted to be at her own home, with her own parents. Mini hadn't visited them since Mrs. Shi had taken one look at Mini's bulging belly and declared it indecent for Mini to go outside.

Mini gave the nurse a few hours off to be with her own son, instructing her to join Mini later at the Paos'. Mini dressed herself and Jing Ling, then packed Jing Ling's milk bottles and diapers. She carried the baby down to Kung Yi's suite with a cotton bag slung over her shoulder.

The house was quiet. The servants were setting the table for breakfast. Mini quickened her steps; she would convince Kung Yi to skip breakfast and join her. *A minute more in this house is a minute too long. I'd rather be with Pa and Ma.*

She knocked on the door gently—one, two, three times. To Mini's surprise, Mai opened the door.

"Oh, Mai, what are you doing here so early?" Mini asked.

"I'm ironing for Young Master," Mai lowered her eyes and bowed to Mini. "The Old Mistress told me to," she added.

Kung Yi came out from his bedroom wearing his pajamas. "Mini, you're up so early today. Oh, my sweet girl is here." He gently pinched Jing Ling on her cheek as the little girl opened her drooling mouth in a smile when she saw her father. "Mai, you can leave now. You can continue later," Kung Yi said, taking Jing Ling from Mini.

"What is *she* doing here so early?" Mini asked pointedly. "It's not like you're waiting for a shirt to be ironed."

"Mother sent her over and she can't say no, I suppose."

"Kung Yi, you should get ready so we can leave," Mini changed the subject.

"Why? It's too early! What about breakfast?"

"I want to leave soon. I haven't seen my parents for a long time. Surely you understand. Right, Kung Yi?" Mini slapped his arm playfully.

"All right, my sweet wife. I'll go change," Kung Yi relented.

He was in a good mood. Putting his daughter down on a couch, he went to his bedroom and Mini followed. On the rumpled bed, there was a freshly ironed shirt along with a pair of trousers. Kung Yi took off his pajama top and was about to put his shirt on. Mini stared, blushing. She missed the smell of his flesh and the touch of his hands. Without thinking, she reached out and touched his back. Kung Yi turned around and embraced Mini tightly enough that Mini could hear his heart beating. His hand reached down.

The baby's cry brought them both back to reality. Mini left the room to attend to Jing Ling and Kung Yi finished washing and changed to go. They quietly sneaked out the front door after Kung Yi informed his mother's maid they were leaving.

It was the first time Mini had been outside in months. She waited patiently in the crisp cold air with Jing Ling in her arms while Kung Yi walked to the end of the lane to hail a rickshaw. When they got in, Mini insisted on leaving the rickshaw curtain open despite the cold. She let out a long breath and inhaled the fresh street air. She faced out, greedily taking in the view of the lively streets.

Though it was an early December morning, the street was still bustling with people. Women in colorful quilted jackets were carrying bamboo baskets as they walked, while others noisily bargained with vegetable vendors. Other food vendors were selling boiling-hot soymilk, scallion pancakes, and fried savory donuts. Men in wool coats with fur collars and newspapers under their arms walked in confident strides on their way to teahouses. Mini sniffed the scented air and sensed a happiness she hadn't felt in many months. She held her daughter tight, pulling Jing Ling up to her chest to keep her warm as she kept her eyes glued to the streets.

"Stop!" Mini suddenly called out.

The rickshaw stopped at once.

"What are you doing, Mini?" Kung Yi asked.

"I'm hungry now. Let's stop for breakfast. There's a stand right in front of us."

"You want to eat on the street on this cold day?" he asked, incredulous.

"I want to. Please, let's eat here. Please?" Mini begged.

"All right, whatever you like." He stepped down, then turned to the coolie. "You wait here. We'll be done soon."

The sweet soymilk and fried savory donuts tasted better than anything Mini had eaten in a long time. When they were done eating, she bought two hot sesame pancakes and gave them to the coolie, who accepted the food with a deep bow. He put the packet carefully in his pocket before picking up the reins of the rickshaw and continuing on to the Pao residence.

Mrs. and Mr. Pao were already waiting for them at the door. Ai May ran and gave Mini a hand as she stepped off the rickshaw.

"Young Mistress, let me hold the baby," Ai May said. Mini handed the bundled-up Jing Ling to Ai May, who took her carefully. "How sweet your girl is! She looks just like you," Ai May crowed. "And Young Master, of course," she added.

"Ai May, come inside quickly. It's too cold for the baby," Mrs. Pao called out.

"Oh, yes." Ai May walked inside with the sleeping baby in her arms.

With Ai May cooing over Jing Ling, Mini went to the kitchen and made tea for everyone. Kung Yi chatted with Mr. Pao over the steaming tea while Mrs. Pao filled Mini in with the latest news.

"Mini, do you remember Mei Fen from the Chang family?" she asked.

"Of course, we went to the same school. How is she? I haven't seen her since my wedding," Mini answered.

"She got married," Mrs. Pao lowered her voice, "to a Japanese soldier. Your father didn't like it at all. He turned down the wedding invitation."

Mrs. Pao glanced at her husband, but he was deep in conversation with Kung Yi.

"But you can't blame her," she continued. "Her father studied in Japan when he was a student, and he works for the Japanese. It's only natural she'd marry a Japanese man."

"I don't think so," Mini disagreed. "I didn't marry an Englishman, after all, and Pa works for the British."

"Silly girl, are you joking? We Paos would never marry a foreigner. What a scandal that would be," Mrs. Pao said, shaking her head.

"How is Ling, Ma?" Mini asked, deliberately changing the subject.

"Ling is fine. She doesn't write much. I get few letters." Mrs. Pao got up and went into her bedroom. She came out with some letters, which Mini eagerly read one by one. Each was short. Ling gave no details about her life except to say that everything was fine. She didn't mention either Jie Xing or their son, Xiao Bao, and said nothing about visiting Shanghai.

"That's strange. Ling didn't say anything about Xiao Bao. How tall or big he is," Mini told her mother.

"Well, you know Ling. She was always too lazy to write," Mrs. Pao said unconvincingly. "After lunch, you'll take down a letter for me. I don't want to bother your father."

Mini reluctantly left with Kung Yi and Jing Ling after dinner. On the way back home, the neon lights of the dance halls lit up the dark sky. Shanghai's famous nightlife was just as it had been before.

They visited her family again the following Saturday. Unfortunately, Mr. Pao had a business dinner to attend and left after lunch. The day passed pleasantly, with the four of them resting quietly in the living room. Mrs. Pao sat in her chair and held her sleeping granddaughter on her lap while Mini knitted a pink baby cap. Kung Yi sat motionless on the sofa, staring at the white steam rising from a boiling kettle on the coal-burning stove, the heat source for the room. Wind was howling outside. The day had since given way to night and it was already pitch dark outside.

"Kung Yi, are you falling asleep?" Mini leaned forward to see his face better.

"No. I'm just thinking," he said vaguely.

"Thinking about what?" Mini pressed him.

"We haven't had any fun for a long time. First the war, then the baby."

"Are you suggesting . . . ?"

"Yes, tonight."

"No, we can't. We have Jing Ling to look after." Mini sighed. Though the idea was so appealing.

"Why not, Mini? The dance halls are still open." Kung Yi got up excitedly.

"So, you want to go to a *dance hall*?" Mini asked.

"I wouldn't mind."

"It's impossible. What about Jing Ling? What about the curfew? What about your mother? She won't be pleased if she finds out."

"Mother won't know. She'll be in bed by the time we're back. She was in bed last week when we returned. As for the curfew, we can leave in time to beat it. But I don't know what to do with the little one." Kung Yi scratched his head.

"Don't worry about the little one," Mrs. Pao interjected. "I will take care of her. The nurse is here. She won't go hungry. You two go have some fun."

Mini's face brightened up. "How do I look?"

"You look wonderful." Kung Yi gave her an appraising glance. Mini looked radiant in the same red qipao she had worn on Jing Ling's one-month birthday. It complemented her fuller figure.

"Which one?" Mini asked.

"The Paramount Hall, of course."

The Paramount Hall was the most fashionable and luxurious dance club in Shanghai. It was air-conditioned in summer and heated in winter, keeping it at a comfortable temperature all year long. Only the most modern of the well-heeled, young crowd could afford the entry fee. Kung Yi and Mini had gone there once or twice before the war.

"But I'm not dressed, not for a fancy place like that."

"Mini, nonsense. You look lovely."

"In that case, let's go then," Mini said, smiling.

The art deco dance hall was on the corner of a busy street in the British Concession. Its entrance was crowded with cars coming and going, ensembles of Americans, British, and Japanese in uniform, and a smaller number of Chinese civilians spilling out of cars or the dance hall. Colorful lights flashed to the quick rhythm of the music.

"Sounds like a foxtrot," Mini said enthusiastically, as their rickshaw pulled close.

"You prefer the waltz and the Latin dances, though," Kung Yi replied.

"Oh, I could dance to anything now. It's been so long since I've been, since we've gotten out to have some fun."

"Maybe the next one will be better," he said.

The girl at the door took their coats. Inside, the dance hall was dark and crowded. Cigarette smoke filled the air. One could barely see anyone's faces. A waiter showed them to a small table on the side of the dance floor and took their orders. Seated, Mini couldn't stop swaying to the music. From where they sat, they could see the pianist bouncing up and down, pounding the keys while a cigarette dangled from a corner of his mouth. The rest of the orchestra accompanied him, eyes closed or half closed, their bodies swaying back and forth languidly as they played the jazzy "Nights of Shanghai." Mini smiled. *What a wonderful place! So much excitement that we've been missing. It's as if nothing has changed.*

Seated closely against the orchestra, Mini couldn't see the dance floor properly—only the flashing of smooth, curved, silk-wrapped legs alternating with straight, sharp trousered legs, all moving quickly in time as the dancers spun around the floor. She couldn't see anyone's face without craning her neck up, and when she did, faces swirled in and out of focus too fast for her to recognize anyone. Mini took a sip of Kung Yi's scotch. A hot line trickled down her throat to her stomach. She turned her flushed face to Kung Yi and squeezed his knee under the table.

"It's been so long. I almost forgot what it's like to be here," Kung Yi said, taking the glass from Mini and lifting it to his lips. Smacking his lips, he added, "This is good. I haven't had scotch in a long time."

He finished his drink in no time and waved to the busy waiter. Ignored, Kung Yi soon lost patience, got up, and left Mini alone at the table to watch the orchestra and sip her fruity drink. When the song ended, the crowd dispersed from the dance floor, among them a woman in a sky-blue satin qipao, half-leaning on the arm of a uniformed Japanese official. Fanning herself with a white handkerchief, she giggled and said something into the soldier's ear. The man laughed, patted her rear, and shot her a lustful look.

Mini blinked, standing up as they passed her table: "Mei Fen Chang. Is that you?"

The woman stopped and took Mini in for a second. "Mini?"

Mini reached out to take Mei Fen's hand.

"Mini, what a happy coincidence! I haven't seen you since your wedding. Is Kung Yi here with you?" Mei Fen sounded very happy to see her old friend.

"Yes. He's over there." Mini motioned toward the bar with her chin. "He's getting another drink. It's our first time out since the bombing. What's wrong? Do I look different?"

"A little . . . more mature," Mei Fen laid her warm hand on Mini's shoulder.

"Well, that's because I'm a mother now!" Mini said, beaming.

"Congratulations! How old is your little one?"

Mini and Mei Fen were so drawn into their conversation, they forgot the Japanese official until he cleared his throat behind Mei Fen. She blushed and turned on her heel.

"Mini, let me introduce you to my husband."

Kung Yi returned, drink in hand. He quickly put down his drink on the table on seeing the Japanese soldier with Mini and her friend.

The man extended his hand to Mini, then to Kung Yi. "I am Lieutenant Sasaki, the husband of Miss Chang," he said in halting Chinese. "I am very pleased to meet friends of my wife. How do you do?"

"Very well, Mr. Sasaki," Mini shook his hand and met his smiling eyes. His uniform made her uncomfortable. Other than those fraught times that she crossed the city's checkpoints, she hadn't come into contact with any Japanese soldiers at such close range.

"Please call me Yoshiro. My wife's friends are my friends. Please give us the honor of joining us," he said graciously.

Mini looked at Kung Yi. He nodded slightly and picked up his fresh drink. They followed the Sasakis to a much better table with a full view of the dance floor. They sat and Yoshiro raised his hand, snapping his finger. A waiter came right away. Yoshiro ordered cocktails for the ladies and a scotch for himself.

For a while, the four of them sat there, barely talking. A few Japanese soldiers passed their table and saluted Yoshiro, who replied with a casual wave of his hand. Kung Yi's eyes met Mini's, as if to ask her who this man was. Their minimal conversation ran dry quickly. To Mini's surprise, when the music picked up again, Yoshiro invited her to dance with him. Though he was not tall, his trim body and good posture made him look much taller as he held out his hand to Mini. He was a graceful dancer. Yoshiro's strong arm guided Mini effortlessly. She stole a few glances at him, avoiding direct eye contact. Yoshiro was not so discreet, his smiling eyes focused cheerfully on her as they swirled around the floor.

The song ended and he escorted Mini to the table, only to extend his hand to Mei Fen for the next song. Mini and Kung Yi sat there and watched the two dance. Their eyes locked tight and the couple smiled at one another as he guided Mei Fen around the floor. The two didn't talk, but most of the other dancers on the floor didn't talk either.

He's really a handsome man, Mini thought. She felt happy for her friend, and for a moment, Mini didn't think of him as an occupying soldier. The couple soon returned to the table. Somehow, the ice had broken, and conversation became easier. Mei Fen confided in Mini about their romance. Yoshiro's father was a classmate of her father's at Tokyo Imperial University. That was long ago, but Yoshiro's father wrote to her father when Yoshiro was stationed in Shanghai, which was how they had met. He had been in China now for several years, though in Shanghai for only half a year. Yoshiro would come to check in on his father's friend weekly, bringing food and taking dinner with the family. Soon enough his visits became even more frequent, and Mei Fen found herself getting to know him better. She even began to learn some Japanese—at least enough for simple conversations. Yoshiro was working under Lieutenant Colonel Haruke Yoshitane, she added casually.

Mini had heard of Yoshitane—the famous counterinsurgency specialist—and of the new *baojia* system that he had implemented in rural Shanghai. Mini's father had told her about it, and how Yoshitane had turned the ancient Chinese community law enforcement system into a tool to control and spy on people, capturing anyone who opposed the occupation. Mini sipped her drink to mask her discomforting thoughts. She listened and smiled, but she understood why her father refused to let anyone go to Mei Fen's wedding. She looked at her wristwatch, then at Kung Yi, who was watching the dance floor and sipping his scotch.

"Kung Yi, it's 9:30. We have to go. We have to be home before the curfew," she said.

"No worries, Mrs. Shi. You can stay longer. I'll send you home."

"Thank you, Mr. Sasaki, but we have to leave. We have a little baby waiting for us."

"All right, but still, let me send you home." Sasaki left a few notes on the table.

A few more Japanese soldiers stopped and saluted as they passed by on the way to the dance floor.

Sitting in Yoshiro's jeep, the four of them zoomed past the sentries, the soldiers saluting along the way. They went first to get Jing Ling. Mini persuaded Yoshiro not to stop at the front door of her parents' house, afraid of agitating her father should he see them in the company of a Japanese soldier. She and Kung Yi walked inside and quickly retrieved their daughter before continuing on to the Shi mansion.

Before they parted for the night, Yoshiro invited them to visit and Kung Yi enthusiastically promised they would do so. Kung Yi helped Mini down from the jeep and held her tight against his side as they walked to the mansion gate. Aided by the warmth of the scotch, he freely caressed her waist and behind as they walked to their quarters. The couple found that their long separation had added extra spice to their lovemaking that night. It was as if they were on a second honeymoon. Kung Yi moved back to their bedroom that night.

24

MINI AND THE MAID DEPART

Nothing is forever! Mini remembered the moment when she should have realized that she and Kung Yi had no future together. She couldn't see it then.

Mini had been shattered after overhearing the gossip among the servants of the Shi household. She holed herself up in their room, wallowing in anger at Kung Yi and feeling sorry for herself in the dark. When Kung Yi came up to check on her, he walked into a storm.

"You dirty bastard!" Mini shouted the moment he opened the door.

"What's going on?" Kung Yi asked innocently. He shifted his weight from one leg to the other, his face flushing.

He knows I found out, she thought. *Mai—that little whore—she must have told him.*

"You and that tart, Mai. You slept with her!" Mini replied ferociously. "She wants me dead. I heard them talk."

Kung Yi stepped forward. He tried to pull Mini into a hug, but she dodged him and ran to the other side of the room. Her shaking hands gripped the back of the sofa. Raising her tear-streaked face, she looked at Kung Yi with contempt.

Kung Yi bowed to Mini. "Please, Mini—forgive me. I lost my head after you rejected me that night, after the banquet, when you turned me away."

"So, you sleep with a *maid*?" Mini asked. "*Mai*?"

"I'm a man and I have needs," Kung Yi responded. "She seduced me and I was weak and gave in."

"A *child* seduced you? You!" Mini laughed bitterly. "You *lie*. You don't have to have her around, and yet she's in your room—in here—every time I turn around! You've fallen for her."

"No, really. Please, Mini, she is just a lowly maid," Kung Yi reasoned. "You shouldn't be so mad. She's just a maid. Mini, listen to me—"

"Your mother did this to me," Mini cut him off. "*She* brought Mai into this household."

"Maybe. I guess she's desperate to have a grandson, even if it's from a servant," Kung Yi agreed noncommittally. "But, no, I was aware of the situation. I took precautions." Kung Yi shook his head at the foolishness of his own words and slapped himself. "Mini, please. I've never touched anyone when I've been with you. I'll send her away and I promise I'll never see her again!"

Mini stood rigid, staring at him without a word.

"Come on, Mini, let's forget this," he pleaded. "*You* are the mistress of the house. You shouldn't be agitated by a maid."

"What's Mai going to do now? You're a selfish person, Kung Yi. You ruined a young girl's life." Mini was surprised by the calmness in her voice. She was no longer crying, though she was shaking all over.

"Don't mind Mai," he said. "I'll see to it that she marries a farm-hand. Mini, you forgive me, right? I swear it won't happen again."

Mini sighed. She went to the bedroom and closed the door behind her.

That night, Kung Yi slept on the sofa. Two days later, Mai was gone, replaced by Ying, a skinny girl whose front teeth were missing.

Mini didn't leave, not yet. After all, she loved Kung Yi so much. She was willing to overlook his weakness. Forgiveness proved harder:

Though she stayed, Mini was constantly troubled by doubt and distrust. She found, too, that she was less eager for his embrace. There was no more anticipation. Each time he touched her and she gave in to his desire, she thought of Mai and felt disgust.

Nearly two years passed and Mini didn't conceive. Mrs. Shi declared that she could wait no longer: Kung Yi must take a second wife.

The next morning, Mini gathered her and Jing Ling's things and left with the wet nurse. Kung Yi followed her to the Paos', begging for her to return. Mini would only live with him if he agreed that they would move out of the Shi mansion and run their own household, but Kung Yi didn't know how to live without the support of his family.

"I can't. You know that," he said. "I have only ever worked for my parents. Mini, don't be so hard on me, please. Concubine or no, you're still first in my heart."

"No. It matters to *me*," Mini answered. Covering her face in her hands, she cried. Kung Yi surprised Mini by crying, too, but she found that she no longer cared.

It was another day before her in-laws came to claim Jing Ling.

"Jing Ling is the Shi offspring and her proper place is in the Shi family home," Mr. Shi told Mini and Mrs. Pao.

Mrs. Shi ordered the wet nurse to tear the sobbing Jing Ling from Mini. As they retreated with the little girl, she screamed for her mother. Mini begged hopelessly for them to change their minds, chasing after the car as they drove off—giving no care to the crowd of neighbors who had assembled to stare.

"Jing Ling, my baby!" she cried. "I will have you back. I'll have you back!"

When he returned from work, Mr. Pao was enraged. He phoned and visited the Shis but was told they had gone to their country home and didn't wish to see him. Mr. Pao didn't give up, despite the advice of a lawyer friend who said that the Shi family had a legal claim to their granddaughter, and that no court would rule in Mini's favor. Mr. Pao continued writing the Shis until, eventually, he reached Kung Yi himself. Mini's estranged husband wrote back, promising to let Jing Ling see Mini as often as he could manage.

Mini only saw her daughter once in the next six months—and she wasn't invited to her daughter's second birthday.

25

PURPLE BELL-BOTTOMS

"I'll study when I return," I said and stormed off to my room, closing the door behind me.

"What about your upcoming college examination?" Father called after me from the other side of the door.

I stared at a map of the world that Father had hung above my desk—a prize he had traded for some favor—and thought of how proud he'd seemed to hang it.

"It'll help you for your geography test," he had said, tacking the map to my wall. If only he had stopped at just the map, but I wasn't that lucky.

"Here," he continued. "Have I ever told you the story of Sun Jin?"

Before I could respond, he launched into the story, and I watched in horror as he unrolled yet another poster and tacked it up on the wall alongside the map.

"'Hanging from a beam and stabbing with an awl,'" he said, admiring the scene that now unfortunately plastered my wall. "See, during the Tang Dynasty there was once a young man who came from a poor family. He didn't have tutors to help train him for the court examinations the way the children of wealthy officials did. But he had a good mother and father who encouraged him to rise up and become a high official. So, he studied and studied, never leaving his room—in fact he studied so long in his room that his hair began to grow longer and longer. He insisted he would not cut it until he passed his examination. It grew so long that if he didn't tie it up, he would trip over it when he went to the toilet—the only break he allowed himself.

"Now one day as he was getting close to the examination, he decided he couldn't sleep. He didn't have enough time, you see. So, he left his room and walked out of his family's little home for the first time in years. His parents were naturally curious and followed him as he walked to his father's workshop off the side of the house. This work-shop is where his father built widely sought-after furniture. Even the local governor had sought him out during a tour of the local area—he was that famous! But that's a story for another day.

"So, Sun Jin goes to his father's workshop and digs around until he finds what he wants and walks back to his room. He walks right past his parents without any explanation. They shrug their shoulders, wondering to themselves what he could have wanted from his father's workshop. They knew better than to prod. Their son was *that* diligent.

"Later that evening his mother walks into her son's room to bring him his dinner. '*Aiya!*' she screams and drops the plates of food she was carrying. The sound of his mother's screaming and the break-ing dishes startled Sun Jin, who was sitting on the floor as he always did—back in those days they didn't use desks like you have now, you know—concentrating on his studies. Do you know what startled her so? Picture this: Here's this grown man in his flowing Tang robes sitting cross-legged on the floor, his hair wrapped around the beam of the ceiling. Can you imagine?

"And that wasn't all: In one hand he held his quill and in the other an awl—an awl from his father's workshop. You see, he had taken that awl so that he could poke at his leg whenever he felt sleep com-ing on! If that failed and he fell asleep anyway, once he started to nod off, he would yank his hair that was tied to the beam, which would jerk him awake. *That's* dedication! He studied like that day and night, sacrificing his sleep. When his exams came around, he received the highest possible marks and went to the capital to work for the emperor. That's where the saying 'Hanging from a beam and stabbing with an awl' comes from."

I knew the story already. Father had told it to me before, too many times, but all I could see when he hung the poster was this guy stabbing at his bloody leg with a pointy awl, his head pulled back, his hair tied to the rafters, and his mother walking in on this scene of creepy self-flagellation. *No wonder she broke the dishes*, I thought.

"Now, I don't want you to not sleep," Father continued. "You need to sleep, too, but maybe Sun Jin will give you some inspiration to study hard."

"He was from the Han Dynasty, not the Tang," I said when he paused for my reaction.

"See? That's why you will be the first in the family to go to college."

I knew better than to respond to that, because I was sure I knew exactly what he would say. I'd heard it many times before. Actually, I wouldn't be the first in our family to go to college. Great-Grandfather did and so did Father, who got his college diploma by attending night classes. He insisted night school didn't count.

I shook at the thought of the poster. I took it down the next day when Father was at work, but it still sent chills down my body. I couldn't see the inspiration in it. To me, it just looked like some feudal torture scene.

The school year started Monday. It had only been five days so far, and between school and my parents I was already stressing out. But today was a Saturday, and a shorter school day, so Mien invited me over after school.

"We can study the latest fashions in your magazines and maybe do some dress-up," she said.

That was our favorite thing to do to pass the time. I had just received some outfits Grandma had sent me and I looked forward to showing them off to Mien's friends, who would be there. But for now, I had to listen to this. Sitting at my desk, I closed my eyes and tried to tune out Father's voice—only succeeding in recalling that image of Sun Jin staring back at me.

College entrance exams are a year away, I told myself. But that only made me feel more depressed. It was just the first week of school and already I was tired and overwhelmed.

Our homeroom teacher opened the first day of school with a long speech.

"This is a critical year for you students. At the end of the school year, you will take college entrance exams. These are not like the final exams you have taken at the end of each year so far. The college entrance exams will draw on everything you have learned in high school. The exam is difficult, as you all know. The acceptance rate is less than one in one hundred. Last year, we had two students who passed and went on to college. We didn't have anyone go to a top college last year. That's unacceptable."

He paused for effect before continuing:

"We expect you to do better this year. You all must strive harder. The number of college acceptances reflects on our school—represents the quality of education in our school. Everyone *must* contribute, and the way you students can contribute is by studying hard and mastering every subject."

He rapped his finger on his desk for emphasis. The room was silent.

"You can do it! The party is behind you! We teachers will do our best to prepare you!" he added, pausing again. I guess he didn't want to scare us too much. "Are you ready?" he shouted. "Are you ready to *work* hard, *defeat* your exams, bring *glory* to our school, and bring *honor* to your families? Are you ready?!"

We pumped our fists in the air and shouted, "We are ready!"

But I didn't feel that I was ready at all. As I looked around at the excited faces of my classmates, I wondered: *Their confidence, is it real?* They seemed as if they had already passed the exams. *How can I compete with these people?* I lowered my head again, discouraged by my own thoughts.

I felt a bit better after hearing Mien and her friends mock the teacher when school let out that day.

"Those teachers, they're so nervous they won't make their quota again this year," the daughter of a party member said. Everyone agreed.

"It's so far out of everyone's reach. Why bother to study?" a girl asked.

I nodded, but my mind wandered. I knew what they were saying was probably right, but failing the exam wasn't an option for me. Father and his expectations were one thing, but I also didn't have any well-connected relatives in the party to get me a job after high school. I couldn't get my head around what I would do if I didn't go to college.

I thought of my neighbor Tai Pao. He was working now. I hadn't seen him since school ended, when he failed the college exam and was assigned an apprenticeship inspecting and maintaining machinery at a cement factory on the outskirts of Shanghai. He was still technically working in Shanghai, even though the factory was far from the city and required him to commute long hours each day. It was a good job. I was sure it had something to do with his parents being party members. I didn't know what it meant to work on factory machinery, but Tai Pao wasn't happy about it until he learned that several girls from his class had been given jobs at the various textile mills around the city.

"So, it could be worse," he had said.

I had wanted to feel bad for him then, but somehow, I knew he was making a dig at me. Thinking now of my own chances, and my parents' background, I winced. Tai Pao was right. This time next year I'd be spending long days running kilometers around some mill, replacing spools and fixing tiny breaks in fine thread while trying to avoid losing a finger to the machines weaving thread into fabric.

So, I didn't really need any reminders from Father right now: Studying was the only thing I thought about, day and night. The only good thing to come of it was freedom from doing chores.

"Your number one job is to study hard," Father had said when he relieved me of responsibility for my usual chores. He sounded like one of my teachers.

A knock interrupted my brooding. I had forgotten that Father was still lecturing me through the door of my bedroom.

"I'll study. I promise you!" I shouted.

"Leave her alone. Just let her try her best," I heard Mother say.

I waited. No more knocking came. I smiled as I listened to Father walk away. I so wanted to get out of there, and I remembered why I had come home in the first place. I reached under my bed and pulled out my magazines. There was nothing like them anywhere in Shanghai. They were from Grandma. They were her husband's, she said. They could help me with my English, and I could learn something about America. She had been sending them for two years now.

I had been studying English since my first year in high school, but when I first opened those glossy pages, I couldn't make out anything. I mean, I understood some of the words, but none of it made sense. A caption was the most I could figure out. I tossed them aside then, dejected. But later I let myself just flip through the pictures, and I saw such an odd world, full of so many things I had never seen before—exotic landscapes and people doing things I couldn't even imagine. Many of the people were dressed in such vivid colors and styles. Styles of clothes that I didn't know what to make of. Soon enough, I managed to make out the celebrities from the captions and I showed them to Father.

"Wow," he chuckled at a picture captioned as a singer named Madonna and some guy. "Fashions have changed. I'm not sure you'd catch me with someone like her even if I lived in America," he chuckled some more and flipped through the magazine, pausing at an elegant picture of Princess Diana from England.

"Your mother was quite fashionable when we were young," he remarked. "Well, things were different then."

"Really?" I remembered Mother's reaction the first time I received a magazine in the mail.

"Ting, stop wasting your time with those magazines. They're useless here. Look around you. So wasteful! See, look at the price of postage!" She stabbed at the postage on the big brown envelope with her finger to emphasize the point. "Translated to yuan, this is half my monthly salary. She should stop sending magazines and send a check instead. I'd make much better use of the money than magazine postage."

I tried imagining Mother as an English princess, but I couldn't.

Afraid Mother would tell Grandma to stop sending the magazines, I was quick to write back to her in America, thanking her and telling her how much I learned from the magazines. They kept coming.

I couldn't shake the pictures. They were like windows to a different world. I took the magazines to Mien's house, where we would spend hours studying celebrities with her grandma's magnifying glass. Looking at the pictures, we would fantasize about dressing up and walking down our gray Shanghai streets.

Mien was different. She was very popular in school. Her good nature and nonjudgmental way of dealing with people meant she always had a handful of friends over at her apartment after school. She always made an effort to include me, and once I began bringing Grandma's magazines over, suddenly I was more popular with the other girls too. Now with my new clothes, I was certain to be the most popular girl in school.

I smiled at the thought.

I pulled on my purple bell-bottom pants and a form-fitting floral shirt with a large pointed collar. Grandma had recently sent them to me, along with another top. Hong Kong fashion, she had written in the note with the box. Clothes like these were popular with the Chinese girls in Hawaii.

I stood on my bed looking at myself in the mirror on my dresser. I saw a skinny girl with two pigtails in a Hong Kong rock star outfit. I struck a pose, mimicking the fashion models I saw in my magazines. I shook my pigtails loose, letting my hair reach my shoulders. Satisfied, I gathered a stack of *Time* magazines and walked out.

Father had left and Mother was knitting alone in the big room. She lifted her head, glanced at me, and said, "Ting, why'd you let your hair down? You look older. I don't like it."

"I'm going to Mien's."

"No, you're not, not in that. That outfit of yours will land you in trouble. Grandma should never have sent it. She doesn't know how we live here. Never wear it in public."

"Why? I won't wear it to school. Today is Saturday," I said dismissively. "I haven't been out all week."

"I suggest you don't wear it anytime," she replied. "I can have Aunt Fong adjust the pants and the shirts to make them wearable for you. What do you say to that?"

"No, Mother, I'd rather keep them the way they are. It's the fashion, don't you understand? I don't want them altered."

"What fashion? What are you talking about? You look ridiculous."

"Hong Kong fashion, of course," I said coolly. "Mother, you don't know anything. All you know is Mao's suits." I rolled my eyes.

"Suit yourself," she responded, also cool. I could tell Mother was very annoyed with me, but she pushed no further. She shook her head and went back to her work.

The sun was bright outside. People were looking at me. I felt good. I was the center of attention for once. Head high, I walked fast with the magazines under my arm, the English cover purposefully in view. I made it a few streets further when, about one block ahead of me, I heard a woman screaming and a man yelling. Public humiliation of class enemies wasn't the norm anymore, but I continued a bit more cautiously, just in case. I walked closer so I could see better.

A huddle of older women in blue cotton outfits and wearing red party armbands had formed a circle around a young couple. The girl was scuffling with one of the women. At one point she seemed to break free, only to fall into the street. The others managed to grab her. One held her down fiercely while another old woman bent down and cut the woman's tight red pants down the sides with a pair of scissors.

"How dare you! How dare you!" The young woman screamed, sitting in the street, her pants in tatters around her legs. By now a crowd was gathering to stare.

The old woman shouted back: "This is a lesson to you for following Western capitalist fashion!"

The others laughed. The man, who had been wrestling with two of the other women, took advantage of the distraction to abandon his companion and run off with his pants intact. As she watched him flee, the young woman sat there, choking on her own tears. Her face was red with humiliation.

The assembled crowd joined in whistling and laughing at her.

The old woman who held the shears turned and addressed the crowd: "Now you learn a lesson. We Chinese don't need to dress like Westerners. Westerners are capitalists. Their fashions will corrupt you."

My stomach turned as I watched the woman's self-righteous face lecturing the crowd. I never made it to Mien's that day. I backed into an alley and returned home, all the while checking over my shoulder in case someone had followed to report me. I got home safe, but the moment shook me.

When I arrived back home, Mother barely looked up from her knitting, asking casually, "Oh, back so soon?" She said it in such a way that I knew she didn't really expect a response. I didn't want to give her the satisfaction of telling her why I was back or what I had seen. She didn't say anything else, either, just a knowing "humph" as I walked past her and went quietly into my room.

I closed the door. After sitting on my bed and staring at myself in the mirror, I retied my pigtails and changed into my school clothes. I took out a book and started my math exercise. There was a knock at my door. It was the soft, kind knock of my mother.

She opened my bedroom door and placed a bowl of rice with a fried egg on top and a warmed glass of milk on my desk. "Eat. You need a lot of nutrition to give you more brain power and to improve your memory."

I accepted the food quietly without thanking her. I ate and continued with my math. *Maybe Father is right. Maybe college is my only way out.*

One year. That's all. I can make it. I have to.

26

COLLEGE BOUND

I was napping at home and wasn't sure just who or what I had heard. Whatever the sound had been, it was followed by Mrs. Yung's voice.

"What is it?" she asked.

"Scores from the college exam," someone answered her. "Everyone gets them today."

The mailman! I realized with a start.

I bolted up on the couch, wiping off the sweat that had beaded on my forehead, listening intently, still groggy from my nap in the agonizing afternoon heat that couldn't be broken by a fiercely oscillating electrical fan only a few feet away.

"I can get it for her," Mrs. Yung said.

"I'm home! I'm home! I can get it myself!" I cried out, realizing they weren't just voices in a dream, but the voices of my neighbors.

I opened the door to the mailman, and Mrs. Yung standing behind him. She flashed me her fake smile.

"Oh, I thought you were out with friends," she said, stealing a glance at the sealed envelope.

I ignored her, only taking the mail and closing the door. Should I open it? Should I wait? I sized up the envelope, seeing if its shape or markings would give me some clue as to my fate. I placed it on the table and considered it a bit longer. I thought about leaving it for Father to open and read for me, but I had second thoughts.

I want to know before . . . If today is the day, then they may already have heard . . .

Before I could even straighten out my jumbled thoughts, I was tearing open the envelope. My heart was pounding and my sweaty hands shaking, seemingly disconnected from me as they struggled to remove and open the single folded sheet of paper.

My heart skipped a beat.

Yes! I'm going! I'm going!

I was bursting inside, but afraid of uttering the words aloud. I wanted to yell, to scream to the world that *I was going to college*, but a perverse notion took hold of me that if I did so, fate would retract my good fortune like a cruel joke. My emotions ranged from trembling anxiety to jubilant disbelief and back again.

Did I read it right? I placed the letter on the table and smoothed it out, reading it again carefully to assure myself it was real, that I read it right.

> *Congratulations! You have passed the national college entrance exams and are accepted into the college of your first choice. Your major will be assigned to you by the college based on your test scores. The college will contact you to provide further information.*

It then listed out my individual scores for each subject. I read it again. That was it. I didn't know yet what the sentence about the major meant, but right now it didn't matter. I paused, taking it in. I felt a sense of calm, a physical certainty I hadn't felt before. *It was real.* With that thought, my body relaxed.

Fudan. I'm going to Fudan. Not even Father could've imagined that.

I ran outside to the local phone booth, passing Mrs. Yung and Mrs. Yi by the kitchen door.

They both yelled after me, "Are you okay? Did you pass?"

"Yeah!"

All I wanted at that moment was to phone my parents; I couldn't wait for them to return home. I was so proud. I wanted to make them proud—especially Father, who had put so much pressure on me. I could hear his excited voice in my head: *You're the first, the first in the family to go to college!* I wouldn't argue with him this time.

That night, Father insisted on going out to celebrate. At that time, the restaurants were still few, and going to eat at one near the Bund was a real treat. Unless Grandma was visiting, we never ate out.

Mother suggested we call Grandma after dinner. I hesitated. It was likely a month's wages just to eat at a restaurant on the Bund. I knew calling her would be nearly as expensive. I promised to write to her. But Mother was happy and insisted that it was okay, Grandma would be happy to hear the news.

It was a short walk from the restaurant to the Peace Hotel on the Bund, home of the only international long-distance phone in Shanghai. Mother gave the number to the clerk, who ran it and directed us to wait in booth number five. The three of us squeezed into the tiny booth and closed the door. The telephone rang. Mother looked at me and I picked up the receiver quickly.

"Hello? Hello?" I yelled into the phone. I hadn't written Grandma for a year because I hadn't wanted to give her false hope. Now I was calling her.

"Ting? Is that you? What's going on? Is someone sick? Is everyone all right?" Grandma asked urgently on the other end of the line.

"No, no," I reassured her. "We are all fine."

"Good." A pause. She must've been wondering why we had called then, if it wasn't an emergency. We had never called her before.

"Mother wanted me to call because I received my college exam scores. I did well. Grandma, I'm going to college." I tried to deliver the news calmly, but I could feel my heart jumping in my chest.

"Oh! I am so happy. I knew you could do it. I am very proud of you."

I closed my eyes and saw her bright smile.

"Thank you, Grandma." I didn't know what else to say. I opened my eyes and looked at Father. He beamed at me. "Yes, I am very happy, too," I added.

"Ting, you will come to America. Graduate from college and then come here to continue your studies," she said at the other end.

"What?" I asked, confused. "Grandma, I don't think that's possible. Plus, I can learn just as much here as in America. I'm going to *Fudan*, Grandma, here in Shanghai. It's a top university! One of the best in the world—they say it's better than any you can go to in America *or* in England. So, you see, I don't need to go to America anymore."

"Ting," Grandma raised her voice, her tone stern. "You will study in *America*. You hear me?"

Mother took the receiver from my hand.

"Mother," she said calmly, "we can talk about Ting's future later." She paused, then, listening. "Yes, we are very happy that she is college-bound. Listen, we have to go. Goodbye!" She hung up briskly.

I wasn't ready to think about my future beyond college just yet. I never really had. College was the destination. Being a college graduate would already set me apart. Why worry about the future? I wouldn't be working in the city mills! I had a bright future waiting for me, though I had no idea what that would be.

It didn't matter what came after. I didn't need America anymore. I had proved I was better than all the popular girls, better than everyone in my school, better than all the other kids in my neighborhood. I couldn't wait to tell them all, and I spent the rest of the evening planning how I would visit everyone in the neighborhood—everyone in my class—and tell them.

Yet, when I woke the next morning, I didn't have any desire to see anyone. I woke instead to an embryonic feeling that I couldn't explain. I had done it. Everyone was proud. I was proud. But what it meant now that I had achieved the goal I'd worked so hard for, I had no idea.

I didn't go and see anyone that day. Instead, Mother gave me money at breakfast and told me to catch a movie.

I had two choices at the cinema, and I picked a detective story from Japan, one the censors had so mutilated that the dialogue didn't make sense and I'm sure I missed any number of clues. I didn't care, though. It was better than the alternative, which was a documentary about Chinese-Cambodia relations that I safely assumed was propaganda. So, for eight cents, I enjoyed the few hours of air conditioning and took my mind off everything I had thought about in the days and months that had come before.

I didn't see anyone the next day, either. In fact, I never did see anyone from school after that, other than Mien. She was leaving to visit her paternal grandmother in Beijing and would not come back for a few weeks before taking up her work assignment.

27

YOU NEVER KNOW WHEN CHINESE HISTORY WILL COME IN HANDY

TING, SHANGHAI, 1985

Weeks later, at the end of August, I was withering under the scorching mid-morning sun. We had reached Fudan University on the outskirts of the city. After a near-suffocating two-hour bus ride east, we got off at a dusty construction site where they seemed to be simultaneously digging and laying new road. Others got off at the stop with us and we all trudged up a dirt path for another twenty minutes. The saplings' autumn leaves fluttered, teasing us with the promise of shade, but provided no respite as we walked beneath their almost-barren branches. When we reached the Fudan gate, Father stopped to ask for directions.

My hands full of luggage, I couldn't wipe the dripping sweat from my forehead and so shook my head instead, letting the droplets fall to the ground and mark the dirt path leading up to the gate. My arms were tired from carrying my overstuffed bags, but I knew Mother would have a fit if I set them down in the dirt.

"Almost there!" Father shouted. I stared at his sweat-soaked back as he tried to lift his arm to point and managed to raise only his shoulder. He pointed with his chin to a monstrous gray building several hundred yards in front of us. Father's jerky awkwardness was silly, but his cheer was infectious. The heat hadn't dampened his enthusiasm and I picked up my pace to catch up with him.

Finally! We reached the building and stepped inside to a dim foyer. Although it was only marginally cooler inside, it was a relief to get out of the sun. As we stood there waiting for our eyes to adjust to the darkness, I noticed I could *feel* this place. It was alive, as if vibrating with an unseen energy. I put down my bags to take it in. I listened to the excited voices around me. I looked up the large stairway in front of us and down the two long corridors stretching right and left. I thought of the hotel that Grandma took us to for lunch on her last visit. The foyer in which we were now standing was Spartan by comparison. It made up for its austere simplicity with a sheer cacophony of voices echoing off the walls in every direction. It had none of the quiet formality of the foreigners' hotel, and I liked it.

I followed Father, who had broken off from us and approached a middle-aged man in a gray polyester shirt. He was sitting at a large wooden desk by an open door to the right of the grand stairs. He was studying several sheets of paper spread out in front of him while his free hand absentmindedly fingered an unlit cigarette tucked behind his ear.

Father cleared his throat to get the man's attention. "Please, Comrade, my daughter is moving in today," Father said. "Can you please let us know which room she is in?"

The man looked up. "Oh, you are one of the lucky parents. Let me see your paper. I need to check the list."

"Thank you, thank you for your compliment. Here is the paper," Father said, smiling broadly as he looked down at me. He had heard such compliments often over the past summer, and he still beamed in response to each one. Now, with the light from the man's desk lamp reflecting off Father's glistening face, he looked even happier. He carefully took the notice from his breast pocket as if it were a fragile treasure. I was so embarrassed by his shameless display of care that I involuntarily turned, as if to hide, and silently watched behind Father as the man read the paper for what seemed like a long time. Frowning, he put the notice on his large desk, put on his eyeglasses, and moved on to the long list on his desk. He flipped through the list several times, stopped, tapped his pencil on the desk, and looked at the damp notice Father had handed him again.

My name isn't on the list, I thought. *This is all a mistake. He's going to tell us the university didn't accept me after all.*

"Your daughter's room is number 417 on the women's floor," he said finally. "It's at the top of the staircase. Go upstairs, and then go down the right corridor."

The door to Room 417 was half open when we got there. Mother nudged the door open with her foot and we filed in with our baggage. There were two sets of bunk beds against two walls opposite each other in a long rectangular room. Another family had already beat us to the room. A slim middle-aged woman was kneeling on top of the top bunk to the left of the window. Upon seeing us, she stopped with her arms outstretched, sheet in hand. She stayed frozen like that for a moment, as if embarrassed at being caught in an unsightly position. Mother nodded, as if breaking a spell, and the woman quickly composed herself, nodding back. Mother surveyed the room with a brief look and put my bedding on the bunk below. The woman had already picked the most desirable spot in the room—by the window, where her daughter would get most of the breeze in the summer and most of the sunshine in the winter.

Her daughter, a young girl in a pink cotton dress, was fussing around with nothing in particular while a balding man with an important air about himself was arranging two large thermos bottles on the table under the open window. *Had Mother packed my thermoses?* I wondered. Earlier, I had tried to convince Mother that I wouldn't need much, but she would have none of it. When I had caught her packing two tall hot-water bottles, a big washbasin, and a few jars of home-cooked meat sauce, I quietly rebelled and put them back. At least I *thought* I did. Mother had caught me returning the meat sauce and stuffed the jars back into one of my bags.

"Cafeteria food is notoriously expensive and bad," she said. I didn't argue with her.

Now I was regretting that I had taken out the hot water bottles. As if reading my mind, Father moved the girl's thermos bottles to one side and replaced them with mine. They had made the journey with me after all.

"Comrade, my daughter's bottles are already there," the middle-aged man's voice rose as he spoke. "You can put yours next to hers."

"What if I put my daughter's *in front* of your daughter's?" Father asked diplomatically. "That way, they can both access their bottles if they need to without getting up from bed."

"Well," the man replied tersely. "Your daughter is taking the *bottom*, so it is easy for her to get up if she needs to."

I moved my bottles without a word. I hated when Father fussed like that. The girl winked and smiled at me. I smiled back.

She stepped forward and extended her hand. "Hi, my name is Ming Cheng, but my English name is Maggie. You can call me Maggie. I'm an English major."

I took her hand awkwardly, still uncertain about what was expected when shaking hands.

"My name is Ting Li. I'm a history major."

"How interesting! I will be a translator. What do history majors do?" she asked.

She seemed genuinely interested, but I had no answer. The college had assigned my major to me. I would rather have studied Chinese literature if anyone had asked me, but they didn't. I mumbled something about going on to graduate studies after, remembering Grandma's comment and realizing at the same time it wasn't really an answer.

"Really?" she asked incredulously. "You must be so smart!"

"I like your dress," I said to change the subject.

"Thank you!"

She was pretty with delicate features and fair skin. She was tall, several inches taller than me. Her straight black hair was loosely held in a ponytail by a ribbon of pink satin. Her pink dress was bright in the sun streaming through the window, and the hem swayed with her every movement about the room. With her red leather sandals, she looked quite striking in contrast to the gray concrete floor and walls. I must have seemed shabby beside her in my standard white short-sleeved shirt and navy blue knee-length skirt.

"You're also Shanghainese," Father interrupted. "You can both go home together on weekends," he added a little too excitedly.

"Yes, that's a good idea," Maggie's father added.

He then introduced himself and his wife, who had by then finished with Maggie's bedding and climbed down from the top bunk. After chatting politely for a while, Mother and Father left reluctantly, but not before they had made my bed, put away my clothing, inspected the big communal washroom on our floor, and purchased my food vouchers in the cafeteria—where they scrutinized that night's dinner menu on the blackboard. They insisted on touring the entire grounds over my futile protests that it was still much too hot out.

Father only stopped once we had come full circle and reached the gate where we had first arrived.

"Ting, goodbye," he said. "Study hard. Please be sure to visit on weekends. You're not far from home."

"It's okay, I'll walk you to the bus stop and see you off," I insisted.

But they were just as insistent and turned to leave me at the gate. A hint of sadness overcame me as I squinted into the glaring sun and watched until they disappeared from my view. I told myself it was silly to feel this way, but I didn't know why.

I sat on a bench under the trees. It was getting late. The sun was lower, and a breeze had picked up since I had arrived with my family at the gate earlier in the day. The little trees whispered, their shadows dancing in the late afternoon sun. Many more people were passing through the gate loaded with luggage, new students with their parents and siblings, even grandparents. The students usually walked empty-handed as their family carried their bags and cheered them on through the campus gate.

I realized that I was new to everyone and everything. High school and old friends were behind me. I was entering a new world and starting a new life.

I returned to my room only to walk in on Maggie finishing an animated story she was telling two other girls. Maggie's hands gesticulated wildly as she tried to describe something or someone. One of the new girls was still putting some things away in the room, laughing at Maggie's antics.

The new girl was short, slim, and had an unusually narrow face. Her long black hair was tied into a ponytail that nearly reached her waist. The other girl watched from the top bunk, smiling down at Maggie with bright eyes. Maggie stopped her story to introduce us. The short girl with the narrow face was called Ying and the girl on the top bunk was Xia. They were language students, too. Ying was studying Japanese and Xia was studying English, like Maggie. Maggie thought this was funny, three language students in one room and one Chinese history student.

"What an odd arrangement," Maggie said, laughing.

"No fair. I'm outnumbered!" I joked back.

"Well, we'll see, won't we? There are eight of us girls, aren't there?" Maggie asked, pointing to the still-unclaimed bunks.

"Anyway, Ting, I now dub you an honorary language student, like us! What do you girls say?"

"Of course," Ying answered.

"And we may need you," Maggie added. "You never know when Chinese history will come in handy."

"And you all can teach me how to talk to the foreign guys I just saw," I said.

"Foreigners, in our dorm?" Xia asked. There were more foreigners in Shanghai every year, but they remained a fairly rare sight.

"Yeah," I replied. "Three of them—guys. They came up the stairs with me talking in some language, and then they turned down the hall on the floor below us. You can't miss them."

"They can't let them in here," Ying said.

"Are they Americans?" Xia asked.

"Oh, maybe they are Americans who teach in the English department," Maggie answered proudly.

"No, they're African, I think," I said.

"African? What do they look like?" Maggie asked.

"They're black, of course," Ying said. "Now you're the one being silly."

"No, not all Africans are black," I corrected her. "At least, in magazines the Egyptians aren't black."

"That's not Africa," Ying said.

"Sure it is. It's in North Africa," I replied.

"Those are Arabs, not Africans," Ying insisted.

"Come on, so what do they look like? Are they black, or what? What were they wearing?" Maggie pressed.

"Yes, they're black. I don't know what they were wearing. They looked normal enough," I said, uncertain.

"They can't be African then. All the Africans wear really colorful shirts and they have these beautiful rainbow-colored hats," Maggie explained.

"Not them. Maybe they're from somewhere else," I said.

"Blacks aren't allowed to go to college in the US, so maybe they're Americans," Ying guessed. "Maggie, you and Xia can practice English on them!" she teased.

"Maybe I will," Maggie answered cheekily.

"Come on, let's go see. We're sure to find them. Everyone was watching them."

"We can't go down there. That's the boys' dorm," Ying said.

"Sure we can," Maggie insisted.

"No, the dorms are separate," Ying insisted. "They can't come here and we can't go down there. We can go and wait on the stairs for them to come out."

"That's so obvious," Maggie chided.

"So what? You've never done that before?" Ying asked.

"What do you mean, hang around waiting for a foreigner to come out of his room?" Maggie asked. "No. I've never even spoken to a foreigner before."

"I tried once, when I was in high school, but my English wasn't good enough to carry on," Xia answered, surprising us.

"Have *you*?" Maggie asked me.

"No, but I've seen foreigners before, at the airport and hotels, anyway," I added.

"You've been to a foreigner hotel?" Xia asked. "They don't allow Chinese unless you're an important party official."

"Wow, who would've thought? Somehow . . . Oh, I don't know, I don't know what I thought," Maggie said. "What was it like?"

"I've been to two hotels," I boasted. "They were both beautiful, very grand. One even had a fountain inside. Everything is polished so much that you can see your own reflection. And the lobbies are big, like I don't know, as big as an auditorium. You walk in and they have chairs and couches all around and once you sit down, you sink in them, they're so soft. If you sit long enough, someone will come to you and offer you tea and cake. You have to pay, of course. The cakes are delicious! Like nothing you've ever had before."

"So, can you take us there?" Xia asked.

"I don't think so. My grandma took us. She's from America. When she came to visit last time, she took us for lunch and Mother liked it so much that my grandma took us back just to sit and have tea and cake in the lobby."

"What, your grandma is American?" Ying asked. "Wait, I'm confused. How can your family be party members then?"

"They're not." I shook my head vigorously. Father was a supervisor at a state-owned transportation company who had been passed over for a promotion many times because he wasn't a party member.

"Ying, you assume only children of party members can enter the top colleges. That's no longer true," Maggie said.

"Go back to the hotel," Xia interrupted. "How did you get in if your grandma wasn't staying there?"

"I just followed my grandma. Nobody even asked a question when she walked in. The hotels have these tall, grand doors and there's a man, actually a couple men in hotel uniforms, and when we walked up to the door, they just opened it for us."

"Just like that? You walked in?" Xia asked.

"Well, with my grandma and my parents," I said.

"So, did you talk to the foreigners?" Ying asked.

"No, not at the hotels, anyway. I talked to one at the airport once. He was an American."

"Ting! I don't believe it!" Maggie exclaimed, excited. "Come on, let's go wait for the Africans downstairs."

"Not me," Xia said.

"Come on, Xia. Don't you want to see them?" Maggie pressed.

"No, go ahead. I'm sure I'll see them eventually."

"Let's go," Ying said.

The three of us walked downstairs. A number of students, mostly guys, were milling around on the third-floor landing.

"Hey, what's going on?" Maggie asked one of the guys.

Ying elbowed me. "Is that them?" she asked, pointing.

"Yeah," I confirmed.

"Can any of you girls speak Arabic?" the guy asked.

"She knows about Egypt," Maggie said, pulling me forward.

"I can't talk to them," I said quickly. "Anyway, I don't know Arabic."

"They're from Africa," the guy said.

"Somalia. They're our Communist brothers," another guy explained.

"You're right, they dress pretty ordinary," Maggie whispered to me. "But that other guy is cute."

She meant the Chinese guy who was with the foreigners. The three guys I had seen on the stairs were hunched together with a tall Chinese student outside one of the rooms, grinning and making hand signals. The rest of us watched them, not knowing what to make of these foreigners in our building.

"It's one thing to see them, but to have them live in our dorm, just one floor away from us?" Ying said, voicing my own hesitation.

"They're not," a guy answered her. "They're in a special dorm for foreigners on the other side of campus."

"So what are they doing here?" Ying asked.

"They can visit, of course," the guy said, shrugging his shoulders.

Maggie had no fear. "I want to meet them," she said. "Who's the guy they're talking to?" She pointed to the tall Chinese student.

"Ni Ming."

"That his room?"

"Yeah."

"Okay, not much to see. I'm going back," Ying said.

"Don't you want to meet them?" Maggie asked.

"If they're on campus then you're sure to run into them. Not like you can miss them," Ying replied.

"Seriously? They're from outside China!"

"I don't even know where Somalia *is*," Ying said.

"Ask them. I dare you," Maggie teased. "What about you, Ting, are you gonna ask them?"

"Me?"

"Yeah, you know all about Africa."

"No, I don't."

"I'm just joking. Well, if you girls aren't going to talk to them, then let's go. Let's get Xia and walk around campus."

I'll admit, I was curious. Maybe not so much so that I was willing to walk up to them and try to strike up a conversation. I thought about the foreigner I met with Grandma at the airport, and the others that I had seen come off the plane with her and at the hotels. I was so awkward when Grandma came out of customs with that big American man—he even tried to shake my hand. She was so natural talking to him, laughing even. I looked at Maggie laughing, leading the three of us as we walked around campus. I thought of Grandma, wishing I could be more confident and outgoing, unafraid of anyone and anything.

28

WHEN IT'S
BETTER TO LIE
AND DANCE THE
NIGHT AWAY

TING, SHANGHAI, 1985

Maggie held a large mirror up in front of me. But instead of looking at my own reflection, I looked at her. She was striking as usual in a black mock-turtleneck sweater under a bright red ski jacket. No ponytail today. She wore her black hair loose on her shoulders, contrasting with her fair skin and pink cheeks.

"Hurry up," Maggie said playfully.

I quickly pulled on a new green sweater that Mother had recently made for me. I combed my short hair, looking at myself in the mirror.

"What do you think? Do I look okay?" I asked.

Maggie nodded approvingly. "Your mother did a great job. The sweater fits you so well."

"Not too plain?"

"You look *good*."

I looked at myself again in the mirror and smiled back.

"Let's go then. Tong Tong, sure you don't want to come with us?" I asked our roommate, a quiet girl from the Anhui countryside, and the only one still in that evening. She had been quietly studying as we dressed. I knew what the answer would be but asked anyway.

"No, go ahead. I'll see you when you return," Tong Tong answered.

"Okay, if you get bored, come join us in the cafeteria. Okay?"

Tong Tong nodded as I pulled on my faded gray wool overcoat.

"You gonna dance again with that guy from the political science department?" Maggie asked as we left.

I shrugged. "Maybe."

"He had his eye on you last time. He's not bad looking."

I looked at her. "He's too serious. Not my type. But if he wants to dance, why not?"

"I bet he offers to take you on a ride around campus," she said, squealing with delight as she mimicked him steering a bicycle.

"Ew!" I said and punched her in the arm.

"I'm just saying . . ."

"Keep it to yourself then!" I said in mock-disgust. "How about you and Ni Ming. You get a ride yet?"

"Soon," Maggie said shamelessly, "and he won't give rides to other girls after that."

Maggie and I had become fast friends over the past four months. I didn't have much in common with her—or any of my roommates— but it didn't matter. The great thing about college was how little we talked about where we came from. I mean, I knew Maggie was the niece of a famous Chinese opera singer in Shanghai, the only daughter of a district government chief, and that Tong Tong was the daughter of peasants who lived in a mud house somewhere in the countryside in Anhui. But otherwise, who our parents were, what we did, or who we were before didn't matter, because at the moment our lives were so full of excitement that we hardly looked back as we ran toward the future—whatever that was. Maggie stood out, though. She wasn't merely indifferent to my background or, like others were, studiously avoiding the past. Like her compliment about my sweater—she may not have worn it herself, but she was quick to find good things to say. It was the same with people: She often found some quality I didn't see. She liked showing me how to use a scarf to add color to a gray sweater that Mother had knitted, but not before praising Mother's handiwork. Maggie was refreshing that way, and her confidence was infectious. I felt so much more modern, as if I were playing out the fantasies I'd had back when I pored over my grandma's magazines and played dress-up in the clothes she sent. That was me now, real, a college girl—sassy and sophisticated.

Tonight, we would be dancing! The parties at college were frequent, and I had learned some basic dance steps from Maggie. I looked forward to escaping the monotony of my studies as we got close to finals. Maggie had heard about the dance party the day before and told me over dinner.

"Tomorrow night, here in the cafeteria. You'll come, right?" Maggie asked. It was more a statement than question. "Ni Ming will be there," she whispered in my ear.

When we arrived at the party, a contraband tape of Teresa Teng's "The Moon Represents My Heart" was playing. Officially, the school had banned her songs, along with other pop songs from Hong Kong and Taiwan. It was soft, spineless music that would weaken our revolutionary spirit, the school explained. The ban didn't stop us from listening, and Teresa Teng and her ballads were a favorite at these dances. The girls liked her sweet songs of love and the guys enjoyed it because the slow tempos gave them an opportunity to hold girls a little closer.

Maggie saw Ni Ming at a table by the wall, surrounded by several girls who were flirting with him. He looked over as we came in and waved to Maggie with a slender hand holding an unlit cigarette. Maggie made a beeline for him. I watched her and hummed along with Teresa Teng's lilting voice.

Maggie leaned into Ni Ming, apparently sharing some witty comment as they both laughed. The other girls lingered a little longer only to trail off one or two at a time.

Ni Ming was a law student. "The most handsome guy on campus," Maggie had said once. She had a crush on him since meeting him weeks earlier at a different dance. Although I suspected she had had her eye on him since that first day when we saw him outside his dorm talking to the three foreign students. You couldn't miss him around campus. He'd take girls for a ride around campus on the back of his bicycle, though never the same girl twice. I didn't have the guts to say hello to him even though he was just one floor below us in the dorm. I was sure he'd never waste a glance on me, plain girl that I was.

Maggie looked over and I winked. She smiled back and I turned to take in the crowded room. What was an ugly cafeteria by day had been transformed tonight into a makeshift dance hall. Tables were pushed to the side and stacked on each other. More people were coming in. The guy from the political science department that Maggie had mentioned earlier wasn't in sight. *Just as well,* I thought. Instead, another guy I didn't know came up and asked me to dance. He looked especially nerdy with his glasses and boyish face. *The evening is still early*. I shrugged and went with him. *I'm going to enjoy myself.*

Soon he had me swirling to a fast waltz. When he asked me to dance to another song, I found that I was actually enjoying his lead. He moved on when another guy cut in at the start of the next song. The evening passed quickly like that, as I danced and danced, forgetting everything in that steamy cafeteria until, instead of a guy tapping my shoulder for the next dance, I turned around to find Tong Tong behind me.

"Wow, Tong Tong, you came!" I said smiling. "Isn't this fun? Take off your jacket and we'll get you someone to dance with."

She shook her head. "Your mother is here looking for you."

"What?!" I stopped and my dance partner left without a word.

"She's outside. Come on, quick. It's cold."

A sharp December wind whipped at my face as I pushed the door to the cafeteria open. Mother's dark shadow stood a few steps away, arms crossed as if she were hugging herself, feet stomping as if dancing deliberately out of step with the music still audible from inside—a cadence I immediately recognized from our time standing together in lines to purchase our rations.

"Ma, why are you here?"

"Don't you have a jacket? It's too cold to go around in just a sweater," she said.

I looked down at myself, realizing I was sweating from all the dancing. "I left it inside. Ma, come inside? It's warm in there."

"No, I prefer to talk," she said, looking at the steamed-up doors to the cafeteria-turned-dance hall. "It's quieter out here."

"Okay, but it's too cold to stand outside. Let's go to my dorm. There's no one there but Tong Tong. Let me get my jacket." I disappeared inside and reappeared moments later with my jacket in hand.

"Put on your jacket. You'll catch pneumonia and you won't be able to study," she said when I didn't put it on immediately.

"I'm not cold Ma. I'm sweating."

I felt irritated and braced for another admonition. She silently hugged my arm to herself instead. Her affection was enough to melt my annoyance, and in its place, I felt guilt creeping in. I took her arm and gently led her to my dorm. I hadn't been back home for four, maybe five weeks—I couldn't remember. I hadn't phoned either. At first it was the dread, but as the weeks passed, I had simply forgotten to check in. At that moment, though, I realized that I had missed her motherly touch, and slowed down to enjoy the warmth of her arm linked in mine.

When we reached my room, Tong Tong was back at her desk. The room was lit by a bare light bulb hanging from the ceiling and a small desk lamp, one of the few personal possessions Tong Tong had brought to school.

"I'm going for some hot water for tea. Would you like some?" Tong Tong asked.

"No thank you. It's getting late," Mother said. She sat quietly waiting, looking around the room until Tong Tong left to fetch the hot water.

"Why haven't you come home for so long? Your father and I are worried," she finally said once Tong Tong was gone. "We miss you."

I looked down at my lap. I knew this was coming, but still I didn't want to face her and have her see the guilt on my face. After the excitement of college, home was so boring. *Why haven't I come home? No grand philosophical discussions, no stimulating friends, and no dancing. It's always so boring. No, I don't miss home. I'm having fun here. I have nothing to talk to Mother about and I'm tired of Father's endless interrogations about college.*

I wanted to say what I really thought, to get it off my chest, but I didn't. When my friends and I had talked one night about what we missed most, I said I missed Mother's delicious cooking. I wasn't the only one: It was a common theme that night. Sitting there and facing Mother, I thought that was really the only thing I missed, and not even that much. I knew it was wrong to feel this way, but it was true.

"I'm busy with finals," I said. *Better to lie.*

"But you were dancing away," she said, not backing down.

"I'm sorry. I've been so busy. I needed to break up my studying for a bit." I gave her a quick glance.

She looked intensely at me and simply sighed. "I came because I wanted to make sure you're okay," she said. "Now that I see you're doing okay, I want to tell you your grandmother is coming. She arrives in four weeks, and I want you to promise me that you will be home for her as often as you can."

"I'll be home. I get a break for Chinese New Year," I said impatiently, hoping to end the awkward conversation.

"Yes, but she will stay longer than the three weeks. Please come home every weekend, for her," my mother repeated, insistent.

"Mother, you came here on such a cold day just to tell me that?" I asked.

"Yes . . . and I wanted to see you," she said, reaching out and swiping a stray hair away from my face. Once again, I felt my icy heart melt at her touch. I took her cold, coarse hand in mine and squeezed it gently.

"I have to go," she said. "I came from work and Father will be waiting."

"Tell him I miss him," I said. "And I'll be home soon, after exams."

"Let me take your laundry," she insisted. "You can pick it up on the weekend, have lunch, and go right back."

"Ok, Ma."

I turned off the overhead light, leaving Tong Tong's desk lamp on and walked mother to the bus stop over her protestations. It was cold, but the wind had died down and I held Mother's arm while we waited silently for the next bus. When it came, I stood back and watched as she stepped onto the empty bus. She was not yet forty-five years old, but she looked tired. I noticed her white hair and remembered holding her coarse hands and seeing the shadows in her lined face. I suppose she had been that way for a while, but it was only now, watching her board the bus in the dark, that I appreciated how much she had aged. Mother climbed up the bus steps with difficulty, her hands full with a bag of my dirty laundry.

The excitement from the dance hall had long since dissolved. In its place, I was filled with guilt. I didn't go back to the dance, instead returning to my semi-dark room lit only by the small lamp over Tong Tong's desk. Tong Tong hadn't returned, and so I sat on my bed, staring at the vague outline of the hot water bottles and washbasins until I fell asleep.

29

WHAT HAPPENS AFTER DIVORCE

Heavy rain hit the window rhythmically. It was only five o'clock in the afternoon but the darkness outside was complete. I sat on my bed, fully dressed as if to go out. Even so, I shivered in the unheated dorm room. I pulled my bedding over my legs as I considered where to start. The end of my first semester was fast approaching. In a week, I would have five finals and then winter break.

The eight of us were quiet, all of us studying for finals, until Xia broke the silence.

"It's dinnertime. Anyone want to go to the cafeteria with me?"

"I'm ready," replied Maggie.

I looked out through the window. "It's pouring and cold."

I wished I were home. Mother would serve piping-hot chicken noodle soup without me lifting a finger.

"We should all go. It's not going to let up and once the cafeteria closes, you'll go hungry," Maggie said.

I rolled my eyes.

"It's unbearable studying overnight when you're hungry," she insisted. Maggie always made sense, but I was too comfortable in my warm bed to head out into the cold.

"I can bring you something if you want," Xia offered.

"If you don't mind," I said. "And you can take my raincoat."

Xia always liked my fashionable yellow raincoat, a gift from Grandma. She smiled and removed the coat off the hook. Everyone else left and I returned to memorizing my notes on the dynasty that gave us Confucianism.

I was in the middle of my note review when Xia returned with my dinner. "Old Tang at the front desk told me your mother is on the phone," Xia said as she put the food down on the table.

"Oh? Thanks for the rice. You didn't have to come back so quickly," I said.

"It's ok, I just had noodle soup. They're all chatting, and I wanted to get back. You should go before Old Tang hangs up on your mother."

I grunted, put on my shoes, and went downstairs to Old Tang's office. He pointed to the phone without prompting.

"Your mother," he said and turned back to warming his hands with his tea.

"Hello, Ma, why are you calling?" I asked, hurried. "You know I'm busy now. I was just about to eat my dinner. Now I have to eat it cold."

Mother's voice was faint. "Hello, Ting?"

In my mind's eye I could see her making the call from a storefront in the open air, shivering. "Why are you calling in this pouring rain? You must be getting wet."

"No, Ting, I'm still at work. I'm sorry to interrupt. I called because your grandmother—she will arrive this Saturday. Will you be able to go to the airport with us, to welcome her?" she asked.

"I don't think so. I have an exam early that morning. Tell Grandma I'll try to come home once my exam is over. I'll *try*. I have no time until I'm finished. I can help with the New Year after that," I replied.

"I'll tell her," Mother hesitated. "I'm sure she'll be disappointed, but she'll understand. Don't worry about the New Year. Your father and I will take care of everything. You just come home after you're done with your exam."

I *wasn't* worried. I hadn't given New Year's a thought until then and I knew they would take care of everything. "Okay, Ma. I've got to go. I have a lot of studying to do."

"Bye, then. Good luck on your exams." I could hear her sigh. When the phone clicked, I nodded my thanks to Old Tang and went back to my room.

Xia was still alone in our room when I returned. I picked up the rice and began to eat.

"Thanks again," I said.

"Sure. Everything okay?"

"Yeah, my mother can be annoying," I responded. "My grand-mother is coming to visit for the New Year and she called to remind me even though she already told me weeks ago. She wanted me to go with them to pick her up, all the way to the airport! I don't have time for that. It's a long wait and then once I go, I'll have to go home with them and everything. My day will be shot."

"This is your grandma from America?" she asked.

"Yeah. My only grandma. It's her first Chinese New Year with us. It's kind of a big deal for her. She hasn't celebrated it, at least in China, for more than thirty-five years."

"You miss her?"

"Yeah, I guess so," I said. "I miss her stories."

"That's nice."

"Yeah. Are you going home this weekend?"

"For sure, I need to help out," Xia said.

"But your studies," I replied. "Even with finals?"

When Xia didn't respond, I imagined my own parents running around buying food and otherwise spending late hours in the com-munal kitchen preparing dishes. I looked forward to those dishes as I finished off my cold rice bowl. Xia made me feel a little guilty for not going to the airport or helping out. She went home almost every weekend to help her mother or to tutor her younger sister. I looked over at her. She was by then absorbed in her studying again. Xia was a puzzle to me. She never talked about her family and, to this day, nearly five months after living in the same room, I still didn't even know where she lived. It wasn't as if we ever talked about it, but somehow her silence around the rest of us was different. She didn't talk to anyone much.

Tall and broad, Xia was as big as a lot of the guys here. Her straight aquiline nose, bright eyes, and delicate skin seemed to instantly attract the eyes of guys around her. Yet she never showed any interest. As far as I could tell, all she did was study. *She didn't show interest in anything,* I realized as I thought about it. *Well, that's not true. She watches us, watches when we talk, watches when Maggie tries on a new shirt, watches when we discuss music smuggled from Hong Kong, or who has a crush on whom.*

I shrugged and went back to memorizing facts about the ancient dynasties from my Chinese textbooks and notes. That's what it would come down to. Finals would be little different than any other exam I had taken: a test to see how many facts I could regurgitate. Fortunately, I found I enjoyed history a lot more than I thought I would. I was actually learning where the Han people came from, who Confucius was, and how Confucianism almost didn't survive the early dynastic struggles. It gave context to some of the early Chinese poetry and stories Father had read to me.

Funny, I thought, *I look forward to telling him.* I hadn't felt that way in months.

That week and the next were tedious with studying and exams. But time moved quickly and before I knew it, it was the last day on campus before winter break. I didn't bother going home to see my grandma that weekend. I planned to call, but then I was in the middle of exams and then, well, I forgot.

Now with exams over I could rest, and I was in no hurry to leave. I sat on the bed in my heavy sweaters and thick socks, holding a cup of hot tea and chatting with Maggie while Xia smiled and listened. Ying had just left for home. Tong Tong was still making the rounds, and when she returned, she let in the sound of indistinct whispers from the hall.

"Hey, what's going on outside?" I asked, too lazy to get up.

"A foreign lady is coming upstairs."

"A foreign lady?" Maggie and I repeated together.

I got up to see for myself. As I did so, I saw the foreign woman herself, stopped at the open door to our room.

My mouth dropped open.

"Grandma! Ma! Pa!"

Behind them, a swarm of people—cafeteria workers, the cleaning crew, and students had gathered.

Grandma was dressed impeccably in a light green embroidered satin Chinese-style jacket and a pair of black woolen pants. She carried an overcoat, slung casually over one arm, and she had covered her hair with a colorful woolen scarf. Standing in our open doorway, she towered over me. She looked so much younger than her seventy-one years would suggest.

She smiled. "Well, aren't you going to invite us in?"

"Of course. Grandma, why are you here?" I heard hushed voices from the group of people behind them. I sensed my roommates surrounding me at the door.

Grandma stepped inside, her pleasant scent filling the room as she scooped me into her arms. "Your mother said today is the last day of school, so I decided to give you a surprise. I've got a taxi waiting outside. I hope you're all packed."

I struggled free from her embrace, embarrassed at her public affection. I stole a glance at the bag on my bed and nodded.

"Go get your things then," Mother said.

I grabbed my bags and darted for the door, leading them out. In my rush, I wanted only to get away from the scrutiny of so many people, and I entirely forgot about Maggie, Xia, and Tong Tong.

"Wait," Grandma said, stopping me in my tracks. "Aren't you going to say goodbye to your friends?" She nodded to my roommates politely.

I turned around and mumbled an introduction. "This is my grand-mother, visiting from the USA."

Tong Tong and Maggie came forward and shook hands with Grandma. Xia smiled at Grandma, nodding slightly and then taking a step back to rest her hand on the desk under the window. *How odd the way Xia looked at me*, I thought as we were leaving moments later. *No, she's looking at Grandma.* Xia's lips had parted a little and her pretty face had turned golden when she stepped into the sunlight coming in through the window. The intensity in her eyes, however, made it seem as if she were somewhere else.

"Goodbye. Enjoy New Year's!" I said to everyone and grabbed Grandma's arm to lead her out.

Once we reached the taxi waiting for us outside the gate, I thought of the long walk to the bus stop and an idea came to me.

"Grandma, can we give my friends a ride? Tong Tong has to go the train station. It might be hard for her to get on the bus with all her luggage. She's been eating a five-cent vegetable dish every day to save money and bought loads of stuff for her family with the money she saved. She's from the countryside, you see," I explained.

"No problem," Grandma said. "Go get them . . . as long as they fit in the car."

I ran back and announced breathlessly, "Hi girls, who needs a ride?"

"Me!" Tong Tong jumped up. She grabbed her bags with haste, giddy at the opportunity.

"Maggie, come on, don't be shy." I took up Maggie's bag and looked at Xia, who was staring absentmindedly out the window. "Xia?"

She smiled back at me briefly but turned to look outside. "No, it's okay. I live close by and I don't have much to carry. I will take the bus."

"You sure? It's so crowded. The taxi is comfortable," I said. "It's free, you know. My grandma will pay for it."

"Thank you. I'm sure," she demurred again.

Xia looked back at me then. Her face was red by now and she looked as if she was blushing or close to tears. I never understood her, and so I didn't insist. Maggie, Tong Tong, and I ran downstairs and out the gate to the waiting taxi. The taxi driver somehow managed to put all our bags into the trunk and we climbed into the back of the taxi. Grandma was already sitting in the passenger seat. Tong Tong, Maggie, and I piled in on top of each other next to Mother and Father in the back seat and off we went. As we took off, I realized I didn't know how we all would have fit if Xia had joined us.

It was nice and warm in the car with the six of us, even if the seats really were uncomfortable and we were much too squished. The three of us students sat quietly. No doubt Maggie and Tong Tong were listening, as I was, to Grandma chatting with the driver in her old-fashioned Shanghai dialect, her language stuck in a time decades away from us.

At the train station, the three of us tumbled out. Tong Tong thanked Grandma, patted my shoulder, and said goodbye. "You're lucky to have a grandmother like that," she added before running to the platform with bags in tow.

I saw admiration in her eyes as she said that. *Was I lucky?* I wasn't sure. I didn't know how to articulate what I thought. I wanted to agree that Grandma was indeed great, but she was also so far away, and I had seen her only three times in my life. I had been looking forward to my break and sleeping in as much as I'd been looking forward to seeing her. I climbed back into the taxi and sat on Maggie's lap until we dropped her off on our way home.

After a feast of a dinner, Grandma and I settled into Mother and Father's bed in the front room. I was content to rest there, my stomach full, without talking. In the quiet of the house, my dorm seemed far away. My mind eased back to home and Grandma after months of thinking about anything *but* home. I felt sleep coming, and the story she had told me when we were in this same bed on her last trip came back to me.

I bathed in a flood of vivid images of war, of a family I never knew huddled in a dark storeroom, of the Japanese sentries and checkpoints that Grandma had navigated, and the birth of my mother in the middle of all that. *How did they survive it all, especially Grandma, after divorcing her husband?* I had seen many images of the war and could imagine all of that, but divorce? No one ever divorced in China, certainly no one that I knew of. It just wasn't spoken of. The idea of Grandma's life after her divorce was such a vague abstraction. Thinking of this, I was surprised to find myself wide awake and staring at the ceiling, eager to ask her what happened next. I listened to her breathing quietly beside me.

"Grandma?"

"Yes, dear?"

"Grandma, what happened to you after your divorce?" I finally asked.

30

BACK WHERE THEY STARTED

MINI, SHANGHAI, 1941

The Mahjong tiles were silent. Mini coming home had brought an end to that. The clicking and the endless chattering gossip had been replaced by a perpetual quiet.

Mrs. Pao was too ashamed to bear her friends' glances, some sympathetic, at Mini when she greeted them or helped Ai May serve tea and dim sum. Like any curiosity, they said nothing, but Mrs. Pao felt it all the same. She was considerate of Mini, for the most part, but the difficulties their household faced had increased and, with them, the tension at home. It didn't take much for Mrs. Pao's mood to change in the gloom. She alternated between self-pity and anger.

"Kung Yi is a good man. You were *fortunate* to marry him," she would start. "You wouldn't have lost him if you put your own pride aside. So what if he took a concubine? You'd be the first wife and the boss of her! Now it's too late."

Mini could ignore these comments. Others were harder.

"Shame, Mini. You brought shame to this family," Mrs. Pao might say instead. "I don't have the face to see anyone anymore. My friends are laughing behind my back."

In these moments, Mrs. Pao would pull out a silk handkerchief from under her arm and wipe her eyes. How to respond when—cloistered at home, friendless—Mini's mother blamed her for the shame that had befallen the family? Mini didn't argue, just simply lowered her head and tried hard not to cry. She had written to Ling once for comfort, and Ling responded with a few sympathetic lines, but that was it. Nothing about Xiao Bao or Ling's life in Suzhou to distract Mini from her circumstances.

Mini took on knitting work in the neighborhood to feel useful and earn extra cash. It didn't bring in much, but it was her way of showing her parents that she didn't want to be a burden. She didn't mind it; she even found that knitting day and night gave her some solace. It helped take her mind off her daughter. She passed her days like this with her mother and Ai May, quietly waiting until Mr. Pao returned in the evening. Their only visitor was a haggard woman who would come daily to their gate and beg for rice.

Until one day after lunch, when Mini and Ai May heard someone jiggling the doorknob to the gate outside. The two were methodically hanging freshly laundered sheets out in the yard. Mini was holding one end of a sheet while Ai May twisted the other end to squeeze out the excess water before hanging it on the line to dry. They both looked at the door.

"Who could that be?" asked Mini, puzzled.

"Aiya! I gave the beggar lady rice already," Ai May declared, marching to the gate. "I'll be just a moment, Mistress. I'm not giving her any more. Once a day is enough; rice is hard to come by."

Ai May yanked the door open violently, only to be reduced to silence by whatever she had seen. Mini pinned and then smoothed the sheet on the line, and when by the time she had finished Ai May hadn't returned, she called out, "Ai May, what's going on?"

Ai May didn't respond. Mini lifted the hanging sheet and could see that the door to the gate was still open, and Ai May was just standing there. On the other side of the threshold stood Ling, staring back at Ai May, waiting in silence.

"What's going on?" Mini asked. It took Mini a moment to recognize her sister. "Ling! What are you doing? Why—why are you wearing that peasant's outfit?"

Mini rushed to the gate. She stared at Ling, dressed in bleached, gray cotton pants and a tunic. She held two large parcels. A snot-caked, dirty little boy, his eyes set wide apart, stood close to her, his hand gripped tightly to her shirt.

"Ling! Oh my God, Ling!" Mini cried out as it dawned on her why Ling was there, and in such a state. "Come in! Don't just stand there."

"Mini, I am back—for good this time." Ling struggled to smile, instead breaking into tears.

Mrs. Pao called out from the house. "What are you two doing out there? Why all the noise?" She shaded her eyes with her hand, trying to see what the commotion was about. Startled, she made her way over to Ling as fast as her tiny feet allowed. Mrs. Pao reached out and pulled Ling into her arms.

"Ling, oh, Ling . . ." her voice broke.

"Forgive me for showing up like this, Ma." Ling broke loose from her mother's embrace and bent down to the little boy. "Go. Say hi to your grandmother," she said, pointing to Mrs. Pao.

The little boy looked around but stood rooted where he was.

Mini picked the boy up. "Xiao Bao, you are much taller."

He looked at her with his flat, empty expression.

"He doesn't understand, Mini," Ling said matter-of-factly.

Mini held him tight and, accentuating every word, said, "I am your aunt. Do you remember me?" Hot tears rolled down her cheek. Xiao Bao touched her wet cheek with his little finger and put it into his mouth.

A coolie knocked on the open door to get their attention. "Miss, your luggage," he said.

With the coolie's help, Ai May carried a large, intricately carved wooden trunk, Ling's only luggage, down from the rickshaw. It was an heirloom Ling had taken as part of her dowry when she left her childhood home.

"Where to, Mistress?" Ai May asked.

Mrs. Pao hesitated. "Upstairs, Ling's old bedroom."

She looked at her mother, who avoided her gaze. Mini knew. *Just like me. Poor Mother, poor Father.* Mini felt a lump in her heart weighing her down and expanding, her stomach queasy, lost in her dizzying thoughts. *What did we do to deserve this? They thought they'd be happy when Ling and I married well. But now . . . How's father going to take it? Why did we both end up like this? If I hadn't . . . Was I wrong to be so uncompromising? If only I wasn't so proud. Ma is right. I should be with Kung Yi and his family.*

Mini fought the urge to cry and busied herself with the little boy, carrying him inside and cleaning his face and hands. She changed him into his pajamas and put him down to sleep in Ling's room before joining her mother and Ling in the sitting room.

The three women settled into silence, remaining like that as the hours passed. The only sounds in the house were Ai May's footsteps as she went back and forth between the kitchen and dining room preparing dinner. Darkness gradually descended, and Ai May lit a dim lamp that cast a faded orange glow over the room. Ling kept to herself. When Mini occasionally glanced over, she couldn't tell whether Ling was still or crying. Her sister seemed to hide in the shadows. Eventually the quiet was broken by the familiar sound of a rickshaw stopping. Ling snapped to attention and stood, waiting. Just as suddenly, she dropped to her knees when Mr. Pao entered.

"Father, your useless daughter has returned home," she cried.

"What? Ling, is that you? What's going on here? Come up, please. No need to do this. Please get up." Mr. Pao bent down and rested his hands on Ling's shoulders. "Tell me what's going on. Why are you dressed like this?" Ling hadn't changed since she arrived.

"Oh Pa, I am sorry that I brought shame to you. I should've listened to you." Ling's voice was trembling.

"Ling, you are home now. It's okay. It's okay. Where's Xiao Bao?" he asked.

"He's here," Ling said.

"He's asleep," Mini added. "Upstairs."

"They threw us out. I'm sorry. I had nowhere to go," Ling continued.

"As long as your mother and I have a mouthful of food, I will not see you and Xiao Bao starve," Mr. Pao said.

Mini stayed in Ling's room that night. She told her story of Kung Yi and the Shis to take Ling's mind off her own troubles. Ling listened quietly, interrupting occasionally to ask a few questions in her low, soft voice. The sisters held each other tightly, sobbing. Both were overwhelmed by sorrow for their shared misfortunes. They could hear their mother sob downstairs, but neither of them spoke of her or their father. They were ashamed. Mini dared not speculate on how their father felt. They had failed him.

It took a long time before Ling told her story. When the Japanese invaded, she and her household had left Shanghai to join Jie Xing's family in Suzhou. But Jie Xing returned almost as quickly: He had to manage the family business. It started out at first with just small slights and critical remarks—her in-laws blaming Ling for Xiao Bao's condition. After the first night, they had refused to eat with the boy. Seeing him struggle to eat only reminded them that their only grandson was now mentally incapacitated.

"I cannot bear to see my grandson," the Wang matriarch had declared.

That statement marked the end of Ling's appearance, as well. From then on, she tried to live in the shadows. Ling was careful to not get in anyone's way. That wasn't enough. When everyone had given up any hope that Xiao Bao would return to normal, Mrs. Wang all but banished Ling and Xiao Bao to their quarters. Jie Xing's first wife cut off Ling's allowance. Ling remembered the bitter exchange clearly.

"I don't need to waste a dime on you and your *retarded* son. Both of you are useless to the Wang family," she had announced.

"I still have a chance to have another healthy son," Ling argued.

"Stop dreaming," the first wife had sneered back. "You think Jie

Xing will ever desire you again? You're a widow, except your husband is still alive."

"You are in the same boat as me," Ling answered. "No better—"

The hard hand of Mrs. Wang across Ling's face was her only response.

Ling ate leftovers in her room with her son from that point on. Not long after, Ling sold her jewelry and furs for the money she needed to clothe herself and Xiao Bao and pay for decent food. She took on sewing jobs for money. Her aunt, the matchmaker, felt terrible. She tried helping, initially—though she, too, was shunned and was only allowed to send some treats for Xiao Bao through the back door. Her husband also lost his favor with the Wang patriarch when Xiao Bao was disowned as the heir.

"Why didn't you write and tell us?" Mrs. Pao cried.

"Ma and Pa, I didn't want you to see what I was going through," Ling confessed. "I didn't want you to worry."

"Why didn't you tell me?" Mini asked.

"I didn't want to. You had your own troubles. What could you do, anyway?" Ling said in her soft, calm voice. She had resigned herself to her fate.

"Oh, Ling," was all Mini could say. *Ling is right. What could I have done to help her?*

"Why didn't your uncle and aunt say anything?" Mr. Pao asked, angry. "They never mentioned your . . ." He searched for the appropriate word, but ultimately gave up.

"Pa, don't hold it against them. I pleaded with them to not say anything," Ling said. "I thought I could stay there forever. I didn't think my in-laws would be so heartless to their own grandson." She broke down.

"I'm sorry." Mini reached out and took Ling's hand in hers.

"What did Jie Xing do?" Mrs. Pao asked.

"He disappeared. Busy in Shanghai with his business. He said he deferred to his first wife on all household decisions. In four years, he only showed up over the holidays and he always stayed with his first wife. He wouldn't bother to say hello to me or our son." Ling buried her face in her hands.

"Bastards!" Mr. Pao pounded his fist on the table.

"They cannot return you like this," Mrs. Pao protested. "There is no justice. I will have a word with them."

"Ma, they can. I am nothing to them. They gave me some money and that was the end of it," Ling said, resigned.

As if life had come full circle, the Pao family was back where they started. No one ever mentioned again what had happened. Each member of the family focused on the present. Ling helped Mini get more knitting work and took up sewing as well. Ai May pitched in whenever she could, as did Mrs. Pao.

Shanghai had held on to its veneer of calm in the four years since the Battle of Shanghai. It was what had ensued in the capital at Nanking, in fact, that continued to hang over Shanghai. Memories were still fresh of the gruesome ways the Japanese had slaughtered hundreds of thousands of innocents in Nanking, and the memories became fresher with each retelling. Everyone had either seen themselves or knew someone who had seen the corpses floating down the Yangtze River—pulled daily from the river's mouth after the Japanese captured Nanking.

Life went on, but the fear ran deep. By November 1941, rumors returned of a new Japanese offensive. The cold of late fall was pressing in, but Mini felt there was more to it than that. Her father stayed longer at work and was quiet and preoccupied after he returned home. It was one such evening when Mini opened the door to her returning father and, instead of going directly to his study after changing into his house robe, Mr. Pao sat down among the ladies in the sitting room and asked Ai May to bring tea. They looked at him, wary whenever he changed his routines. Mr. Pao cleared his throat.

"Mr. Robinson has asked whether I would move to Hong Kong," he finally said.

"Why?" Mini asked.

"The war in Europe isn't going well. The Germans continue to advance. The British are too stretched to give any support to China. Many British have left Shanghai with their families for Singapore or Australia. Mr. Robinson thinks the Japanese will take over all of Shanghai sooner or later. He thinks it would be better for me to move to Hong Kong."

"So, the rumors—" Mini started.

"Master, we will follow you wherever you want to go," Mrs. Pao declared before Mini could finish.

Mr. Pao was quiet for a while, his brow knitted with worry. Mini wished she were a man. She wished she could share her father's burden.

"I gave a lot of thought to the offer this afternoon. Our livelihood is here, in Shanghai. I cannot imagine uprooting my family and moving to an unfamiliar place," Mr. Pao said. "Also, I cannot imagine selling our properties in such a short time. They are worthless now."

But Hong Kong can give us an opportunity to start all over without shame. I can go to a new place where no one knows me.

Mr. Pao continued, "Our best option is to remain in Shanghai. I am too old to start all over again. Mini, come see me after dinner, please."

"Yes, Pa."

He picked up his tea then and left for his study. Mini had been worried about her father for a while now. Often, he returned to his study after dinner, closed the door, and stayed the whole night there, sleeping alone on the couch. His salt-and-pepper hair had turned completely white over the course of that year. His face was covered in deep lines, his once-proud posture was now stooped, as if the weight he carried on his shoulders was too heavy.

Mini blamed herself. *If only our life could be the same as it was, when the four of us were under the same roof and the house was full of laughter. I try my hardest to do what I can, but nothing seems to relieve the burden. Father only stoops more, stays withdrawn in his study longer. What little I can do is insignificant compared to what Father is facing. I know nothing will be the same ever again. And Mother, she's all but stopped talking. I have to do more or . . .* Mini couldn't bear to think the rest of the thought her heart was telling her. Tonight, she wanted to reach out to her father, to have a heart-to-heart talk—to redeem herself.

When Mini went to his study after dinner, she was surprised to find her mother and sister in the anteroom to the study, sitting silently on the couch. Both gave her an expectant nod as she passed through to her father's office. Mr. Pao directed Mini to the chair facing his simple wooden desk. Mini sat down, avoiding his eyes. She looked over his shoulder to the two Chinese calligraphy scrolls hanging on the wall. Mini had never paid much attention to them before. One told of a horse leaping a thousand *li*, and the other spoke auspiciously of good fortune and happiness. She shifted in her seat and glanced to the side, taking in framed maps of Britain and China. She felt as if she were avoiding something, and when after a while her father still hadn't said anything to break the silence, she turned to look at him, his face in the shadows. A single desk lamp spilled its dim light almost in a perfect circle over the desk, where his hands rested on a stack of paper. He spoke clearly.

"Mini, the reason I wanted to see you is that I want you to make a promise to me."

"Father, I will do anything you want me to do," she said firmly.

"I want you to promise me that you will take care of Ling, her child, and your mother *in case*," he emphasized, "anything happens to me."

"But why? Nothing will happen to you, Pa. What are you talking about?" Mini's heart had started racing when he'd spoken the words.

"Nothing will happen, most likely, but I don't know what the future holds. I have decided that I am not moving. I am too old to start all over. I will stay in Shanghai no matter what. Many of my colleagues have gone to Hong Kong, Singapore, or Australia already. I have no ties there. My life's work is here in Shanghai, but I also know that Shanghai will soon fall to the Japanese. That means I will lose my job, and maybe worse, since I work for the British. Mini, you are the only one who has the ability to shoulder the responsibility of our family. I know it isn't fair to you, but you are this family's only hope."

"Things won't be so bad," Mini said, desperate to reassure him. "You'll be all right . . ."

"I hope so," her father said. He paused for a moment. "Our British tenants are moving to Hong Kong. I just got word today. Most foreigners are leaving Shanghai. We will have no rental income for a while. Times are hard enough. Our rental in the Chinese territory still lies in ruins from the bombing. Building materials remain impossible to obtain. Even food, as you know, is hard to come by. What's available on the black market costs more than I can afford on my salary alone. And our circumstances are certain to get more difficult. This war is not ending soon, and it will take a long time to find another tenant."

"Pa, things will be fine. Ling and I will take in more sewing and knitting work, and I will watch expenses."

"Even so . . . Mini, can you please give me your word?"

"Yes, I promise," Mini complied. "Oh Pa, I just want you to know I am grateful to you and Mother for taking me in, for taking me back. I want to do something to help—help you and Mother . . ." She couldn't finish. Her emotions overcame her and Mini started sobbing.

Mr. Pao stood and reached over, putting his hand on her shoulder. "Mini, it's not your fault. It's my fault. I failed you and Ling. I should have prevented Ling from marrying Jie Xing, and I should have found a better family for you, a family that suits you," he said and sighed.

"Pa, don't say that. It's our fate."

"No, I was useless in finding you two suitable husbands," he insisted. "I was too proud, and your mother was right. I never liked bringing up the marriage of my daughters to my friends. I felt like I was putting you on the market for sale."

"Pa, please," Mini pleaded.

"I was always afraid that you—no, that *I* would be looked down upon. I never had the family background that my friends have. I was a coward. It was my fault."

"Please, Pa, don't blame yourself." Mini sobbed harder.

Mr. Pao got up and paced back and forth in the dimly lit room. "I am useless," he said. "Marrying one daughter to a scoundrel and the other to a spineless man who couldn't take care of anything in life. They ruined you both. *I* ruined you." His tears were visible to Mini now. It was the first time Mini had seen her father cry.

"Please stop. Please, Papa," she pleaded. "What happened has already happened. I want to help, Pa—please let me. I will do anything you want me to do. I will look after Ma, Ling, and Xiao Bao. Tell me how I can help. I can find a job. Please tell me how I can make it up to you and Mother."

Mr. Pao took a deep breath. "I gathered this for you," he said, his hands resting on the stack of paper on his desk. "I want you to go over the deeds to our properties and the bank accounts. I want you learn everything."

Mini hugged her father, leaning in and resting her forehead on his chest, her tears staining his cotton shirt.

"Yes, Papa."

31

HOURS
BEFORE DAWN

It was past midnight. Stars twinkled a little brighter in the moonless sky. Mini was standing by the window, a corner of the curtain pulled aside. She peered into the darkness that blanketed the city, listening to the light snore coming from Ling's room across the landing. She thought about her daughter.

Kung Yi had called out of the blue that morning. He said his wife's family had come to Shanghai. While she was busy entertaining, he'd take the little girl to the park on the Bund. Would Mini care to join them? Jing Ling had to be back home for a late family lunch. He could drop the girl off at ten in the morning so Mini could spend an hour or so with her, alone if she liked. Mini thanked him for his thoughtfulness. Yes, of course she would be there, she had told him. It was the first time she had seen Jing Ling since Kung Yi had married his new wife.

She set off for the Bund dressed in a plain cotton qipao, an old wool coat, cotton shoes, and no makeup. As a divorcee, her status in society was that of a widow. Mini felt that she *was* a widow. She shied away from the fashionable, colorful clothing that had once been her passion. She had carefully packed anything that reminded her of the good days in a wooden trunk and slid it under her bed after she moved back home. She hadn't opened the trunk since.

The roads were congested. It took a lot longer than usual to get to the Bund, but Mini, anxious to see her daughter, had left early and arrived before the hour. The park was empty. Few in Shanghai would brave the cold wind to visit the park on a December day. She pulled her coat tight to keep warm and sat on a bench under a tree at the children's playground. The trees were bare and the grass yellow. She watched the shadows from the trees frolic playfully with the bare boughs cast about by the wind.

Mini heard Jing Ling before she saw her. Jing Ling's high-pitched giggle penetrated the still air, clear as a bell. Mini looked in the direction of the giggles and saw Jing Ling high up in the air, her hair and scarf flying behind her. *At least the old man got one thing right. He gave my daughter an appropriate name,* she thought.

Kung Yi had lifted Jing Ling over his head. His hair was combed back slick and shone with hair jelly. He was looking up at his daughter and saying something to her. She was laughing. He saw Mini and put the girl down, taking her hand as they walked towards Mini.

Mini felt butterflies in her stomach. She wanted to face Kung Yi calmly, indifferently. Instead, she blushed as she faced him. She hated the feeling.

Kung Yi was equally ill at ease. His free hand reached out to Mini's, as if to shake hands with her, only to stop mid-motion. Finally, he bent down and gestured to their daughter.

"I'll pick her up at a quarter to noon." He squatted down and faced Jing Ling. "You behave well, okay?" He pinched her face gently and stood up. He nodded slightly to Mini and left.

Mini picked up Jing Ling and carried her in the opposite direction, away from Kung Yi. The little girl wasn't sure what to do. She kept glancing back at her father as he walked away. The wind was strong, and it was too cold to stay in the park. Mini left the bare trees and their dancing shadows and took her daughter to a coffee shop just outside the park.

A welcoming warmth and the smell of coffee and cakes enveloped the pair as they pushed the door open to the café. Mini picked a booth next to the window facing the park entrance so she could see Kung Yi when the time came. Jing Ling instantly crawled to the window, pressed her face hard into the cold glass, and mimicked the rumbling engines of the cars that passed by. Mini smiled. She waved the waiter over and ordered a coffee for herself and a piece of cake for her daughter.

"Little baby, can I help you with your coat?" Mini asked.

The little girl turned and paused to stare intensely at Mini with her coal-black eyes. She slowly nodded yes.

Mini took the little navy wool coat and matching scarf and mittens off her daughter's tiny body. She was three now. Mini thought Jing Ling was shorter than the average three-year-old and on the skinny side. Her skin was pale. She had never been a talkative child. Now she was completely silent as she looked at Mini with her serious black eyes.

The cake arrived. Mini smiled again at Jing Ling.

"Would you like to eat your cake?" she asked.

"Mother said I shouldn't eat cake before lunch," the little one answered.

A sharp pain stabbed Mini. She took a deep breath.

"It's okay if you have it once in a while," she said. "I won't tell on you."

Her daughter continued to stare intensely back at her, as if trying to see if she could trust this woman sitting beside her in the booth. She reached for the cake. Jing Ling's tiny finger jabbed into the cream, and she licked it clean. Mini reached across and gently held her daughter's hand, wiping her finger with a napkin.

"Would you like to sit on my lap? I can help you."

Jing Ling nodded. Mini lifted her up and put the little girl on her lap. She buried her face in the nape of her child's neck while the girl ate cake, smelling Jing Ling's sweet scent.

"How does your new mother treat you?" Mini asked.

"She's nice," the little girl said.

"Oh, really?"

"She cooks my favorite dumplings for me."

"Oh, that's nice."

"I'm going to be a big sister now," Jing Ling said. "Papa said I'm going to have a little brother."

The sharp pain in Mini drove deeper still, only to swell and expand into a burning knot in her throat. She remained quiet for a minute to collect her composure.

"A little brother? Really? That's nice. Do you know when?"

"Papa says soon."

Jing Ling's mouth was stuffed with cake. She was so focused on the cake that she had difficulty talking. Mini took sips of her coffee, fighting back tears and the pain in her heart. She didn't want people to see her cry, and she turned to face the street outside. It was busy as usual. Cars honked impatiently at the pedestrians and rickshaws that couldn't get out of the way fast enough. Two prostitutes were pacing in front of a hotel across the street, one of them grasping at a man's coat sleeve as he emerged from the hotel. *They both look so young and so desperate, trying to solicit business in broad daylight.*

Mini turned her attention back to her daughter, who was happily licking her plate to get at the remaining cake frosting. She realized the hour was up when she saw Kung Yi approach the park.

"But we only just sat down," she said, as if she were talking to him across the table.

Mini returned Jing Ling to Kung Yi at the park and took her leave quickly for home. The news that Kung Yi was expecting a son occupied her the whole of that day and night. She couldn't sleep and gave up trying. Sitting at the window in her bedroom, Mini stared into the black night and imagined the life Jing Ling would have as a girl born to an outcast mother. She would be at the mercy of her step-mother, who would now have her own child.

Mini determined to bring her daughter back home. *That's the best option for Jing Ling. She should be with her own mother. There's no reason why I couldn't take care of my daughter. Yes, I'll make my case to Kung Yi when the time is right, but I need to discuss it with Father first. I'll need his permission, of course.* Mini was confident her father wouldn't let her down. He was a compassionate man and understood his daughters' pain. The more she thought about it, the more feasible it seemed. *I will talk to Pa first thing tomorrow.* She was happy.

Mini's heavy heart lightened, and a sharp whistle rose through the air outside, as if the heavens had responded in agreement. A quick flash lit up half the sky. The vibrations from the explosion that followed were loud enough to shake the house. Mini, disoriented, thought a fire must have broken out somewhere near the Bund. A second and then a third explosion followed in rapid succession, banishing her bewilderment. Mini bolted for the door and pushed it open. Her hand was shaking. Ling was at her bedroom door, dressed in a nightshirt, holding her boy tightly to her chest.

"What's happening?" Ling cried to Mini.

"Bombs!" Mini grabbed Ling's elbow and turned her to the stairs.

Ai May and their parents met them at the downstairs landing. Mrs. Pao, also in pajamas, gripped Mr. Pao's nightshirt in one fist. Ai May was dressed hastily, her buttons and buttonholes clearly mismatched, her hair in disarray. Mini's heart beat fast. They stood looking at each other and listened as the booms shook the house and furnishings.

"It is a bombing, Pa," she whispered in a low voice. "What do we do now?" Her question broke the trance that had seemed to overcome the family.

"Pack our valuables in case we have to escape," Mr. Pao ordered. "Nothing big, only small things like cash and jewelry. Now! Go pack, fast!"

Everyone rushed to their rooms, even Mrs. Pao on her little bound feet. Mini didn't have much. Just a few pieces of jewelry that she had refused to part with for sentimental value. Within minutes, they were all back at the landing again, everyone looking at Mr. Pao.

It was still hours yet before dawn on December 8, 1941. The Japanese Navy had opened fire on the British and American warships docked in the Huangpu River in Shanghai. At the same time, Japanese dive-bombers roused a still-sleepy Pearl Harbor, five thousand miles away.

32

TIMES ARE
HARD NOW

Mini tightened her scarf to cover her face as best she could. The damp cotton clung to her. It had been drizzling the whole week and the air remained heavy with a steamy mist. She prayed the rice wouldn't grow moldy before she got back to Shanghai. It was a typical day for May—well into the rainy season— the kind of day when mold grows within hours on any exposed surface. Mini wiped her face dry. She couldn't worry about that. Right now, the mist just gave her an excuse to hide her face behind a scarf.

Mini was biding her time, standing outside the train station, scanning the food stands in the square. She was early and she was hungry. Beggars loitered around the stands, ignoring the vendors yelling at them to leave in the hopes of getting a few discarded scraps. Mini walked toward a stand where steam was rising from a pot full of eggs soaking in soy sauce and tea leaves. Mini's nose twitched at the smell. The old lady behind the pot stared at her in anticipation. Mini longed for two of the hot eggs for breakfast, but they were too expensive. She bought two plain pancakes instead. Her eyes fell upon a soot-covered little boy standing next to her.

She hadn't noticed him when she walked up. Now she watched him as his eyes followed the pancakes she stuffed into her parcel. He looked up at her in silence. Mini sighed, reached back in, and handed the pancakes to him. He accepted the pancakes with both hands, dropped to his knees, and kowtowed.

Mini turned quickly and walked across the square to the station entrance. It was jammed. A stream of incessant noise filled the air like discordant bells. *Good. The more people, the better.* She lowered her head and entered.

Mini looked like one of the thousands of ordinary peasant women going through the train station daily, dressed in a coarse blue cotton shirt, gray baggy pants, and black cotton shoes. The normally crowded station was even busier these days. The relative peace of Shanghai had drawn refugees from the surrounding countryside—through which the Japanese had marched, brutalizing the locals. Mini welcomed the chaos. She allowed herself to be swallowed by the crowd. She had become invisible.

She maneuvered to her favorite spot where she could set her large cloth parcel down and scan the station. The train to Suzhou was in twenty minutes. She watched the two Japanese sentries standing at each side of the gate leading to the platform. They stood tall over the cowed Chinese around them, rifles slung on their shoulders and bayonets stabbing the air. Mini knew the risks. They didn't even need a reason to stop her. She knew it was a bad idea to travel alone. Soldiers like them had been raping Shanghai women every day, even in broad daylight. If they discovered that she was smuggling cigarettes to Suzhou, then Mini imagined she would be among the many stabbed by those bayonets and left for dead in the street.

She waited as long as she could, only to join the rush to board just before the last whistle. A large group of people began to converge on the gate. Mini worked herself into the middle and, bowing like everyone else, walked past unmolested. The loud, hurried, and disheveled group trying to catch the train put off the Japanese soldiers, who were either too lazy or too disgusted to search the throng of peasants. Like many of those around her, Mini made the chaos her ally.

She quickened her steps and hopped onto the train, pushing herself deep into the already-crowded carriage. With nowhere to sit, Mini held her parcel tight to her with one hand and gripped the back of a bench with the other. Able to relax at last, Mini realized she was drenched in sweat. She untied her scarf and used it to wipe her face and neck as she silently observed the compartment. It was packed like a sardine can, full of people with tired faces.

Mini wasn't as afraid of the sentries as she once had been. She had made her first trip in late February, not long after her father lost his job along with most of their savings when the British bank closed. Mini and Ling's knitting and sewing jobs dried up when their foreign neighbors were sent to the camps. Mr. Pao could still count himself lucky, even if it meant he was without a job. He could've been hauled off with his British colleagues, or worse. At least the Chinese-run bank remained open so Mini could withdraw money to buy food. This would only last so long, especially with unpredictable black-market prices. She'd decided then to give smuggling a try.

Mini had visited her aunt in the Suzhou countryside and scouted out the black market there. It seemed safer. She left again for Suzhou one week later, cartons of cigarettes packed neatly in her suitcases. Again, she went through the checkpoint unharmed. Once in Suzhou, she offloaded the cigarettes, filled her empty suitcases with rice, and returned the next day. The run had been successful. In no time, Mini had recruited Kung Yi and her aunt to help. Mini would bring cartons of cigarettes to Suzhou, where her aunt and uncle would trade them for rice. Kung Yi would buy the rice from Mini on her return. The profit in it was small, considering the risk involved, but it was better than the alternatives. She ran the trip once a week, each week wearing a different disguise.

Mini had shed her furs in favor of peasant clothing today. She had picked well, given the many peasant women cramped into the third-class compartment with her. Mini held her parcel tight. She looked no different than anyone around her, for whom their meager belongings were likely their only remaining possessions. The train lurched forward and she shifted her weight to find a more comfortable position, but it was futile. The train was so crowded that flesh pressed on flesh, the compartment hot and full of the sour smell of human sweat. She closed her eyes, drifting in and out of a stupor.

After a journey that seemed an eternity, Mini was startled by a loud whistle. This was her stop. She retied her headscarf as they pulled into the station. Mini got off the train with hundreds of others. She was tired and badly wanted to catch the first rickshaw she saw—but peasants didn't travel by rickshaw. Only after walking some distance, when she was sure she was out of the guards' sight, did she dare to wave at a passing rickshaw. The short ride took her to a three-room brick house on the outskirts of Suzhou. The house sat in a jungle of lush green bushes, almost invisible from the street. The door swung open before the rickshaw had completely stopped. Mini's aunt stood waiting in the doorway. She was a smaller version of Mrs. Pao, maybe comelier even, despite her plain brown cotton dress.

"You must be tired. Come, change and wash your hands. Lunch is ready."

Her aunt pointed to a square wooden dining table on the dirt floor in the middle of the living room, surrounded by four wooden benches at each side. A big bowl of braised pork, a plate of sautéed bok choy, and a clay pot of winter melon soup sat in the middle of the table. *That last batch of cigarettes must have fetched a good price. Good enough to buy pork.* The aroma from the braised pork made her empty stomach growl. She sat down and attacked the bowl of rice set out before her. There was no talking over lunch; there was nothing to talk about anymore. Everyone was in bad shape and there was no sense dwelling on it. No sense talking about the smuggling either—that would just bring bad luck.

Mini ate quickly and carried the empty dishes to a pot full of water. "Where's the rice?" Mini asked as she washed the dishes.

Her aunt pointed with her chin to a back room. Mini looked over. Two large sacks of rice sat by a bed.

"Old Lui will come to take you and the sacks to the station," her aunt said as if reading her mind.

Mini nodded. *Fifty kilos*, she thought. *About two hundred yuan after expenses. Not much, but enough to get by for another week. I might not even need to go to the bank this week. And Xiao Bao will have braised pork, as I promised.*

She spent the rest of the afternoon and evening helping her aunt with chores and ate dinner with her aunt and uncle once he returned from work. It was well after sundown when Old Lui arrived with his rickshaw. Old Lui was a reliable coolie who helped Mini every week. He knew one of the Chinese puppet soldiers who manned the station late in the evening. For a carton of cigarettes, Mini could get through the gate and onto the train without any problems. Without a word, he carried the sacks onto the rickshaw and took Mini to the station, arriving just in time for the last train to Shanghai. Old Lui helped Mini carry the sacks onto the train. She found a seat on the floor by the restroom in between two carts and was soon joined by many others, all carrying large pieces of luggage.

Mini was exhausted when she finally reached Shanghai. She had ridden through the countryside in total darkness and wanted nothing more than the relative comfort of her home, but she wasn't yet done. She called over a peasant in rags and gave him a few coins to help her carry the sacks from the train out to the square. Mini followed the man closely, pretending they were traveling together. She saw Kung Yi on his tiptoes out in the square, standing next to an empty rickshaw. He was searching the crowd, and when their eyes locked, Mini smiled. With the rickshaw loaded up, Kung Yi and Mini quickly climbed on and rode off.

"How was the trip?" Kung Yi asked.

"Not bad," Mini said, too tired to add much more. They sat in silence the rest of the way.

When they reached the Paos' house, Kung Yi took out a few bank notes from his pocket and handed them to Mini. His hand touched Mini's for a brief moment during the transaction, and she pulled her hand away as if burned by his touch. Mini folded the notes into a tiny square and stuffed them into a small pocket she had sewn into her pants.

"Mini, can I take you out for a late-night snack? I mean after dropping the rice off at the store?" Kung Yi glanced at her briefly. Mini didn't respond.

"What am I saying? I'm being stupid," he said. "You'd never want to dine with me."

Again, Mini said nothing. She wanted to get away from him as fast as she could. Not because she hated him, Mini found, but because she was still very attracted to him. He was *so* handsome. Earlier, when he had seen her across the train station, Kung Yi's smile had made her heart leap.

He accepted her silence as reproach and said no more.

Mini reached home just before curfew. Once again, she had completed the treacherous journey without incident, and she sighed in relief. Her satisfaction was quickly replaced by frustration when, upon reaching the gate to their house, the door didn't automatically open as usual. *What? No one bothered to wait up? How can they sleep while I risk my life?* Resentment rose in her as she fumbled in the dark for her key, unlocked the door, and walked through the garden. *Not even a light for me to see by?* Mini opened the door to a house that was quiet and completely dark. There was only a dim light coming from her parents' bedroom in the far back of the house. *Strange*, she thought. *They're up, but where is everyone, especially Pa? He never goes to bed without making sure I return safely.*

Mini walked down the hall to their bedroom and knocked quietly. Ai May opened the door holding a wet towel.

"What's going on?" Mini asked.

"Shhhh," Ling said.

Mini pushed past Ai May.

"He's sleeping now," Ling added. Her eyes were puffy.

Mini saw a bloodied towel in a washbasin on the nightstand by the bed, her father's chest rising and falling as he slept. His face was bruised, with one black eye, and his head was wrapped with a blood-stained white cloth.

Mrs. Pao sat by the bed, her right hand resting on her husband's hand. She was no longer crying, though her eyes were sunken.

"Ma." Mini stepped forward.

Her mother stood up, trembling, only to wobble and fall into Mini's arms. She hugged Mini with all her strength.

"Thank Buddha you're back," Mrs. Pao murmured.

Mini sat down and put her arm around her mother. Ai May sat quietly on the floor by the door. They stayed there in silence, four women in the dim candlelight.

Mini felt a small hand touch her shoulder. Startled, she woke to find Xiao Bao standing in front of her, pointing to his belly. Dawn light filtered in through the shuttered windows. *Ling and Ma are still asleep,* she thought. *Oh, you poor boy. You dared not wake the others, even though you must be starving.*

Mini stood up and led him outside to the kitchen. She poured hot water into a bowl of leftover rice, put some pickles into it, and gave it to Xiao Bao.

"I want meat, the red pork."

I forgot I'd promised him roast pork before I left.

"Xiao Bao, I will get meat for us today, I promise," Mini said. "Eat your porridge now. You will have meat for lunch."

He sat down at Ai May's big butcher table, slurping down the food as Mini watched him sadly. He was six but had the coordination of a four-year-old. Short and thin as a rail, Xiao Bao was perpetually dirty, even though Ling and Ai May constantly cleaned him. As he ate, he dropped rice grains everywhere: on his shirt, on his lap. He didn't seem to notice as they stuck to his face and hands. Mini waited patiently. When he finished, she picked the grains of rice from his shirt and pants and helped him to the kitchen sink, where she washed his hands and face.

She sent Xiao Bao back to bed in Ling's room. Only after Mini had covered him with a thin blanket and promised him several more times that he would have meat for lunch did Xiao Bao let go of her hand.

Her father was awake by the time she returned to her parents' bedroom, where her sister and mother sat in silence. One of Mr. Pao's eyes was swollen shut. He exhaled deeply upon seeing Mini, reaching a hand toward her. Mini took it gently and cupped it in her own.

"Pa, I am so sorry I wasn't with you," Mini said.

"You were busy trying to feed us." Mr. Pao's voice was coarse. "And it's a good thing you weren't with me. God knows what those Japanese ghosts would have done to you." He paused before continuing, "Now promise me you won't run rice anymore."

"But Pa, we need to eat," Mini argued.

"I'd rather starve than have you risk your life. These Japanese ghosts are vicious," he said. "Look what they did to me."

"Pa, what happened?" Mini asked.

"I went to the Bund for our monthly withdrawal. As I passed the checkpoint on Fuzhou Road, I bowed to the Japanese bastards. One of them was drunk. He came to me and said that I didn't bow deep enough. He wanted me to kneel in front of him, kowtow to him. I refused, and he hit me with his rifle butt. The other bastards saw what he did and joined in too. They kicked me when I fell to the ground. They meant to kill me, I'm sure. I was lucky. I didn't die, only because a German gentleman came forward and intervened. A brave man . . ." Mr. Pao stared into space, swallowing his words. He closed his eyes.

Oh, if only I'd gone one day earlier, Mini thought. *We got enough on this run; we could have waited to make a withdrawal.*

"He hailed a rickshaw and paid for it to carry me home," Mr. Pao continued.

"We need to thank him," Mrs. Pao said.

"We cannot. I didn't even ask his name," Mr. Pao whispered.

"Pa, don't worry about this now," Mini said. "How do you feel?"

"Tired and in pain. I . . ." He struggled for words and decided he had none.

"We should call a doctor," Mini said.

"We insisted when he came home but Pa refused," Ling said, resigned.

Mr. Pao waved his hand, indicating that he wanted to be alone.

"You can't stop going to Suzhou. We need the money," Ling said once they had left the room.

"Pa doesn't want me to," Mini said. She was annoyed by her sister's suggestion that *she* should be the one to risk her life, but at the same time she was worried herself.

"Maybe it's time to visit Jie Xing," Ling continued. They had discussed it before. "Xiao Bao is his son," Ling said, looking down at Xiao Bao, who had emerged from the bedroom and was holding his mother's hand. "It's time for him to be a father."

"You mean—"

"Yes," Ling said firmly.

"Ling, we are not going to beg," Mini said firmly.

"What choice do we have, Mini?"

"When will you go?"

Ling slowly shook her head. "No, I can't face him. But please, take Xiao Bao with you."

Mini said nothing more after that, but she also couldn't let the idea go, however distasteful she found it.

When after a few days Mr. Pao still didn't improve, they called a doctor. He told the family that Mr. Pao was likely still suffering from internal bleeding. He would need more medical care than they could afford.

Ling was correct. They had no choice.

Mini looked at her reflection in the mirror. She saw a tired woman losing her youth. *I don't have the luxury to think about that.* Mini averted her eyes and got on with her task. She powdered her face to cover the black shadows under her eyes and applied lipstick to bring color to her lips. She bent down and pulled out the large trunk from under her bed, choosing a sky-blue silk qipao and a pair of black Mary Janes. She dressed and walked to Ling's room.

"Is Xiao Bao ready?" Mini asked through a closed door.

"Just a minute," came Ling's answer. "I just washed him and I'm dressing him. You can come in."

Mini pushed the door open. The boy was wearing a pair of navy blue shorts and was halfway into his white shirt. He was smiling and couldn't wait to go out with his aunt.

"Are you happy to see your father?" Mini squatted down so she could look Xiao Bao in the eyes. He continued smiling.

Mini and Xiao Bao took the tram to Jie Xing's house. Xiao Bao, ever a busybody and fascinated by crowds, fidgeted and pulled in different directions, oblivious to Mini's unease. She held his hand tightly to prevent the child from jumping off the tram at every stop.

They were going unannounced. Mini had no idea whether Jie Xing would be home. Afterwards, they would visit her friend Mei Fen, who lived two tram stops from Jie Xing. The last time she had seen her friend was when Mei Fen had delivered her first baby. She still remembered her friend's husband, drunk as he was with happiness. Mini couldn't help but smile as she remembered how the exuberant new father had forced sake on Kung Yi and Mini in celebration. But this visit wouldn't be a social call. If she must swallow her pride and beg Jie

Xing to help feed his son, then she would ask her friend for help, too. At least Mei Fen might be in a position to find a Japanese official to rent the family house in the British Concession.

Mini and Xiao Bao arrived at Jie Xing's house, an imposing three-story stone building surrounded by high walls with a tall iron gate at the front. Mini could see azaleas blooming on both sides of the interior walkway leading to the house. Mini paused and unconsciously tightened her grip on Xiao Bao's hand as she took a deep breath and pressed the doorbell. A young maid ran out. She eyed Mini suspiciously.

"Who are you looking for?"

"Mr. Wang Jie Xing."

"Who are you?"

"Please tell him Mini is here to see him."

"Mini," the maid repeated the name as if she wasn't sure how to pronounce it.

She ran back inside, reappearing a few minutes later to open the gate. She cast a curious look at Xiao Bao as he and Mini walked past.

The sitting room was different. The walls that had been white when Ling lived there were now blue. The mix of Chinese- and Western-style furniture was gone, replaced with Japanese pieces. The exception was an old sofa, next to which stood Jie Xing, all smiles. He appeared to be bigger. His face was red and had a greasy sheen, as if he had been drinking.

Jie Xing stepped forward.

"Well, well, Mini. To what do I owe the honor?" He ignored Xiao Bao and grabbed Mini's hand eagerly. "It's been a long time. Join me on the couch for some sake?"

"No, thank you. This is Xiao Bao." Mini tugged the hand of the child hiding behind her. "Say hello to your dad."

The boy gave no sign of recognition.

Jie Xing tapped Xiao Bao's head. "Oh, you're taller now."

He snapped his fingers and the young maid reappeared.

"Tea and cake," he said. "Take the boy with you. Feed him whatever he likes."

The maid bowed. She took Xiao Bao's hand and pulled him from the room.

"It's okay," Mini told him when Xiao Bao resisted.

He walked sideways, pulled along by the maid, all the while glancing back at Mini. Mini nodded at him with a reassuring smile. After another maid brought tea and cake, Jie Xing closed the door.

"Mini, what do you want?" he asked directly. "I was never your favorite person, and now you show up unannounced at my house. I am sure you have a purpose. What is it?"

"Times are hard now," Mini began. "We are hoping you can help out, not for Ling's sake, but for your son's."

"Ha, thirty years feng shui goes around," Jie Xing laughed. "I gather your father is no longer working for the British. How much do you want?"

"Whatever you can help with," Mini said coolly.

Jie Xing left the room and returned with a thin wad of notes. "Three thousand—that is all I can do now," he said. "But I do not wish to see Xiao Bao in this house again. Luckily, my new wife is out today with our baby son. She would be very upset if she were to see him."

He found Ling's replacement, Mini thought. She took the notes and put them into her handbag.

Jie Xing moved closer to Mini, laying a hand on her lap.

"Mini, if you want to have more, we can discuss it."

Mini moved away. "Discuss what?"

"The conditions," he said, smiling. "You know I have always been fond of you. You are different from Ling. You may not be as pretty as her, but you always stood out. I heard you are single now, right?"

His mouth hung open like a drooling dog. Mini felt his eyes undressing her and her face turned red. She stood up.

"There is nothing to discuss, Jie Xing. But I can promise you one thing," she said. "This is the last time you will see me."

"Well, well, very proud, just like your father. Being proud is doing you no good right now. People have to eat," Jie Xing said. He picked up a piece of cake and took a bite.

Mini didn't respond. Instead, she stood up and marched to the kitchen where Xiao Bao was eating under the maid's watchful eyes.

"Xiao Bao, it's time to go."

The child stopped chewing his sweets and stared at Mini with his expressionless eyes. Mini pulled him up from the chair.

"I said we're going!"

She dragged him to the front door, where Jie Xing stood waiting, smiling as he watched them leave.

Once she was sure they were out of his sight, Mini let her tears flow. She wiped at them with her free hand as they reached the tram stop. The child hung on to her other hand, trailing a step behind. She realized people were staring. *I must be a complete mess. Oh, why does it have to be like this? Why are some able to survive? No, people like Jie Xing aren't just surviving—they thrive in these horrid times. One man's disaster is another's delight. I need to get it together. Oh stop, unpleasant thoughts! I can't see Mei Fen like this.*

Mini continued on for a few blocks until she was sure her emotions were in check. Finding herself only one tram stop away, she decided to continue walking to save the fare.

Mei Fen lived in a small Japanese-style house with a small, neat front yard. A chrysanthemum bush was bare of flowers, but lushly green. Faint Japanese music and the sound of a woman and child singing hung in the air. The maid answered the door and, recognizing Mini, directed her to the nursery where Mei Fen was sitting on a bench, singing along with her toddler son, Dai.

"Excuse me, Mistress," the maid announced. "Your friend Ms. Shi has come to visit. I will bring tea to the sitting room."

She, too, gave Xiao Bao a curious look before disappearing into the kitchen.

Mei Fen let out an excited cry when she saw Mini.

"Mini, what a nice surprise! I'm so glad you came to visit."

Mei Fen struggled to stand up. "I am ridiculously big," she laughed brightly. "I can't even see my own feet." She was visibly at the end of her pregnancy.

"Who is this little fellow?" Mei Fen pointed to Xiao Bao.

"This is Xiao Bao, Ling's son," Mini rubbed her nephew's head fondly.

"Oh, the one..." Mei Fen didn't finish her sentence out of politeness.

Mini nodded and pulled Xiao Bao closer. "Xiao Bao, call this lady aunty."

Xiao Bao didn't say a word, only looked up sullenly at Mei Fen.

"Xiao Bao, why don't you stay here and play with Dai and the toys? I will ask nanny to bring some sweets," Mei Fen said to him. "What do you say?"

He didn't say a word, but he didn't move either. They left him in the nursery and went to the living room where tea and biscuits were already waiting for them on the coffee table.

"Sorry that I didn't call—" Mini started to apologize.

"Nonsense!" Mei Fen said cheerfully. "You know you're welcome any time. In fact, I'm so happy you showed up. I get very bored with Dai. I have nobody to talk to most days. Yoshiro is hardly home. He's busy at work all day long, sometimes all night long too."

She caught herself. "Sorry, I keep blabbing about myself. How are you? How are Kung Yi, Ling, and your parents? How's your little girl? I haven't seen any of you for ages. Since I had Dai, I haven't had time to go out. Now I am almost due again and I haven't got the energy to go about town. Yoshiro wants to name our second son Daijiro. It means 'second great son.' That is, if I'm having a boy. I don't think we have a name for a girl yet—"

Mei Fen went on and on like this, only stopping once she saw Mini's tears.

"What has happened, Mini?" she asked, suddenly concerned. "Oh, please tell me!"

She pulled Mini over to the sofa and forced her to sit down.

"Please tell me. What's happened?" she repeated.

"Mei Fen, I didn't call because we no longer can afford a phone," Mini began. "Kung Yi and I are separated. Father lost his job. Worse, he was beaten up by Japanese soldiers and is now bedridden. We're proof of the old saying that 'disasters do not walk alone.'" Mini's sobs choked off her words and prevented her from saying any more.

"Oh, poor Mini." Mei Fen covered her mouth with her hand, shocked by all the news. "And Mr. Pao! I can't believe it. What savages! Do you know their names? I have to tell Yoshiro."

"No, we don't. Mei Fen, our whole family has bad luck."

Through sobs, Mini told of Ling's return and her divorce. It was the first time she told anyone of her family's misfortunes. Mei Fen listened patiently, the tea cooling and untouched. When Mini finished, Mei Fen handed her a clean handkerchief. She sat next to Mini and rubbed her shoulder, trying to comfort her, embarrassed by her own good fortune.

"Tell me, Mini, how can I help? I'll do anything."

Mini dried her eyes. "Honestly, that's why I came. Your husband must be very connected, I think, so maybe you can ask him to help us find a renter for our vacant house in the British Concession," Mini said. "It is a nice house. Small but nice, you know? If you can find a Japanese tenant, then we won't have to worry about being harassed by the . . ." She was going to say "Japanese ghosts," but she didn't want to offend her friend.

Mei Fen nodded in understanding. "I promise to talk to Yoshiro."

"I shouldn't have come and asked, but I don't know where else to go," Mini said.

"Shush. Don't say that. I only wish I had known sooner. I should've checked in. I've been so preoccupied here," Mei Fen chided herself. "I'm sorry, that's no excuse. Is there anything else we can do?"

"No, I'm the one who is sorry. You have your family. I should be going," Mini said. "Ling will be worried about Xiao Bao."

"Okay. You'll at least let me see you off with something. I can't let you go empty handed." Mei Fen got up and waddled to the kitchen, where she pulled together a large parcel of ham and other dry goods. "For your father. Ham soup helps healing bones. He needs it now," she insisted. Smiling, she stuffed a handful of candy into Xiao Bao's pocket.

It wasn't but a few days later that Mei Fen showed up at Mini's doorstep, breathless as much from her condition as her excitement.

"I have a tenant for you!" Mei Fen said. "His name is Matsuda. He's Yoshiro's new boss, and he just arrived from Japan. He is a fine man, well educated, with high social status in Tokyo. He wants to see the house tomorrow. He asked that you meet him there at ten tomorrow morning."

"Oh, thank you, Mei Fen!" Mini threw her arms around her friend, giving her a big hug. She was unabashedly happy to have a tenant and the income, but she was unsure just what to expect.

Our family has suffered so much because of the Japanese, she thought. *Now I'm the one putting our fate in their hands.*

33

I AM A SERVANT

Standing behind an ironing board, Mini thought back to her first meeting with Matsuda. She set her iron down. *That was two years ago.*

Mr. Matsuda had liked the house. He also wondered if Mini might be his housekeeper as well? He had a three-year assignment in Shanghai, and with his wife and children left behind in Tokyo, he would need someone he could trust to take care of daily things for him. Mini came highly recommended by Yoshiro. He offered to pay handsomely.

Mini had swallowed her pride—not just at being a servant, but a servant *in her own house.* She was also nervous. She didn't know this man and was afraid she might be in danger. But she couldn't afford to worry about that. Her family needed the money. Her father was still injured and unlikely to work again as long as the war went on, and then there was Ling and Xiao Bao to consider, so what choice did she have? Mini had hated begging her friend Mei Fen for help, let alone Jie Xing.

What's the point in thinking about the past? In all that time, Matsuda has been nothing but a gentleman, courteous on every occasion when he calls and asks me to prepare dinner or to take care of something beyond the daily cleaning.

Mini returned to the chore in front of her. She folded the finished shirt and put it neatly on the chair to her right, pausing to wipe the beads of sweat pooling on her forehead. She looked outside at the shriveled green bushes against the low wall of the garden. They appeared livelier than usual under the cloudless blue sky. In the room warmed by a heating stove, Mini forgot it was a bitter winter day. She turned to take in the domestic scene she found herself in. Beside her was a chair full of freshly laundered men's underwear, shirts, and pants, along with sheets still to be ironed. The room was otherwise tidy, austere even. Her eyes wandered, settling on the far wall, where a portrait of the emperor of Japan hung. The ringing telephone interrupted Mini's thoughts.

"Mr. Matsuda's residence," she answered.

"Nori Matsuda here."

"Oh, Mr. Matsuda. What would you like?"

"I will be late today. Would you be kind enough to wait for me?"

"Yes, of course, Mr. Matsuda." *I am a servant, after all.* She softly put the phone back onto its cradle. She would be serving him dinner again. Despite her reflexive resignation, Mini found she didn't mind anymore.

By the time she finished ironing the last pair of trousers, darkness had descended. She gathered all the clothes and walked into the tidy upstairs bedroom. A family portrait stood on the nightstand next to a small stack of books in Japanese. Mini picked up the picture and studied it closely. Matsuda sat next to a willowy woman in a kimono. She smiled elegantly at Mini from the picture. *Strange, his pretty wife has never visited. For that matter, as long as I've worked here, I haven't seen any women visit him. He is handsome in that uniform. He looks more suited to being a businessman with that bookish way he stands. Except for his eyes, maybe. They seem too sharp, and a bit frosty. Maybe it's the photo. He seems so much mellower. But what do I know? It's not like I see much of him—at least, never outside this house.* She set the photo down and looked at the two serious-looking teenage boys standing behind the couple and staring back at her.

How could a man abandon his lovely family and live like this? He must be lonely.

Mini put the photo down and continued to puzzle over Matsuda. *Not once has he mentioned his personal life. In fact, he hardly ever talks. His Chinese is clearly very good. But maybe his heavy accent makes him self-conscious. No, I don't think that's right either. He never brings anyone home. And the few times I stay late to cook he spends his time like a monk in his study.* She shook her head as if she were shaking the thoughts away from her. *It's none of my business. Luckily, he is an easy master to work for. He may never say anything, but he also doesn't complain about my cooking.*

She put the clean clothes away and went downstairs to the kitchen. The Japanese food she had learned to cook from Mei Fen was still warm on the stove. Mini made herself a pot of green tea; she enjoyed the conscious ceremony in making and drinking tea. She would have to wait a few hours until Matsuda returned, so she took the tea and cup to the living room and sat down on the sofa.

Maybe it was the mood that had taken hold of her earlier, but she chose to sit in the darkened room without turning on the light. The house was eerily quiet, the stillness interrupted only by the occasional car that zoomed by outside. Her thoughts drifted to Jing Ling, whom she was now seeing every two weeks. *I never had the chance to talk to Father about taking Jing Ling back. Now, here I am working as a maid. The years are passing. But I mustn't give up on the idea. How can I take care of a five-year-old girl?*

Mini paused and sipped her tea. She didn't want to contemplate how long it would take to have an answer to that. *I must remember, this is temporary. It's not time yet. I don't want Jing Ling to live this life of hardship. I don't know when I'll get her back, but at least now I'm able to save some money. I must do that first. As long as I can continue to visit her. At least now she understands that I'm her mother. I just wish she were less distant. I so desperately want to get close to her.*

Mini sighed and took another sip, distracting herself with the tea. She breathed in and savored its warm scent. *This is good tea. Father would appreciate it. Maybe I can ask for some from Mr. Matsuda.* In thinking about how her father would enjoy it, her thoughts turned to him at home. He was no longer bedridden, but his spirit was broken. He spent his time in the house with his grandson and left everything to Mini.

These thoughts were too depressing to bear. To banish them, Mini took out a new album that she had bought earlier in the day and turned on the gramophone. As the record spun, a melancholy voice filled the room.

Before she knew it, Mini's eyes were watery.

She was wiping her tears on her apron when she heard Mr. Matsuda's familiar knock and went to open the door. Mr. Matsuda nodded slightly as he walked in and passed by. She didn't look at him. When Mini didn't move to close the door, he stopped.

"Miss Pao, is something bothering you?" he asked.

"Everything. I am a most unlucky woman," she said. "That's what's bothering me. I have to support my family like a man. I have a daughter who won't call me mother. I ... Now I am nothing but a servant—your servant. What did I do wrong in my last life to deserve such bad luck?"

Tears filled her eyes again. Mini didn't know what had taken hold of her, but she didn't care. She wanted to shout and complain. Instead, she slumped back to lean against the wall, staring, her eyes fixed on Matsuda's, but not seeing him.

Mr. Matsuda held her gaze but didn't say anything. He waited quietly for her to continue. Mini felt his eyes sweeping her tearful face, and she lowered her head.

"I should serve dinner now," she said.

She turned and walked past him toward the kitchen. With her back to him, she added: "And you can fire me if you like."

Mini immediately regretted it. *What have I done? I've put up with so much. Why did I have to break now? He will fire me. He might even want to move out of the house. Who wants to deal with a mad woman?*

"Wait, Miss Pao," Matsuda said. "Would you do me the honor of joining me for dinner?"

Mini turned around. Matsuda's eyes were studying her. His piercing eyes were so sharp.

"No, I don't think it's a good idea. I will *serve* dinner," Mini said, avoiding his eyes.

"Please, Miss Pao," Matsuda bowed to her. "I'd love to have your company." He paused and continued, "I want you to know I don't see you as a servant. You help me, yes, but I simply can't manage my life here without you. Please, give me the honor of sharing my meal with you this evening." He bowed again.

Mini didn't know whether he was mocking her. She stood there and waited for him to continue. He looked expectantly at her.

What's it going to hurt me to stay a little longer? Home isn't pleasant, not anymore. What am I rushing there for? To face endless responsibility, to see Xiao Bao's dirty face, Ma's grief, and Ling's misery? I might as well stay. But . . . she shifted her feet and faced him directly. *Having dinner alone with a man, a Japanese man . . . that's too much.*

"Miss Pao?"

"Yes," Mini finally answered.

"Very well. I will change and join you in a moment."

Mini set the table and Matsuda returned in his blue cotton *yukata* house robe, looking very relaxed. They were quiet for much of the dinner. Mini at first felt awkward with the intimate informality of a Japanese meal. She was self-conscious as she sat cross-legged on the tatami mat on the floor, just inches away from Matsuda at the small, spare table. But as Mini ate and enjoyed the sake, she found herself talking about her troubles. It wasn't long before Mini's random comments became a monologue, pausing only to drain the thimble-sized sake cup. Matsuda listened patiently, refilling Mini's empty cup. She found herself feeling better as she told him her troubles. Soon a second bottle was empty and Mini picked it up.

"I will heat some more," she said as she tried to stand, pushing herself up from the low table.

The sake had overpowered her, and she fell back down onto the tatami. Matsuda was quick to catch her before she crashed onto the table.

"Sorry," Mini slurred.

"You shouldn't drink anymore," he advised.

"I can have more," Mini argued. "I'm having fun."

The warmth from Matsuda's hand on her back radiated through her body. Instinctively, she leaned on his arm. She rested her free arm on his chest, her hand slipping under the fold of his yukata and touching his bare chest. *When was last time that Kung Yi touched me? I can't even remember.*

"Let me get you home. It's getting late."

"I'm fine. Don't worry," she mumbled.

Matsuda insisted and escorted her home that night. It was well after curfew. She was giddy all the way home.

Mini stayed late again the next day. He hadn't called that afternoon, but she waited anyway. They had a nice meal and it wasn't long before they had finished a bottle of sake. Mini returned with another and sat down, closer this time. She poured some for herself and downed it in one sip. She rested her head on his shoulder and Matsuda ran his fingers through her hair. She delighted in the tenderness of his touch, his fingers soft and sensuous. She let him continue like this, letting her body relish the tingling feeling that rippled through it. She imagined his warm fingers sliding down the back of her neck and down her back, pulling her close.

Mini looked up at him, paused briefly, and finally reached to kiss him. He returned her kiss passionately and held her tight, letting go only to look into her eyes. Matsuda's eyes were intense and desirous. She leaned her head back, cupped his face in her hands, and brought his lips to hers as she slid down onto the tatami. Mini let him continue kissing her like this, moving slowly down to her neck before carrying her to his bedroom.

She was not expected at Matsuda's the next day. It was his day off, and thus hers also. Mini spent the weekend thinking of that night, how it had come to be, and felt happy in the memory. She bore no illusions that it was anything more than pleasure—the pleasure of being wanted, of having company, and of not having to think only of surviving.

The following week, Mini continued her duties there as usual. When she didn't stay to greet him for two days in a row, Matsuda called to say he would be returning early from work, and to invite her for a drink and then to a Chinese opera. She accepted without hesitation. Mini enjoyed the opera that night, but more than that Mini delighted in the attention and his charm. When her worried mother interrogated her after she got home the next morning, Mini said she'd had too much to do, and by the time she finished it was too late to return home, given the curfew.

"Curfew?" Mrs. Pao asked incredulously. "What does the curfew have to do with it? Mini, he's a high-ranking Japanese officer. His jeep can drive through Shanghai anytime, curfew or no curfew."

It was obvious that her mother knew. Mini felt shame but ignored it. She made little effort to hide her new exhilaration in being desired and desiring another. She avoided her mother's angry eyes and made no more attempts to reason with her.

Mrs. Pao sighed. "The world is turning upside down," she said before turning her back on Mini and walking out of the room.

Ling, who had been listening quietly, looked at Mini with sad, knowing eyes.

"Be careful," was all she said once their mother had left the room. Mini knew better than to ask what Ling meant.

Mini wasn't proud of what she had done. She also couldn't and didn't want to stop. She was happy thinking back to Matsuda's touch. She felt safe in his embrace. She had made her choice.

34

HIS EMBRACE

The change in Mini was gradual but unmistakable. She was not the last to realize it, and even reveled in her transformation: She was head of the household, she kept a lover, and she was Jing Ling's mother. Mini developed a new confidence in knowing all of this and felt no shame. When exactly she had managed to shed her past anxieties she didn't know, but she didn't linger over it. Mini didn't need to speak of it, nor of the suffering from which this confidence had been born.

Mini and Jing Ling grew closer. Her little girl was often on her mind, and she promised that it was only a matter of time before they could live together the way a mother and daughter should. While Mini didn't have the means to take Jing Ling home, she was quite comfortable demanding the time she wanted to spend with her daughter.

It was no surprise, then, when Kung Yi phoned her at Matsuda's residence one evening. Jing Ling was sick and wanted to see her mother—her real mother. Would Mini come the next day? Mini replied that of course she would and took a day off to see her girl.

The Shis continued to live comfortably, but even they had clearly felt the hardship of war. It was well known they had let much of their house staff go. Their vast lands that had once produced the rice eaten by most of Shanghai were now mostly left to rot in the countryside—what hadn't already been seized by the Japanese or raided by Chinese fighters. What they managed to sell was only through great difficulty, given the hazards inherent in bringing the rice into Shanghai.

The Paos were no better off, of course, but Mini was by now a survivor and took comfort in being nobody's dependent. The irony wasn't lost on her.

The rickshaw dropped her off at the gate to the Shi mansion. She asked the coolie to wait for her as she stepped down. She banged the lion knocker and took in the neighborhood as she waited. Mini usually didn't visit Jing Ling at the Shi mansion. She had no desire to see any of the family—least of all the new wife—and hadn't been to the Shi household in some time. The bright March sun did nothing to distract from the gloom of the lonely mansion, surrounded by ruins. Countless beggars occupied the hollowed-out buildings that lined the street leading to the Shis'.

Mini was more than a little surprised by how far the family had fallen, such that even they could or would not keep up their once-grand entrance. Mini banged once more on the door. *I should discuss my situation with Matsuda*, she thought as she waited. *Maybe he'll give me a raise. I can hire some help and bring Jing Ling back. Ha, why would he give me a raise? Because I'm sleeping with him?* The thought made her blush. *But why should there be any shame in that?*

She banged the doorknocker harder, impatiently. A young maid finally answered, whom Mini didn't recognize. She didn't care; she waved off the coolie and walked past the maid.

"Wait, Miss?" the maid called out, trailing Mini as she walked briskly up the short path and into the great hall where Kung Yi sat alone, reading a newspaper.

"You're here," he said, standing at once.

"Yes," Mini said, pausing long enough to take in the same decay she had observed at the gate, as if a malady had set in and taken hold.

"I'm so glad you came. She's been asking for you."

Mini ignored him as well and continued up the stairs to the nursery. A red-faced Kung Yi dismissed the maid and quietly followed Mini.

The little girl was in bed. Her pale and sunken face made her eyes look bigger than usual. She was pushing away a bowl of black Chinese medicine the nurse was trying to feed her.

"You can go now. I'll take care of her," Mini announced. The nurse put the medicine down on the bedside table, bowed, and left.

Mini sat on the bed and gently touched Jing Ling's forehead.

"How are you feeling, my sweet girl?" Mini asked.

"My head hurts," Jing Ling said, closing her eyes. Her soft little fingers touched the back of Mini's hand lightly, like a feather.

She bent toward Jing Ling. "You will feel better soon if you take medicine. Should we try?" She said soothingly. "I'll give you a piece of chocolate if you drink your medicine."

The girl opened her eyes. Her face alternated between suspicion and mischief. Mini took a bar of chocolate from her purse and Jing Ling grinned.

"Now, how about that medicine?" Mini said as she lifted the bowl carefully. She grimaced involuntarily at the bitter aroma, but Jing Ling didn't protest. The girl pushed herself up and stared at the bowl in Mini's hand, working up her courage.

"Jing Ling, my brave girl, you can do it. Just pinch your nose and take a sip." Mini held the bowl to Jing Ling's mouth.

In this way, Jing Ling slowly drank the medicine. When she finished, Mini rewarded her with the candy bar, which Jing Ling hungrily unwrapped and bit into straightaway. She handed the bar back to Mini.

"Mama, would you like a bite?"

"What a sweet girl you are," Mini said. Happiness filled her. Jing Ling had only recently begun calling her Mama, and each time she melted with joy at hearing that simple word uttered from her daughter's lips. "No, my baby, it's all yours."

"Mama, can you tell me the story of the pretty lady who went to the moon?" Jing Ling licked her fingers.

"Of course." Mini wiped the melting chocolate off her girl's fingers. "Would you like to lie down and listen?"

She did just that and Mini pulled the blanket up and tucked her in.

It didn't take long for Jing Ling to fall asleep. Mini sat there, looking at her child. *Poor motherless child! She needs to be with me. I will hire someone to care for her so she can be with her real mother.*

She heard the door open. She turned and saw Kung Yi walk into the room. Mini had forgotten him.

"How is she?" he asked.

"She's asleep." Mini avoided his eyes.

"Would you like to have a cup of tea in the sitting room?"

Mini knew what he meant by the sitting room. *Our sitting room. No, I cannot. I should be leaving now.*

"Mini, no one is here today," Kung Yi said. "Father and Mother are in the country, and my wife and kids are with them."

My wife, he says. She looked up and found Kung Yi smiling at her with that same disarming smile, the one that always melted her heart. She nevertheless remained distant and unmoved.

"You can share a cup of tea with me and spend more time with Jing Ling after she wakes up," said Kung Yi.

Hmm. That I can't refuse.

"Fine," Mini said, quietly standing and leaving Jing Ling's room.

Kung Yi opened the door to the adjacent sitting room. Everything was the same, from the little round rosewood tea table and carved high-backed chairs to the rosewood sofa covered with the light-green fabric Mini had picked out before their wedding. She couldn't believe his new wife didn't mind living in the exact same room as his ex-wife.

"Please sit down," Kung Yi said, and rang for the maid.

Mini sank into one of the plush chairs. The maid brought tea and dim sum. She set the tray down, poured tea, and left, closing the door behind her.

Mini glanced at Kung Yi sitting casually on the arm of the chair across from her. She liked how he looked in his brown sweater and gray wool trousers, with his hair combed back. Like this room, he hadn't changed either. *He looks good.*

"Mini, you don't know how much I miss you," he said, breaking the silence. "Not one day passes that I don't think about our life together."

"Thinking about the past isn't going to help," Mini said shortly.

She was not as cold as her words might suggest, and she betrayed a sad smile. Mini didn't want to admit her conflicted feelings and yet, as she looked down at her lap to avoid his eyes, she betrayed those very feelings.

"I wish time could be turned back," he continued.

"No, that's not going to happen," Mini said. "You know that."

"Mini." Kung Yi looked at her. He stepped closer and embraced her.

Mini couldn't breathe. Her heart felt like it could jump out of her chest. Without knowing it, she had returned his embrace, holding him and resting her head on his shoulder. She realized she was sobbing. He held her tighter, gently caressing the small of her back. Mini didn't know how long they held each other. She didn't know how they ended up in their old bedroom.

35

A MAN WON'T WANT A WIFE WITH SIX TOES

Mini leaned against the door frame of a mud hut, one hand under her huge belly and the other hand rubbing her back. A familiar crow rested on a bare branch of the lone tree in the yard. Its piercing cry made Mini shudder. Gray clouds hung above, threatening snow.

Dressed in a quilted gray cotton jacket, pants, and black cotton shoes, Mini looked like a poor young peasant woman pausing before stepping into a mud yard to head out into the expanse of frozen yellow fields. Mini often stood like this. She watched a hen pecking near some farm tools scattered next to a straw-covered chicken coop.

It was December 1944. Mini had moved in with Ai May's family in Anhui province—an impoverished village hundreds of miles from Shanghai—when she could no longer conceal her pregnancy with baggy clothing. Mini had watched this scene for four months now. She had witnessed the fields turned from green to yellow. It seemed that as her body grew bigger, the scene before her grew grimmer.

Bored and cold, Mini waddled back inside the mud hut. She passed the all-purpose room where Ai May's family of six cooked, ate, and slept. Beyond it was a back room with a door. This room was Mini's world. It consisted of a small wooden bed and a chair. Thick satin bedding lay folded on the bed. Mini was grateful to Ai May for insisting that Mini bring her own bedding. She wouldn't have been able to sleep on the straw bedding that the rest of Ai May's family was accustomed to.

It was June back when Mini had become certain she was pregnant. The shame returned, and it overwhelmed her. How could she see anyone, how could she admit her affair? She was certain it was Matsuda's child, but told him nothing. More than anything, she felt guilt in knowing that she was carrying a child fathered by a Japanese soldier, whose lot had disabled her own father. Abortion was an option, but she couldn't gather the courage to go through with it. Days became weeks, and weeks became months. She would have to tell Matsuda. There was no escaping the obvious. She often relived the night she told him.

Matsuda had asked Mini to set up the dinner table in the garden under a full moon. It was a hot summer night. Matsuda was unusually tired and somber. He quickly downed a few cups of cold sake and moved closer to Mini.

"I have an unpleasant job here, but you have made my time in Shanghai bearable. I enjoy my time with you," he said as he poured sake into Mini's cup. "Drink more, Mini. It is a wonderful night, here with you."

Mini took a sip. "I have something to tell you," she said.

"In fact, I have something I must tell you too," he replied. "But go ahead, you tell me first." Matsuda looked at her expectantly.

"I . . . I am pregnant."

Matsuda slowly put down his cup. "Are you sure? I took every precaution, you know."

"Yes, I am sure. I don't know what to do. Tell me what to do."

Mini looked away, unsure how he would take it, or rather, how she might take his reaction. She studied a patch of silver moonlight resting on a bush.

Matsuda sat quietly. Finally, he cleared his throat, "Mini, you know, I am a married man and I cannot accept this child as my legitimate child. And you are an unmarried woman. Having a child will—I suggest you find a place far away where no one knows you and come back once it's done."

"What about the child?"

"I leave it to you. I will take care of your expenses." He took Mini's hand in his. "Your hand is cold. I am sorry that I cannot do more." He paused. "I'm sorry, my own news comes at a difficult time. My assignment in Shanghai ends in November. Things are not going well for the Great Japanese Empire. I received my orders today," he said, caressing Mini's hand gently. "I want to thank you for the good time we have had together."

Mini sat silently. Her head drooped and she wanted to cry. Matsuda waited patiently. The hot summer night was still, and the moon cast its light over the two of them. They sat in the garden, in silence, for a long time until Mini, tired, suggested they retire for the evening.

That night was the last Mini spent with Matsuda.

She left Shanghai a week later, accompanied by Ai May. Ai May's parents and siblings treated Mini like a princess—one to be left alone and, she suspected, talked about behind her back. *Whore.* Mini ate alone in her room. Her meals contained strips of meat while the family ate porridge and wild vegetables. *Pampered while the rest of us barely make ends meet.* Mini's guilt-driven mind had become irrational in her self-imposed exile. *A whore discarded by some loathsome Japanese soldier.* Mini was certain they knew every little detail of her affair with

Matsuda, even though she was just as certain that Ai May would never betray her shame.

She spent her days looking at the yard or sitting on her bed in her room, rubbing her growing belly, brooding over her situation, and wondering about her future. As summer turned to fall, an early snow threatened to isolate her even more. *Soon I won't even be able to leave this little room*, she thought as she watched one snowflake fall past her window, then more. They floated in the gray sky like feathers drifting in the wind. *How long will I be here? And I have to leave the child behind. I don't know how I can do that. Another motherless child!* Mini shivered and pulled her loose quilted peasant jacket tight around her. She thought of the small wood pile outside that would remain untouched until Ai May's mother fetched some logs to cook their mid-evening meal. They wouldn't waste their precious firewood to warm the hut, certainly not for a few mid-day snowflakes.

Mini wondered if the baby inside her was warm enough. "Of course, you must be nice and warm." She sat on her bed and rubbed her belly just in case. The tightness in her belly seemed stronger today.

"You cannot wait, ah? Just a little longer," she said softly to her unborn child. "What am I going to do with you? I'm a bad person. Your mother is a mistress, worse than a concubine. You don't deserve this. You did nothing. You're not even born yet and I've let you down. I cannot keep you. Not now. I'm sorry. I have no choice. You understand, don't you? I have no choice. Please forgive me."

Mini didn't know when she fell asleep. When she awoke, the room was completely dark. She lit some candles and waited patiently for her evening meal. When Ai May's little sister came in with a bowl of rice and a plate of cabbage and a few slices of meat, Mini pulled up a corner of the bedding, baring some of the wooden boards of her bed, on which the girl set the meal down.

"Thank you," Mini said, picking up the hot rice bowl without waiting for the girl to leave.

Mini was hungry every hour of the day and by now she was starving. She took a bite and swallowed. Before she could take another bite, a stream of warm fluid gushed between her legs. A splitting sensation overcame her. She nearly dropped the rice bowl in an attempt to set it down and she gripped the upturned bedding for support.

"Someone!" she screamed. "Please! Fetch the midwife!"

Mini was exhausted by the time it was over. When she came to, the midwife was holding a little bundle. There was the murmur of hushed voices outside her room.

"What is it?" she asked the midwife, her voice dry and coarse.

"A girl, unfortunately," the midwife said with a pitiful look. "Such a tiny little thing and six toes on her right foot. Poor girl, a man won't want a wife with six toes. Bad luck. She'll have a hard time finding a man."

Mini closed her eyes hard. She was tired and didn't even have the strength to reply.

"Mistress, I'm ready now," the midwife said, breaking the silence. "I'll feed the baby some rice water and take her to another village near here. You needn't worry. The wife of the house just had her baby and she has enough milk for two. I told them you'll pay fifty yuan a month. They will take good care of your baby."

Mini opened her eyes. "Please hand me my baby. I'd like to feed her now."

"No, Mistress, this is no good. Once you see the baby's face, it will stick with you the rest of your life. You shouldn't look at her."

They think I am abandoning this child for good. But I won't. I can't. I will take her back when I can. I want to remember her face.

"Please," Mini said. "I'd like to feed her at least once."

The midwife reluctantly handed over the bundle. Mini undid the swaddling and touched the tiny fingers and tiny toes of her daughter.

Yes, a little stump right next to the small toe of the baby's right foot did look like a sixth toe. The baby opened her eyes and stared back with intensity. Her eyes were almond-shaped and coal-black, like Jing Ling's. The baby yawned and closed her eyes. Mini knew it instantly. *She is Kung Yi's child, Jing Ling's sister.* Mini pressed the baby against her breast and murmured, "My treasure, my precious."

The tiny girl kept her eyes closed. Her little mouth latched onto her mother's nipple and greedily sucked, as if she did it with the knowledge that this would be the last time she would ever drink her mother's milk—her only chance for succor from the mother who would abandon her.

36

REST IN PEACE

Mini's absence had been like a chronic illness felt throughout the Pao household. Her father seemed to have been affected more than the others. The indignity he felt in failing his family had grown all the more palpable, as if a heavy stone were cast on him and he couldn't remove himself from under it. Mini had left for Anhui only a few short months before, but in that time what little health he possessed had seemed to drain away.

When Mini had first returned, there was little spirit left in her already frail, spindly father. That was months ago. Today was the last day of Mr. Pao's three-day wake.

His coffin rested on a stand in the living room below a portrait of him, newly hung for the occasion. The silk-lined coffin was open to reveal Mr. Pao, wearing a three-piece linen suit and two-toned shoes. His eyes were closed, and his lips parted slightly—as if he were smiling in a pleasant dream. Four monks in yellow robes sat at the altar. Incense burned beside white votive candles, an offering of rice wine, a bowl of rice, and various dishes. The monks chanted in unison, praying that he would be reborn into a life without suffering.

The humid May weather didn't allow for the customary one-week wake. Three days didn't even leave enough time to run the obituary in the newspaper, and so only a few people came. But Kung Yi visited each day with their daughter. Ai May had sent word to him without telling Mini. A very pregnant Mei Fen came with her husband, Yoshiro, on the first day. He looked tired and hardly said a thing, though at least he came dressed as a civilian. Mei Fen returned on the second day with only her parents. They had been the Paos' neighbors and comforted Mrs. Pao, reminiscing for several hours over shared memories of their daughters, back from when the world was innocent.

The funeral had started late in the afternoon on the third day. The monks' low, even, calming chant carried through the air, interrupted only by the occasional bang of a gong. Burning incense could be smelled throughout the house. The Pao women stood, dressed in black from head to toe with white flowers pinned in their hair, feeding stacks of fake money into a coal stove in the atrium where they prayed for Mr. Pao. The money-turned-ashes ensured that he would never worry about money in the other world.

After some time had passed and the women had tended to Mr. Pao's needs, the funeral director came over and whispered into Mrs. Pao's ear. She nodded and motioned to the girls to toss the remaining money in the stove. The funeral director walked over to the head monk and whispered into his ear. He, too, nodded and then hit the gong. The chanting stopped and the monks stood up, bowed to the coffin, and backed out from the living room. Mini whispered her gratitude to the head monk and stuffed an envelope into his hand, which he received with both hands as he gave a deep bow.

Mrs. Pao, Ling, and Mini walked up to stand before the coffin. One by one, they kneeled and kowtowed three times. After the last bow, the funeral director set the coffin cover, pulled a nail from his pocket, and held it as he hammered it down, sealing the coffin. Mrs. Pao, who had been quiet up until then, cried out at this final act. She was helped, still weeping, into a black car parked behind the hearse.

The drive to Jingshan was only some fifty miles from Shanghai, but it seemed like hours on the battered road. The town had once been popular with city folk, who enjoyed picnicking in the foothills of Jingshan Mountain, for which the town was named. Mini didn't know why, but she had assumed that such an idyllic place would have been spared. Instead, as they drove through the town, Mini witnessed rubble and charred timber piled up at every corner along the quiet streets. Hollowed-out buildings framed the sky, and those few still-intact buildings were riddled with bullet holes. The town had been hit very hard by the US air raids since the last time Mini made this trip.

The Americans and National Army are closing in, Mini thought. *I had heard the rumors, but can they be so close? Why didn't I find the time to ask Matsuda, or even Mei Fen when she visited these last few days? I've been so consumed by sorrow I've ignored everything else. Why didn't I recognize it? Mei Fen complained that Yoshiro was working harder than ever and was never home. Could it be the bombing? Oh! Mei Fen, you've been so worried, and I missed it until now. What had she said last? Poor girl.* Mei Fen's last words to Mini took on new meaning.

"Stay by my side, will you? I need your support more than ever," she had said when she took her leave on the second day of the wake, asking Mini to be with her when she gave birth to her third child.

"Of course I will," Mini answered absentmindedly.

"Please, Mini, promise me," Mei Fen had replied forcefully.

"Yes, of course, I promise. Thank you for coming, I can't say enough."

Mini had grasped her friend's hands in thanks, but it was the despair and fear in Mei Fen's eyes that Mini now remembered most. *It must be true. The Americans are coming. Mei Fen is preparing for the worst. Oh, I wish Father had lived long enough to see this day.*

Mini sighed and wiped her damp forehead, shaken out of her memories. Looking at the handkerchief in her hand, she realized it had been a gift from Matsuda. She spread it out on her lap and stared at the two embroidered birds landing on a pink plum blossom. Her chest tightened. *Matsuda was good to me. I can never forget that he's a Japanese soldier, but . . .* Her thoughts trailed off.

She didn't want to think about him, but she couldn't help it, her mind returning to the memory of their last night together. He had been so tender as he held her, comforting her in his arms as they lay quietly. They both knew they'd never see each other again. The next morning, he left a sum of money on the table for Mini. "For the child," he had said. Then he turned, and Mini had watched longingly as he walked out the door one last time.

The hearse stopped, interrupting Mini's wandering mind. They had arrived. Jingshan Mountain rose up gradually to one side and the sea spread out behind them. The workers carried the coffin up to the grave, already dug. Mini and Ling helped their mother, who struggled to climb up the slope on her lily feet. Yellow and purple wildflowers danced in the wind around them on the path. Not a single soul was to be seen. The graves were overrun by growth, but there was an odd beauty to it, as the tall grass rolled like waves with the wind.

The coffin was lowered into the grave and Mrs. Pao's wailing renewed, reaching a crescendo. Ling and Ai May both dabbed at their eyes with handkerchiefs. Mini felt she should've been crying too, but she had no more tears. She had cried so much the last three days that her face was swollen and her eyes dry. She felt nothing but exhaustion.

Rest in peace, Father. I will carry on, taking care of Ling and Mother as I promised, she swore silently one last time, before releasing a handful of earth onto her father's coffin.

Mr. Pao's tombstone stood next to a tiny tombstone that read: *Wang Xiao Bao, February 14, 1936 to January 28, 1945.*

Mini was still in Anhui, having just given birth when it happened, and so she didn't learn of the accident until her return. Piles of red firecrackers on a stand had caught Xiao Bao's attention at the local market and he stood there, lingering a little longer than he should have. Ling had moved on, walking deeper into the crowded market. She didn't notice that he had fallen behind. He had panicked when he couldn't see his mother, witnesses said afterward. The boy cried out for his mother, ran wildly into the street calling for her. The passing car couldn't stop in time. It had been the last straw for Mr. Pao.

Mini couldn't bear thinking of the image of her father crying over Xiao Bao's grave as she stared down at the two of them. She walked away, toward the edge of the hill overlooking the sea. She watched as the wind blew the clouds apart, revealing a patch of blue sky, which was slowly replaced by more clouds and then clear sky again. Mini could see a faraway beach, where yellowish seawater was washing the sand. The ocean stretched out before her without a single fishing boat in sight. *Too bad Xiao Bao didn't live long enough to see the beach and the sea. He would have liked it.*

At least I arrived in time for the burial service. Upon returning from Anhui, the news had been a blow to her, and she cried for days. *Now, thinking back, I wasn't crying only for Xiao Bao, but also for my abandoned daughter. But I had no choice,* she reminded herself once more. *Oh, poor Ling. I was so wrapped up in my own misery that I forgot all about you. I'm so sorry. I should have—I didn't notice how sad you were. Jie Xing, that bastard, why didn't he come, at least make an effort instead of . . . What father, what kind of man sends a letter saying that he regretted the fact he wasn't able to attend his own son's burial service? What a coward. No, that would assume he feels something.*

She thought back to his brief letter, which included a small check to help cover the burial costs. The letter closed, saying "Xiao Bao is on his way to a better place, because there would be no place for him on earth." *I cursed Jie Xing as heartless—we all did—but maybe it is a blessing. Little Xiao Bao, you were loved. This world is so cruel. What would've happened to you had you outlived us, and nobody was there for you?*

Mini turned and walked back to Mrs. Pao and Ling. Mrs. Pao sat by the newly erected tombstone, tracing her husband's name with her finger. Ling was on the other side, cleaning Xiao Bao's tombstone with her handkerchief.

Ling had aged so much. One easily could have mistaken her for Mrs. Pao's younger sister, her face pudgy and sagging, her body bloated and shapeless. She no longer smiled. She hardly said a thing these days.

Mini had caught a glimpse of Ling sitting on Xiao Bao's bed one afternoon, murmuring to herself, her face buried in one of Xiao Bao's jackets. Mini had left quickly and silently, both sad and ashamed at having been witness to Ling's despair.

The once-beautiful Ling was gone without a trace.

37

NO JEEP GIRL

Mini had longed for the war's end. Yet it was of little comfort when it finally arrived.

She had lost everything she held dear: her marriage and Ling's, her father, Xiao Bao, and even her dear friend Mei Fen, who seemed so blessed. She died giving birth to her third son the day his father was captured, when his intelligence division surrendered to the Americans. Mini recalled seeing Yoshiro a month later. Mini was helping Mei Fen's parents with the children when he showed up at the door to their home haggard, hair full of lice, only to learn that he was returning a widower. He and his sons left for Japan the next day.

Mini had all along assumed life in Shanghai would return to its normal prewar ways, but the sudden fall of the Japanese changed little for their family. Soon the little bit she had saved from renting the house out to Matsuda would run out. Nobody wanted to rent it. She didn't even know where to turn to rent it. She had no ties to the Americans who occupied the city. She expected the Brits to call on her father and offer him back pay, but she grew restless as the months passed. She steeled herself to write to Mr. Robinson, her father's former boss at the consulate. She couldn't help feeling she was begging, even knowing that it was her father's due. But she didn't know where Mr. Robinson was, let alone if he survived the war. She was pleasantly surprised when just three days after she posted the letter, she received a reply from the consulate. It was from Mr. Robinson's secretary inviting Mini to see her, setting an appointment for that Friday afternoon.

Mini arrived at the appointed time and found the reception area full of people who seemed to be purposefully milling about. There were a few ladies, but most were men in civilian clothes or military uniforms, waiting to be called on. Two receptionists calmly worked the ringing phones, their occasional frown the only mark of their frustration at the constant stream of calls. Mini waited and walked up to the younger receptionist as she hung up, smoothing out Mr. Robinson's letter on the desk.

In halting English she said, "My name is Zhi Fen Pao. You can call me Mini." She paused. "I am here to see Mr. Robinson's secretary," she continued, more comfortable as the English came back to her.

The phone rang again. The receptionist took the letter while she answered the phone. She glanced at it and handed it back. She waved Mini to a door that led down a hall and, covering her mouthpiece, added, "Mr. Robinson's office is two doors down on your left."

She knocked on the door lightly once, then twice a little louder.

"Come in," a woman's voice called out from behind the door.

Mini walked in to find a light-haired young woman typing behind a desk and looking up at Mini. "You must be Miss Pao. Please give me a minute to finish a sentence here . . ."

She went back to her typing for a moment and then stood up and went to knock on the glass door to an inner office. "Mr. Robinson, Miss Pao is here."

"Send her in, please." The voice seemed to boom in reply.

The young lady showed Mini in. "Should I bring some tea?" she asked.

"Yes. Thank you, Miss Wilson."

Mr. Robinson's hair had thinned and his round, red face was sagging. He stood up and extended his thick hand to her. "Good to meet you, Miss Pao."

"Thank you." He didn't remember her and Mini wasn't about to correct him, even though she was a little let down. It had been more than ten years since Mini had met him, but she had made a point of wearing her navy blue wool dress, the same one she wore to the British picnic party. Now it looked faded on her and hung loose, like a hand-me-down meant for another. Mini had also changed in other ways. Had Mr. Robinson remembered her, he would have noticed she was no longer the young girl who shyly hid in the shadow of her father.

"Sit down please, Miss Pao." He sat back down onto his chair as Mini sat facing Mr. Robinson across the desk. She forced her trembling hands into her lap.

A light knock on the door distracted Mini as Miss Wilson came in with a tea tray. She set it on a side table and poured two cups of tea, closing the door softly on her way out.

"My condolences, Miss Pao. Your father was a jolly good fellow and I was fond of him. It's a pity he didn't witness Great Britain's victory. He'd have liked that."

"Yes, he would have," Mini murmured in a low voice. *How do I start? I wish I had prepared something to say,* she thought to herself.

"It must have been hard for you all. Now tell me, Miss Pao, what can I do for you?" he asked, his voice quieter, as if aware of her awkwardness.

Mini picked up her teacup with her slightly shaking hand and took a sip to calm her nerves.

"Mr. Robinson, our family fell on hard times after the British left. Things happened so quickly."

He nodded, encouraging her.

"Father didn't have time to withdraw any money from the British bank and he was not paid for December, the month when the Japanese attacked. I understand we will be able to withdraw our funds, but I do not know when. Is there anything you can do with the bank and also," she paused, "to collect his pay?" She looked down at her lap again, feeling small.

"I see," Mr. Robinson said, rubbing his red face with his hand. "Yes, I understand it's been difficult still for many to get back on their feet. It's only fair that I see to it, Miss Pao."

He wrote something on a piece of paper and rang a bell. Miss Wilson walked in and he handed the paper to her. "Please take care of this."

He stood up and extended his hand to Mini again. "Miss Pao, it was nice to see you. Please do come if you need any help. My condolences again."

"Thank you very much." Mini took his hand and bowed slightly before following Miss Wilson out.

In the outer office Mini looked blankly at Miss Wilson, unsure of what to do next.

"One minute, Miss Pao. Once I type up this letter, you can take it to your bank. They have to be very careful, you see, because in all the chaos, how do they know who's really who they say they are? This will authorize you to make withdrawals on your father's account. Now, what's the bank?" she asked as she sat down and started typing.

"HSBC. And my father's pay?"

"Once I finish here, I'll phone payroll. A check should arrive at your house soon, Miss Pao. I'm sorry to say you're not the only one. And I'm very sorry for your loss." She finished her letter and handed it to Mini, smiling. "Good luck, Miss Pao."

Mini left the consulate as evening was descending. The dimming fall light made sinister the bare-branched trees looming over the sidewalk. It was too late to take her letter to the bank and she hesitated, not wanting to go home just yet. What was there at home to go to? As she paused, a tall brown-haired woman in uniform walked past. They made eye contact as she passed Mini, who was still standing at the gate to the consulate. The deep-set blue eyes looked familiar. The woman stopped and turned back.

"Mini, that's it. Your name is Mini, isn't it?"

"Yes, it is," Mini replied warily. "And you are . . . ?"

The woman extended her hand to Mini. "Mary Jenkins . . . no, Mary Hayworth, my name was Mary Hayworth then. We met at a party, remember? It was in a park on the Bund before the war. Oh, it must have been ten years ago? I'm afraid you don't remember me."

"Oh, yes, I remember. It was a long time ago." Mini shook her hand.

"You must be visiting your father. I remember your father works at the consulate."

For a second, she couldn't find her voice. She swallowed the lump that rose in her throat. "My father passed away during the war. I came to visit Mr. Robinson."

Mary's kind eyes caught everything. She stretched her hand out as if to touch Mini, but stopped in mid-air, only to look at her watch. "I really don't have anything important here. What do you say we go for a cup of coffee?"

Instinctively, Mini wanted to refuse. The time she spent at the picnic party was one of the loneliest experiences she had ever had in her life. She still thought after all these years it was strange how one could feel so lonely with so many people around you. She wanted to politely decline but she reflexively glanced at her wristwatch in response to Mary's expectant look. *It's not even 5:30. Why not, when nothing's waiting for me at home?*

"Yes, Miss Hayworth, I'm free for a bit. I know a small café around here that's good and cheap." Mini thought of the café she used to go to with Kung Yi.

"Lovely, let's go then!" Mary said cheerfully.

Her spirits lifted once she walked into the café with Mary. It had been a while, and the warm, smoky interior called back memories from just before the war with so many blond, blue-eyed uniformed men and their lithe white Russian companions. Raucous English mixed with a contemporary jazz piece gave it a lively atmosphere. They sat down and Mary told Mini a long story about her life in Chongqing over coffee and cakes. She had married a US Navy captain at the wartime capital deep in the mountains in Western China. He was an advisor to the Nationalist government.

Mary had done her part, too, she stressed, and described her time helping in a hospital. Her last name now was Jenkins; Mrs. Jenkins, she preferred to be called. She was working at the Red Cross now, distributing food and medicine to the Westerners who had recently returned from the concentration camps. Many had no homes to return to, their homes destroyed or damaged by the Japanese. They were set up and living in the camp barracks, dependent on the Americans for shelter and food until they could rebuild.

She paused before continuing. "I can't begin to imagine how they lived, how they cope now." She looked away and dabbed her eyes with a napkin, softening her otherwise cool, regal demeanor. Mini was touched by Mary's emotions as she recalled the sight of the refugees.

"I appreciate how they must feel. It's been so hard, and then with the war over you want everything to be normal again, but it never will be. Fortunately, we still have our home, and I was able to rent out our other house . . ." Mini bit her tongue. *I don't know Mary well enough to mention our tenant, let alone that he was briefly my lover. People have been shot as collaborators for less.*

"Oh, poor dear. I read how horrible it was. Those Japs are the devils. What they did to the people. But you're safe, and your family is safe, I hope."

Mini told Mary how her father died, of his beating. Mary was horrified and held Mini's hand as she listened.

"Those bastards. But, how did you get on then? I don't know how I could survive." Mary shuddered.

"We got along," Mini said simply. "We took in some needlework, and for a period I smuggled rice for my ex-husband."

"Oh, my!" Mary gasped. "I heard stories of course, but as a woman with all that the Japs were doing, weren't you afraid?"

"Yes, of course, but I was desperate. It was dangerous and Father made me quit. We struggled to live off savings after that. That's why

I was at the consulate today. We cannot access Father's savings at the British bank."

"Oh, but I have an idea!" Mary said. "Why not work at the Red Cross with me? I'm sure I could get you a paid position. Would you want it? We need translators. You know, when we distribute food. And the Americans need help, too, to talk to the local refugees who are repairing the local airfields for the Air Force."

"Yes, anything, please." Mini brightened at this turn of good fortune.

"You may have to work alongside American soldiers."

Mini looked around the café at the Americans there. *I survived the Japanese, I can do this,* she thought.

Mary laughed. "Oh, sweetie, I don't mean to scare you. They're fine men."

"Of course. When could I start?"

"I'll see what I can do tomorrow—oh, it's so dark already. Mr. Jenkins will wonder whatever happened. Let's keep in touch and hopefully I'll have good news soon."

Mary came through, and in a few short days Mini was working for the Red Cross. The money wasn't much, but it didn't matter. It was something, and it got her out of the house. Compared to everything Mini had known until then, it was more liberating to put up with the American GIs (and their catcalls, even the cruder ones) who saw all Chinese women as if they were for sale.

"I am not Jeep girl, and stay away from me," she would say dismissively. Most left her alone, impressed by her confidence. For the first time in her life she felt legitimate, earning her own wages without having to smuggle rice or serve as someone's maid.

Though happy with her job, she generally kept to herself, especially around the loud GIs. Occasionally Mary would swing by at day's end and invite Mini to a nearby café to chat. She enjoyed these moments, but remained careful even with her new friend, who, seemingly oblivious to Mini's hesitation, repeatedly encouraged her to go out.

When Mary invited Mini to a Christmas party on one such mid-December evening, she wouldn't accept Mini's excuses any longer.

"You know, Mini, I insist. It's Christmas, after all. You should get out and have a little fun," she said. "You take care of everyone else. Time for me to take care of you."

"I'm not sure. I have to ask my mother," Mini tried to excuse herself.

"Mini, you're a grown woman. You don't need your mother's permission. I promise you it will be fun. George is dying to meet you."

"I'm not sure; you know, being around foreign men. I am shy," Mini demurred.

"Oh, is that your real concern?" Mary asked. "Don't worry—George and his friends will be nice to you. You're my dear friend."

Mini just looked back at Mary. She dreaded the thought of being propositioned and having to use her now-standard *Jeep girl* line.

Mary seemed to read her thoughts. "Don't worry," she said. "They're all decent people, the men are all gentlemen, and George promised me none of them would dare give you a hard time."

The party was at the Cathay Hotel where Ling had stayed with Jie Xing during their honeymoon. It now housed mostly British and US military officers. Mini walked into the high-ceilinged dance hall decorated with a giant Christmas tree. Mini's outfit matched her mood. She didn't want to stick out, so she put no makeup on. She made a point of ordering a new qipao for the occasion, but the black dress with a below-the-knee slit up her calf looked serious, almost somber, on her. Her only jewelry was a single pearl pin that held her curled, shoulder-length hair back above her right ear. She felt uneasy as she walked through the room full of strangers, nearly all of them big, tall Western men, many in uniform. She watched the men and women, wine glasses in hand, casually chatting, and thought back to that picnic a decade ago. To calm her nerves, she picked up a glass of wine from a tray held by a waiter, took a sip, and decided she didn't want it. She had just found a table out of the way where she could set it down when Mary spotted her and glided effortlessly through the crowd to her, one white-gloved hand guiding a stocky, sandy-haired man's arm.

"Mini, this is my husband, George Jenkins," Mary said. "George, this is Miss Pao."

"It's my honor to meet you, Miss Pao. I've heard a lot about you and I'm glad we've finally met," he said, taking Mini's hand and kissing it.

"Let's join the group," Mary suggested before Mini had a chance to say anything. "They're over there in the far corner, by the band."

Mini followed them to a group of about seven people. She was relieved to see another Chinese woman. *At least I'm not alone this time.* Mary introduced her to everyone, and Mini nodded politely to each. *Even if I could remember all these foreign names, I'm sure to mispronounce them.* The last introduction was to a lanky young man in a crisp US Navy uniform with intense gray eyes and a slightly hooked nose. He extended his hand to Mini.

"Robert Weingardener, Jr. Lieutenant, US Navy," he said.

Mini shook his hand weakly. "Mini Pao. It's nice to meet you."

The band had switched from a Christmas song to a cheery dance number. A man in a black tuxedo stood up and blew his trumpet hard, as if to announce the real start of the party. The trumpet distracted Mini. She smiled at the trumpet player as he fell into a private reverie, his eyes closed and his body swaying with the notes coming from his instrument.

"You like jazz, then. Would you care for a dance?" Robert asked, bringing Mini back into conversation.

"I'm afraid I forgot how to dance. I haven't danced for years," she replied.

"Please, Miss Pao. Let's put your dancing to the test," Robert insisted, and Mini nodded, following him reluctantly to the dance floor.

Robert proved to be good on his feet. He had a slight limp that did nothing to deter his infectious enthusiasm. He offered his hand to continue dancing when the next song started and Mini readily took it. They danced to most of the music that evening, leaving their friends alone to their conversation in the corner. Robert didn't try talking.

His big, sincere grin conveyed more than words. She smiled back and was even laughing after a few glasses of wine between sets. As the party wound down, Mini realized she had stayed far longer than she'd planned. She knew her mother had learned to not ask questions when she came home late, but still, it had been some time since she had been out. She should be getting home. Robert walked her out to the curb.

"May I invite you out sometime, maybe for another dance and perhaps dinner?" he asked as they waited for a taxi.

"No, my mother won't allow it," Mini said, still giggling.

They stood like that, quietly, until a taxi arrived. Robert held the door open, thanked her for the good time he'd had, and waved at her as the taxi pulled away.

Mini looked back and watched him standing there, smoking. He looked in the direction of her taxi as if lost in thought in the cheery neon light of the Cathay Hotel. *He's handsome—surprisingly so. Oh well, it was a fun night, but I'll never see him again.* Mini shrugged and turned away.

38

A PROPOSAL

What did I get myself into? It's starting to rain! It's just a matter of time before a real downpour forces me inside. I'm sure to catch a cold. Mini looked up at the darkened sky as if beseeching the heavens for relief. Instead, the unforgiving wind hurled rain in her face.

Mini had nothing to shield her from the fat raindrops but a thin housecoat and cotton slippers, and both were soaked through. *Just a little longer,* she thought as she stomped her feet. *If only Robert would leave! What's taking him so long, and what's he doing all this time?* Cursing under her breath, she peeked into the house from the unlocked door, hoping to see Ai May coming to announce that Robert had left. *Where is she?*

Mini hadn't thought about Robert since the Christmas party. She hardly had any spare time during the week, between her full-time job and her weekends with Jing Ling. But one Saturday afternoon in early January, Robert surprised Mini by appearing at her doorstep. Mini politely invited him in and offered him a cup of tea. He invited her out. Mini was quick to decline and send him on his way. The next Saturday he appeared again, and then the next, and every Saturday after that. By now, Mini could recognize the way he rang the doorbell:

two short rings and one long one. The last couple times, Mini had run out the back door at the sound of the doorbell, telling Ling to inform Robert she'd left to run an errand. Robert would leave and eventually Ai May would appear at the back door to call Mini back in.

The last few times took just a minute or two. Why hasn't Ling sent him off? Mini cursed a little more, and stomped her cold, soggy feet. *This downpour is getting heavier. I can't stay out in this cold rain.* She pushed the door open an inch and was about to walk in but caught herself. *Why am I sneaking in through the back door of my own home? If I have to see him . . .* her thoughts trailed off as she walked around to the front door and rang the doorbell. Ai May looked at her soaked mistress.

"Mister wouldn't leave. He insisted on waiting."

Ai May's whisper turned into schoolgirl giggles, and Mini frowned and walked past her to the movable coal stove. Rainwater dripped from her hair and the damp housecoat clung to her body as she warmed up her freezing hands. The glow from the stove was the only light in the semi-dark hallway. After drying her hair with a towel Ai May handed her, Mini steeled herself to greet Robert. *I'll be polite and say hello. When I excuse myself to change, he'll leave.*

Robert shot up from the sofa as Mini entered the dim living room. She took Robert's extended hand and gave him a limp shake.

Since the start of the war they had taken to keeping the blinds down at home, and now Mini was glad for the dimly lit room. With Robert standing there, she couldn't help but notice the threadbare sofa covering, the fading lampshades, and the yellowing wallpaper. They stood there awkwardly as Ling and her mother sewed quietly on the couch. There was no lingering sign of conversation among them.

Robert cleared his throat, "Miss Pao, I'm glad you're home. You're hard to find." He chuckled.

"Excuse me, I'm not dressed for visitors." Mini smiled, but she really wanted him to leave. "I was caught in the rain on the way home. Thank you for coming, but I really need to dry off and change."

"Of course, of course. If you don't mind, I'd like to wait for you."

By the way he looked at her, Mini could tell she wouldn't get rid of him easily.

"Please sit," she responded.

Mini went upstairs and dried off, taking her time as she wondered how to get rid of him. She changed into a heavy red sweater she had knitted herself, and a pair of loose black wool pants. *If I have to meet him, at least I'll look presentable.* She sat down and looked at herself in the vanity mirror. Mini combed her hair, powdered her face, applied lipstick to her lips, and rouged her cheeks. She smiled at herself in the mirror. *I still look good. Robert must think so, too, or he wouldn't be so annoyingly persistent.* It flattered her.

But this is dangerous. He's a nice man, but what will come of this? If I go out with him, where will that lead? I have a daughter and I abandoned another daughter in the countryside. I promised myself I'd never allow myself to fall into that same trap. I need a new life without any shadow of my past. He'll only make it worse. I'm a divorced woman over thirty with no prospects in Shanghai, aside from being a mistress or a concubine—and maybe not even that after rumors that I've dated an American GI get started. At least as it is now, I still get a few proposals through Ma's friends.

"They're wealthy," her mother would always start.

"And they're *married*," Mini would answer simply.

A few of her prospects even had more than one wife already. After her mother's last attempt to mediate a proposal by such a man, a disgusted Mini finally convinced her mother that her salary was enough to sustain the family and that she could stop entertaining marriage proposals. Mini was getting heated just thinking about her mother's last proposal.

I will not *be a concubine—let alone a wife number three or number four. But I am going to have to do something. This job isn't permanent, and I have no idea what I'll do next, but I have to get rid of Robert. His attention isn't going to help. No doubt the neighbors are already spreading rumors. My already dim prospects will be reduced to . . .* Mini didn't want to finish the thought and, seeing her now-flushed face in the mirror, she dabbed away some of the rouge and got up to go downstairs. Mini paused again in the hallway to listen. *Maybe he left?* The living room was quiet. She stepped into the living room and Robert stood up once again, more expectantly this time. His teacup hadn't moved an inch.

"Miss Pao, would you give me the honor of taking you out for a cup of coffee?" he asked.

Mini was taken aback. She had come down hoping to get rid of him. This wasn't how she'd planned it. Mini looked at her mother, but her head was down. She was focused on her needlework, but Mini knew without a doubt that her mother was watching, even if she couldn't catch her in the act.

"That would depend on my mother," Mini replied. "We Chinese cannot go out with a man unless her mother gives permission. And it doesn't matter how old we are." She knew her mother would say no.

Robert turned to Mrs. Pao and bowed slightly. "Madam, would you please give me permission to take your daughter out?"

Mrs. Pao looked up at him, puzzled at his English. Ling translated. Mrs. Pao turned to Mini as if to ask what she should say. Then, to everyone's surprise, she nodded her head to give her consent.

"Yes," Ling said. "She said yes." She sounded a little too enthusiastic for Mini's comfort.

"Thank you, Madam." Robert bowed to Mrs. Pao again. He then turned to Mini. "When would you like to leave?"

"We can leave now, if you don't mind. I just need to get my coat from upstairs." Mini could sense they all wanted him out of there.

They stepped out and Robert put two fingers to his mouth to whistle, hailing a coolie pulling a rickshaw down the street. *How American, and how embarrassing, out here on the street in front of the neighbors.* Mini felt her face flush once more.

"Where to?" the coolie shouted after he mounted the bike.

"To the Bund," Mini shouted back without lifting up the tarp, and without asking Robert's opinion.

"Where at the Bund?"

"Cathay Hotel," Robert shouted back in his funny-sounding Chinese.

Mini flushed again in embarrassment. *Oh, come on. Let's get out of here.*

Inside the rickshaw, Mini and Robert sat upright, both rigid and quiet. She felt a hand touching her hand. Turning her head, she could make out the outline of Robert's face in the darkness, and from his glistening eyes, she could tell that he was looking at her. His eyes were deep and kind. *He's smiling. That grin.* Mini smiled back, her nerves settling, and turned to look out the little rickshaw window. As she watched the wet streets, she thought of how Kung Yi had come to fetch her in this way. She thought back to her first rickshaw ride with him. *It was sunny and warm. I was young then. It was so long ago and so many things have happened.*

"You have been avoiding me, Miss Pao," Robert said, interrupting her reverie.

"No, I . . . I was just busy . . ." Mini's face was flushing again. *Darn it. I'm glad it's dark and he can't see me like this.*

"No need to make excuses," Robert said. "It was obvious. May I ask why?"

"Why?" Mini repeated the word incredulously. "You're an American and I am Chinese. We have nothing in common."

"Well, that's not true. Many of my colleagues are dating Chinese girls."

"That is because many Chinese girls are Jeep girls," Mini said.

"That's what you think? You think I have mistaken you for a Jeep girl?" Robert asked. "I can promise you my intentions are honorable. I just want to know you better and to have a good time along the way." He laughed. "I knew you were a decent girl from the day we met. Mary told me your late father worked for the British for many years. I'm very sorry about your family's loss. I'm sure he must have been very successful to have secured a job working with the British." Robert looked at Mini, took her hand, and kissed it genteelly. "Mini, I like you very much. If you'll allow me, I'd like to spend some time with you. I am sure we can have a swell time together."

"But once you leave, I will be seen as a Jeep girl by my own people," Mini informed him. "I will have no reputation left. The neighbors talk."

Robert pulled his hand back a little too suddenly. *It's too late now, silly.* She realized she liked the feeling of his large, warm palm on her hand, but she didn't want to say anything that might encourage him, either. They continued to ride on in silence until finally Robert said, "Help me to understand you Chinese. Do young men and women meet before they are married, generally speaking?"

"No, marriages are arranged by parents," Mini said. *Except mine! I made a dumb mistake with my marriage.*

"So, a person has no say in who they're going to marry?" he asked.

"Yes, generally speaking."

Robert let out a sharp whistle.

Silence fell again. As they neared the Cathay Hotel, Robert cleared his throat. "Miss Pao, I am going—"

He was interrupted as the rickshaw stopped suddenly. They had arrived.

"We are here, Mister," the coolie announced in English. A taxicab honked impatiently behind them.

Robert jumped off, paid the coolie, and helped Mini down. Rain was still coming down and the wet ground glistened, bathed in the neon lights from the Cathay.

"Come on," Robert grabbed Mini's hand and ran to the lobby café through the rain, laughing like a schoolboy.

They settled into a booth and Mini dried her damp hair with a napkin as he watched her. *That grin.* She smiled back. Mini's mood had lightened. She enjoyed coming to this café and she found his boyish grin infectious.

"What were you saying back there in the rickshaw?" Mini asked. "You were about to say something, but you didn't finish."

"Oh, that . . ." Robert trailed off, looking around for a waiter. He snapped his fingers to get someone's attention and a waiter came.

"Good evening, sir."

"Vodka for me, please," Robert said.

"And the lady?" the waiter turned to Mini.

"A coffee, please," Mini answered.

When the waiter returned with the coffee and a shot of vodka, Robert downed it in one gulp. He wiped his mouth with the back of his hand and ordered another. Mini watched curiously.

The second arrived, and Robert downed that one too. Only this time he put down the glass and looked intently at Mini. That grin of his was gone.

He's so odd. She sensed he was summoning the courage to say something.

"What?" she asked, though it came out more a statement than a question.

"Miss Pao, I want to finish what I was about to say in the rickshaw," Robert started. "I will be deployed to Japan soon, in two months' time."

"Oh?" Mini was surprised to find that she was strangely disappointed, but she didn't know what else to say. Picking up her cup, she took a sip. She put it back down and turned to look to her right, to the booth next to them. A Western couple occupied the booth, both in their twenties and in uniform. They were deep in conversation. The woman giggled. She reached out across the table and touched the man's hand. He leaned forward, listening intently as the woman said something. His eyes were absorbed by her face and his lips curled into a smile. *Such a beautiful couple, clearly in love.*

"Miss Pao. I'd like to know, would you marry me?"

Mini turned back to Robert suddenly. She blinked several times, as if to clear her head. *Did I dream that?* Robert was looking at her. He rubbed his hands together nervously.

"You must be joking, right?" she responded when he didn't say anything more for a moment. "You are making fun of me."

"No, I'm serious," he said. "I gave a lot of thought to this on the way here after you told me about Chinese marriage customs. I haven't been able to forget you since I saw you, and I don't want to leave and never see you again. I figure that my only option is, well, to propose to you. So, yes, I'd like to marry you."

"You don't know me, and your family doesn't know me," Mini said, still shocked. "Don't you need approval from your parents?"

"I know you are beautiful," Robert replied. "My parents wouldn't object. It's my life. If you agree, I'd like to get married in a couple of weeks so we can at least have some time together before I leave for Yokohama."

"I don't know . . . ," Mini stammered, confused. "I have—I have to *think*. I have to talk to my mother and sister. I don't know any life outside of Shanghai. I've never been out of Shanghai, except to Suzhou."

"You do that. You don't have to worry about life outside of Shanghai," he assured her. "I promise I will look after you, no matter what, wherever we are."

Robert's eyes were serious. Mini couldn't bear to look back at him, and picked up her coffee cup instead, only to give up midway. Her hands were shaking too much to drink without spilling. She put the cup down. Robert reached out and wrapped his big hand around her two shaking ones.

"Miss Pao, *Mini*," Robert said gently. "Please think about it—but I don't have much time. I'm a soldier and I have orders."

Mini pulled her hands away and rubbed her forehead gently with her fingertips to ease the throbbing headache that had overcome her. *This is too sudden, too outrageous—dangerous, even. I don't even know him.* But there was something that pulled her back from rejecting him right there. They sat like that, wordless, as Mini struggled to make sense of her jumbled thoughts, the one constant being that she couldn't continue to just sit there and feel him staring at her, waiting. Mini called out to the waiter to send over another vodka, which she threw back with a quick gulp before finally looking back up at Robert. He had that same expectant expression.

"I will think it over," Mini said. "Now I have to go home. My head-ache is too much."

Robert wordlessly escorted her outside and waved over a taxi to take her home.

Mini couldn't sleep for days. *Why didn't I reject him there at the table? That would have been the sensible thing to do. Though I've been with a foreigner before—the enemy even—and why was that any different? I had fallen for him, of course. And there was the war. Now it's different, things are returning to normal; slowly, but they are. And Robert's not even Asian. How could he ever understand me? I don't even know if I like him.*

She thought of his wide, boyish grin. *He's cute in a way. And he seems a gentleman, but do I really know him? I certainly don't know what to expect of his family. But did I really know Kung Yi, for that matter, before I married him? Could Robert's family be any worse than my in-laws? What if things don't work out? What would I do in America?* Mini thought of the scenes she had seen in the movies and tried to imagine living in such a strange place. It was just too scary to uproot herself from Shanghai. She had spent her entire life here.

Yet, for some reason the opportunity to start her life anew in a place where no one knew her was appealing, and she continued to debate it in her mind, though she couldn't articulate why. The idea of a fresh start was too powerful to dismiss, even as she held out hope for a proper, respectful marriage. She confided in Ling, who was no help. According to her sister, Mini was mad to even entertain the idea. *Why*, Mini wondered, *did I assume Ling would answer any differently?* She asked her mother's advice, who told her to forget the idea, but only after Mini explained how far America was from China. "With an ocean in between, I won't be able to see you every week," was Mrs. Pao's only concern.

After a week of this, Mini made up her mind and phoned Robert. She met him at the same café the next day. Mini headed there straight from work, her uniform covered with a thin layer of dust. She didn't think twice about her appearance as she walked in. Whether from her striking figure or determined stride, the café patrons lifted their heads and briefly appraised her as she entered. Robert clearly enjoyed the scene. He stood up, again with that broad smile on his face, and waited for her to walk to his table before pulling the chair out for her to sit.

Mini hadn't noticed the staring; she was preoccupied. She sat perfectly upright and looked directly into Robert's eyes. Without a hello or even a pause, she said, "Robert, I agree to marry you. Before I marry you, though, I want you to know something about me."

His smile grew broader still. "Shoot," he said.

"I was married before and I have a daughter. My only condition in agreeing to marry you is that I want to take my daughter with me wherever I go, and you have to promise me that you will never mistreat her."

I have two *daughters,* Mini chastised herself. *I practiced saying it! Oh, why don't I have the courage to say so now?* She looked down at her lap, ashamed, thinking of the black eyes and lazy yawn. Sadness gripped her. *How will I bring my little precious back into my life?*

Robert waited. "Anything more?" he asked finally.

She took her time responding. "No, that's it," Mini said when she was ready. "I am a divorced woman with a child. This is a bad thing in China."

"Well, it's not a bad thing for me," Robert said. "I love you the same. I accept your condition. When will you marry me?"

"One more thing. Please take me away from Shanghai."

"I can promise you that much!" he said.

He stepped around and sat down on her side of the table. Wrapping her in his arms, he gently kissed her on the cheek. Pulling her close again, he kissed her tenderly on her lips. Mini closed her eyes. Her heart was racing.

They married two weeks later with Mary and George as witnesses. Nobody questioned why the family wasn't there. They signed some papers and were declared husband and wife. George slapped Robert's back and shook Mini's hand. He congratulated them sincerely. Mary hugged Mini warmly and whispered into her ear, "Marvelous, Mini. I hope you're happy."

They spent their honeymoon in a small room Robert rented on Nanking Road. He carried her into the room from the landing and dropped her onto the bed. Mini couldn't sleep that first night. She sat on the bed after making love with Robert, watching him sleep. His hairy chest rose and fell, his arm stretched out as if he were trying to touch her even in his sleep.

I am alone from this point on. My fate is entirely controlled by this man, a man I don't know anything about. Who is he? I know nothing about him. I know his name and his age. Why did he want to marry me? What does he get from a Chinese woman six years his senior? He seems to be genuinely in love with me. He is tender and seems attracted to me. How long will this last? It's my life I'm gambling with, but what choice do I have?

She got up, opened the window, and lit a cigarette. The cool night air gently touched her naked flesh. A cat was mewing on the black roof below her. She put out her cigarette and flicked it out onto the roof. The cat fell quiet. Mini looked back at Robert, quiet on the bed. *It is nice to be loved. Robert loves me and I shall love him back. Simple as that.* She went back and lay down quietly next to him.

For the entire week, they didn't leave their room except to eat. Robert was head over heels. He couldn't get enough of Mini. She was content to forget about life outside of their little room, beyond the present.

39

A YEAR IS A LONG TIME

Robert left for Yokohama in June. More than a year passed. Mini had moved back to her family home after two weeks of marriage. She waited for papers to arrive informing her that she could travel to join her husband.

The wait was painfully long. The letters from Robert came few and far between. She wondered often whether their honeymoon had been a dream, and whether he had used her and was now gone from her life for good. Just as Mini felt she was giving up hope, she received papers delivered by a US serviceman. She had been granted permission to join her husband in Japan. She was advised to take the next ship out, in a week's time. There was no mention of Jing Ling. Mini cabled Robert. He replied that the adoption was a separate process and would take some time. Mini should join him in Japan and they would pick up Jing Ling once the adoption was approved.

Today she would be settling this business once and for all. Mini stepped out of the rickshaw to a quiet, deserted mid-afternoon street with only cicadas to greet her with their tired songs in the blazing

July sun. The gate opened and she strode across the garden and into the familiar mansion. She came today to see Kung Yi's wife.

A maid must have announced her arrival, as Kung Yi's wife was waiting for her, holding the door open to their quarters. Mini held her head high as she entered the apartment, barely glancing at the skinny woman.

Mini sat down on the sofa. Kung Yi's wife rang a bell for tea before sitting opposite Mini.

"Where's Jing Ling?" Mini asked.

"Napping, in her room," the current Mrs. Shi whispered back, avoiding Mini's stare.

"Napping? In three months she'll be nine. She shouldn't nap anymore."

Kung Yi's wife started to say something but thought better of it and closed her mouth. A maid brought in a tea tray, set it on the coffee table, and closed the door behind her.

"Now, let's get down to business," Mini said, pausing to look at the woman.

Kung Yi's wife sat, hands folded on her lap and eyes still averted from Mini.

"I am leaving tomorrow, and I want you to know I will pick up Jing Ling in a year," Mini said, more confident than she felt. "You had better take good care of her. If I find out she has been mistreated, I will give you one hell of a time. I *mean* it." She paused again.

"Yes, I understand," the other woman whispered. Her face flushed, and she seemed to sag in her chair.

Pathetic. I don't know how Kung Yi can be attracted to her. But then, she wasn't his to choose. Mini's eyes left the small woman with her long, narrow face and looked around the room. *Everything is the same. It's obvious Kung Yi misses me. He's kept everything exactly the same.* She smiled at the thought but stopped when she saw the pictures of two boys on the end table. Mini's hatred surged. She stood, towering over the woman, and slapped her hard across her face.

The woman's face turned a bright crimson. "Why?!" she exclaimed before catching herself and dropping her voice. Her body trembled. "I said I understand. She'll get good care."

"No," Mini said coldly. "*That's* for breaking up my family." *It's what I wanted to do—should have done—when I stood outside their wedding. I finally did it.*

"Mrs. . . . ," the younger woman fumbled. "Uh, it wasn't my fault."

Mini knew it was true, but it was also easy to blame this woman.

"Remember, be nice to my daughter," Mini replied. "I will be back."

Mini left her there and went to see Jing Ling, who wasn't napping at all, but instead sitting wide awake in bed, wearing a pink cotton dress that Mini had made for her. An electric fan buzzed next to her, blowing her black hair back. Jing Ling was absorbed in a picture book and didn't notice her mother slip in. Mini sat quietly on the edge of the bed.

"Mama!" Jing Ling cried out when she noticed. The little girl jumped up and wrapped her arms around Mini's neck. Mini held her tight. She couldn't stop kissing the girl's head and cheeks.

"My precious, my precious. I miss you so much."

"I miss you too, Mama. Are you picking me up? You never come here. Am I finally moving in with you?" Jing Ling asked.

"Oh, you will, my little one," Mini said tenderly. "I promise you. You will be with me soon. Promise me you will be a good girl."

"I will, Mama."

Mini took a bar of chocolate she had gotten from the Red Cross out of her purse.

"Can I eat it now?"

"Of course you can," Mini said, smiling.

"Second mom said I shouldn't have sweets, because they will make my teeth rotten," Jing Ling said. "But I don't care." She winked and Mini laughed.

"She gives chocolate to my little brothers," the girl continued. "She only gives sweets to them, but not me. She said they are the Shi family's future."

Mini hugged her little girl tight, as if she were afraid that she would lose her if she let go. *My poor child, I am sorry you have to endure this one more year*, she thought. *I wish I could take you away with me this minute.*

"I promise you I will pick you up," Mini said. "And you will have lots of chocolate, as much as you want." She closed her eyes and felt the softness of her daughter's cheek. Jing Ling wiggled out from the tight embrace and took a bite of chocolate. "Listen, my little one," Mini continued. "I will be leaving Shanghai for a while. I won't be able to see you for about a year. When I see you next time, you will be mine."

"A year—you mean on my tenth birthday?" Her face lit up.

She understands time now. Oh my girl, a year is a long time for a child.

"Yes, on your birthday you will live with me and your stepfather."

"But my father is here," Jing Ling sounded confused, sucking the melted chocolate off her finger.

"You will have a *new* father," Mini said. "He looks different. He looks like a foreigner." *He is a foreigner. Why can't I just tell her?*

Jing Ling was quiet and thoughtful before speaking again. "Blue eyes and yellow hair, like the one I saw in the picture book, right Mama?" she asked. "Will he like me?"

"I'm sure. Who wouldn't?" Mini hugged her little one tightly. "You are the sweetest girl on earth. Everyone likes you."

"But big grandma doesn't, and second mom doesn't," Jing Ling answered matter-of-factly.

Mini smiled at Jing Ling. "Don't mind them. I know you are a good girl, and everyone else likes you." *Neither the old woman nor Kung Yi's wife care for my girl. That only means I'll be able to take her without any trouble when the time comes. Good. Jing Ling will be mine, finally. It's just a year.* "I have to go now," Mini said. "Promise me you will be a good girl."

"Okay, Mama," Jing Ling said happily.

Jing Ling walked with her mother to the front gate and waved at Mini as she turned back to look once more at her little girl. Mini waved back and blew her a kiss. Jing Ling's smile faded from her pretty face, replaced by a lonely, worried look. Mini glanced back every three steps until she couldn't see the girl anymore. She let her tears flow once she was well out of Jing Ling's sight.

One year, one year. That's all I need.

40

WHATEVER
IT TAKES

Maggie and I watched the families strolling by, kids squealing in play as we sat beneath a huge billboard in People's Square that shouted: "Speed Up the Four Modernizations!" Happy couples and parents strolled by with children. The laughing families, the sunshine, none of it made a difference. A little girl fell and looked around for her parents. She cried when she didn't see them. Her mother ran up and consoled her. *How sad it must be to grow up without a mother.* It should've been a cheery afternoon, but it wasn't.

"What are you thinking?" I asked, looking at Maggie to distract me from my melancholy.

"Po."

We had just left Po, Maggie's old boyfriend. We'd come from his farewell party. Maggie didn't want to go, but I wasn't about to go without her, so I dragged her along. The party, the mood, everything about it was joyous—exciting even. His mother had cooked up a storm to send him off. Po would be making real money in Japan, which was all we talked about. *Japan. He's going to Japan.*

It seemed everyone knew someone who was going to Japan these days. Though it wasn't just Japan, and it didn't matter where people were headed off to—leaving Shanghai for anywhere was enough to get people talking. The prospect of going anywhere for any reason was exciting. Nobody acknowledged that Po was going to a bogus school or that the "school acceptance letter" he'd received was just another name for a visa his family couldn't obtain by other means. Scores of people left to fill laborer jobs in Japan that no Japanese citizen would take. No one mentioned that part either. Po was two years ahead of us in school and had been working at a teaching job assigned to him at a village school in Jingshan after he graduated last year. Though it was only fifty kilometers from Shanghai, it was really a world away. A brilliant Chinese literature student, Po was destined to be a great writer. But no one mentioned that either.

"Why Japan? He's got a secure teaching post," I asked, though I knew the answer. Somehow, I had thought Po was different.

"And be stuck out in Jingshan?" Maggie replied.

"Why trade it for some bogus language school in Japan?" I asked. "His brother told me that he doesn't know the first thing about Japan. At least in Jingshan he can focus on writing."

"His brother's just jealous," Maggie said. "I bet his brother didn't tell you how miserable Po was. This move gets him out of his lousy job, and out of the countryside."

I struggled to answer. "For what, washing dishes in Japan? At least here he's a teacher. That's *respectable*."

"Would you want to be stuck in the country teaching peasants?" Maggie asked bluntly. "Even if they respect you for it now, who's to say what will happen in the future?"

Maggie didn't need to say any more to send shivers down my back. The thought of Po being denounced or beaten by his students for being a teacher . . . You could see the horror of it reflected in the dead expressions of the teachers who had survived the Cultural Revolution and returned to teaching when the schools reopened.

"Still, I feel sorry for him," I insisted. "He's wasting his talent."

"Oh Ting, come on, really?" Maggie asked.

"He'll be second class or worse over there working as a laborer, looked down upon. He will work so hard just to survive that he'll have no time to think, let alone write anything."

Maggie sighed. "I know. Shanghai at least would be better. He wanted to transfer, but his parents used up all their connections, and couldn't do anything to help him. He was fed up. I get it." She caught herself reflexively and looked around to make sure nobody was listening. "His dorm in Jingshan is a mud hut. He doesn't even have running water or a toilet. There's no library to speak of. He has no one to talk to there. The peasants don't care about his writing or his ideas."

"But his parents are party members, right?" I asked. I thought about my own family. *What would I do? Only another year and I graduate. Will I get sent to Tibet?* "And he's been a Youth Communist forever. Doesn't that count?"

"Come on, really?" Maggie said. "You of all people. Don't be so naïve."

I didn't tell her I had applied for membership myself, hoping to boost my chances to land a job in Shanghai after I graduate. *It's not like I have anything else to hold out for. A step away from my not-so-red— who am I kidding—my* black *family.* I didn't think I was eligible, but the political counselor had encouraged me.

"You need to be a party member," he'd said at the time, as if it were as simple as that. "Times have changed, and family background is no longer a consideration."

Maggie broke my thoughts. "His parents are very low-level party members," Maggie said. "You're a history major. You know power is the only thing that matters. It's been that way for a thousand years."

"But times have changed," I said, weakly echoing my political counselor.

"Really? Give me one example," Maggie challenged me.

I searched my brain. "What about Sung Qing? She was smart enough to be accepted into a master's program in the US."

Maggie laughed. "You mean the Industrial Bureau Party Chief's daughter?" She didn't need to say more, but she did anyway. "The person who sponsored and promised to pay for her tuition is some Chinese-American businessman who was seeking a permit for the industrial zone they're building across the river."

"What about Wu Han?" I moved on. "He was accepted into a master's program in the physics department. He had no connections, I'm sure of it."

"He'll have to find some if he's to get anything close to that research job he wants," she replied.

I couldn't come up with more examples to support my theory, so I turned my head to watch a girl in a red jumpsuit waving a wooden sword and charging straight at a boy, who backed off quickly as other kids laughed at him. I smiled.

"Po should apply for a master's program here," I said finally. Maggie ignored me, lost in her own thoughts. "He writes so well. Things are changing and in two years things may really be different. He can fulfill his dream and write."

"Ting, he's tired of being poor," Maggie said. "He can't even afford a bike on his salary."

"Still, he's so talented," I replied.

"His parents spent their savings on a ticket to Japan, hoping he'll be able to lift the family out of poverty." Maggie went quiet and I had nothing more to say.

I hadn't thought about Maggie the same way before our conversation. I had assumed, maybe incorrectly, I realize, that she would always stay in Shanghai, that her famous aunt would pull some strings and she'd get a teaching job in the city.

We sat in silence. The discussion had become too depressing to continue, and I stopped thinking about Po and the future and reflected instead on the park and the kids playing around us. A soft wind brushed our faces ever so gently. My thoughts were swallowed up by shouts from the karate kids.

Eventually Maggie's voice brought me back.

"It's late. I have to study for my last final," she said.

We got up and parted at the edge of the square, with Maggie heading off to study as I made my way home. I was done for the semester. Except for my class on modern Chinese history, I had done well. I was still smarting over my grade and even more so over my professor's comment that all I did was regurgitate what was in the textbook. *What did he expect?* "You need to learn to think on your own," he'd said. *That stung.* I tried forgetting my teacher, Maggie, and Po. I didn't need to return home just yet, but I didn't want to stay out late either. My parents were expecting me. So, I skipped the bus and walked home. I was tired after two very busy days. Fresh air would do me some good. Just yesterday, I had made a long journey with Xia, starting at 5:30 in the morning to catch the bus to a countryside clinic.

Xia surprised me when she asked for me to go to the clinic with her. I had just finished dinner and was reading in the cafeteria when she walked up and set down a big bowl of rice and a bowl of soup with almost nothing in it. I smiled perfunctorily and returned to the open book in front of me, pretending to be absorbed in my reading.

"What are you reading?" Xia had asked after waiting patiently for a minute or so.

"Somerset Maugham's *Of Human Bondage*." I lifted the book and showed her the cover. The Chinese translation was popular on campus.

She took a bite of her food and chewed loudly, her mouth half-open. Xia closed her mouth quickly and swallowed, as if realizing what she was doing.

"Ting, can you spare a few minutes? I'd like to tell you . . ." She trailed off.

I closed my book, "Yeah, sure."

She glanced around at the few others in the cafeteria, none we knew.

"I'm three months pregnant. Will you go with me to an abortion clinic?"

"What?" I thought I heard wrong. *It's impossible to get pregnant without being married.*

"I need to go to a clinic, and I don't want to do this alone," she repeated patiently.

"Who's the father?"

"I don't know."

I had nothing to say to that. How *could* I? The school prohibited dating, yet many did it. They all planned to marry after graduation. I just assumed that was the case with Xia.

No wonder Maggie always says I'm naïve.

"Can you go with me or not?"

"When, and how much time will it take?" I asked. "Can I let you know?"

"Tomorrow. All day. It's not near here and we have to take a long-distance bus."

"I'll check my calendar," I replied, then paused. "Xia, how can you not know the father?"

"Let me know as soon as possible," Xia said without missing a beat, and started eating her meal again.

I sat waiting for her to answer my question, waiting for her to talk, but she didn't. So, I got up and left.

I couldn't focus after that. *Why choose me to confide in? Abortions outside of state hospitals are illegal. Can I get in trouble if—? No, I don't want to think about doing that. But how's she to get one without a marriage license?* None of this sounded right, and I felt a little disgusted thinking about the whole thing. I can't say what I was most put off by. *I won't go with her,* I decided. *Why should I? She has family. Any one of them can go with her.*

But my decision didn't sit well. I hadn't known anyone who had gotten pregnant, or at least, anyone who had admitted it. I had no frame of reference, and in trying to imagine what this clinic must look like, I kept seeing my grandmother sitting in a dark room in a desolate country house, pregnant and absolutely alone. I saw Xia again back at the dorm later that night. She was calm, preoccupied. The others were also in the room, so I waited until Xia left for the washroom and followed her out.

"Xia, do you have anyone else who could accompany you?" I asked.

"No," she said matter-of-factly. "And you've always been so kind to me. So, I thought you might help me out."

"What will happen? I mean after."

"I don't know. I think it hurts a lot," she said. "My sister-in-law had one when she got pregnant with her second. She had to stay in bed two days."

"Will you be able to walk?"

"I think so. I will have to." I sensed her fear.

"I'll be with you," I said, though I didn't know what had got hold of me, where that came from. But I was going now.

Xia reached out and grabbed both of my hands. "Thank you so much, Ting. I *knew* you'd help me out. I *knew* you'd be the only one who wouldn't judge me."

I smiled warily, unsure of what I'd signed up for. Xia was wrong. I *had* prejudged her. *She's so stupid. What an irresponsible idiot. And how many men could she have been with to not know who the father is? So disgusting!* I couldn't shake that thought. But then I thought about Grandma again. Did I judge her too?

"Why Qingpu? Why so far?" I asked.

"Village regulations there are more relaxed, as long as you pay their asking price. I want to face it soon. You can go tomorrow?" she asked again. I told her tomorrow was perfect. I had no class, since I had finished all my finals and I was going to Po's party the day after. Xia was relieved.

"If we leave early, we can get back the same day."

Xia and I left the dorm quietly the next morning. The bus was empty, with only a handful of passengers on it. All of them were red-cheeked, coarse-skinned country folks wearing bulky padded jackets and carrying empty bamboo baskets. They noisily chatted amongst themselves as we found bench seats at the front of the bus. *They're all returning home from selling their products at the morning market in the city,* I thought.

Our bodies bumped into each other as the bus traveled along the rough country road. We would be riding this bus for three hours. I stole a glance at Xia not long after we left the city. I had never heard of Qingpu and, other than going to Pudong across the river, I had never left Shanghai before. She stared straight ahead, stone-faced. I could tell she was looking at nothing in particular. Her lips were pressed hard together, as if she were fighting a thought or suppressing an urge to cry. Her hand gripped tight on the shoulder strap of the small army bag she carried everywhere as a school bag.

Discouraged by the weight of Xia's silence, I turned and looked out the window. Rows of gray, boxy buildings stretched out for kilometers as we drove by. I eventually drifted off to sleep until a violent jerk yanked me awake again. I wiped the drool from my face with the back of my hand. Xia didn't notice. Nobody did. Xia sat in the same position. By now, the bus was well outside the city limits, maybe twenty or thirty kilometers outside Shanghai, I guessed based on the time. The dirt road we traveled on now was sandwiched by rice paddies and country houses. It was still spring, and signs of life were everywhere. Green sprouts covered the fields on both sides of the road and colorful wildflowers bloomed fiercely. Houses were scattered about in the fields. I could see dirty piglets in pigsties next to the houses closest to the road. No one was at work in the fields. We passed a water buffalo lying contentedly by the side of a rice paddy, napping in the early spring sun. Xia continued to give no sign that she wanted to talk. I was hoping that she'd fill in more of the blanks during the ride, but that didn't seem likely. Instead, she just sat quietly, staring into space. I turned back to the window.

When we finally arrived, the bus driver stopped for a few seconds to let us out at the village center. There was nothing there that suggested a town—there was little to even distinguish it from the surrounding countryside. A few food stands were clustered around a one-room general store. We stood in the middle of a muddy square, not knowing exactly where to go. Xia went up to the store and an old woman came out. After a brief exchange, the old woman pointed to a white house in the distance. She gave us a curious look, and I regretted coming.

The clinic was simple, not much more than a small cement box divided into two halves by a plaster wall. The inner half of the clinic was semi-visible through the fogged-up interior windows. The outer half had a desk near the wall dividing the rooms. A young woman in a white uniform sat behind the desk. Opposite the desk was a bench that I assumed must be for relatives to sit and wait. The room was empty. We were the only people there besides the woman who sat behind the desk.

A little window mounted high above the bench was the only window. The small frosted glass panels allowed for little light. It took a bit for my eyes to adjust after the blinding sunlight outside.

Xia gave the woman a fake name and one hundred yuan, easily three months' worth of food back at our cafeteria. The woman took the money and asked for Xia's marriage license. Xia said she didn't know that she needed to bring it and had left it at home. She quickly offered up her brother's name when asked about her husband. The woman behind the desk gave Xia a long knowing look. Xia didn't blush or flinch, and I was amazed. She just casually looked away.

Initially, I had envied Maggie for her boldness, but I had soon realized that she was more brash than confident. If she offended someone, she didn't care. Offense was never her aim, but it was never her aim *not* to offend either. No, Maggie *was* confidence, I decided. Xia, on the other hand, I realized, was quietly different. She was maybe even more self-assured in her silent composure and disregard for what was expected of her than even Maggie, who would never sleep around. Maggie had many boyfriends in the three years I knew her, but it was all just fun, and she would discard them as quickly as she picked up a new one. For all her bravado Maggie was very traditional—no, she was thoughtful in what she wanted.

"None of these guys are serious," she would say, or perhaps it was that they were a bore. "I'm not ready for a real boyfriend but when I find him, I'll marry him." I realized as I compared Maggie and Xia that I had never articulated to myself—let alone anyone else—what *I* wanted. And not just about guys, either.

I'm moving along, doing what's expected of me, and here I am sitting and watching while Xia just tells this woman that she's someone's wife. She's paying one hundred yuan for an abortion. Could I do that?

No, I couldn't, I concluded simply.

I was stuck, in a way, between them. I could be outgoing. My natural state, though, was to be quiet. Only I didn't have the confidence of either of them. Maybe more importantly, I didn't even know what I wanted. Up to now it had all been so simple.

I studied. I did well on my entrance exam and was told I would be studying history at Fudan. I studied even harder. But how much of that was my choice? I thought it was at the time, but how much of that was some survival instinct? It must have been my own will or I wouldn't have made it, but was it really a choice I had made? In a year I'll graduate and, like Po, I'll be sent off to teach somewhere. I never thought I had choices to make. I didn't need to. But that hasn't stopped others from choosing. Like Xia, or Po, or even Maggie. She picks up and leaves boyfriends quicker than she cycles through clothes. She's no doubt planning something. The way she talked about Po's choice, she has plans, no doubt, and won't wait for her future to be decided for her. What am I going to do?

I had no answer to that.

With nobody there, Xia didn't have to wait, and a nurse called her into the inner room almost immediately. Through the fogged-up window, I saw her stretch her arms up—taking off her sweater, I assumed—before a hand pulled the window cover down. I nervously stared at the wall for what seemed like forever. At some point, it felt like all the warmth in my body had completely drained away in this shadowy room. I put on my jacket, wrapped my scarf around my neck, and took my book from my leather bag. I resigned myself to a long wait.

I had difficulty reading at first, but eventually got so engrossed in the story that I forgot the time until I felt someone's eyes on me. I looked up. The woman behind the desk was looking in my direction.

"Nice bag," she said.

"Thank you."

"Overseas?"

"Uh, yeah . . ." I said vaguely, not wanting to reveal too much.

"Hong Kong?"

"I guess so." I looked down at my book again. Minutes passed quietly.

"What are you reading?"

I showed her the cover.

"Fancy book. College student, eh? Not from around here."

"Fudan." I tried saying it as nonchalantly as I could, self-conscious with the awareness that my college must seem a world away from this woman and the clinic.

"You must be smart. Is the other girl your friend?" she asked. "She looks a lot younger than twenty-eight."

Xia is only twenty-two. I didn't say anything. I just nodded with a smile and returned to my book. This time she left me in peace.

A scream startled me. I sat up abruptly and looked at the nurse. She had heard it, too, though she didn't say anything. Just as suddenly, the room went quiet again. I heard the clinking of metal instruments hitting a metal plate and whispering between the doctor and the surgical nurse, or so I guessed.

I don't know how long I sat there listening, as much to the silence as the sounds, before the door opened and a very pale Xia walked out. She was bent forward, one hand pressing down on her abdomen. Sweat covered her forehead.

I put my book into my bag. I hadn't read much.

Xia smiled—for the first time in quite some time—and nodded slightly.

I helped her sit down. She got up after only a few minutes and walked slowly to the front door.

"Let's go," she said. "I want to get out of here."

I pushed the door open and she went out without looking back. I turned around and waved to the woman behind the desk.

Xia leaned on my shoulder as we slowly walked to the bus stop. She was in obvious pain. There would be no bus for another hour. Buses out in the countryside were few and far between.

"I'm starving," she said. "I could eat a whole pig."

"Let's go over there." I pointed to the food stands not far from the bus stop.

"I have no money. I spent every dime in that clinic except for the bus fare home."

I pulled a few rumpled notes from my pocket. I had three yuan, more than enough for two bowls of noodles and bus fare to get back to our dorm.

"Let's eat," I said, though I wasn't sure it was such a good idea judging by the large bucket filled with dirty bowls.

"Are you going to eat yours? It's getting cold," Xia said after finishing her bowl of noodles. After getting a good look at the food stand, I hadn't eaten much.

"I'm not hungry," I said.

"Can I have yours?" she asked.

I pushed my bowl of noodles toward her.

Xia brought it closer and stared into the bowl, stirring the noodles with her chopsticks. "I bet you the doctor and the nurses pocketed my money. I paid five times more than I would have at a state hospital," she said. "But . . ." Xia never finished her thought. She didn't need to.

Color slowly came back to her cheeks as she finished the soup. She was a pretty girl, really, with her two large, deep eyes and her thin, arched eyebrows. Two deep dimples made for a striking oval face.

"Was it very painful?" I asked.

"Yes, they didn't use anesthesia."

"Oh . . ." I couldn't find words to respond.

"I screamed and the doctor told me it served me right," Xia said.

Again, I didn't know what to say.

"People are so judgmental," she continued. "Ting, I owe you a lot. You asked me how I got myself into this trouble? To tell you the truth, the father, he isn't Chinese. I had met a few Americans and a German and, well . . ." She moved on to sipping my soup, but never finished her sentence.

"Oh, Xia, my goodness, you'll be arrested if you're caught," I said. "Foreigners? It's a crime to *talk* to them, not to mention . . ." I couldn't bring myself to say the word "sex."

She didn't say anything.

"Why?" I finally asked.

"Ting, you and I are from different worlds. You'll leave and go to America. Your grandma will take you there. I have a barber and factory worker for parents with no education and no connections. The only way to get out of this country is to meet someone who will marry me. If it takes me having sex with a foreigner to get out of China, then yes, I'll do it."

"I'm sure there's another way," I said. "Xia, you don't need to leave China."

"Really?" she asked. "My family has no connections, no back doors, no money. I'll be assigned to the worst post after I graduate, I can only guess where. Either I rot in a remote village or I leave the country. I don't have the fifty dollars needed for the TOEFL test."

That hurt. She knew Grandma had offered to pay for my test should I want to go to America. Xia and I were well into our third year in college. The future weighed on our minds like a huge stone. I thought about it, too, but I hadn't figured out what to do. Did I want to be assigned somewhere far away from home, away from Shanghai, where there weren't even movies or books?

"You could be expelled and go to jail for what you did. It's a huge risk, Xia," I said.

"I know," she said. "But it's a bigger risk to do nothing. I've never asked them for money. I'm not a prostitute."

"Oh . . ." Again, I was at a loss for what to say. I swallowed hard. "Be careful," was all I could manage to summon when I found my voice again.

We didn't talk upon the return to our dorm. I kept the secret to myself, but I often wondered over summer break about what Xia had said about getting out of the country to live with true freedom. *Is that freedom? Is it worth so much?*

I spent my last summer mostly doing nothing. Mother insisted that I shouldn't do any housework because, as she put it, it would be my last summer off for the rest of my life. My parents were worried that after college I'd be assigned somewhere so far away that they'd only be able to see me once a year. The three of us spent many sleepless nights discussing what we should do about my job assignment, but we couldn't come up with any solutions. I wrote letters to Grandma, who still insisted that I should continue my studies in the United States. I couldn't make up my mind. Once my application to the Communist Youth League was rejected just after the school term ended, I knew my chances of getting a job in Shanghai were slim. My family background still determined my future. I didn't know what to do.

By the time senior year started I had figured out nothing. As usual, I was the second to arrive at the dorm. Maggie was already there writing a letter when I walked in. Her belongings were stored neatly in their place. She stood up when she saw me and gave me a hug. Maggie looked stunningly beautiful in a flowing red silk dress and a pair of black sandals. I always envied the way she carried herself.

It was true that she wore beautiful clothes, but her elegance did not come from her clothes. She made whatever she put on look unique.

"Writing a love letter to your new boyfriend in Utah?" I joked.

I had bumped into her one late night on the Bund. The Bund was my usual spot to hang out at night to escape the heat after taking a long afternoon nap at home. I'd take a book with me and read under streetlamps while enjoying the breeze coming across the river. When I got bored, I'd watch lovers huddle together, leaning on the railing along the Bund, stealing a kiss or caressing each other when they thought no one was looking. One night I spotted Maggie with a short, stout young man. They stood facing the river, side by side. The man had wrapped his arm around her shoulder. She gently brushed it away. I walked up to them. Maggie introduced him as Mr. Huang. He was visiting Shanghai from Utah. He greeted me in halting Mandarin. I shook his hand and quickly excused myself.

"No, I am writing my friend in Beijing. Remember Ni Ming, the guy we used to dance with?" she asked. "He's in Beijing now, in graduate school."

"Of course I do," I replied. Ni Ming was the tall, handsome guy all the girls fought to dance with, though I never had the honor. Maggie and Ni Ming had been an item on campus until he'd graduated the year before.

"Tell me, what's the deal with Mr. Huang?" I asked.

"Nothing! He's not my type," she frowned. "Though he was very impressed with my English," she said proudly and took out a compact from her purse.

"A gift from the new boyfriend," she said sarcastically.

"So, you *aren't* dating him, then?" I asked.

"Oh, no!"

"How'd you meet him?" I asked.

"My mother's cousin said he's looking for a wife, and if I marry him, he'll take me to the US."

"I didn't know you wanted to leave."

"I don't, but my parents think it'd be good for me," she said. "I'd rather work as a high school teacher and marry someone I have something in common with here in China."

"So why go out?"

"My mother insisted. She kept saying I should marry him, before I even met him. Then he just showed up like it was a done deal."

I shuddered at the thought.

"Yeah, that was my feeling, too." Maggie continued. "I only went out to the Bund with him to get her off my back. We've nothing in common. He doesn't read and I'm reading English literature *in English*." I had teased Maggie earlier about her boyfriends, but I hadn't appreciated until then the way she was choosing not just the man, but her own time and place. *What would I do if my parents arranged for me to marry someone?* I didn't want to think about it.

"You'd rather marry someone like Ni Ming," I joked. Maggie threw her pencil at me, but bit her tongue as two more roommates arrived, cheerily interrupting us with chatter about their summer.

Evening quickly descended as we caught each other up on what we did and didn't do over summer break. We split up after dinner, going off into different corners of the campus to meet other friends.

I didn't get back to the dorm room until close to midnight. I was surprised when I opened the door to find the lights on and my roommates wide awake, though nobody was talking. All the beds were occupied except Xia's. Judging from the grim look on everyone's face, something bad had happened.

"What's wrong? You look like someone just died," I joked.

"Close to it," Maggie said.

"What happened?"

"Xia was expelled," Ying jumped in.

My heart sank. "How?"

"She was caught in a hotel room with an American engineer who works at the McDonnell Douglas Shanghai joint venture."

"When?"

"Two weeks ago. The hotel guard saw Xia with the man several times. He followed them upstairs and called Public Security."

"Was she arrested? Will she go to jail?" Our little secret trip together came vividly to my mind.

"No, she was lucky because it was a first offense and she is from the reddest family background. Also, the man insisted they were boyfriend and girlfriend. She was just expelled from the university. Her parents came to the dean's office, kneeled down, and begged the dean not to expel her. But the decision was already made," Ying said.

"How do you know all this?" I snapped. I didn't like the way she talked, with so much contempt. I didn't want it to be true.

"I have my sources," she said, haughtily lifting her head.

I couldn't sleep that night. The conversation between Xia and I on the ride back from the abortion clinic went around in my head, over and over.

The next day, I had lunch early and cut my afternoon class. I boarded the bus to go find Xia. Before we parted for the summer, Xia had finally told me where she lived. I didn't know whether she'd be home, but I wanted to take the chance.

Xia's home was in a narrow alleyway sandwiched between shacks built with tin and dark wooden planks. It had been a shantytown before 1949 and was not much better now. The doors to all the houses were open. Men, young and old, sat outside naked from the waist up, wearing only boxer shorts. Women of all ages wore shapeless housedresses so thin that their nipples and the shape and color of their underwear could be seen through the fabric. Except for the occasional flick of plastic slippers against heels, they all sat lazily in the afternoon heat, fanning themselves with bamboo fans. They watched me suspiciously. They knew I didn't live there.

I found Xia's address. Peeking through a wide-open door, I saw a girl napping on a bamboo lounge chair. I knocked on the door frame. She opened her eyes, saw me, and got up.

"Who are you looking for?" she asked.

"I'm looking for Xia. Is this the right address?"

"Yeah, Xia is my sister. She's not home now. What do you want?"

"I'm her dorm mate. I just wanted to say hi."

"She doesn't want to see anyone from her school, you hear me?" The girl's eyes were hostile.

A door that led to a back room opened and Xia walked out. She had lost weight. Dark rings under her eyes and a pink mark on her slightly swollen cheek were the only color on her otherwise pale face. Her mouth drooped, giving a hint of sadness.

"Ting, I'm here." She tried to smile but couldn't quite manage it. "Nice of you to come all the way to see me."

"I just heard the news last night."

"Don't you have class in the afternoon?"

"I skipped. First day, nothing important is going to happen today."

She smiled for real this time. Her pretty face briefly returned before sadness overcame it again. She looked around.

"Let's get out of here," she said quickly.

"Slut, you're not allowed to leave the house," her sister shouted. "Pa and Ma told me to watch you. You better stay."

Xia shouted roughly back at her sister in a manner I'd never seen from her before. "I'll slap you if you call me slut one more time. I am going out whether you like it or not!"

"I'm going to tell Pa and Ma and you will get another beating tonight."

Xia grabbed my hand and pulled me out as quickly as she could, slamming the door behind us.

"Let's walk through the alley. Come on," she whispered.

We walked fast, almost running through the alley under the watchful eyes of her neighbors. Xia's eyes were fixed on the ground the whole way. A few children ran after us chanting, "slut, oh, slut," as we got close to the main street.

Xia pretended not to hear and soon their chants were buried by the noise from the traffic.

We stopped several blocks away at a store selling fruits and ice cream. I bought two red-bean popsicles and we found a shady spot under a tree.

We sat licking our popsicles and watched the busy traffic on the street.

"So, you heard," Xia finally said after a few minutes.

"Yes, that's why I came," I said. "What are you going to do now?"

"I don't know."

There was silence, and she started crying. Tears streamed down her contorted face. "My father slapped me so hard and my mother cried and called me a useless slut. She said I was stupid to throw away something so wonderful. I made them lose face in front of everyone. I let them down so badly." She stopped to stare at a passing bike. A young man was riding it and a young girl sat on the back, holding the base of the seat tight without touching him. They were laughing.

"I was their source of pride just weeks ago," Xia said, miserable. "The first in my family to go to college, you know. I am nothing but shame to them now. I can't go out without being called a slut and I don't know what to do. I'm ruined. What do I do?" She buried her face in her hands.

I didn't know. I wanted to tell her everything would all be okay, but that was a lie. I just sat there, wordless.

We sat there like that for more than half an hour as she sobbed. I wanted to ask her whether it was worth it to risk all this for the potential freedom. I didn't. I couldn't add salt to her fresh wound. She was a mess when she stopped sobbing. I handed her my clean handkerchief. She blew her nose, wiped the tears from her face, and handed it back to me. I looked at it.

"Keep it," I said.

As she put it into her shirt pocket, I suggested getting another popsicle, but she refused. After a while I got up.

"I have to go," I said.

"Ting, this time it's different," she said suddenly. "It's different with Tom. I feel something here," she said, touching her heart. "I feel something *here*. I was always happy each time I saw him, and I wanted to be with him. Oh, why am I Chinese? I'm so unlucky."

I sat back down next to her.

"What about him? Does he like you?"

"I think so."

"Will you contact him again?" I asked, feeling sorry for her, but also incredulous that Xia would fall for a foreigner. Then again, why not? My own grandmother had married one.

"I don't know how. I'm not allowed to go anywhere close to where they hang out. I'm on the neighborhood watch list."

"Oh, Xia."

That was all I could say. I felt so sad for her. But now I was sadder still for myself in my perpetual, though invisible, confinement.

I sat alone for a long time at a quiet corner when I returned to campus. The sun went down and I let the darkness swallow me. I wanted to cry, but no tears came.

Everyone was asleep when I finally returned to the dorm. I undressed and sat on the bed. With my flashlight, I wrote to my grandmother.

> *Dear Grandma,*
> *I changed my mind. I'd like to continue my studies in*
> *America. Is it still possible?*
> *Love,*
> *Your granddaughter Ting*

41

THE TREASURE

TING, SHANGHAI, 1989

Mother told me to stay in China no matter what.

"I lost my mother once and I don't want to lose my daughter," she said. "Ting, America is rich, but I'd rather live a hard life together than send you away to your grandmother."

I didn't think about that when I posted the letter. I'll admit I didn't think about them at all in that moment. My mind had conjured up thoughts of Xia, Maggie, and others like them. It was only after posting the letter that I thought about the consequences. I felt terrible. It was like a betrayal, I know, but I also felt I had no choice. Still, I didn't have the guts to tell my parents. A month went by. On a Saturday afternoon, I returned home to find my parents waiting inside. Mother jumped up as soon as I pushed the door open.

"What were you *thinking*? Asking to go abroad without even discussing it with us! You think your wings are mighty now so you can fly away from us?"

"What are you talking about?" I asked. My stomach dropped.

"Jing Ling, stop. Let's have a calm talk." Father came up, pulling my mother aside gently.

"No, I won't have it. She clearly doesn't respect us. Such a big decision and she made it all alone." She pointed her finger at me as if I were her enemy.

"Why, Ting?" Father interrupted. "There are plenty of schools here. You can do a master's and even a PhD without leaving China. How do you think you'll get a visa? Less than five percent get one." I groaned internally at the thought of the lines outside the US consulate.

I took a deep breath and sat down. "Pa and Ma, I'm sorry for making the decision without asking for your permission. But I gave it a lot of thought."

"But Ting," Father continued. "America is so far away, an ocean and a world away, really. When will we see you again? Did you think about that?"

I lowered my head. No, I hadn't thought about it. I couldn't tell them that the possibility of a long separation from my parents never crossed my mind.

I struggled for words.

Mother was crying. She dabbed her eyes. "Ting," she said more quietly. "My mother left me for an American. I didn't see her for twenty-seven years. I won't be able to handle it if I cannot see you for so long."

I cried too and held Mother tightly. Deep in my heart, I knew Mother had already decided to let me go. That was why she was so sad.

It took almost a year to apply, get accepted by a US college, and get a passport in China. On the day I went for my visa, I was one of forty-five people in line. Hours later, when I walked out of the US consulate, I had a visa. I couldn't believe my luck. I was free to go to the US.

After that, my whole family was caught up in a whirlwind of preparations for my departure. My parents bought a one-way ticket to San

Francisco. It took their life savings. First, I would stop in Hawaii so I could visit Grandma.

"You must visit her, for us," Mother said.

I was excited, but extremely nervous. I had never left home before, except for short trips near Shanghai. I had never been on a plane. Now I was going to a place so far away that it required a ten-hour plane ride.

How would I survive? When would I see my parents again? Did Grandma share these worries when she left China with Bob? She placed her fate in the hands of a man she hardly knew. I busied myself by going all over Shanghai to say goodbye to friends or to buy necessities, avoiding sitting with my doubts.

Before I left, I wanted to say goodbye to Grandaunt Ai May. More importantly, I wanted to find out what happened to my lost aunt. The visit to Anhui was a five-hundred-kilometer journey from Shanghai. To my surprise, Mother agreed to the trip on the spot, without even mentioning the cost. Father volunteered to go with me. It was a good excuse for him to go back to the countryside, he said. He missed the land and the smell of the country.

Ai May and her husband came to pick us up at the station with a borrowed donkey cart. Her husband, a rough-skinned old man with hard, wrinkled hands, carried our luggage to the cart. He smiled widely, showing his missing teeth.

"I know you city people aren't used to the bumpy road here. It will be a short ride and we'll be home soon," he apologized.

"Old brother, no worries here. I am from the country, too," Father said as he climbed into the cart.

Ai May's husband then lifted me onto the cart, even though I was perfectly capable of climbing up myself. Ai May gave the old man an approving nod. With that, he sat down behind the donkey and set off down the road.

The donkey cart bounced along the muddy road, preventing me from falling asleep, even though I was dead tired from sitting for a night and nearly a day on the hard train bench, scarcely able to sleep. I held on to Grandaunt's hand, trying to steady myself during the two-hour ride to their village.

We reached their house in darkness. By then I was too tired to pay attention to anything. I took a cold shower with a washbasin in the yard and went straight to a mosquito-net-covered bed in a small room in the back of the house. Soon I was dead to the world.

The crowing of the rooster outside my window woke me. I sat up on the wooden plank bed, disoriented for some time until I realized where I was. The room was small. There was a single window stuck on a mud wall, through which I could see kilometers of green fields. I thought about my dream. A young girl with long black braids hanging down her back told me she was looking for her mother. It had been strange and unsettling and left a bad taste in my mouth.

I felt thirsty and hungry. I went to the front room, an all-purpose room that served as a kitchen, dining, living, and bedroom all in one. *It's smaller than our little two-room apartment, but at least they don't have to share a bath or kitchen. Though I'm not sure which is worse: sharing a bathroom or doing my business outside in the cold.* A wood-burning stove and a water bucket stood against a wall next to a wide-open front door. The room was completely quiet. No one was there. I poured some cool boiled water from the kettle into a bowl and drank it all. I then took a basinful of water from the bucket and went to the yard to brush my teeth and wash up. The birds were singing their sweet songs from the treetops on the other side of the low mud wall that separated the yard from the fields. I stood between the empty pigsty and a chicken coop, looking out at the gleaming field in the rising sun.

My empty stomach rumbled. I went back to the room and looked for leftovers. I couldn't find anything. I sat down, disappointed, on a handmade wooden bench by the open door, staring at the empty pigsty, wondering if this was what Grandma saw when she was here, pregnant with the child she had given away. Could the girl in my dream be my lost aunt?

A warm hand touched my shoulder. I looked back. A sweaty Aunt Ai May stood behind me.

"You must be hungry. You didn't eat last night."

I nodded. She bent down, lit the stove, put a kettle on, and started kneading flour to make buns.

"Where's Uncle?" I asked.

"He's out working in the field. I'm taking the rest of the day off so I can be with you."

"Where's Pa?" I asked.

"He's out in the field. He wanted to see the crops."

We continued in silence and soon the room was filled with the aroma of the cooked buns. She took two out. "Be careful. They're hot."

I picked up a bun, only to drop it back onto the plate. It really *was* hot.

I reached out and took Ai May's hand. "Is this the place where Grandma left her treasure?"

I had figured out what the treasure was after Grandma told me about the secret birth of her second child.

She almost dropped the plate in her hand. Ai May looked at me intensely before responding: "So, you know then."

"Yes, Grandma told me," I said. "Was the baby born in the room where I slept?"

She nodded. The wrinkles on her forehead deepened.

"What happened to the baby?"

Aunt Ai May was visibly saddened. "I cannot find her. I lost the baby."

"How?"

"It's a long story."

"Please, tell me. I want to know."

"The midwife took the baby and gave it to . . ." She paused. "The baby was taken from your grandmother right after she was born. The midwife gave her to a family who lived in another village. The family promised to look after the baby and return her to your grandmother when she was ready to claim her. The family was decent. They had a small plot of land they worked on. They wanted the extra income so their kids could go to school. Your grandma agreed to the arrangement because she thought she would come back for her soon."

"I don't understand why Grandma didn't claim her when she was born." I paused. "It's cruel," I added.

"Ting, you don't understand. It was very shameful to have a baby outside marriage—and to a Japanese soldier," Ai May said. "Your grandmother thought she could leave the baby where she was until things got better. But with your great-grandfather dead, your grandmother was carrying the whole family by herself. It was a very, very difficult time. She quickly married again and before she could do anything, she had to leave the country. She still wanted to claim her baby. She told me so before she left. It just didn't happen."

"She didn't come back for my mother," I said bluntly. "She said she would."

"Ting, you have to be fair to your grandmother. She came back for your mother, but she couldn't leave Shanghai with her," she explained. "Your Grandma left in 1947. She returned two years later, during the revolution. She had to leave in a hurry. And then . . . she couldn't come back after that." She looked at me and nodded at the food. "Go on. Eat."

I had forgotten I was hungry. I picked up the now-cooled bun and took a big bite. It was fluffy and sweet.

"After the revolution, the family who took in the baby was given a landlord title," she continued.

"But you said they only had a small plot of land and worked it themselves," I said.

"That's true. Things changed after 1951. Before then, only people who owned large land holdings were landlords. After that, anyone who owned land was a landlord. The state took the family's land for the people. I heard that the man of the family killed himself after he was tortured, and his land was confiscated. His wife was forced to leave home with their children. She moved to her mother's home, several villages away. I rushed back home after I heard the news. My little sister told me but it was too late. They were gone. I was told she left for a nearby city because her landlady title had brought misfortune to her family."

"But what happened to the girl? Where is she now?"

"I went to the city where the family moved, to the address they gave me. No one lived there. It was a small city and I asked around. Someone told me he knew of the family and said they had left. He said she gave the six-toed girl away to someone as a maid."

"Who took her in? Were you able to find out?" I asked.

"No, I couldn't." Ai May paused, lost in her thoughts. "I've been looking ever since but haven't found any trace of her." She dabbed her eyes with a dirty handkerchief. "I will look for her as long as I live. I promised your grandmother that I would keep an eye on her. Oh, I lost her!" Ai May cried out in distress. "I can't die peacefully unless I find her. When you see your grandmother, please tell her that I'm still looking."

I hugged her tight. So much sadness, I just couldn't bear it. I looked at Ai May. Her deeply lined face was full of guilt.

"It's not your fault," I said. "Grandaunt, it's not your fault."

We left after two days. Again, they borrowed the donkey cart and took us back to the train station. Ai May gave us a large bamboo basket filled with dried vegetables and bamboo shoots. She embraced me so tight I couldn't breathe.

"Come back soon," she whispered into my ear. "I don't have another twenty-seven years."

42

MOTHER AND DAUGHTER TALK

Father and Mother took the day off before my departure and did a last round of shopping for food and extra rolls of toilet paper to stuff into my suitcase.

"Everything costs money," Mother insisted. "You have to make five hundred dollars stretch."

I stopped protesting and let them do whatever they saw fit. It took many hours packing and repacking, shifting things around, but finally, the small mountain of supplies that had been piled on the floor was packed into three giant suitcases.

All I could think as I looked at the suitcases standing by the door, with my leather schoolbag containing my passport, was that I'd be leaving my home tomorrow and I had no idea when I'd return. I wandered aimlessly between the two rooms where I grew up, pacing back and forth.

"Ting, relax." Father smiled at me. It wasn't a happy smile, though. "Why don't you go out with your mother for a while? I still have little things to pack. It'd be nice if you two had a mother-daughter talk before you leave."

There was nothing left to pack. I was dripping with sweat from all the packing and repacking. The weather was hot and the little fan just moved the humid air around the room. I paused.

"Pa, I'll stay and help you pack."

"No, go out with your mother, please. She'll be pleased if you go."

Mother looked back at me expectantly. She looked old, and a lock of gray hair drooped over her forehead. Her eyes were surrounded by tiny wrinkles. I wrapped my arms around her thin shoulders.

"Where do you want to go, Ma?" I asked. "I'll take you wherever you want."

I was feeling rich with the money Grandma had sent me.

She broke free from my embrace. "Let's go to the neighborhood coffee shop. They have that fresh cream cake you like."

"Okay," I said and turned to my father. "And I'll bring a cake and an iced coffee for you, Pa."

"Nice girl," he replied, and quickly turned away.

The heat had driven people out of their houses. The coffee shop was very crowded, packed with chic young couples slowly sipping their iced coffees. A melancholy pop song from Taiwan played in the background. The song sounded so sad that I almost decided not to go in. But Mother wasn't bothered and soon found a small round table at the back. I ordered a slice of cake and an iced coffee; she ordered a cup of green tea.

We just sipped our coffee and tea for a while, not knowing what to say to each other. I searched my memory and couldn't remember another time when Mother and I sat in a restaurant or coffee shop alone. Never once had we been alone just for the sake of being alone, to talk. Now we were sitting here, in a place Mother was usually too frugal to visit, for the sole purpose of being together. It felt so strange.

I took a bite of cake. "Oh, it's very fresh. Would you like to try it?"

She leaned over, picked up my fork, and took a small bite. "Oh, it is very good today."

"Why don't you order one for yourself, Ma?"

"No, it's too expensive," she demurred.

"I insist." I went to the counter, brought back another piece of cake, and placed it in front of her.

"Thank you." She smiled.

After a time, it was Mother who broke the silence.

"Ting, you're leaving tomorrow. I'm sad, but also happy for you. I think it's good for your future. But I also know we'll be separated for a while. It's very expensive to fly back to visit us."

"Ma, you and Pa can visit me in a few years. I'll send money for the airfare."

"You're joking, right? It's even more expensive to travel with two people, not to mention that we'll never get visas. Too strong of an immigration tendency."

"You will," I insisted. "Ma, I'll take you there so you can spend some time with Grandma at her house. I know you never had any chance to be with her when you were little."

"It's true, I was a motherless child," she said then. "I knew how hard it was to grow up without a mother, so I made sure to give everything I had to you."

Tears were suddenly rolling down her face. I was speechless. I reached out to her across the table. Her hands were rough.

I waited till she calmed down before asking, "Ma, tell me what happened to you after Grandma left."

She looked around the shop. "These young people are so fashionable," she said.

I thought perhaps she didn't hear me, and I was about to ask again when she started talking.

"A life without a mother is not a nice life," she said. "Your grandmother promised me she would take me with her to America before she left. I believed her. I waited for two years before I saw her again."

"So she did come back for you . . ." I was holding my breath.

"Yes, she did. But it was too late. She came back in May 1949. I was close to eleven. She took me to the photo shop to take a picture for my passport and we went someplace to fill out papers. She brought a Girl Scout uniform for me. She took me to the Bund to have cakes. A week later, the Red Army marched into Shanghai. The Kuomintang government closed all its offices and ran away with everything they could lay their hands on."

"What happened then?"

"The Americans left too," she said. "Your grandmother rushed to a US Navy ship here in Shanghai. She took me with her. I remember it was docked on the Bund. She tried to convince the officer to let me on. She argued, she cried, and she begged, but he refused. Only Americans were allowed. That was the order. I didn't understand it at the time. All I knew was that she boarded the ship without me, and I just stood watching as it left the dock so slowly."

She looked into the distance, as if everything around us had vanished. Was she replaying the scene again in her mind? I touched her hand. It was covered in cold sweat.

"I could see my mother was crying, shouting my name," she continued. "I had no idea what had happened. I thought I'd be with her. I didn't even cry, because I was so confused. Ai May took my hand tight and held it. We just stood there, watching the boat leave."

"What happened afterward?"

"Ai May took me back to my father."

"Did you love your father?" I felt incredibly stupid asking, but it was too late. I had said it. I used to hate my grandfather, whom I had never met, because he had been an anti-revolutionist. I blamed him for all of our misfortune.

"My father was a good man. He was kind and generous. I heard stories—that he would take off his own coat and give it to a shivering man on the street. But he was a useless man too, a man with high aims and no ability to achieve them. He couldn't make any decisions in life, and always listened to other people who were no good for him. That tendency eventually did him in."

"But he wasn't a good father to you . . ." It was something I had always assumed, since Mother never mentioned anything nice about her childhood.

"He tried," she said. "He married his second wife because he listened to his mother. That was when all the bad things happened. Your grandmother is much smarter than your grandfather was. If only she had stayed with him, things would have turned out very differently." She took a sip of her tea. "Your grandfather loved me."

"Because he bought you things? He had money, after all," I said.

"No, he squandered his fortune in very little time," Mother said. "But he loved me. He tried to give me some comfort, knowing I was a motherless child." She paused before continuing. "When he inherited his parents' stores and land after they died, a friend convinced him to sell all the rice stores and put the money into the stock market. It was just before the revolution in 1949. The market bottomed out quickly and he lost everything."

"Is that when he was sent to prison?"

"No, well yes, but not because of that. He was jailed right after, you're right. That same friend also advised him to join the Kuomintang just as they were on the cusp of defeat, and he bought a gun. So there was no question that once he was arrested, he would stay in jail for a long time. His wife left and took the kids to her parents' home in the countryside. She divorced him. I returned to live with Aunt Ling and Ai May until I married your father. Ai May left Shanghai after Aunt Ling died. She didn't want to become my burden. She married a widower, the man you and your father met in Anhui." She paused, looking at my hands holding hers.

"How did he die?" I asked gently.

"Your grandfather?"

"Yes."

"I don't really know," she said. "I was told he committed suicide."

She looked away again with that vacant look, as if she saw the ghost of my grandfather standing in front of her.

"My father was released for good behavior in the late '50s," she continued. "He didn't want to go out into society. He didn't want to be tormented by the heartless young people outside, I guess. So he volunteered to be a janitor in the prison. By then he had spent many years there. But then the Cultural Revolution started, and he was jailed again. One day, I went to visit him and was told he was dead. That was it. They didn't even let me see his body. I don't know where he's buried."

She covered her face with her hands, her thin shoulders shaking as she sobbed quietly. In a half audible voice, she said, "I regret all my life not bringing him the chicken soup he wanted. He asked me to bring a pair of rain boots and said he craved chicken soup. I only had money to buy boots. I couldn't do both. He needed the boots, you see. So, I sent over the boots and promised I'd bring the soup next time. But by then it was too late."

I picked up a few napkins and handed them to her. I didn't want to ask any more questions. They upset her too much.

She wiped her face and smiled at me bravely. "Silly that I've told you so many old things. I haven't thought about any of that for a long time. They are behind us now. We should celebrate your bright future."

"Yes," I said. I picked up my cup and noticed it was empty. I got up again and brought back one more iced coffee for me, a green tea for mother, plus two more pieces of cake for us.

"Was your stepmother awful?" I had just told myself I wouldn't ask her more questions, but I couldn't stop from asking this one. I needed to know before I left. "Was she mean to you?"

"No, she wasn't mean to me at all. She treated me as she would a potted plant. I was fed and watered, but otherwise, I didn't exist to her."

"I am so sorry." I picked up my mother's cold hand and tried to warm it with my own warm ones. "Let's not talk about the past anymore. Let's talk about the future."

Mother and I then imagined my life in America. It was so hard to envision anything beyond Grandma's tales and pictures, and so Mother imagined me playing on the beach after my days in class, only to then admonish me for being so frivolous.

We knew it would be years before I would see my parents again. I was determined, though.

It won't be another twenty-seven years, no matter what!

43

OVER EASY
OR SCRAMBLED

I pushed a luggage cart piled high with my mismatched suitcases through the doors to the US Customs area. I spent what seemed like an inordinate amount of time with the customs agents. My unusually large pile of luggage had, no doubt, caught their eye. I watched on in embarrassment as an agent pulled apart two bags, searching through my clothes and various other items that Mother had insisted I pack, though for what, I didn't know.

"You sure brought enough pots and pans," one of them chuckled after they completed their search and helped me load the suitcases back onto the cart. I thought of my mother and gave him a silly smile before I struggled with the cart, pushing off toward the exit.

I stopped my cart outside the customs area and was greeted by a stout white-haired foreigner smiling at me. "You must be Ting. Welcome to Hawaii. Welcome to America!"

I understood his words and this man looked vaguely familiar, but I couldn't make the connection. I was still trying to take him in when suddenly he spread his arms around me and kissed both of my cheeks. That caught me by total surprise. I didn't know how to react. I simply let my arms dangle by my sides. I had never spoken to a foreigner, let alone have one hug me.

"I'm Robert, your grandmother's husband. You can call me Bob," he said.

I blushed. I still didn't know what to say. How strange for him to introduce himself as "Grandma's husband." Shouldn't he be my grandpa? In China, I called everybody who was older than me "uncle" or "aunt." If they were much older and I knew them, they would be "grandpa" or "grandma." I called my friend's grandfather "grandpa." Yet this man in front of me told me to call him "Bob." There was no way I could call this old man by his first name!

All the while, Grandma was beaming behind him until, seeing the bewilderment on my face, she stepped forward and gently pushed Bob aside. She put a purple-and-white lei around my neck and hugged me.

When we stepped outside to the parking lot, I was instantly wrapped in unfamiliar warm, humid air. It smelled thick and salty. The sky was intensely blue, and the sun was blinding. I lifted my head and, shielding my eyes from the sunlight with my hand, I took in the bluest sky I'd ever seen in my life. Two white seagulls swooshed overhead, wings spread, soaring into the sky and disappearing from my sight.

I didn't say much during the hour-long car ride. I said I was too tired, but the real reason was my unease. Somehow Grandma was different here. It wasn't so much that she *looked* different. It was something I couldn't figure out. Maybe it was the sight of her standing next to a white-haired foreigner. Or was it the way she switched back and forth between languages, translating something for me and for Bob? I wasn't sure. I felt distant so I kept quiet.

I rolled down the window and let the moist sea air cool my hot face. The wonderfully silky and cool lei resting on my sweaty neck gave off a pleasant fragrance. My eyes fixed on the passing scene outside the car. Our car moved at a speed I had never experienced before, rushing down a four-lane freeway. Everyone was moving just as fast. *How orderly,* I thought. *No one honks.* I heard nothing but the zoom of the moving cars. I closed my eyes.

"Almost home," Grandma's voice reached me, and I opened my eyes. I must have fallen asleep.

The car turned onto a small road and stopped at a paved driveway next to a single-story white house perched on a low hill.

"We're home," Grandma announced.

Bob got out and, after opening the door for Grandma, he held the door for me, too. I didn't know what to make of the etiquette here and just followed along.

Finally, I had arrived at the house, the house I'd seen pieces of so many times in my life, the house I thought I knew *everything* about. Really, I knew nothing. It was not as big as I had imagined. Of course, it was *enormous* compared to our two-room apartment, but somehow still smaller than what I had imagined.

A low wall surrounded a sandy little yard planted with aloe. I stared at the odd, hard, pale green leaves of the plant, stretching out like the arms of the thousand-arm Buddha. Strange that I'd never seen this part of the house in the photos.

I helped Bob move my luggage into a room facing a high fence in the backyard.

"This is your room for the week," Grandma said.

She prepared a meatball and spaghetti lunch that was peculiar, though surprisingly tasty. Grandma gave me a tour of the house when Bob retired to his study after lunch. She pointed to a room next to mine.

"This is Bob's room," and then to a larger room at the end of the hall. The curtains were half drawn, and a TV stood right in front of a comfortable-looking bed. She walked in and signaled me to come in as well.

"My bedroom. I watch Chinese shows on TV every night. You can join me tonight if you're not too tired."

She then showed me to a musty-smelling back room where a pool table with a ping-pong cover sat in the middle of the room. It looked lonely, and obviously hadn't been used for a while.

"The kids used to play pool and ping-pong back here, but this room hasn't really been used since they left."

"Am I going to meet them?" I asked.

"Maybe next time," she said.

I wondered how much her children knew—or cared to know—about me.

The tour ended at my bathroom.

"Why don't you take a shower and a nap?" Grandma suggested. "You must be tired."

I was indeed tired to the bone and happily agreed.

Grandma wasn't joking. It was *my* bathroom, and I didn't need to share it with anyone. The whole room was scrubbed clean, and bottles of shampoo and conditioner stood on the counter. I took a long shower. The warm water fell on my head, my face, and my body. What a sensation! I had never experienced anything like it. I smelled the shampoo, conditioner, and soap, inhaling deeply and breathing the fresh lavender scent into my lungs. In my mind's eye, I saw my mother washing her hair with coarse industrial soap and waiting in line for the bathroom shared by four families.

The rhythmic sound of waves woke me up. I didn't know that I had fallen asleep, but in the faint moonlight coming in through the uncovered window, I found myself on a soft bed, fully dressed. I rubbed my eyes and tried to figure out where I was before I realized I was sleeping at Grandma's house. The house was so quiet that I could hear my growling stomach compete with the sound of waves. I must have slept so soundly that Grandma didn't have the heart to wake me for dinner.

I quietly tiptoed to the kitchen and found a few pieces of leftover chicken in the refrigerator. I couldn't find any plates. Giving up, I found a napkin on the table and ate with my hands. Though it was very late I was wide awake. I sat on the sofa so I could stare out the window, watching a pale moon in the sky behind some clouds. In its dim glow, I could make out the faint outline of mountains in the distance. I listened to the powerful ocean waves. I couldn't see the ocean, but the sound of waves reminded me of its presence. It sounded so strong, so close. At times I was afraid the waves would wash the house away. It was frightening. Eventually I drifted back to sleep.

The smell of frying meat reached my nose. I got up and went to the kitchen, finding Bob at the stove.

"Good morning!" he said cheerfully.

"Good morning. I fell asleep on the couch," I said.

"I figured," he replied. "You'll have jet lag for a few days."

"What? Jet leg? What is a jet leg?" I asked, confused.

He laughed. "Jet *lag* is the physical effect of the time difference between Shanghai and Hawaii. For example, it's morning here but it's night in Shanghai. So, naturally, your body wants to sleep now and stay up late into the night here. But don't worry, it'll pass."

In China we followed Beijing time no matter where we were. This was the first time in my life I had traveled anywhere that could cause *jet lag*.

"How long does it take to get past this jet lag?" I asked, since Bob seemed to be the expert.

"You're young. My guess is it'll be two or three days," he advised. "If you keep busy during the day and have a good night's sleep tonight, you might be over it by tomorrow."

It occurred to me that I hadn't called my parents. I had promised them! Father had gone to a lot of trouble to have a telephone installed just before I left so they could take calls at home. The phone could only *take* international calls—it couldn't make one.

"Grandpa," I mumbled. "Can I make an international call?"

He must have sensed how awkward it was for me to call such a big-nosed white man "Grandpa."

"Call me Bob," he said. "Who do you want to call?"

"My parents. I forgot to call my parents to tell them I arrived safely."

"Ah, don't worry," he said. "Your Grandma did after you went to bed yesterday afternoon."

"Oh, good. I was too tired. I couldn't sleep on the plane." I looked down.

"Why?"

"It was my first plane ride and I was afraid," I admitted.

"Afraid of what?"

"Well, it was so high above the ground," I said.

"You'd be surprised," Bob said. "Flying is much safer than driving. But since it's your first time, a little fear is to be expected. You'll feel better next time." He smiled briefly before turning back to his cooking.

"Aha, bacon is done," he said. Bob loaded bacon onto a big plate and placed it in the middle of the table. "Would you like some eggs for breakfast?"

"Yes, please," I said.

"How do you want them? Over easy or scrambled?"

"I don't understand what you mean," I said, lost. His questions sounded right out of my TOEFL test, but "over easy" and "scrambled" were new terms for me.

"Don't worry. I'll fix something and you eat. How's that?" he laughed.

"Where's Grandma?" I looked around.

"Getting ready, I suppose. It usually takes a long time for her to get ready in the morning."

I remembered her morning makeup ritual while she'd been visiting us in Shanghai. Indeed, the process seemed complicated.

He set the table with three empty plates. "We call these scrambled eggs," he said as he put a plate of eggs next to the bacon and poured orange juice into three glasses without asking me whether I wanted any.

He went and knocked on Grandma's door. "Breakfast's ready."

Grandma came out as I served myself some scrambled eggs and a piece of bread. I picked up a piece of bacon but put it back down warily.

"Ting, try it," Grandma said. "It tastes just like fried pork. There will be a lot of new things. Just try it and see if you like it."

I reluctantly took a strip.

Bob told Grandma that he was going to be a good host and take me to the beach. I looked at Grandma. "Maybe Grandma can come too?"

"Your Grandma doesn't like to walk on the beach. She can't handle the sunshine," he said.

"You go and enjoy yourself," Grandma told me. "I've seen the ocean too many times, and I can use the time to clean the house and get lunch ready."

"Okay," I said, figuring it was impossible to avoid being alone with Bob.

"Don't be afraid," Grandma whispered into my ear. "Bob's all right." Then, more loudly, she added, "I will take you to Waikiki in a few days. We can do some shopping together."

"Where is Waikiki?" I asked Bob as we left the house.

"It's where all the shops are on this island. It's very busy, full of tourists, mostly Japanese. I stopped going there because I find it uninteresting, but your grandmother likes it. She goes often, not to buy anything, because she doesn't buy expensive things. She's too frugal for that. But she likes window-shopping."

I understood the words, the individual words, but not how he used them. I figured he didn't mean Grandma liked to shop for windows, but I wasn't sure what he *did* mean. I didn't say much after that.

Bob led me behind the house onto a sand path, which sank under my steps. Seagulls cried overhead. After a few minutes of walking, we were out of the jungle of houses and facing an open beach covered by smooth, golden sand. It was so long that I couldn't see the end of it. The waves pushed in, crashing on the beach and receding instantly. I stopped, mesmerized.

"Go on, go closer. Dip your toes in and feel the waves," Bob encouraged.

A big wave caught me. My shorts were soaked. The water was so cool, yet so warm at the same time. The edge of the bright blue sky and the vast ocean blurred together on the horizon, making me feel so small. I was filled with a strange feeling that I couldn't identify or explain. I guessed I was happy, but I felt sadness as well, without knowing why.

Bob left me alone for what seemed like a long time. Eventually he came up to me.

"You like it, don't you?" he asked. "It's really close to home. You can come here every day while you're here." He studied me for a moment. "You know, you remind me so much of your grandmother when she was young. I'm glad you could come."

"Thank you for sponsoring me," I said sincerely.

"It's my pleasure," he said, also sounding sincere. "I didn't need much convincing from your grandma. I was happy she brought her kin here, to be close to her."

Yes, I came here in my mother's place. She should be the one here now. She should've come here forty years ago, I thought.

We walked along the beach for a while, and I relaxed enough to start running in and out of the waves, laughing like a child, while Bob watched me and laughed along. The distance between Bob and me narrowed a little. We stopped at a local coffee shop on the way back home for a glass of iced tea. The sun and beach had parched us.

As we sipped our tea, I summoned my courage. "Tell me about my Grandma, please. I want to know what she was like when you met her."

"Oh my. She was an elegant lady. I can still see her in my mind's eye." He looked ahead, into the distance. "So tall, so confident and elegant. I was smitten instantly."

I smiled shyly.

"I know life wasn't easy for her in this country," he continued. "But she was a courageous woman. She took an opportunity and made the most of it. She was a sensible woman, too. Without her, I wouldn't be where I am now. She's a good money manager." He laughed at that.

I didn't know what he meant, but I was more curious about how she had made her life here. "Why did you say life was not easy here? She had you to take care of her, no?"

"I promised to take care of her and I'm glad I kept my promise," Bob said. "Now, let's go home. I don't want to get in trouble with your grandmother. She must be expecting us back any minute now."

Waikiki was a busy place, even on a weekday morning. Grandma guided me through Waikiki's outdoor market, full of stalls selling toys, pearls, and almost everything else. I took my time to look over every stall, but I didn't buy anything. We strolled through the street and looked into the windows of the expensive stores.

"This is called window-shopping," Grandma told me.

The mannequins in the windows looked down at me haughtily. Grandma suggested we go inside, but I said no. This was beyond me. I knew I didn't belong there.

She took me to a small, unpretentious Japanese restaurant in a back alley for lunch. After a cup of tea, I asked about her other children.

"Grandma, is it strange to raise someone else's children?"

Grandma had spent her life raising two adopted children, while my mother had been left behind in Shanghai. It had always bothered me a great deal, and I had never found a way to ask her when she visited us.

"Why would it be strange?" Grandma asked. "I adopted two lovely kids when they were very young, and I raised them like my own. They're my children just as much as your mama."

Yet, in the meantime, my mother had been raised by someone who barely acknowledged her existence.

"Where did you adopt them from?" I asked.

"They were orphans in Hong Kong. After I married Bob, I couldn't have children . . . we tried and tried. Then, I was finally pregnant, but I miscarried," she said, her eyes moving away from me. I followed her gaze to see what she was looking at, but there was nothing there.

"The doctor told me I wouldn't be able to conceive again," she said. "I was fine with that for a while, and Bob said he didn't mind. But then he started to have affairs, one after the other. I found him in bed with the wife of his superior. I was so furious that I reported him. He was demoted and transferred."

"Why would he do that to you?" I asked, shocked. "Why didn't you *leave* him?"

"I threatened to, but it was complicated," Grandma said. "He told me that I was always sad, and he just wanted to be with someone cheerful. I missed your mother so much and that made me sad. I was alone all the time. I didn't have many friends at the navy bases where I lived. Most navy wives were white people. They were nice, but distant. I could never get into their circle. I stayed home most of the time. I found things to keep busy. There weren't even Hong Kong shows on TV here back then. Bob was the only one I had. I had nowhere to go and felt trapped.

"Eventually, it got to me. I had a nervous breakdown and went to a hospital. I had long talks with a doctor at the mental hospital I stayed at. I told him everything: how I'd married Bob, about the daughter I left behind, how I was afraid that Bob would divorce me. I wouldn't be able to survive on my own, I was sure of it. At some point after I had been in the hospital awhile, the doctor had Bob sit down with us and I told him my fears. Bob cried and said he was sorry, and he promised me again that he'd take care of me. The doctor suggested we adopt. He said it'd help me to heal. We decided to adopt from Hong Kong because Bob said having Chinese children might help me to heal more."

"That was very thoughtful of him. Did he stop cheating?" I asked. Why I asked such a personal question I didn't know. Grandma gave me a sharp look, and I was embarrassed. I didn't mean to be nosy, but I had this feeling Grandma wanted to tell me. She didn't have anyone to talk to all these years.

"Bob is not a bad man. He stayed with me. He had women here and there. I told him as long as he didn't leave his family behind, I would look the other way. He was very good to our children. They adore him. The children helped me as well. They kept me busy. I had a family to take care of, so I had less time to think about your mother. But she was always on my mind."

"Why did you leave my grandfather when he took his concubine but stay with Bob when he cheated?" I asked, immediately regretting the words.

Grandma looked as if she was on the verge of tears but composed herself. She took a few sips of tea to calm down.

"I wouldn't have been able to survive if I left Bob," she said matter-of-factly.

A waitress interrupted before I could continue. She set down two bowls of soup, a big plate of fried vegetables and shrimp, and a small bowl of sauce. She placed them on the table and bowed slightly to us.

"What is this?" I looked at the light-brown soup with a few small pieces of seaweed and tofu floating on top.

"This is miso soup. It's made with bean paste. And the fried food is called tempura. You'll like it. You eat it like this." She picked up one of the vegetables and dipped it into the sauce before she bit into it. I followed her example.

"It's good," I said.

"I lived in Japan for many years after I left China. I know Japanese food very well."

"How many years?" I asked.

"Five years. Then I went to Guam."

"What happened to your friend's husband? The lady who died in childbirth? Did you see him while you were in Japan?" I asked.

"Yes, I did. He never remarried. He raised his three boys all by himself. It was bad in Tokyo after the war, and they were starving all the time. I helped him with military supplies, chocolates, canned ham and fish, milk powder—anything I could get for the children. I had promised my friend Mei Fen I'd take care of her children, and I did. They lined up and bowed to me each time I visited them. Now the boys are all in their forties." She smiled and seemed very proud of herself.

"And what happened to Mr. Matsuda?"

Grandma stopped eating. She looked at me and lowered her eyes. "He committed seppuku, what they call ritual suicide, before he was taken into custody by the Americans for his war crimes. He made it home, but . . ." She trailed off.

His hands must have been bloodstained, being the head of the military intelligence. He got off easy. I bit my tongue.

"Did you see him in Japan?" I asked instead.

"No."

The air felt heavy. We stopped talking and fortunately the waitress brought rice and chicken, lightening the air somewhat. We ate quietly.

From where I sat, I watched the lunch crowds fill the street outside. A young couple stood in front of an Italian place, maybe discussing whether to go in. The blond-haired man in a blue, white, and red Hawaiian shirt caressed the brown hair of a young woman in a white halter-top and pink shorts. They looked into each other's eyes and smiled. It was just a small moment, but something you'd never see in Shanghai.

"Ting, I've thought a lot about this," Grandma said, startling me.

"Thought about what?" I said.

"I struggled all my life just to survive," she said. "You're different from me. You're young and educated. You should make a life for yourself, an independent life, so you can be on your own *no matter what*. Learn as much as you can in school. People who drink lots of ink always do better in life."

I had pushed my pending trip to San Francisco to the back of my head. After a couple of days of being pampered in Hawaii, visiting with Grandma, and touring the island with Bob, I hoped I wouldn't have to leave. Grandma's words reminded me this was all temporary. I'd leave soon and face a life with no one by my side. I stopped eating and looked back out the window. The happy couple was gone.

"Grandma, I'm very worried," I confessed finally. "I don't speak English well and I don't know anything about San Francisco. I wish I could stay here."

"Your English is good!" she insisted. "You don't have any problem with Bob. You will do fine. My friend Mary promised me she'd help you whenever you need it."

I remembered the English lady from Grandma's stories. "Mary—Mary Hayworth, your friend from Shanghai?"

"Yes. We kept our friendship up all these years. She and her husband were very kind to me."

"Will she be kind enough to meet me at the airport?"

"I'm sure she will," Grandma said.

"I've never met her. Will she recognize me?" I no longer wanted to eat my lunch. My nerves were now wrestling with my stomach.

"You can't miss her. She is tall and has a full head of silver hair. I'll show you a picture once we're home. I've been talking about you to her so often, I'm sure she'll recognize you. Let's get on the phone with her as well. You should introduce yourself to her."

I nodded.

"It is scary, I know," she said. "I was very scared when I got on the boat to Japan to meet Bob. Everything was bleak and I didn't know whether I'd return alive."

The waitress brought more food to our table. Grandma picked up her chopsticks. "Now, let's eat. Leave the worries for tomorrow. Let's enjoy ourselves."

44

A NEW BEGINNING

Bob parked the car at the curb in front of the airport departure area and popped open the trunk. I pulled two suitcases out and walked with Grandma to the check-in counter while Bob went to park the car. I had shed much of my luggage after Grandma convinced me that my dorm room wouldn't have enough space for everything I had brought from China.

The airport was full of smiling new arrivals, looking forward to days spent at the beach doing nothing but soaking in the sun and the sea, and red-faced departures who had doubtless overindulged themselves in both. Somehow, I felt apart, isolated from all of them. I was extremely lonely in the busy crowd, as if there was a whole world separating them from me. Everyone else had purpose—they were sure of what they were going to do. After having fun on the island, they would return to their lives at home. I didn't know what to do or what to expect. I had no idea what was waiting for me. I was stuck. It was too late to turn back, as I was no longer legitimate in China. I didn't even have a resident registration anymore. The government had canceled it when I left. Officially, I no longer existed in the eyes of my birth country. My path was simple: Go forward.

I moved rigidly in a stylish blue cotton dress that Grandma bought for me in Waikiki, as if my limbs had lost all their flexibility.

The loudspeaker announced my flight would board soon. We stood up. Bob gave me a hug and a pat on my back.

"Ting, you'll do well. You're a smart girl, I can tell."

Grandma and I embraced tightly. I didn't want to let her go. She pushed me back and looked at me intensely, her arms outstretched and hands resting on my shoulders.

"Ting, call me as often as you can," she said. "I want to hear everything. Come visit me during your break. Mary told me she'd arrange your ticket for you."

I looked down at my feet, nodding. "Now, go on," she said with finality.

I turned and walked to the gate. I dared not look back for fear I'd run back to her. I only looked back after I handed the agent my ticket. They were still there. Bob held Grandma's shoulder with one arm and waved at me with the other. She smiled at me and gave me an encouraging nod.

Once on the plane, I sat down by the window and turned to watch as a long train of luggage carts came out. Workers unloaded the luggage from the carts and loaded them onto the plane. I wondered whether my two suitcases were there. *They must be*, I told myself. The carts were emptied in no time. A moment later I felt a jolt. The plane started moving. The pilot announced something I didn't understand, and a pretty blonde stewardess started her safety demonstration as the plane moved slowly toward the runway.

I felt the engine vibrating under my feet. Before I knew it, I was no longer on the ground but shooting into the air. The airport, which had looked so big just a few minutes ago, became smaller and smaller. Soon, I watched as the whole island, gleaming in the blue sea, was reduced to just one dot among others, before disappearing from view entirely.

I closed my eyes. I saw Mother and Father waving at me. I saw Xia sitting by the curb, crying. I saw Grandma sitting wordlessly across the table from me, her eyes full of hope. I touched the golden-leaf bracelet and earrings I wore, gifts from my grandma and her legacy. I saw myself spreading my wings and soaring into the air.

"Would you like something to drink?" a pleasant voice asked, interrupting my thoughts. "Juice, tea, or coffee?"

I opened my eyes and looked at the smiling flight attendant. "Coffee, please." I breathed deep and smiled back.

I felt joy. And what a wonderful feeling it was.

THE END
&
THE BEGINNING

ACKNOWLEDGMENTS

In memory of Jay Carr.

I'd like to thank my mother and Kate, for your love, and Nora, for your encouragement. Also, Robin, for giving me a chance to know what life could be as a child. I am thankful to my father, for his belief that girls are as good as boys, or better.

My special thanks to Christina Kovac, Charlotte Irion, Peter Pearson, Hildie Block, and Jim Mathews for being at my side as I shaped my story.

I am grateful to my editors Alex Posey and Amanda Hughes, for perfecting my imperfect English, and Elizabeth Brown for your heart-felt comments.

I cannot thank enough my husband, Noah. Without you, I wouldn't dream to write this story.

ABOUT THE AUTHOR

Dina Gu Brumfield was born and raised in Shanghai, China. She resides in Maryland with her husband. This is her first book.